THE BERLIN GIRL'S C

Leah Moyes

Production by eBookPro Publishing
www.ebook-pro.com

THE BERLIN GIRL'S CHOICE
Leah Moyes
Copyright © 2020 Leah Moyes

Edited by Irene Hunt

Proofread by MJ Jones

Previously published by SpuCruiser Media as
"Berlin Butterfly: Ensnare"

Leahmoyesauthor@gmail.com

Facebook @BerlinButterfly

Twitter @authormoyes

ISBN

The Berlin Girl's Choice

A Historical Fiction Novel

LEAH MOYES

I dedicate this book to the person who, despite my many faults, never hesitates to stand by my side, many times lifting me up when I'm unable to do it myself. He was the first to believe in me, and I am lucky "forever" is a very long time.

I love you, Greg.

ReadMore Press

Sign up for **Readmore Press'** monthly newsletter and get a FREE audiobook!

For instant access, scan the QR code

Where you will be able to register and receive your sign-up gift, a free audiobook of

Beneath the Winds of War
by Pola Wawer,

which you can listen to right away

Beneath
The Winds
of War

POLA WAWER

Our newsletter will let you know about new releases of our World War II historical fiction books, as well as discount deals and exclusive freebies for subscribed members.

PROLOGUE

M ay 7, 1945, Germany surrenders to the Allied Forces. The European conflict of World War II is over. Adolf Hitler is dead. The Third Reich has fallen, and Hitler's brutal war atrocities are exposed. The city of Berlin—although technically in Soviet-occupied East Germany—is in rubble, broken and divided into four sectors: American, British, French, and Soviet zones. The eastern side of Berlin is under complete Russian Communist control, and friendly relations with the Allies turn hostile.

June 1948, the Soviet Union blocks Western Berlin road access from food, water, and supplies. In response, a massive Allied airlift is executed. Fuel and food are received by aircraft until the blockade is lifted in May 1949.

In the 1950s, East and West Berlin function as different countries, governing under very different leadership and laws and even issuing their own currency. The Soviet zone of East Berlin finds they stand alone in their politics; a satellite occupation far from its mother country and facing what they believe to be a rebellion from the Allied forces. Their grip on the residents of East Berlin tightens as more and more people flee. By 1961, it is estimated two to three million people have already deserted the eastern side for better opportunities in the West.

As August 1961 approaches, nearly a thousand educated professionals, skilled laborers, and families make an exodus westward each day. East Berlin is hemorrhaging, now on the verge of total ruin. Leadership panics and Nikita Khrushchev gives the Deutsche Democratic Republic official approval to seal off the western side of Berlin from all of East Germany. While it appears as though the wall is to keep the Allies detained, its real purpose is to keep the East German residents from reaching democratic freedom.

Used with Permission from http://www.berlin-germany http://
www.berlin-germany-fanclub.com/berlin-wall-map.html fanclub.
com/berlin-wall-map.html

Author's note

The German language is intertwined often in conversation throughout
the story, and although the author attempted to make it simple enough
for the reader to understand the context, a German glossary can be
found at the back of the book.

CHAPTER ONE

1961

The wood floor creaked under pressure at the same time a cold hand swiftly shot across my mouth. Shock prevented me from screaming. Despite sudden awareness, fear paralyzed my eyes and they remained shut.

My first thought should have been about my safety, but my concern shifted to the couch next to me. Papa's labored breath remained steady. He had not awakened. I then feared for myself until I heard a familiar whisper in the dark.

"Ella, it's me."

I took a breath. My arm stretched to turn on the nearby lamp, but Anton's touch warned me not to. "It's too dangerous. The soldiers are coming."

"Why?" My voice staggered with unease.

In the shadows of the light from the streetlamp that seeped through a nearby crevice, I could see his face cringe with fear, a fear I had rarely seen. Anton had been my constant, the only reason I lived to see my fifteenth year.

"It's happening," Anton whispered as he wiped his forehead. Possibly from the August heat wave or from running, but he seemed nearly out of breath as he continued, "They're closing off Bernauer as we speak."

I gasped and moved swiftly to my feet, separating the thin curtains from the frame. Looking past the decorative bars that covered our main window facing Ackerstraße, I caught sight of the military trucks. They hummed slowly down the cobblestone street less than a kilometer away. Soldiers dragged something like wire rolls from the back of the vehicles.

Immediately my eyes shot toward the door of the connecting room where Josef, my eleven-year-old brother, slept.

"So the rumors are true?" My heart sank. I had remained by Papa's side since he fell ill a few weeks ago. The disturbing news Anton delivered from the shadows revealed that the Soviet sector of the city was getting desperate. People were leaving East Berlin by the thousands.

"I've found a route to the West, but we must leave now." Anton took his turn at the window. He surveyed the neighborhood carefully as it filled with soldiers. Their voices rose steadily as they demanded that the curious people who had wandered outside go back in. I pressed my lips together and forced the tears back, staring poignantly at the frail body nearby.

"I can't leave him, Anton," I whispered weakly. I couldn't imagine abandoning the only father I'd ever known, the man who had rescued me from a lifetime of loneliness and the cruel fate of being an orphan.

"He can't make the journey, Ella." Anton reached for my hand. He tenderly caressed it, but I could still feel his anxiousness. "If we hurry, we can get to Wedding before they get the blocks up, but the construction has already begun."

A tear fell on our conjoined hands and pooled on my dark skin. Anton let go and wiped the steady stream of tears clumsily from my face with his sleeve. A stray curl stuck to my cheek from the increasing moisture. Anton twisted the long strand in his fingers before he tucked it behind my ear.

For one moment, we were children again.

"You must go." I gently brushed his hand away despite my desire to linger. I quickly reached into the nearest cupboard and grabbed the remains of the dinner loaf, wrapping it in a thin towel. I knew this would be Anton's first meal of the day even though it was after midnight. He hadn't been as lucky in finding a family and had turned to the streets. This was how he always knew what was happening before any of us, but it was a hard life. Papa tried to help, only we had little to give after Mama passed.

"I can't leave you, El," his voice cracked. I stood still. Visions of a young boy surfaced. I'd forgotten how small and sickly Anton appeared when he first arrived at the orphanage. Especially the way he looked now, so tall and strong. His confidence, like many youth, arose from the streets.

With the many pressures weighing on the people of Germany since the end of the war, survival was a priority. Our pride was all we had left, as the world cut up our country like a *Zwiebelkuchen*. Only, our slice of the onion pie was dished out to Soviet Russia.

I reached out for him. Anton's hands found their way to my shoulders, and he pulled me in. The strength of his arms had always brought comfort, and they didn't fail now. We had never been apart, and as he held me, we trembled with the idea and fear of the unknown.

"Please . . ." I whimpered. "Please go. You'll get caught if you don't!" I looked once more toward the adjacent room then begged, ". . . and please take Josef with you."

Anton's lips brushed my cheek. We were motionless, neither one of us ready to let go. "I found it, El." Anton's whisper forced my face to whip backward just enough to see his eyes. I knew Anton had no reason to lie to me.

"I saw it last night off Kastanien and Schwedter." Anton looked as though he failed me. "I couldn't get it." My grip tightened with the news.

The noisy commotion nearby rocked us back to reality. His body shuddered as he pulled away.

"They're getting closer!" I choked.

The darkness shrouded Mama's cuckoo clock on the wall, although I could hear the chains clink slowly against the pendulum. It was a deafening reminder that the longer we waited, the less chance they had of attaining freedom. I rushed to my little brother's side and shook him awake.

"Josef! Josef!" He awoke frightened. "Quickly . . . get up. You're leaving with Anton." They were like brothers. I knew he would be safe, but where they were going was a mystery to us all.

We had heard life with the Allies was much better. Food and resources were abundant, and one did not live in constant fear. The boys simply had to get there first.

I found Josef's worn *Tasche* and stashed a few clothes and his most prized possession, his *Kasperle* puppet, inside. It was still dark; therefore, I packed blindly and lightly. His tiny body couldn't be pulled down by the weight. The noise outside grew nearer. The sound of screams came simultaneously to doors being kicked in or slammed shut. Panic echoed through the neighborhood. It was hard to tell what was happening; Mitte was under attack.

Josef clung to me and cried, "You and Papa are coming too . . . right, El?"

I grasped his hands. "You must say goodbye to Papa." I held my voice as steady as possible. "Quickly, Josef. Do it now." I pointed to our father and then reached for the ceramic teacup on the shelf that had a crack in its handle and tipped the contents into my hand. I slipped the few coins into his sack and sealed it tightly.

Anton moved back to the curtain. Headlights glowed only a block away. People were dodging the uniformed soldiers. Cries of desperation surrounded us.

"Hurry, Josef." Anton's voice cracked.

The piercing squeal of brakes signaled a truck had stopped directly in front of our building.

My throat strained, fighting the lump that grew as I watched my little brother grip his father's arm and kiss him tenderly. When Josef faced me, a streak of light from the increasing headlamps penetrated through the slit in the curtains. It innocently created a boundary line of illumination between us, Josef and Anton on one side . . . I on the other. The separation had become all too real.

"El?" The sound was barely a purr, but there was no doubt where it emerged from.

I glanced at Anton then down to Papa. The commotion must've startled him awake. I went to him but delayed my touch, knowing he would sense my uneasiness. I kneeled to the side of the couch and leaned my face in until his breath warmed my cheek.

"Go," he mumbled.

I looked at him alarmed, although the darkness hid my face. *Is he really telling me to leave?* I waited for a confirmation that came within seconds.

"You . . . must . . . go," he gasped with very little strength.

I placed my trembling hand on the side of his face. "Please, Papa. Don't make me choose." My eyes stung from the strain. I looked back at Anton, my heart emotionally torn between the people I loved the most.

"Please come, kleine Maus," Anton whispered.

My throat was too dry to even speak. I looked at Papa once more, his body frail and limp. How could I desert him now, knowing his life hung in the balance? I peered back at Anton's pleading green eyes and lowered my head. I couldn't even motion *no*. It was too hard.

I reached for a faded, blue cloth that rested on the nearby desk, small white marks stitched into the corner. I pressed it into Anton's hands.

"Don't forget me," I cried, my voice barely audible. Anton's fingers gripped the fabric tightly. He didn't have to look to know what it was.

"Ella, you're coming, right?" Josef's voice had not yet changed, and the high pitch of his cry sailed through the room. Anton quickly reached for him and pulled him toward the back of the flat. He opened the window that led to the side alley with one hand. We were fortunate to live in a street-level apartment. With his other hand, Anton pushed Josef through the window.

My heart ripped open.

His little hand stretched back for me. I was motionless. Once they were both outside and pressed against the brick, I lunged for them. I wanted to memorize every possible detail I could.

"Ella?" Josef whimpered.

My hand squeezed his tightly. "I love you, Josef. You will be safe with Anton. Listen to him!" I gazed at the older, wiser person Anton had grown into. The closed, quiet orphan who had sat across from me every meal for many years had become a man. A man who I desperately hoped would get to the west side of Berlin in time.

"Take care of him, Anton!" I begged through a controlled sob. Anton faced me conflicted. He rushed back toward me, placing both of his hands on my cheeks as his lips pressed urgently against mine, then he vanished.

The empty sensation of his touch lingered as my fingers clenched tighter to the concrete sill. Agonizing cries swelled in the alley the moment their shadows disappeared. I hardly recognized my voice as the torturous feeling of abandonment resurfaced. Only this time, the choice to separate was mine and mine alone.

CHAPTER TWO

The moment the sun's rays hit the rift in the curtains—the exact location the military truck headlights had lit only hours before—my eyes flashed open, red and inflamed. Bouts of tears coursed down my cheeks as the screams and chaos robbed my silence and left me with little comfort in the form of a thin blanket overhead.

Even with the daylight, I feared what I might witness beyond our front window, although I dreaded even more the fate of Anton and Josef.

Had they made it to the West? Would I ever see them again?

I studied Papa. He remained completely still, having weakened in the last forty-eight hours, and while he had moments of consciousness, like last night, they were short.

A flash across the room caught the incoming light at just the right angle. I stood up and walked to the desk. Right where the handkerchief had rested the night before was a small round object. My heart instantly sank. I reached for the piece. My thumb traced the front where a series of small, raised dots surrounded a tiny red jewel. It was Anton's tinnie pin.

The ornament's shape was that of a shield representing his Germanic history. It was the only thing he owned of his family, . . . and he left it to me. I wrapped my fingers tightly around it as if it were Anton himself. I pulled my fist to my mouth and squeezed harder as I fought my desire to scream. Everyone I loved was slipping away from me, and I couldn't stop it.

I pinned the shield to the inside of my dress. Its cold surface pressed against my skin as I bent over to buckle my shoes. In a way it helped me feel as though Anton was still a part of me, strengthening me . . . knowing hard times were still to come.

Despite the images my mind conjured up from the constant noise throughout the night, I was not prepared for what I was about to experience when I stepped out our front door.

Stunned by the eerie silence within the halls, I hesitated. Our large apartment building housed over twenty families on five floors, but not one sound could be heard within.

I had a single *Mark* in my pocket, and without Father's wages, we were nearly destitute. I knew food was the priority, but I was undoubtedly tempted by Anton's discovery. Kastanien and Schwedter were nowhere near Krzinsky's; it would have to wait.

I pushed the main door open but remained frozen in place. The street was filled with confusion as everyone was attempting to flee. I jumped as a man dropped his suitcase in front of me, its contents scattering about on the brick. As he looked up, his eyes briefly locked on mine. The fear was evident, splattered across his pale countenance. He reached for a fistful of clothing with one hand and his sobbing child with the other and then disappeared in a sea of similar sights. The road had turned into a footpath. Cars could no longer drive along Bernauer Straße.

My eyes darted about until they reached the other side of the street. There, in a meticulous line, stood a multitude of soldiers along a razor-wire fence. Each soldier faced the crowd, his hands gripped tightly around a weapon.

Onlookers stumbled in disbelief. Women cried for mercy and freedom. Some of the men chanted, "Schweine!" and raised their fists angrily to the soldiers. The young squaddies seemed mostly unaffected by the insults but clutched their long rifles carefully across their chests, ready to use if the command ever came.

A similar scene developed across the newly formed border. Parents, children, siblings, cousins, friends, and lovers separated by a mere moment. Simple choices made one day resulted in life-altering effects the next.

As my eyes followed the curve in the road and over the top of the cemetery walls, a row of apartment buildings directly on Bernauer had actually become the border line overnight.

Astonished, I watched desperate people tie linens together and make a rope as their only means of escape. A couple slid down with only the clothes on their back. Toward the opposite end, a family took turns as they leaped from a second-floor window and into the arms of firemen on the west side. A young girl, frightened to jump, clung desperately to the windowsill as her feet flapped wildly beneath her. I watched as her fingers lost their grip one by one. My ears rang with her screams as she disappeared from my sight.

My throat strained as if it were on fire. Choking sharply, I turned back toward my own building to catch myself from collapsing. One hand pressed heavily up against the rough surface while the other shook uncontrollably. I should have listened to Anton months ago. He warned of the gossip developing, but Papa and I didn't want to believe it. Life in East Berlin was difficult but not hopeless.

After all, the Deutsche Democratic Republic, our own government, denied the possibility of such a separation. Even Herr Ulbricht, the council chair, publicly stated, "Niemand hat die Absicht, eine Mauer zu errichten!" No one has the intention of erecting a wall! And we wanted to believe him; this was our home.

Now it was too late. This was not one of those horrible nightmares I used to have in the orphanage, the type that would jolt me awake, feeling as though the torment and anguish I experienced were way too real. No, this was, in fact, very real; only Anton wasn't here to comfort me.

Time after time, Anton was the only one who could calm my fears. Before he arrived at the home for unwanted children, the nurses would lock me in a closet at night. This was the only means to silence my terrifying screams from those around me. Tears started to sting as a recollection of those dreadful times resurfaced, triggered as the cries from the street intensified.

I scolded myself for my earlier selfish thoughts. Anton's "find" would have to wait. I needed to get to the shop quickly and back to Papa. I took a deep breath and steadied myself. My small-brimmed hat was pulled low over my dark curls as if that could block out the noise. Truthfully, nothing could. I kept my eyes downcast and took a step forward.

The sound of a single gunshot stopped me cold. One soldier along the fence had blasted a warning shot into the air as people pressured him. The sound amplified the fear tenfold, if that were even possible.

I wrapped my light sweater tighter around me and fought my desire to merely return home and curl up under my bed. Once I mustered the strength, my body hastily maneuvered back through the narrow brick opening of Friedhof Sophien across from Anklamer.

I rarely used the cemetery as a path, but as I leaped over the closest headstones onto a grassy lane, a strange comfort enveloped me. The thick foliage and sweeping branches of deep-rooted oaks momentarily camouflaged the frenzy outside the graveyard walls, tempting me to take refuge inside the columned mausoleum, an unsettling site avoided in times past.

As my proximity to Berg neared, my ears were once again met with terrifying cries and I launched into a dead run toward Krzinsky's *Geschäft* near Invaliden park, now only minutes away.

I found the shop surrounded by an unruly gathering. My attempt had begun too late. His door was closed and locked as desperate, frightened citizens pounded on his small windows. I was afraid they would shatter under the strain. One mother cried for milk, her baby wailing in her arms. A man demanded liquor while the children at his side bawled in confusion.

I stood up on the bench near the streetlight. I hoped to get a better glimpse of the entry from there. My eyes squinted anxiously to read the sign he had posted. I feared his sudden closure was permanent.

Herr Krzinsky pulled the curtain back from the small window on his door and screamed, "Ich hab geschlossen!" His hand continued to wave angrily behind the glass as if that would automatically send the people away. "Geschlossen!" he cried once again.

Herr Krzinsky was a large-statured Russian with a full, heavy beard and thick eyebrows. Under normal circumstances, people would be intimidated to confront him. Only now, their desperation and numbers added to their confidence. That is until the sirens suddenly wailed to the left side of me. The *Polizei* vehicles, at first, could barely move down the street, but their sirens grew louder indicating their approach was only mere seconds away.

The uniformed officers pushed forward, and the people scattered. Two men clambered over the bench I was standing on, and it collapsed beneath me. Thrown to the ground, I rolled to my knees.

All I could see was a frantic clutter of shoes. Someone's leg hit me in the face while another stepped on my hand. I had to move or be trampled. I crawled toward the shop, my knees and hands covered with scrapes and bruises. Before I reached the window, another man tripped over me and knocked me flat. My hat flew off and disappeared in the crowd.

"Ella!" I heard my name called simultaneously to a loud tapping against glass, but I could not focus. Dizzy and lightheaded, my head spun.

"Ella!" The word was repeated anxiously. I rested my head on the ground. A moment later, a large pair of hands reached under me and lifted my body so easily it was as if I weighed nothing at all. One hand held me tightly against his chest while the other physically created a path the short distance back to the shop door. Inside, I was set down quickly as Herr Krzinsky bolted and locked the door behind him once again. He carefully helped me to my feet and brushed the dirt off my dress.

Herr Krzinsky and Papa were close. They had a unique brotherhood as soldiers in the *Wehrmacht*, the German Armed Forces. Their involvement in the invasions of both Poland and France was rarely spoken of except in Herr Krzinsky's gratitude to Papa for saving his life, not just once, but twice. The heroics came with a steep price though. Due to the shrapnel Papa received, he lost the use of his right knee, forcing him to use a cane the rest of his life.

"Ella! Your father is he . . .?"

"He is still alive." I inhaled deeply to catch my breath. This news brought a great deal of relief to his face. He reached for a cloth.

"But Anton and Josef are gone," I continued.

Herr Krzinsky turned sharply back to face me. "Where?"

"The West, I hope!" my voice cracked. The memory of our tearful goodbye remained fresh. "They left last night as the wire was going up."

"Where, Ella?"

"I don't know . . ."

"Where were they crossing?" his voice rose unexpectedly.

"I don't know . . ." I sniffled. "Anton mentioned Wedding." Herr Krzinsky's face lost color.

"What?" I demanded.

"The border guard stopped nearly three hundred people at that crossing this morning alone. Sixty-nine border crossings are completely sealed off now, and people who resist are being detained—"

"Children too?" I questioned, as tears easily slid down my cheeks.

"Anyone . . . any age."

I continued to follow Herr Krzinsky to the storeroom. I slid into a chair across from his family, huddled in silence. His wife, Greta, and their two children, thirteen-year-old Andres and eight-year-old Freddy.

They listened to the radio announcer shout the news with exasperated breath.

"The U-Bahn is closed!" The man hollered, and Greta gasped. Her twin sister rode the D line weekly from the West to visit them. "Residents of the DDR are now only allowed to cross with special papers . . ."

Greta turned to me and immediately reached for the towel her husband held and moistened it. As she wiped the dried blood from my fingers, she spoke of the news that had been announced earlier.

"A woman almost died this morning . . . only a few blocks away." Greta held up her already soaked handkerchief to her nose. "The radio said she tried jumping out her window to freedom."

My thoughts went to the images I saw prior to coming here and then shifted to Anton and Josef. I imagined the terror they must have faced.

So much to say, but no words followed. The silence was confirmation that we had all begun to comprehend our losses.

"You must stay here until the streets become safe again," Herr Krzinsky insisted.

"Papa needs me. I must go now." I stood to leave. Herr Krzinsky's mouth was hidden by his heavy beard, but I knew it was curved into a frown.

"Ella, it's dangerous."

"I'll take the back roads and go through the cemetery again. I can't leave Papa alone for long."

Herr Krzinsky sighed. This was an argument he would not win. He pulled a small sack of flour, a bag of noodles, and a handful of chicken bouillon cubes off a shelf. He wrapped them tightly in a hand towel and showed me how to stuff it in my sweater to make it look like it was part of me.

When Papa fell ill a month ago, Herr Krzinsky took on a personal responsibility to make sure our little family would not starve, even though we had very little to offer in return. He said it paled in comparison to what he owed Papa.

I reached into my pocket and held out the single silver coin in my palm. Greta grasped my hand and closed it tightly as she wept. She left the mark inside and then kissed my hand sweetly. It took all my willpower to not openly cry. Herr Krzinsky led me toward his back door.

"Do not stop for anything, Ella. Lock your doors, and do not come out until things have settled down." He kissed the top of my head, and even though I turned my back on him, I was sure he watched me until I was out of sight.

I did exactly what he told me. My feet barely touched the ground as I sprinted home. Once there, I found Papa still motionless on the couch. His face looked as though life as he knew it had not completely turned upside down.

"Papa?" I kneeled on the floor next to him and slipped my hand through his. "Papa, Herr Krzinsky sends you well wishes."

Papa's eyes fluttered, he took a deep breath and exhaled. I brushed my hand across his forehead and through his light-colored hair. He was a handsome man. However, now in this condition, he looked as though he had aged twenty years in the last six months. The doctor said he never fully recovered from his combat injuries. Ultimately, it was the diagnosis of sarcoidosis that would kill him. Papa hardly had the strength to fight it.

"El?" a faint sound emerged.

"Yes, Papa, I'm here," I said as my face remained close to his. "Please, rest yourself."

"El?" he said again. My face burned as tears broke through.

"Papa?"

He fought to speak. "S-sorry."

I couldn't hold back, and a fresh stream rolled down both my cheeks. I knew that despite his condition, he must've recognized the scope of my decision to stay.

"I love you, Papa." I lay my head against his chest and felt the weak vibration of his heartbeat. His hand moved slowly toward my cheek as his finger caught my tears. His eyes closed, and he was asleep again. It had only been four short years together, but it was the best four years of my life. I could have never left him here to die alone.

It would be several days before I attempted to leave the flat again. I blamed it on Papa's steady decline, but truthfully, I feared what I had witnessed. From our main window, I continued to watch the turmoil unravel by the hour. Not one day resembled the next.

By Sunday, Papa's deterioration accelerated. He stopped eating, his skin appeared clammy and pale, and although I could still feel his heart beating, a shadowy sensation seemed to linger across him. Different parts of his body slowed down, some stopped. As I cleaned his waste, my thoughts went to Anton and Josef. It had now been one full week since they left.

Were they safe? Were they free?

I placed clean linen under Papa's body; his only acknowledgment was a brief flutter of an eyelash and a lingering moan. I somberly sat at his feet as the room grew darker with the setting sun. Although the silence was both encouraging and frightening, I found myself searching for the small phonograph box that remained untouched in the front corner. Memories of a happier time flooded my thoughts. I needed to find the place Anton told me about.

I placed my hand on Papa's cheek, and his skin felt warm. He stirred, yet his eyes remained closed. This small reaction brought immense comfort to me.

"Papa, I'll return shortly." I expected no response as I grabbed my sweater and headed for the door. I took a deep breath before I opened it.

This time, there were no crowds, no cries, and no chaos. Either everyone was gone or in hiding like me. Besides the soldiers, only a few scattered people appeared.

As I passed by the now darkened Chapel of Reconciliation, its pencil-sharp steeple pierced black clouds that hovered heavily. Two lone women stood near it, opposite each other, and tenderly held their toddlers up to touch hands over the fence. They could be family or friends.

Despite the unknown bond, the separation was heart-wrenching to watch. Again, I fought to keep Anton and Josef's parting images tucked away.

Within twenty minutes I arrived on Kastanien. Another couple of minutes passed before I reached the crossroad of Schwedter. My breathing hastened at the thought of my search finally coming to an end.

As I turned the corner, I saw shattered glass spread across the ground. An ear-splitting crash continued as my eyes followed the startling sound. The boys, younger than me, turned at their sudden detection. One held a fragmented board in his hands. The other gripped a pipe. All the shop windows between us had been destroyed.

My feet seemed cemented in place. They faced me fully now and began their approach. My eyes widened with each looming step.

Move, Ella! I demanded in my head. *Run!*

My breath amplified as I willed strength into my limbs. It was completely dark now, and the vandals were only a few yards away. Finally, my feet shuffled enough to wake me up. I leaped backward and turned the corner, taking the longest strides I could render until I felt far enough and safe enough away to finally breathe. By the time I reached Acker, my heart no longer felt like it was beating out of my chest.

My ventures rarely occurred without Anton, and alone, vulnerability consumed me. Once inside, I quietly locked the door behind me, light enough to not alarm Papa. I sank to the floor, my knees pressed heavily against my chest. The struggle within my mind exhausted me. My head fell into my hands. I wanted to disappear. Lifting my face, I studied my empty fingers and envisioned how close I had come to holding the recording.

Some people would say such a search was insignificant in comparison to the madness I now faced, but the song "La Vie en Rose" always brought such peace to me. Memories of Edith Piaf's smooth vocals swirled about me as I pictured Mama and Papa dancing around the sitting room. It was their love song. I yearned to hear that music again.

Despite the heartache that could accompany it, the risk seemed worth it. This made my empty-handed return that much more painful. Anton and I had been searching for it for nearly a year.

I dejectedly rose to my feet and pulled the loose cover close to Papa's chin. From the curve of his mouth, it appeared as though he had seen Mama again. I knew it wouldn't be long before he joined her.

CHAPTER THREE

My hand skimmed the edges of the simple pine box that housed Papa's body. The dismal clouds that weighed heavily above seemed to parallel the gloom in my heart. Darkness overpowered any light, and like the absence of rain, my tears no longer stained my cheeks.

It had only been sixteen days since Josef and Anton left. Now as I stood here alone near a shallow gravesite burying the last remaining person I cared for, I had very little reason to go on and lacked the strength to say goodbye to yet another.

"Ruhe in Frieden." The priest's hollow words of peace moments earlier produced a sour taste in my mouth as I fought the urge to insult an ordained man of the cloth. I knew he spoke more from obligation than attachment. It was part of the "deal" I fashioned with the mortuary near the Frieden-Himmelfahrt cemetery, but despite not having any money for a proper burial, I could not bring myself to have Papa cremated.

Herr Krzinsky had used the relationship of an old military comrade to make the arrangements for me. He put me in touch with Herr Koen Franke of Berlin Niederschönhausen. His family's fourth-generation mortuary in the borough of Pankow had been passed down to him.

Unwilling at first, he claimed his clientele came strictly from the government, but Herr Krzinsky could be quite persuasive. Consequently, with Herr Franke's change of heart and my own will, I agreed to work off my casket debt as a servant in his family home for the next two years.

As I contemplated this decision, I picked a small blue flower bunch sprouting near my feet. I lifted it to my nose to inhale a memory and laid it lovingly on Papa's casket. Appropriately so, the blossom was called "forget-me-not". Despite our short time together, he was the only father I'd ever known.

I had no recollection of my birth father. It was always inferred I was probably just one of many unintended results of war passion and abandoned as an infant. If it weren't for the Kühns' infertility, I would still be in that rat-infested orphanage to this day.

My fingers trembled as I blew one last kiss.

"I love you, Papa," I whispered and then turned my back. My entire soul wanted to crumble and be buried with him.

I clutched Anton's tinnie pin through my fabric top. It had remained next to my heart continuously since its discovery. Its constant presence had crafted a welt with identical design marks barely above my left breast. To me, this was more of a gift than a discomfort; Anton could never leave me.

I squeezed my eyes shut only to open them to an audience across the acreage behind the vast estate. I flinched. A young man leaned quietly against the brick siding. He pulled a drag on his cigarette and watched me intently. My eyes were blurred, and my head felt light, but I stood upright. I didn't want anyone to think I was broken.

The man with light-blond hair and tall, lanky form simply stared, emotionless and cold like the rest of this place. My wavy, dark strands whipped wildly across my face until I twisted their disobedience into a tight braid. The angry glare I shot toward him was filled with vengeance as if he was personally responsible for my father's death.

"You can bury him now," I cried heatedly, ". . . and tell Herr Franke I will be here as determined tomorrow at eight."

He didn't say a word. I didn't expect him to. I stumbled behind the large stone crematorium that anchored the building and disappeared in a rush down the street. I boarded bus B109 toward Mitte but got off much later than the stop closest to my home near Bernauer and Acker.

I deliberately walked toward the Brandenburg Tor. It was not a common path, though one had developed as of late. I watched angrily as soldiers worked diligently to reinforce the segregated cage that now cut Berlin in half.

The barbed wire that had originally been rolled out the night the boys left proved to not be strong enough to keep people in. Efforts for a crueler deterrent were being developed, but nothing—not even concrete blocks or wire—could stop some people from trying . . . thus the steady sound of gunshots from day one and nearly every day since.

I paused briefly near the recently closed checkpoint, the red-and-white access gate heavily guarded. Two large water-cannon tanks held their threatening positions dead center.

I watched as mobs of desperate people still gathered with very little hope of crossing. It was now possibly more about catching a glimpse of a loved one no longer within arm's reach than it was about actually crossing the border.

I'd passed here often but never saw *my* familiar faces. I didn't even know if they were on the free side or in the only other place worse than the city of East Berlin . . . a *Stasi* labor camp.

The stories on the street said the DDR's secret police, more commonly known as the *Stasi, Staatssicherheit* (state security), were dispatched to do their dirty work. Only once again, the powers-that-be denied it publicly. All the Stasi really seemed to be was a network of commissioned thugs and spies. They answered to no one, made their own rules, and cast a very dark shadow on a crippled and dying city.

The superintendent of my building said that in the last week that the Stasi had arrived twice in the middle of the night and seized multiple residents without any explanation at all. He also claimed his friends in other buildings near the wall had seen the same strange occurrences. This would have been a more frightening thought if I felt I had something to live for.

My eyes tore away from the sad images at the checkpoint before me, yet I still had no tears to wipe away. I hadn't cried since I said goodbye to Herr Krzinsky and his family four days ago. He had been evicted from his shop and their livelihood when the DDR closed all the businesses along his street for undisclosed state reasons. Of course, we all knew it was because of his proximity to the wall.

He came to bid farewell to Papa right before he passed. It was tormenting to watch their final goodbye. Papa never woke again after that and took his last breath less than an hour later.

Anger stirred inside me as my thoughts instantly went back to Anton and Josef. Walking slowly in a trance, I recalled the last moments we shared. Josef's quivering voice and trembling hand, then Anton's intense mixture of fire and fear. I'd only seen that look on Anton's face once before, many years ago. I had nearly forgotten where I'd seen it—that first day, the day we met.

***

It was an unusually early morning as Nurse Margret rubbed the rough rag against my dirty cheek hard enough to make me believe that if she pressed any firmer, the color might come out of my skin as well.

"Owww!" I screamed.

"How do you do it, kleine Maus?" Nurse Margret complained of my inability to stay clean as she referred to my nickname of "little mouse". She said I could find trouble in all the farthest corners of the orphanage.

Normally, this wouldn't matter because we never left the building, except now something seemed different. Even at the age of six, I sensed an urgency in her touch and noticed her eyebrows didn't meet in the middle when she spoke. I knew today had to be special.

I only had three dresses, two for everyday wear and one I'd only seen twice. They packed it away for special occasions. So when she pulled my day dress up over my head, ready to replace it with the pale one that had only one small tear, I knew for sure we would be going outside.

However, before she could get it over me, I bounced from bed to bed with excitement until I came face to face with this quiet boy who stood motionless at the door. My squirrelly frame froze in place. I'd never seen his color of eyes before. It was difficult to describe. My life was as colorless as it could be with white walls and white clothes and white mush. The thought of anything *that* shade of green actually stunned me.

His reaction, I later learned, was not the shock of a little girl standing only in her underpants, but that he had never seen anyone with brown skin before, and he found it fascinating.

A whack on my butt brought me to remember where I was. Nurse Margret grabbed my small arm and held me tightly between her thighs as she pulled my dress on. I didn't fight, moved by what I'd just seen.

"One more move like that kleine Maus, and we will lock you in the closet while we all go out to the youth festival without you!"

I didn't know what a youth festival was; I merely wanted to get out more than anything. I wanted to see something other than the damp, smelly walls and broken toys. Being in the closet was worse than that, and I spent enough nights in there to know. Thus, I behaved.

When I trailed through the front door to the steps below, we were warned to remain in a single file line. Nurse Gitta led the way while Nurse

Margret took the back. With the addition of the new boy, we numbered nineteen; the three babies remained with Nurse Irma.

I inhaled long as I stayed in step behind Frederick. The smell tickled my nose, and my brow crinkled at the unpleasant odor. A lot like the stench of our own toilet. I was disappointed that the odors were nothing more than what I smelled inside day after day, with an added ingredient of unwanted smoke and other things I could not identify. I pinched my nose as we marched past piles of broken concrete and scattered rubble.

The view from our single bedroom window was limited. Much of the destruction I was used to seeing, only not on this grand of a scale. The fallen buildings multiplied the farther we walked away from our two-story home.

Despite my nose being discouraged, my eyes and ears were not. Sights beyond anything I'd ever seen ignited a fire within me. Each step we took drew us closer to music and laughter and crowds of people. More than I'd experienced in my whole life.

"Stop." Nurse Gitta raised her hand. I was so distracted that I bumped directly into Frederick. He, in turn, pushed me roughly to the ground as if I'd done this on purpose. My fists curled as I scrambled back up to hit him, but I was too late. The new boy, hardly bigger than me, had already pounced and had Frederick down flat. His fists landed blows on Frederick's face and chest until both nurses took hold and grabbed the little, scrawny fighter to his feet.

Nurse Margret was a large buxom woman and used her size often. She heaved the boy up close to her face and gripped his arms tightly to his side. Her face turned a deep red, and she spat when she shouted. I counted to ten, three times in my head, as I watched. Once she was finished, she set him down on the closest partition. There was such a great deal of noise around us that our little congestion was most likely neither heard nor seen.

"All of you, up. Get up on that wall." Nurse Gitta set us all on the same block barrier. "Watch the parade and don't move," she warned.

We stared in awe as all of Berlin marched in the streets that summer day in 1951. They carried signs and played music, laughed, and danced. It finally occurred to me that this must be a celebration of sorts. I was only beginning to learn the alphabet—I could not read the signs—but smiled at the excitement I felt. Once again, I saw color and happiness like never before.

Nurse Gitta disappeared momentarily and returned with several young people. They handed each of us a long candy wrapped in a paper similar in color to the new boy's eyes, only lighter. I smiled as I held it. I never had anything that beautiful. Each child excitedly opened their wrappers and started chewing on the taffy inside.

I looked down the row beyond a handful of kids and saw the new boy's empty hands and his head, hung very low. I hesitated, looking longingly at the rare prize in my fingers and back at the boy who had weirdly fought for me. I glanced at the nurses. They swayed in rhythm, clapping and watching the parade more than us.

I slithered carefully past the others and plopped down next to the new boy with the stringy brown hair and long eyelashes. He didn't move. I opened the wrapper, twisted half of the candy off in my dirty hands and handed it to him. His face wrinkled in confusion, and *that's* when I saw the look. His reflective green eyes revealed unexplained anxiety.

"Hier." I said as I pushed the candy into his hands.

He didn't say anything. His eyes finally relaxed, and his thin lips curled a little as he took a bite. We continued to watch the sights and sounds for another hour before we returned to the *Waisenhaus*.

Anton and I connected that day. It almost seemed as though our spirits had already known what our bodies did not. We were meant to find each other somehow, somewhere, because despite Anton's uncertainty, he hardly left my side from that point on.

***

A newspaper flapped wildly across the sidewalk in front of me. It was stamped with the bold black date of 31 August 1961. It was a sad reminder of the present state I found myself in, trapped and alone.

I reached for the *Morgenpost* as I walked. I skipped past the front pages, which were always a parade of proud military pictures, the stories of sacrifice, bravery, and risk the *Volksarmee* took by protecting the people of East Berlin. It was what the government wanted us to believe. Reaching the back page, I scanned the published lists of detained, missing, or dead "perpetrators". The title said it all, "Enemies of the State". I tried to be positive when neither Anton Schulze nor Josef Kühn appeared; nevertheless, . . . I still had no answer.

"Stehen bleiben!" Angry voices echoed all around me. I squeezed my eyes shut. If I concentrated hard enough, maybe the sounds would disappear.

"Stehen bleiben!" The voices grew louder.

"Bleiben Sie stehen!" My eyes opened to the cold barrel of a rifle nudging my arm roughly. A boy similar in age to Anton screamed for me to step back. I'd wandered too close, nearly face to face with the fence. I shook my head and looked around; my sleeve touched the wire.

"Gehen Sie!" he cried sharply. I had no reason to doubt he was serious in his insistence for me to leave. I put my hands up and slowly retreated. His loud exclamations had attracted a small crowd. They all seemed to pause and watch as they anxiously anticipated something tragic happening.

"OK, mach ich." I snapped irritated. Although I moved to leave, I deliberately dragged my feet. I've always had trouble following directions, and this was no exception. Only here, it was from someone who epitomized my rift.

The soldier used his rifle to briskly push me again. What this boy did not realize was that I was at a point where I didn't care what happened next. I swung around and shoved the barrel forcibly away. I could live or I could die. Either way, it didn't matter.

The soldier's eyes widened like marbles. It was obvious this was unexpected. I stood my ground as his reaction grew. His face curled with disgust, and his hands started to shake. He raised his weapon to the firing position as a bead of sweat rolled down his nose. I was not going to back down; whatever happened next was meant to be.

"Halt!" The order came from a much older officer nearby. The younger one ignored him. His hand purposely chambered a round in preparation to shoot as if we were the only two present.

I should have been scared. I should have been shaking as the long, black barrel hovered inches from my face. It was so close I could smell the scent from his most recent discharge and wondered if it was accidental or deliberate. My eyes narrowed with hatred. I was angry. Everything about this soldier epitomized loss to me . . . loss of my brother, loss of Anton, and now the loss of my father.

"Erschießen Sie mich" I cried. The stock wobbled a little. The soldier's staunch pose shook with surprise once again. I'm sure he had never had anyone tell him to "shoot".

He quickly regained his composure and started to continue just as the clearly higher-ranking officer smacked the rifle down. The older officer looked around and angrily pointed out the now larger crowd of spectators to his comrade.

"Nachgeben!" The officer yelled at the boy to stand down. The young soldier's eyes narrowed with obvious disgust. His rifle aimed downward, but his finger still rested on the trigger. The officer turned to me and shoved me backward. He pointed in the opposite direction and shouted for me to leave.

I slowly backed up, although I couldn't resist the temptation to flash a childish smirk at my assailant. Enraged by my insolence, he attempted to argue with his commanding officer as I walked away.

People stared at me with undeniable shock. I could see the twisted queries in all directions as I approached the walkway that led back to my home.

I said nothing.

I felt nothing.

It was apparent they wondered why I had a death wish yet managed to cheat death.

CHAPTER FOUR

Although my father's body was removed from the apartment the night he died, it never felt like he was completely gone until last night.

I didn't even try to sleep. I knew it was nearly impossible. My mind wouldn't allow me to rest. It was full of teasing thoughts. Imaginary ideas that tricked me into believing there was still a future for me to thoughts that laid out the bleak reality. I couldn't turn them off. It was a miserable night of seesawing as my outlook seemed as imbalanced as the childish beam itself.

Before I knew it, the doors on the clock opened, and the dancing figurines appeared with a warning. It was seven o'clock, and I realized life as I knew it had vanished. Today would start my subjection in the home of strangers. That is until I could somehow find an alternate path.

I pulled my key from the rusted brass lock and paused anxiously in the dark hallway. My eyes lingered on the large brick barrier before me. It had recently been constructed in the frame of the main door of the building.

Similar obstacles had been compiled in each of the apartment windows near Bernauer. Additionally, rolls of barbed wire were placed along the edges of the roof. From my bedroom window, I could no longer see the sun shining or the rain falling. It was as if a prison was being assembled around me, right before my eyes.

"They are trying to discourage escape." Frau Ingobert stepped out of her apartment across from me and called for her cat. She was an older woman who lived alone. I didn't speak as she continued, "I think they're trying to force us out."

I gaped at her in shock. "They wouldn't do that, . . . would they?"

She shuffled past me in her cotton robe and slippers. Her face twisted in a frown. Dotzi, her unfriendly cat, cowered in the corner. *She must know something we don't.* "They can do anything they want, dear," she said as she bent over to pick her up.

I glanced back at the barrier then toward Frau Ingobert. Her words resonated in my mind; *they can do anything they want.* I solemnly slipped out the back entry and buried the threat. I had other things on my mind today. I couldn't be late as I ran through the alleys toward the bus stop.

So much unknown lay before me. I didn't mind working to pay off the debt on my father's casket, even if it was for a wealthy family like the Frankes. My apprehension now was more out of inadequacy and doubt. I wasn't sure I was truly qualified for the job. *What if I wasn't good enough? What if I messed up and did something wrong?* I cared for our little home without a problem after Mama passed away, but it was just that . . . little.

I'd never been in the actual residence of the Frankes. I'd only seen the outside cemetery yard. Even from that angle, their home was enormous. It was a formal estate adjacent to the Schönhausen Palace grounds.

Many Berliners knew the palace to be the former residence of the East German government elite. This was before they moved their business to Wanderlitz last year; thus, the Frankes' close alliance with powerful authority was not imagined.

I arrived ten minutes early. A butler ushered me into a drawing room off the main entrance before I could pause long enough to scan the intricate, elaborate detail of prosperity.

"Frau Franke will arrive shortly." His head lowered slightly, while his mouth sulked. I wasn't sure if this was a response or a habit.

I gazed around. The quaint room burst with beauty. It was small enough to entertain privately but large enough to make a statement about Herr Franke's success in the business of death. Gold and crystal lamps adorned glass tables. Gilded mirrors hung in succession, and spotless white cushions topped handsomely carved wooden mounts. I was afraid to sit. My dress would surely leave a stain on such a perfect piece of furniture.

A woman entered the room with a sigh. "I am Frau Franke," she announced. Her auburn hair was pulled up in a tight bun, which made her appear older than she probably was, but her high angled cheekbones and porcelain skin revealed a flawlessness I'd never seen. I could not take my eyes off her. She didn't seem pleased with the arrangement her husband had made to accommodate me. "*You* are the new girl?"

I nodded. Frau Franke didn't hide the surprise of her first impression. It was one I'd seen hundreds of times, yet it no longer affected me. Her eyes went from my face to my feet.

"*You* are Fräulein Kühn?" Her face turned rigid.

"Yes, Frau Franke," I responded confidently. I'd chosen my best working dress, pulled my dark locks into an immaculate braid, and washed my face three times. Yet, somehow, I still felt inadequately presentable under her scowl. "Ella. You can call me Ella," I continued, respectfully.

"I will not," she snapped. "Much too informal." She handed me the apron she was holding and advised me to put it on. "You will arrive precisely at eight o'clock each morning and not leave until five each evening. Workdays are Monday thru Saturday unless told otherwise. You will receive seven marks per day in living wages, and the remainder will be applied to your debt for the next twenty-four months. If you are so much as late or absent, any day, you will not be given a warning, nor will you be released of your debt. However, you will be reported to the authorities on your delinquencies and face severe consequences. Do you understand?"

"Yes, Frau Franke." I acknowledged.

"Fräulein Kerner?" Frau Franke called to an adjacent room as a young woman approached very quickly.

"Please see that Fräulein Kühn is shown to her duties immediately." Then she turned back to me. "Lunchtime will be precisely at twelve o'clock for thirty minutes in the staff kitchen. Bring your own food. If you are caught taking anything from our home, even the least bit of scrap from the table, you will be released and arrested. I will not tolerate stealing."

I lowered my head. It was hard to appear grateful under the circumstances, although I was. I couldn't live with myself if I sent Papa to the chimney, something Germans cringed about since the horrors of Hitler's death camps were exposed. It was a dark history for Germany regardless of whether we believed in the regime or not. It was a scar the world would never let us forget.

I followed Fräulein Kerner, who introduced herself to me as Lena, to the laundry room. She was—thankfully—very kind in her instructions and thorough in her training. Nevertheless, she aptly warned me not to consort with the family or guests. With the type of work Herr Franke did, along with his connections, his home had become a central point for entertaining many political leaders and the elite. As hired help, Lena insisted, we stayed out of their business.

I never perceived this would be a problem. I was much more skilled at avoiding than interfering. The business Herr Franke conducted in his home was of little concern to me; my only focus now was to complete my obligation and then find my family. Nothing else mattered.

When five o'clock came, I was more exhausted than I imagined I would be. I'd scarcely untied my apron and folded it in the back room when a young woman came floating by. She stopped and looked at me curiously.

"Who are you?" she asked inquisitively.

I hesitated as I recalled the strict warning.

"It's OK," she laughed. "I know you were told not to talk to me, although, if you don't, then it'd be considered rude." She appeared smug in her calculation.

"I'd rather be rude than without work," I whispered flatly as I placed the apron on a shelf, which had been recently labeled with my name.

She smiled warmly. "Welcome to our home." And she was gone nearly as quickly as she appeared. She had to have been around my same age, maybe a bit younger—although her countenance seemed so light and free of burdens.

She left me with a twinge of jealousy in her wake. *How would it be to have everything?* I wondered as I stepped out the side door into the glow of a descending sun. To never fear poverty, loss, or loneliness . . . something I would never know.

I fell into my daily routine easily. It was not a hard trade. Somewhat physically demanding from what I was accustomed to, but I wasn't in the factory assembly line or even the unemployment line, which seemed to grow with each subsequent day. My greatest challenge was the adjustment of being around such enormous wealth while the vast majority of the city was slowly starving to death.

By the time I reached my flat late Saturday night, I was quite fatigued. My thoughts lingered so heavily on Sunday, my first day off, that I almost didn't see the notification nailed to my front door.

Gazing around, similar papers were secured to every door down the hall. The deep-black lettering was titled "BITTE BEACHTEN". It demanded its occupants to vacate immediately. Mere days were provided before entry would be restricted. I heatedly snatched it down and slammed my door shut behind me.

How could this be? I collapsed weakly on the couch; the same couch Papa had taken his last breath on only a week earlier. The salty scent of sweat and anguish still lingered on the pillow. I gripped the paper tighter and tried hard to read the fine print.

"By order of the Deutsche Democratic Republic, all homes next to the border must be evacuated for reasons of high security. Evictions will be enforced through People's Police in three days".

Three days! Where would I go? I didn't know anything beyond the Waisenhaus and here. Frau Ingobert was right. They *will* do anything they want. I gripped the paper and read it again as if the words could somehow change in a matter of minutes.

I knew there wouldn't be any money to relocate until the end of next week. With Papa sick, I'd used the last of our savings to live on for over a month. I sunk to the floor, devastated. The strength that seemed to hold my body together leaked through my pores and left me completely defenseless.

Why couldn't I be more like Anton? He was so resourceful. He had an answer for everything. Suddenly, I recalled the earlier time in my and Anton's life, when our home and security had been threatened.

***

"Beweg dich!" Nurse Margret clapped her hands together and rushed frantically into the playroom. All of us children were circled on the floor for leisure time. It was 1955, and I'd just been presented an *Apfeltasche* for my birthday.

Since I didn't really know my true *birth* day, I picked a different day every year. The nurses didn't mind as long as it wasn't celebrated twice in one year, and this time I chose February 9. I was turning nine and didn't expect much. Only to cut my celebration short— well, I wasn't going to stand for it.

"Beweg dich!" she repeated, and the children all jumped up properly, except me. It wasn't mealtime, why was she taking this away from me? She clapped again, more urgently than before.

Anton reached for my hand and pulled me reluctantly to my feet. We followed the others and took our place along the floor crack in our day room. I quickly shoved the whole tart in my mouth as apple jelly dripped loosely down my chin. Nurse Margret didn't appear to see this, looking nervously at the door and then back to us as she moved swiftly down the line.

"Oh mein, . . ." she would whisper as she ran her finger against her tongue and then brush it against dirty cheeks in a desperate attempt to clean them. Thankfully, a noise drew her toward the door before she got to me.

"Willkommen." She clasped both hands together as Nurse Gitta entered the room followed closely by two men.

Instantly, gasps rippled down the row of indigent little bodies, and I peered at Anton with frightened eyes. I'd seen many soldiers outside, although, not as decorated as these men and never inside our home. Each removed their perfect hats as they shook the nurses' hands and nodded their heads. My eyes widened at the dazzling coins that gleamed on their front jackets. One man had three long silver chains that draped from his shoulder to his buttons.

"Danke." They didn't smile when they spoke, yet their words sounded polite.

We stood very still as they moved about our room silently. Their crisp uniforms made little noise as they glanced at everything but us. Again, I looked at Anton. He didn't return my stare. One soldier went to the window and examined the view as the other pushed on a nearby beam. Finally, the one with more gray hair than brown stared at us blankly. He turned to face Nurse Gitta.

"Sind das die Waisen?" The man pointed to us as if we were bags of flour and not children.

"Ja." Nurse Gitta nodded her head to confirm we were discarded children.

The same man put his finger to his cheek and tapped it slowly like it helped him think better. He then walked over to the other man, and they whispered back and forth.

It was very hard to stand completely still for long. I sighed loudly and shifted my weight noisily to the other foot. Nurse Margret responded quickly, putting her finger to her lips with a threatening *Sshhh* in my direction. I crinkled my nose.

Again, we waited as they conversed. The nurses appeared uncomfortable and confused. Even *schüchtern* Melania, as quiet as she was, tapped her shoe twice. The air suddenly felt like a piece of heavy linen was pressed against my face. I just didn't know why.

The soldiers then turned to the nurses and motioned for us to leave. Nurse Gitta clapped her hands together and ushered us out. I followed the others until I realized Anton remained near the outside of the door. Silently, I crouched down next to him, glancing around carefully to make sure no one had seen us. Nurse Gitta did not close the door behind her when she returned to the soldiers.

"Something is not right, Ella," he whispered and inched his ear closer to the frame.

I stood next to him, although I could hear nothing.

Anton turned and repeated what the soldiers said to the nurses. "By order of the National Building Program in Berlin, we are seizing control of this property." He stopped and wiped his forehead.

My eyebrows scrunched, puzzled. Even though the visitors spoke German, I didn't seem to understand their words. Anton ignored my confusion. They continued.

He whispered as quickly as he could follow, "This house has a sturdy foundation, adequate space, and little damage from the war."

In the few times we had ventured out, even at nine years of age, I knew this was true. Anton continued, "The *regierende Bürgermeister* Suhr and his family will become the new occupants here."

My mouth flew open. "Where will we go?"

Anton put his hand gently over my lips. "Sshhh," he whispered as the man continued.

"You have six days to relocate, Frau Dieners."

Anton looked at me, and I mouthed the words "Six days?" My brown skin must've gone white because he instantly reached for me.

I don't know how long there was complete silence in the day room, although it seemed like an eternity before we both heard, "NEIN!" The loud refusal was a woman's voice.

We stared at each other again in complete surprise . . . it was Nurse Margret's voice.

Anton inched up to the frame and peeked around. I tugged at his shoulder. "What's going on?" He brushed me off. I tugged harder.

"Just a minute, El," he said with gritted teeth and turned away. I folded my arms, frustrated.

"NEIN!" Her loud dissent was repeated and echoed around the room with a stomp of her heavy foot.

Anton described Nurse Margret's face, twisted like rotten fruit with both hands curled in fists on her hips.

"You will not put these children out! They have no place to go." Her round face and square chin were only inches from the gray-haired man. "Find another location!"

Nurse Margret was a stern woman who spent her long days barking orders and her long nights sleeping with one eye open. This was the first time we witnessed how she really felt. It was astonishing!

"She will be taken away, Anton."

He agreed. We had heard the stories of how people disappeared over the years for random dissent against the government.

"Frau! Are you resisting a direct order?" one soldier spoke, although there was no strength in his voice. He sounded as shocked as we were.

"Ja!" she demanded. Even though Nurse Gitta's small frame trembled nearby, Nurse Margret continued, "I have worked here every day for twelve years. I've seen hundreds of children get tossed to the street by their own mothers, the very ones who should love them and protect them." Nurse Margret stood her ground. "I won't allow their country to do the same! You tell your foolish building program this home is no longer an option!"

She spoke quite loudly and forcefully until she had driven both men out to the hall where we had unexpectedly been discovered eavesdropping. Nevertheless, even our appearance did not shake her. Both men were stunned to silence. They fidgeted uncomfortably with their caps as they hustled in a panic straight out the main doors. Then, without missing a beat, she turned to us and cried, "Anton! Adele! Verschwindet!" On her command, we disappeared.

Anton grabbed my hand and pulled me into the adjacent room where all the children gathered, yet I could not wipe the silly grin off my face. We had clearly witnessed history. Anton proceeded to tell the story to the others—the story of Nurse Margret, . . . our savior.

From that day forth we viewed her differently. Although she never treated us as if we were special or meant anything to her, now we knew we did.

We often wondered if the soldiers would show up one day and take her away and throw us to the streets. They never did. It was a miracle. One woman against a system, in a world where *one* rarely mattered.

***

But I was not Nurse Margret or Anton . . . I was a young girl who didn't have either the strength or the belief I could stand up to anything. Doubt consumed me and shadowed any possibility I had about rising above the DDR or their evacuation order. I had so little faith.

Chapter Five

It didn't matter how long I lay on the floor and tried to imagine another outcome, I still faced imminent removal in three days.

I had no family, no support, and no options. Then the question suddenly struck me—*what would Anton do?* In the orphanage, he was clever and cunning. Often he could outwit the nurses. When I was adopted, he was only fourteen and moved to the street. His ability to not only survive but function proved he would be disappointed in me right now—especially if I gave up so quickly.

I glanced around. The few furnishings we had wouldn't fetch a price. Papa had sold nearly everything of value, including the automobile, to bury my mother. I, personally, had nothing of importance.

With urgency, I opened all the cupboards and drawers—the very same places I checked when Papa passed, and the same sad result emerged. I deliberately passed by the phonograph; the only thing I could not let go of. I still held the hope of finding "La Vie en Rose". Then I spied the small carton of beeswax and chalk.

It was a long shot. Possibly not even worth consideration, but maybe—just maybe—the drawings I'd done held some slight benefit. Maybe someone would find them useful. Maybe some moneyed parent would buy one for their child. I knew it was a risk, possibly even nonsensical considering the East had so little. Nevertheless, I had no other choice.

It was already dark outside. With no time to waste, I gathered my papers and supplies and walked down to the station. There were always people near Friedrichstraße at this time of night. Surely, I would find someone who would pay fifty pfennigs or a mark for a pretty picture.

I had no specific recollection of when my love for drawing began. The orphanage didn't offer a lot of ways for me to learn or grow, outside of punishment, so doodling became a channel for me to express emotion. Anger, frustration, happiness, and fear— they all came out in my drawings.

It wasn't until Nurse Margret commented on my designs that I started to believe there might be a talent. I used anything I could find that made a scratch. My tenth Christmas, *der Weihnachtsmann* left me a small tin of Stockmar wax blocks. This was the best gift I'd ever received at the home.

My favorite design was the butterfly. I'd rarely seen one in real life, only in books. I was smitten with the size of the wings in comparison to the small yet strong body and what seemed like limitless freedom—to go anywhere at any time and spread beauty along the way. The colors and design were an empty canvas; anything could be created on a butterfly wing.

I sat with folded legs on the cold sidewalk. September nights brought a sharp pinch of chilly air, which indicated the possibility of another harsh winter. I laid several older pictures against the concrete around me and started to sketch a new one. The butterfly I placed in Papa's casket was my favorite creation. The bodice was black with a vibrant glow of red and orange streaks exploding against the yellow wings.

Tonight, though, I would do a green one in honor of Anton. I worked feverishly for roughly thirty minutes without even the slightest response, until . . .

"What do we have here?" A group of mischievous teenagers looking for fun had stumbled upon my makeshift market. The boy who emerged as the group leader reached for the print before I could resist.

"Oops," he sniggered. His finger smudged across the chalk and smeared the right wing into blended destruction. The other boys laughed at what their friend had done.

My face swelled with heat, though I said nothing. He moved swiftly as I reached for the page but pawed at nothing but air. Again, he got a hoot from his entourage. My hands dropped, and I stared at him coldly. I didn't cower under his bullying nor take his bait, but simply said, "Sold. That will be one mark."

"Ha," he chuckled. I'm sure he thought I was joking. I didn't crack a smile. His eyebrow curled with curiosity as his lips wrinkled into a sly, half-grin.

"Well, it's damaged." He laughed out loud and winked at the only girl in the group. She giggled with delight at his attention.

"One mark or I scream," I said, clearly and slowly. My eyes zeroed in on his. His light-blue eyes pretended to be expressionless, yet his pupils dilated. His face tilted slightly. He attempted to play it cool as his hand brushed his blonde bangs aside, but his face angled just enough to prove he searched for confirmation of my bluff. There was no sound. I did not back down.

"Pshhh, Obdachlose." He shrugged his shoulders as if he didn't care. His hand reached into his dress pant pocket and sprinkled a few coins on the ground, well outside my reach. "Keep it. It's nothing." He glanced at me one last time, his mouth turned upward into a calculating grin as his shoe pressed weightily on the picture as he walked away.

I waited until they were completely out of sight before I scrambled to pick up the silver coins. He had paid three times what I had asked and ended his game with an insult. Tears of humiliation filled my eyes; I was like a beggar on the street.

Defeated, I gathered my belongings and fought the urge to openly cry until I got home. Even with my shameful attempt to make some money, the three marks I received wouldn't even get me a room for the night.

Discouraged, my shoulders hung heavy as I walked. The outline of the dirty shoe print, which had distorted my drawing, enraged and pained me equally. I thought about Anton and what he would do. This brought a meager smile to my face because I knew exactly what he'd do. The thought of seeing the arrogant snob flat on his back or forced to apologize was satisfying, despite it being an imaginary scheme.

Anton would never let anyone treat me that way. He made that very clear after a few physical run-ins his first year at the home. Eventually, by the time he was thirteen, his body had started to fill out, and he was no longer viewed as skinny and frail, but by then it didn't matter, because everyone was afraid of him.

***

"Anton, you have to stop fighting!" I cried as we made our way down the hallway.

"They just make me so mad, Ella." His hand rubbed along the top of his very short hair where the strands had recently been shaved off.

"They need to stop calling you Blackie!" Anton's face turned a shade darker the faster he spoke.

"Anton—" I reached for his arm to stop him, "—it's OK."

"But, Ella, you aren't!"

I timidly examined my feet. Anton had become my best friend in a short time, only there were things we still didn't talk about. "Nurse Margret says my papa had to be a Negro."

"Your mama wasn't."

"How do you know?"

"I saw your mama's picture, the one under your bed. She looks like me, only she has really blond hair."

"I guess. I don't remember. She left me when I was a baby."

"Look!" Anton held his pale-white arm against mine. "See, you're only a little darker than me. Like you are sunned!"

I laughed. It almost seemed true.

"It doesn't matter, anyway," Anton whispered, "except, if Frederick doesn't stop, he will be sorry."

For the first time, I saw Anton's face differently. It wasn't hidden anymore. His cheeks and jawbone were more defined than ever before, and those eyes—his striking eyes—were staring right at me.

"What?" he asked as he stopped near the stairway. The small candle's flame on the platter danced before him, his breath moving it unwittingly side to side. Anton's shield, pinned to his collar, flashed in response. I hadn't realized I was staring.

"What? What?" I brushed it off and kept walking, although something felt different inside my chest. I must be getting sick, I thought.

***

As I walked back into my empty apartment that night, after the degrading encounter with the rich boy, I wished rather hard I hadn't taken Anton's friendship for granted. I missed him so much it hurt.

That night, he was all I could think about as I fell asleep and clutched tightly in the palm of my hand was the same tinnie pin Anton wore in the orphanage.

CHAPTER SIX

Despite my first morning away from the Franke home, I could not sleep longer than eight o'clock. I'd returned to my own bed since I no longer watched over Papa, only there was no comfort in it.

The room I shared with Josef was dark and depressing. It didn't matter which way I turned my head; his memory was everywhere. The clothes he wore the day before he left still lay crumpled in a pile. The toy car he would push down the long hall, solely to hear the metal wheels against the tile, sat on top of the chest. The small leather bag of marbles had been dropped neglectfully to the floor.

I reluctantly slid off the bed to the cold floor. When I reached for the pouch, my fingers tangled in the string. Instantly, it reminded me of a similar bag, the one Anton discovered in the secret room.

***

It was the winter of 1953. Most of the children were down with the pox, and the nurses were distracted. Anton and I had wandered away from the group on one of our exploits around the home. It was a perfect cover since they never even realized we were gone.

We hadn't ventured far, just into the closet under the stairs when, unexpectedly, a wall rattled. Anton nudged it barely enough to reveal a tight chute leading downward. It was his idea to go down and see where it led. I was nervous; then again, we had had few adventures to be excited about. My hesitation was short, and the drop was not far.

We found a very small room in a basement, which supposedly didn't exist. The space was quite dark except for a few hand-sized slits. The gaps gave us a slanted view of shoes passing on the sidewalk in front of our building. These, and a few decent-sized holes in the walls, provided just enough light from the outside to move about. At first, I was scared, but then our eyes adjusted to the shadows, and I was eager to explore our new mysterious nook. We spent nearly twenty minutes in the dark space the first time we went.

This was our second visit down the chute, only this time we brought a candle. Anton swiped it from Nurse Gitta's room a week before and let Frederick take the blame. He was known for being a thief anyway, so it didn't matter if he was innocent this one time.

"I don't want to see you get kicked out, Anton. They might decide they've had enough," I suggested as I shuffled around the dusty space.

"I'm not scared," Anton said as he looked around.

We were alone. I wiped my moist hands against my skirt. Anton lifted the flame in my direction. It suddenly brought forth a whole new level of possibilities. I glanced around. My lip curled at the sight of rodent feces that dotted the floor. A handful of copper casings lay in a pile, tempting me forward.

"What are these?" I held them out to Anton. He reached for one and inspected it closely.

"It's from a gun," he declared confidently. I was surprised he knew this. A chill rippled my skin with the thought something violent must have happened here.

I momentarily strayed from our conversation as I eyed a stained and filthy bed roll in one corner and a partially broken stool in the other. Layers of paper were taped to the walls; writings neither one of us could really read, but lots of words were scratched, page after page.

"I wonder what happened here?" I inquired curiously as I brushed some of the garbage aside.

"It was a fight," Anton said so matter-of-factly. "A husband and wife fought, and she shot him . . . dead."

I rolled my eyes. "Why was she the one who shot him? Maybe he was a spy and discovered a secret . . . then he shot her!" I noticed a small stack of linens. I picked up the first one and shook the layered dust off it.

"He couldn't have hurt her—" Anton constructed the crime, "— she was the love of his life, but she betrayed him." He turned over a book with a broken spine. The soiled leather pouch appeared under a brittle newspaper.

My fingers brushed over fine lace that bordered a light-blue handkerchief. I was mesmerized. I'd never beheld anything quite so beautiful.

"They were childhood sweethearts—" I continued the story, "— she didn't betray him; he went to war and left her behind." I moved over to the small candle that flickered on the stool and held the linen to the light. In one corner, two small symbols had been embroidered in white, "כש".

"Maybe her name was Anna—" I wondered what the stitches meant.

"—And her husband's name was Dietrich," Anton said, as he untied the small strap and emptied the contents into his hand.

"He smoked," Anton added as a pipe and small tobacco can rolled out. I went to his side with the satin material still gripped in my fingers. I watched as he inspected the last two contents of the bag, a small photograph of a pretty woman and a crumpled piece of yellow fabric.

I peered at the photograph and whispered, "He was in love." I fought a smile. I wanted to laugh out loud; this had been a fun game.

"He was a Jew." Anton's voice was flat. I looked at his hands as he held the now-open, yellow fabric. It was a star with black lettering. It spelled "Jude".

Anton dropped everything instantly. His reaction startled me, and I dropped the linen as well. We looked at each other with a simultaneous realization. This room had been a hideaway for a Jew!

We had been fairly sheltered in the orphanage, yet the nurses talked. They talked a lot. The stories we overheard about the Jews were confusing and many times frightening. We knew about the yellow badge and that the people who wore them had disappeared during the war. It wasn't until much later that I learned about the death camps, the gas chambers, the ovens, and the scarred survivors.

I was born shortly after the war ended. Anton would have been born during the war, and even though he never talked about his past, rumors circulated. One of the older girls insisted Anton's father was involved in the Third Reich, Hitler's soldiers. Another one said his parents were imprisoned. No one seemed to know the real reason he ended up at our home at eight years of age, and I never asked.

This could explain his anger, though.

"We need to leave," Anton insisted. He grabbed my arm a little rougher than I expected.

"Ow, Anton, that hurt."

"Let's go, now!"

"OK, just let me grab the linen." I didn't wait for his answer. I gripped it tightly between my fingers.

"No!" His voice was sharp. "It's diseased!"

"Diseased with what?" I joked, although his face was dead serious.

"Leave it!"

"No!" I shot back. "I want to keep the handkerchief."

"It belonged to a Jew!"

"I don't care!"

Anton looked at me fairly alarmed. Without another word, he grabbed the linen from my hands. I watched as he threw it to the ground and headed straight for the chute.

"I'm leaving, Ella. Are you coming with me?" He had my only source of light and gave me little choice; I didn't want to remain with the rats.

With my fists tightly clenched, I stomped louder than normal as I made my way to the shaft and climbed up. Once back inside the closet, Anton blew the candle out. I didn't wait for him to check the hall for safety, I simply marched right out and back to my bed without another word.

I didn't speak to him the whole next day. It seemed he was as miserable as I was. The following night, when I pulled my blanket back to go to bed, the corner of the blue linen with the white initials was sticking out from under my pillow. I looked across to Anton's corner of the room. His sad, green eyes were apologetic and sorrowful. I smiled with instant forgiveness.

It was then I realized how much our friendship meant to him . . . and to me. Anton, it seemed, had been raised with such hateful feelings for the Jews, it must've been really hard for him to go back down to the secret room and get the linen for me. It was the same linen I gave him the night he left.

In the eight years I had owned it, the handkerchief had become one of my most cherished possessions, and Anton knew this, which is why he freely accepted it. This was also, most likely, why he left me his pin since it was the only item he ever cared about.

I slumped forward on my stomach as I reached for a wayward marble and let it roll against my fingers. Josef was the last to touch it. *What is he doing at this very moment?* It was nearly one month to the day they left—the longest I'd ever been apart from either one.

Looking around the room, I was reminded of my imminent end. Yet, instead of packing or cleaning, which all seemed useless since there was no place to go, I wallowed in self-pity until it hit me. I needed to draw. It was the only thing that made sense.

I pulled out my colored wax. Without hesitation, I drew the largest outline of a butterfly I'd ever done, and it was nowhere near being done on paper—I sketched it on the front room wall. The plaster crumbled several times under the pressure, yet it didn't stop me. Even when the sun set and the darkness penetrated through, I colored until each wax cube became useless.

With a life of limitations, my art seemed to be the only part I could control. I stood on the arm of the couch and lovingly traced the eyes with my finger. The bold, green shading stared hauntingly back at me. I reached for the last stub of red-colored wax and above the antennas wrote:

"To Anton and Josef, may you be as free as a butterfly."

CHAPTER SEVEN

As I dressed for work the next morning, my thoughts shifted from the butterfly sketch to finding a new place to live.

What I hadn't realized the night before and started to understand now was, that if I was ever to hear from Anton and Josef again, this is where it would happen. This was the only address they had for me. The reality of losing complete contact with them suddenly sank in. I cried the entire ride to work. At the Frankes', I inquired of Lena.

"Do you know of any rooms to rent?"

"Are you OK?" Lena's eyes narrowed. I turned away.

"I'm fine, I just didn't sleep well." It was partly true. My timeline was shrinking, and I feared my options.

"I don't, Ella. I'm sorry." She seemed genuine in her response, nevertheless, she quickly ushered me into the dining room. Today she would show me how to polish the silver. Afterward, her training took us to the sitting room and how to dust the chandelier.

Again, the teenage girl came gliding by like a breath of fresh air . . . like a butterfly. "Guten Morgen, Lena and . . . strange new girl," she greeted me with a giggle. "I'll have to call you all sorts of names unless you give me the real one." She stood still long enough to await my answer.

"I'm nobody you need to worry about," I responded without missing a beat on my duties.

"Well, 'Nobody,'" she cried out loud, "have a wonderful day!"

Once she was gone, I couldn't help a faint smile from surfacing. She was intriguing and seemed honest in her efforts to be kind. Yet, I was warned. Frau Franke was not one to cross. I could not chance doing anything she deemed out of place.

At lunch, I ate some diced tomato and pea pods I had pulled from the small potted plants in my kitchen window. I could not afford to lose any more weight; my rib bones had already started to protrude. There was no food at home, no Herr Krzinsky, and of course, I could touch nothing here.

I contemplated a plan as the other servants laughed and chatted about their personal lives, all with a decent meal spread before them. I kept entirely to myself until I was dragged in.

"Fräulein Kühn," the house driver called from across the kitchen. All eyes turned in my direction. "Why do you sit far away?" The words seemed innocent, the tone did not.

"I—" I actually didn't have an answer. I simply liked being alone.

"Come." He motioned to the table. "Come and tell us about yourself." He patted the stool next to him. Blood drained from my face. There was nothing I wanted to tell. *How can I avoid his request and not make enemies?*

"I'm not feeling well today." I pretended to cough. I was sure my red, swollen eyes would add proof to the charade.

Lena grinned and shook her head. I glanced away from her. I was sure she recalled our conversation earlier when I told her I was OK. I cleaned up my few leftovers and went back to work fifteen minutes early.

When Lena caught up with me in the dining room, she nudged me gently. "You are clever, Ella." I gasped, surprised at her boldness. "Oh, sweetie," she continued, "I know you aren't sick, although I don't blame you either. Max is nosy, gossips, and somehow has a way of getting cozy with all the new girls, so keep your lips and your legs closed when you're around him unless you want everyone to know your business!"

A commotion in the nearby kitchen disrupted our conversation. Lena peeked through the adjoining door.

"Stefan and his friends are here." She shook her head, annoyed.

"Who is Stefan?" I questioned, eager to take the focus off me.

"The spoiled rotten heir to the throne," she confirmed. "The entitled seventeen-year-old son to Herr and Frau Franke."

"Oh," I responded without further inquiry. I recalled my one glimpse of him the day Papa was buried; only it was from quite a distance and a nearly forgotten memory. I felt her staring at me.

"You haven't seen him, have you?" Lena inquired, surprised at my indifference.

"Not close, why?"

She grinned. "Because despite his horrible snobbery and lack of charm, . . . he is something remarkable to look at!" Her answer was meant to get some sort of rise out of me. I continued to work. I was not tempted in the least bit. The only seventeen-year-old on my mind was Anton.

"Who is the girl I see? The Schmetterling?" I changed the subject.

"Schmetterling?" Lena pulled away from watching the boy in the other room and peered at me inquisitively. "Why do you call her a butterfly?"

"Just the way she moves, I suppose."

"Her name is Katharina. She's fourteen and very sweet." Lena started working again.

"Somehow, she doesn't quite fit this family," I suggested.

Lena chuckled. "Yes, I believe you're right."

I thought about the Frankes as I cleaned. Katharina and her brief appearances, possibly the only one I could be fond of. Stefan, I'd only seen from a distance, not close enough for me to even have an opinion on his supposed appealing looks. Herr Franke, leading a dual life. And the one I was most frightened of, Frau Franke. When it came to her, I had no desire to do anything more than my duty and stay as far away as I possibly could. I shuddered, not wanting to dwell on it any longer.

"Why don't you come to the café with me and my boyfriend, Christoph, after work today?" Lena's question took me by surprise. I'd never been invited out with friends on a social call. I was sure to be an awkward guest.

"Um," I choked. I was flattered by the invite but scrambled for a way out. I'd almost forgotten I didn't need to lie to defend my aversion. I quickly responded, "I have to find a new place to live."

"How soon?" she asked, sincerely interested.

"Soon." I didn't want her to feel sorry for me.

"Why?"

"I live near Bernauer." It was all I had to say. Everyone knew what was happening there, we simply didn't talk about it.

"I'll check with Christoph tonight. He has many friends, lots of connections. I'm sure we will find something!"

This time on my way home, I took a bus to the Spree. Despite the secrets it kept, the river seemed calm in the darkness, peaceful and innocent. Lights from buildings on the other side reflected across the water. The faint sound of music carried through the air, and if I stood real still, I was sure I could hear laughter. Amusement was a luxury that rarely surfaced anymore in the East.

I wondered if Anton and Josef were laughing. Maybe eating a nice meal, visiting with new-found friends, or possibly walking along the other side of the river as well, wondering about me . . .

My serenity was disrupted by a sudden commotion near the river's edge. A small group of people had gathered at the bank. They pointed to something moving against the ripples. I squinted as they spoke.

"Ein Mensch!" came the cry. I stepped closer and finally saw what they were pointing to—a person was desperately trying to swim across the river. I'd heard of this as a means to freedom, but it was a perilous choice!

I wanted to look away, but my eyes fixated solely on the determined effort. I had recently read of two other swim attempts that ended badly. It was a very dangerous way to escape.

A man next to me directed my attention to the nearest guard tower; its lights immediately flashed across the blackness then concentrated heavily on the stirring form. The loudspeaker's repeated commands to stop and return to East Berlin seemed to be ignored as the movement appeared to speed up. My hand flew to my mouth in horror. I watched the swimmer shift and turn in a failed effort to evade their line of sight.

Can he possibly not see the reflection against the water or hear the shouts from high above? Or does he believe he still has a chance?

I was afraid to watch, yet curiosity drew my eyes to the tower. Guns had already been directed at their target. I could not pull away. Everything in my head told me to turn away, but I didn't. It was as if my own heart stopped the moment shots rang out.

The body no longer moved. It remained completely still and then began to roll and sink. A woman screamed. Her friend fainted. I turned from the other shocked spectators and leaned against the nearest tree to keep my own legs from collapsing.

Why did I look? Why didn't he stop?

My stomach heaved and convulsed. Thankfully, it was empty. I dropped to my knees weakly. *Why does life seem invaluable here? Why do I feel like we are living in an hourglass with the last remaining sand slipping away?*

My body shook uncontrollably, making it difficult to walk, focus, or think straight by the time I reached my flat. I had to get out of here. Not only this neighborhood but East Berlin. I must find a way.

This government killed for sport, mocking the desire for freedom and paving the path with innocent blood. It was too much to take in. I had to start searching for a way out. I had to escape or die trying.

CHAPTER EIGHT

Despite the difficulty of getting the ugly images of the shooting out of my mind, the next morning was like any other at work. Nobody even seemed to know or care that another innocent life had been violently taken in search of liberty.

On the back patio steps at lunch, the sun was shining, and the air was clean. It was a refreshing alternative to the stuffy, self-absorbed conversation inside. I glanced across the yard toward the cemetery. The tall grass swayed across the headstones. I thought of the rock I'd placed next to Papa. It had been too long since I had visited him.

A small piece of the biscuit Frau Ingobert had given me for retrieving Dotzi from the third floor this morning fell to the ground. I watched as a group of ants scurried from different directions, lining up swiftly and methodically, fixated on the rare prize. I suddenly felt like an ant, focused on one purpose, driven at any cost. Like the ants, I might get stepped on and squashed . . . yet the goal must remain, and despite the risks, I must press forward hoping the next foot that comes down is not on top of me.

"There you are." Lena opened the back door and sat next to me. "What are you doing out here?"

I smiled and pulled my eyes away from the ants. "I wanted some air."

"Well, I have some good news."

My lips pulled into a thin line, restricting even air as I waited. Her good news could be the dirty linen pile was not as high today or that the silver was untouched from dinner last night.

"Christoph has a classmate whose mother might rent out a bedroom." She patted my knee sweetly. This definitely was the best news I'd hoped for. "He will know in a few days."

I hid my frown. *A few days?* I only had one day left at Bernauer.

"Where is the flat located?" I tried to sound grateful. I really was.

"Treptow."

It really didn't matter where, I was desperate. I had hoped for sooner, but it was something. I had no other choice than to wait. Living on the street was an unappealing alternative. Although I'd spent a great deal of time around that lifestyle due to Anton, I wasn't strong enough to live it without him. Memories of Anton crept into my every thought as I worked through the day. He had been such a staple in my life for so long, I never pictured life without him. Even the day I left the orphanage.

***

The morning started out like any other morning. Anton would leave me before Nurse Gitta came to wake us up. None of the other children knew Anton slept with me; he would arrive after they fell asleep and leave before they awoke.

The way he held me at night was nothing more than a brother taking care of his sister. Only we knew if anyone saw it, they would assume the worst. He was the reason my nightmares had nearly ceased to exist.

I stepped onto the cold floor with my bare feet and shuffled to the window. My finger traced along the crack Anton had paid for in blood the year before, but it was the scene beyond that I searched for. I knew I was leaving today. This would be my last day ever in this room, this building, this life.

As excited as I was—especially at the idea of having a real family—the thought of leaving Anton behind tore me to pieces. I turned around—most of the kids were now up and awake—and scanned Anton's bed. It was empty. A sting rippled my soul. I realized I would somehow have to get used to that feeling.

I changed to the rarely used dress I received a year ago as my body started to change. It wasn't really new but new to me. It was the dress I would wear when I left with my new parents. I searched the kitchen, playroom, and hallways but no Anton. The only other place I could search was the secret room, the place we no longer went to. I waited until no one was around and slipped under the stairs to check it anyway.

"Anton?" I whispered, "Anton, are you in here?" I left the door open to allow some light to penetrate the darkness.

There was no answer as I walked toward the back. With the hall light shining through, I could see the panel to our secret room had been moved slightly. A small piece of paper was folded and stuck in the crease. I placed the paper in my pocket and shot out the door quickly, darting straight for my bed.

Again, Anton was nowhere to be found. I unfolded the paper and read the elementary letters, words that spelled out a simple goodbye. Tears clouded my eyes as I struggled to read his humble thoughts of affection, "Ella, Ich liebe dich, bis bald, Anton." I now knew he was gone, really gone. My greatest fear had been realized. Anton would not survive here without me. He had left on his own.

I went to his bed and sat down. The blanket neatly covered the mattress. His few possessions were gone; it was as if no one was ever here. My heart ached, but not in a permanent way, just empty. Somehow Anton would find me. I knew he could never be apart from me. I also knew he was stronger now and older and more resilient, so he'd be able to live like many other teenagers do on the street. No, I had not seen the last of Anton.

***

Looking back, had I known the happiness I would have with the Kühns, I would have wished for them sooner. I don't regret my time with Anton at all, but to have nothing—no warmth or love—then suddenly know what you had missed all of your life, it was like that first day I saw Anton's eyes . . . white, white, white then suddenly dark green, and your whole world changes.

Like back then, I had to believe I would see Anton again.

"Ella? . . . Ella?" Lena repeated my name, although I didn't realize it at the time. "Ella, I've been calling you. You left your apron on the back steps." Even though I faced her, my thoughts were far away. "Ella, you forgot your apron." I nodded. As Lena handed it to me, her face showed slight concern.

I smiled faintly.

"Are you OK?" she asked as we moved down the hallway together.

"Yes." I shook my head. "Yes, I'm fine." I rubbed my eyes.

"Did you hear there was a shooting in the Spree last night?" Lena declared. I stared silently as the image of the man being shot replayed in my head. Lena continued, "My friend Alex was walking his dog near the river when it happened. He said the man was murdered—plain shot to death."

I remained quiet. It was the first time I had ever seen anything like it. It still hadn't fully registered in my head.

"Alex said it took them almost thirty minutes to pull the man's body from the water. They had trouble locating it in the dark even with those bright spotlights. He had already started to sink, so they had to send a diver in." She spoke matter-of-factly. It seemed as though all emotion had been removed.

The troubling recollection brought tears to my eyes. I excused myself and rushed down the hall to the bathroom. I needed cold water or air—anything to help me forget what I'd seen. The man was somebody's son, brother, father, husband, or friend, . . . and his loved ones probably didn't even know he died trying to reach them. The reality of that insight suddenly made Anton and Josef's uncertainty much more difficult to bear.

CHAPTER NINE

The next day, a constant commotion filled the halls. Movement echoed up and down the stairs, out the back door, even outside my bricked windows. I knew the residents were on the move, at least those who had remained after the wall went up. I wasn't close to Frau Ingobert, but it was still difficult to say goodbye. I would not miss Dotzi much.

Out the back entry and around to the street. I watched mothers, fathers, and children carry what little belongings they had and leave their lives behind on Bernauer. Some loaded their furniture into trucks, others carried a simple suitcase each. I knew I would be one of them soon. The heavy burden of ambiguity resonated; I had no place to go.

It was only a matter of time before the soldiers would be here. They were everywhere. I couldn't take a step in any direction of the city without catching sight of the typical green tunic, matching pants, and the visor service cap of a uniformed soldier in front of me. Young, old, officers, conscripted, trucks, and tanks—my whole world had become a military zone.

With no current possibilities, I formulated a plan. My front door was kept locked and bolted at all times. I broke the last two of Mama's wine glasses and littered the glass both in the hall and near my entryway. If I happened to be sleeping when they came, I would at least have enough notice from the noise to get to my kitchen window. The plan was to be out in the alley before they reached the inside. I kept my coin purse tucked into a spare dress in a tasche by the window so I could grab it on my way out if I needed to leave quickly.

Two days passed. I fought hard to stay undetected. Even though I'd monitored and documented the People's Police rounds near my building, I feared discovery with each step. Every movement weighed heavily on my heart. My entry and exit daily through the window occurred under a shroud of darkness. Once inside the flat, the only illumination came from a small handheld flashlight. I also rarely slept. Unaware if anyone else in my building attempted anything similar, I heard and saw nothing. It was like living in a tomb.

By day four, nothing had transpired with Lena and Christoph's friend. I grew weary. Lack of sleep and constant fear affected me deeply, both at home and at work. I didn't know how much longer I could survive this way.

Each night, I deliberately slept in my clothes. The word "sleeping" was an overstatement. It was never a restful sleep. I was terrified. At night, when I lay in bed, I often thought about Josef and Anton. I thought about the life Anton lived on the streets and the choices he had to make because of me.

***

My adjustment with the Kühns was difficult. It wasn't for lack of affection or love. It was trust. Nine months had passed since the adoption, and I still snuck out of the apartment to see Anton. I was afraid if they knew about him, they would stop me. Especially since he was *Straßenkind* now, a street kid.

"Anton," I whispered from behind a post. It was low enough to not alert the group, yet loud enough to get his attention. He turned and smiled broadly. I didn't recognize his new friends.

"Ella." Anton came to me. He hugged me longer this time. It was nice. "Come join us." He kept one arm wrapped snuggly around me. At fifteen, Anton now appeared old enough to join the military. He even wore some of the clothing they did.

"Anton, no." I shook my head, my body trembling. I didn't want him to know I was scared.

"What's wrong?"

"I . . . I'm not sure."

"You will like my friends, Ella." He held me tight, but we still moved in their direction down a dark alley lit only by a bright flame that filled a metal can. There were only three people present. One I realized I *had* met before, the other two were strangers.

"Dirk, you remember Ella?"

The one familiar face peered up and nodded.

"Erich, Franz, . . . this is my friend Ella." The exchange between the two was not as subtle as they thought. Anton didn't seem to notice. I did.

"Ella, come sit down." Anton pointed to a wooden box. I sat, but the hair on my skin still tickled with unease. The darkness outside of our small circle produced shadows and noises I wasn't accustomed to. Anton, sitting on the dirt next to me, picked up a long stick and poked the fire.

Nobody spoke. The heavy sound of footsteps approached us from behind. I jumped at the sight of two more boys who ran anxiously toward us. They slowed to a stop when they reached the group but continued to gaze back in the direction they had come. It appeared as if they expected to be followed.

Both had short hair like Anton. As the light from the fire shone upon one boy's face, most of his cheek and neck appeared disfigured with scars. I didn't hide my surprise very well.

"Oh," I gasped aloud. Anton grabbed my hand.

"Ella, it's OK. It's only Willy and Jurek."

"It's my face." the scarred boy said disgustedly. He sat on the ground to join us.

"No, it's not, Jurek!" Anton defended. "She hasn't been to this part of town before."

"What is she doing here anyway?" The boy Anton called Jurek gave me a nasty look and added, "She doesn't belong here." It was obvious he was in charge. The other boys silently watched the exchange.

Anton put the stick down but still held my hand. "Why shouldn't she be here? She's with me." He stared hard at Jurek.

"Are you joking, Anton?" Jurek sniggered with revulsion in his voice. "You're stupid and blind," he mumbled.

Anton shot up before I even realized he was no longer next to me. His hands went straight for Jurek's throat.

"Anton!" I cried. I reached for him, but Willy pushed me back, and I stumbled over a pile of bricks. I didn't get up. Anton and Jurek rolled across the ground as they threw punches back and forth. Nobody else joined the fight.

"Stop them!" I yelled at the other boys. Their snickers told me they had no intention of complying.

Suddenly, Jurek's head hit a concrete block. Both their bodies went still. I could hear Anton's heavy breath slightly above Jurek's moans. Willy and Erich rushed to Jurek's side as Anton weakly rose to his feet. His hands and face were covered in blood. I reached for him, but he rejected my help, his eyes intently focused in Jurek's direction.

"Get out of here!" Willy hissed. "Take your *Müll* with you!" Anton's anger reignited as he lunged toward Willy and shoved him hard. Willy pushed back.

"Anton, let's go!" I shrieked. Tears streamed down my cheeks. Anton's face was inflamed. He turned from the others and grabbed my arm before we darted around the corner and down a couple of streets only to stop inside an abandoned building.

I studied Anton's wounds. He had cuts along his jaw and chin, and a deep bruise had started to swell at the edge of his right eye. Sweat dripped down his neck. I took out a handkerchief from my skirt pocket and held it up to stop the blood. Anton pushed it away, his breath heavy and labored. He dropped to a squat with his head in his hands.

We both knew why his friends didn't accept me, but we also knew if we talked about it out loud, it would become real. Anton never saw me as different. He only saw me as Ella. This was part of the reason I felt safe around him, only now I knew it came with a cost. I stepped in front of him.

"Anton, let me help you."

"No, Ella, I'm fine."

"Stop it! You're bleeding."

He covered his face as he let out a string of curse words. I knelt down and grabbed his arms. Even when he struggled to pull away, I held on.

"Anton, please stop." I squeezed tighter. "Come home with me." Anton's face was sickened.

"To the Kühns'?" He shot up and paced the floor. "That's your world, Ella, not mine!"

I stood and grabbed the front of his jacket firmly in my grip. Anton was nearly twice my size. I got in his face and forced him to look at me. "*You* are my world, Anton!"

Anton stared at me long and hard, then his eyes dropped to the ground. "OK." He wiped his face with his sleeve. "OK, I'll come."

***

Bam! Bam! Bam! The heavy pounding launched me flat to the floor. Face down, I realized I'd done exactly what I had meant not to do— fall asleep.

I rubbed my eyes and attempted to comprehend what was happening. They were blurry and strained. I heard another loud thud splinter the door as someone busted through. I leaped to my feet the very moment I heard the crunch of glass under heavy boots. They came in like I imagine a herd of wild animals would, how many I didn't know. I no longer had time to get to the kitchen window as planned.

Their inability to be discreet allowed enough coverage for my brazen dash to the bedroom closet. It was the only place I'd possibly have a chance to hide. I maneuvered to the far corner with only a few of Mama's dresses for cover. I smashed against the wall as closely as possible and pulled a long trench coat in front to make it appear as if it was the last item on the rack. A pair of winter boots was pushed forward to hide my feet. My toes curled tightly in the confined space behind them.

The brutes didn't seem to mind that their audacious duty came without restraint or consideration for anyone or anything. The sound of furniture upheaved, and dishes broken amplified with each passing second.

I was fully awake now, struggling to calm my surging breath. I cringed at the thought they would find my small collection of belongings near the back window. This included all the marks I had, yet I knew right now the money was the least of my problems. If they found me, I could be arrested or face far worse consequences. I'd heard stories of young women found at the hands of crazed, irrational soldiers. I had risked everything by staying in the flat.

Someone entered the bedroom and proceeded to flip the bed. If he had touched it, he would have felt the warmth my body heat left against the blanket. It didn't sound as though he had. Another man entered, and they talked about possible hiding places for valuables. The harder I pressed against the inner wall, the more I lost feeling in my limbs. I prayed they would not come over to the closet. It was useless. I knew they would check even before I heard the footsteps turn in my direction.

My breath seemed loud and unsteady, and I was sure it would give me away. The door flung open. The bright beam of a flashlight bounced all over inside. The hat boxes on the top shelf were thrown to the ground and opened with incessant grunts of disappointment.

Beads of sweat rolled down my face, the moisture making my skin itch. If I moved my hands to scratch, the coat would move, so I squeezed my lips and eyes shut. The soldier hit his long flashlight against the dresses, pulled them aside, and smacked the coat. It didn't move much. He hit it again. I could sense his hesitation. He lifted the coat at the hem and saw the boots. His cries echoed through the whole apartment, "Kommt! Ich habe jemanden gefunden!" I kept my eyes sealed shut. He had alerted his comrades that he had found someone. It was over. My face flushed with terror.

As the man reached for the boots, which he believed housed hidden feet, he shot backward with surprise. They moved too easily. The fellow soldiers who had gathered at the door, ready to attack, doubled over in laughter, mocking the man's foolish discovery. I twisted my toes up as tightly as possible, the deformity causing immense pain. In humiliation, the soldier slammed the closet door shut.

If only he had inspected further, he would have seen the *real* feet exposed. In a matter of seconds, the soldiers were gone. I collapsed to the floor of the small space, my body immersed in sweat and tears, weakened from fear and anxiety. I was completely shaken, yet too afraid to leave the closet until morning.

Chapter Ten

A fter work, two days later, Lena and Christoph led me to an area of East Berlin that was considerably more run-down than Mitte or Pankow. I had no choice but to stay positive. The woman who owned the flat was Frau Genau. Those who knew her called her Mama G. She had two adult daughters, but one recently got married, creating the vacancy.

Built in the early 1900s, the building was over sixty years old. I would have to grow accustomed to the stains and rancid smell; yet again, I did not have the luxury of time or choice on my side.

"This is quite agreeable if you will have me," I said, half lying. I scanned past the holes and peeling paint and spoke to Frau Genau in a whisper, "I won't have the money for rent until next week." I didn't want to tell her why. I already felt irresponsible about leaving my purse exposed when the soldiers broke in.

"You can move in next week," Frau Genau declared as she took a seat in her living room chair. I was devastated. I couldn't live much longer under my current conditions. I had slept in the closet again last night and was near a breaking point.

"I'm sorry, Frau Genau." I moved closer to her. "I was hoping I could move in tomorrow and pay next week." I tensed slightly as my lip began to quiver. Lena took my hand, sensing my concern.

"Uhh . . . Mama G?" Lena quipped. Frau Genau eyed us carefully, but Lena had a very persuasive personality. "I can speak for her, and she is trustworthy."

Christoph quickly agreed, although he had only met me an hour ago. "Yes, Mama, you can include me as a reference. She's responsible." Her daughter and Christoph were close classmates, and she had known Christoph for many years.

The silence was awkward. Finally, Frau Genau relented. "OK," she sighed. "You may move in tomorrow, but the forty marks are due by the 18th, then seventy-five by the third day every month following."

"Yes! Oh yes, thank you!" I was quite relieved! I wrote her address down, and even though she didn't seem like a woman who would go back on her word, I quickly said my goodbyes. I moved swiftly from the building and departed for home in case she changed her mind. Tonight, I believed, would be my last night in Mitte.

I strategically navigated the back roads and alleys on my final trek to the apartment. I was a young woman walking after dark, alone, in a city filled to the seams with fear. This thought should have been terrifying in itself, but instead, I found a bizarre sense of freedom. A release from the heavy burdens this place shouldered.

In a strange way, it was almost like the evacuation was doing me a favor. I no longer had to feel the weight of the depressing barrier in front of me every morning and every night nor hear the cries of empty hearts and hands when I saw the tears of children or relived my own painful separation. Yes, I would miss the good times, but the good times were embedded in my mind and not in the cold walls of an empty room.

I located Papa's old suitcase from when he was a shoe salesman. Its hinges had been slightly bent when it had been tossed across the front room. Despite the damage, if pushed tightly, the clasps would keep its contents quite secure.

I placed my limited belongings inside. Mama's brown angora sweater—the one she used to wear on Sunday walks—was found in the closet next to her dresses. I pressed the soft material against my face. Years later, the sweet scent of jasmine still lingered. Her bright smile came alive in my mind as I carefully folded it and placed it next to her wooden hairbrush.

A pile of shattered wood lay in a corner, the small cuckoo bird silenced. I sifted through the wreckage until I located the two small figurines who danced on the hour and lovingly tucked them in the corner.

Josef's *Chatterwell* storybook and his pouch of marbles went into the case next. Then I retrieved Papa's ivory pipe and Iron Cross medal. Luckily, I'd hidden them in a ripped seam in my mattress before the break-in. A couple of dresses later, I sealed the case tightly and set it in the closet.

Even with our few remaining possessions in the apartment, the home still appeared lived in. The phonograph I tried hard to keep safe was nowhere to be found. Only the cover remained, but I refused to let it discourage me. I took one last glance around my home for the last time on Bernauer Straße. It was a full look, committing as much as I could to memory, then tucking it all into a special place in my heart.

I found my way back to the closet, then dimmed the flashlight. Curling up on the floor, silent and numb, I waited for the sun to rise.

CHAPTER ELEVEN

It was a bit of an adjustment to go from living alone to living with complete strangers. Nevertheless, I learned very quickly why everyone called Frau Genau, "Mama G". She was like a mother hen, protective of those around her, and I was no exception.

Despite the unfavorable living conditions, I settled into my new life easily, attributing it to the minimal expectations I'd had since childhood and the ease with which Mama G made it.

One of the wonderful surprises I discovered after my arrival was another phonograph—much older than the one we had at the Kühns', but I was hardly picky.

Mama G only had one record, "Irgendwann Erwacht Ein Neuer Tag" ("Sometime Awakened a New Day"). She had a thing for Camillo Felgen's velvety voice. Watching Mama G's reaction as she listened to him croon nearly every night at sunset, renewed my own desire to search for "La Vie en Rose" *("Life in a Rosy Hue")* once again.

Work at the Frankes' was also going well. Quickly learning everything Lena taught me, I managed a routine of my own with responsibilities in the dining room, kitchen, parlors, and library. Each day was filled with constant labor, dusting, cleaning, vacuuming, washing, and polishing, only to repeat it all the next day.

Hard work was natural for me, so I pulled my weight wherever I went, but it was lonely. I missed my family.

After my adoption, there was very little time to get to know Mama Kühn. She was healthy when I first arrived, but thirteen months later, she fell violently ill. Josef suffered more with her loss. He was adopted a good three years before me, so he had had her for four of his eight years.

That one year with Mama was special. She spent much of our days educating me. I had a five-year-old reading level at the age of eleven, a typical consequence since the orphanage was always filled beyond capacity. Subsequently, education routinely fell far behind basic care.

My drawing was the only literacy lesson I engaged in, and it was self-taught. Art was my outlet in a very isolated existence. Mama worked tirelessly to help me learn to read, write, and discover a love for books.

It was because of that love that my favorite place to clean at the Frankes' was the library. They had an extensive supply and variety of books. On occasion, when I believed no one was around, I would pick one off the shelf and glance through it. Some I could read, others I could not, yet all fascinated me the same.

I had one book at home, besides Josef's childhood storybook. *Immensee* had been given to me from the Kühns the first Christmas I was with them. Written by Theodor Storm, the story follows Reinhard and Elisabeth throughout their tumultuous lives. Over time, what started out as a young friendship—surviving both separations and challenges— developed into love. It wasn't until after I finished it for the second time, I imagined my and Anton's lives somehow paralleling this story. Our own friendship started much the same way, only we faced a much larger division, one with no possible reunion in sight. It was a romantic thought but quite painfully hollow.

"What are you looking at?" The unexpected voice made me jump, and the book I held fell to the floor. I didn't move. Katharina walked over and picked it up.

"Oh, you don't want this one," she said with a wide smile. "I have a good one for you if you like poetry." She placed it back on the shelf and went to the opposite part of the room. Her finger ran along the spines of several books until she found one, removed it, and grabbed the book hidden behind it.

"You will love this one! It's from my secret place." Her happy, energetic personality radiated each time I saw her—a rare attribute in this home. Of course, with the life she lived, why would she be otherwise?

I remained still as she held it out to me. "It's OK—" she paused, "—my parents are away."

I wanted to. I was curious. As she picked up my hand and placed the small brown book in my palm, I glanced at the door for assurance then back at her. The name *Heiner Müller* was deeply engraved on the front cover. I smiled. Katharina knew what I knew . . . if her parents realized she had this book or even read it, they would be angry. His works had recently been banned in the DDR.

"Thank you, Katharina."

Her eyes went wide. "No fair, how do you know my name? I still don't know yours."

I grinned. "It's Ella."

Katharina paused as she stared at my face, only inches away. I hesitated and waited for the questions to come regarding my skin color. They always did.

"I believe you have the prettiest face I've ever seen."

I shifted uncomfortably, slightly shocked at her directness. "I—." My hand brushed a small bead of sweat off my nose. "I don't know what to say."

She smiled and whispered, "Thank you is enough."

I smiled back. "Thank you."

"Ella?" Katharina sat on one of the canapés in the room and patted the seat next to her. "Will you read with me?" I still didn't move. I was too nervous.

"It's OK, I promise," she assured me and patted the seat again.

I relaxed and moved to sit next to her. Opening the cover to the first poem, I handed it to her, indicating I wanted her to read first. Her beautiful, eloquent voice was perfect for poetry, the vocabulary recited was extensive and refined. She handed the book back to me when she finished. I was afraid to read now.

"Come on," she encouraged, "it's your turn." Her countenance was warm and inviting. She had such a natural way of making others feel good. I picked up the book and flipped the page.

"Leichter Regen auf Leit—"

"Leichtem Staub," Her encouragement was genuine.

"Leichtem Staub die Weiden im Gasthof—"

"Katharina?" a voice sailed in from the hall. "Katharina?"

"I'm in the library, Stefan," Katharina answered but didn't take her eyes off the book. "Keep going," she said. She didn't seem to care if Stefan saw us.

He entered.

It's hard to say whose expression was more surprised, his or mine. In the three weeks I had worked at the Frankes' home, I'd never managed to come face to face with Stefan. Nor did I really care. Although here, right now, I wished I'd had some foresight.

"What are you doing here?" Stefan's words came sharp.

"What do you mean?" Katharina missed the fact he directed his question to me. "I'm always in here," she responded.

"Not you." He pointed to me. "Her!"

"She's taking her break with me. We're reading." Katharina once again missed his underlying contempt.

"What are *you* doing in my house?" He stepped closer with a threatening look in his eyes. Those pale-blue eyes I would remember for the rest of my life.

"I'm staff. I work here." I boldly stood up from his sister's side.

She slowly tried to piece our conversation together.

"Not here, you aren't!" Stefan's disgust was clear.

"Stefan!" Katharina exclaimed. "You are being rude!"

"Katharina, she is Obdachlose—"

"No, I'm not!" I shot back defensively. "I'm not homeless!"

"She lives on the street, Katharina! She's a beggar!" Stefan's light complexion turned a deep shade of red. "Mother would be livid if she knew."

Katharina's eyes went wide, glancing at me and then her brother. It was apparent she wondered who told the truth.

"How do you know this, Stefan?" She asked logically, showing maturity beyond her years.

I wondered what he would say. His condescension toward me and my drawing would always be engrained in my memory.

"I saw her," were the only words uttered in response.

I turned to Katharina and pleaded, "I rent a room. I have a home."

"Are you saying you were never selling a painting down at the Friedrichstraße station with the other vagabonds?" Stefan was unrelenting.

"I was selling my artwork to *avoid* being homeless," my voice rose heatedly. I couldn't believe I had to justify anything to this spoiled boy.

"Why don't you tell Katharina how you really behaved that ni—," I bit my lip with restraint. I had more to lose now.

Stefan's stance was unmoved. His eyes narrowed. "You don't belong here!" he snapped.

Katharina held her hand up, "Please, be quiet." She stared at us, then at the door. Her eyes reflected concern as if others might hear.

"Katharina, I am *not* from the streets. Ask Lena."

"Who's Lena?" Stefan asked as he glared in my direction.

"You know Lena, our maid," Katharina answered. Of course he wouldn't know, even though she'd been there for years.

"Get this taken care of Katharina!" Stefan demanded. "The streets are full of resistance to the DDR, and Father's reputation is at stake."

As if he really cared about that with all his own irresponsible conduct.

"She could be an oppositionist." He sneered and walked out.

"I'm not a rebel, Katharina." I placed my hand over hers. "I don't side with anyone politically, . . . and I'm not from the streets."

"I believe you, Ella," she sighed. Her eyes grew sad. "But I must confirm it for Father's sake."

I knew I had nothing to worry about, Lena would clarify the situation. Although, the fact Stefan caused Katharina to have doubts of my integrity bothered me greatly. Additionally, his shallow attitude skillfully managed to degrade me a second time without, it seemed, an ounce of regret in his body. He infuriated me.

Chapter Twelve

Nothing more was said that week about my supposed guilt by association. I assumed my "background" checked out. The fact that I'd been accused of being involved with the opposition was bad enough, but it was worse coming from someone who pretended he cared what his father thought. If Herr Franke knew how reckless and foolish his own son was and the damage Stefan himself caused the family name, he would be the one on the street.

It wasn't a big secret Herr Franke had close ties to the government, especially when their guests were always associates of the Peoples Republic, *der Nationalen Volksarmee,* or State Security. What did surprise me was how Stefan, one of very few young men of age, was able to avoid conscript.

It was the required military service for *every* German boy. Either his father's connections were very high, which was possible, or his bribe was very high . . . also possible. Either way, Stefan lived a very carefree life with no ties to anything, family included.

As repetitive as the days had become, by late October I started a childish countdown in wax on my bedroom mirror. A daunting 674 days left of debt servitude. I should be more grateful. Despite the vacancies in just about every vocation in the East, jobs somehow remained limited.

This was a calculated way the Soviet Union could control the people. If we were dependent on them for basic necessities, we would not bite the hand that fed us. So basically, their success came from starvation first, then minimal sustenance to "save" us.

Too many people in Germany were uneducated and blind. Many Germans were led to believe we . . . (although I call myself a German geographically, I don't believe any German blood runs through my veins) really were the elite race. We deserved more because of who we were. With the loss of World War II and then the smorgasbord of other countries dipping in, many believed we were only in a rebuilding stage to dominate once again.

There were actually people here in Berlin who believed the rhetoric that the wall was placed for our protection *from* the Allies. Despite my own limited formal education, my adoptive parents were very thorough in their social and historical teachings. Papa Kühn, while he fought alongside the Nazis, grew to despise the regime. He spoke very little of the horrors he witnessed, but he emphasized greatly the importance of awareness and knowledge.

The more I read in secret or on breaks from the very books Herr Franke stocked in his own library, the more disgusted I was with ignorance. It was the ability to keep citizens unaware that led to dictatorship and control. Ignorance led us to follow Adolf Hitler, and it was ignorance that allowed a senseless wall to be built. If more people took the time to educate themselves on the simple workings of their own government, Berlin would be a completely different city.

Despite the steady economic decline in East Berlin, Herr Franke continued to entertain as if he was the King of England, and his house was Buckingham Palace. No expense was ever spared for his guests. Imported wine from Bordeaux, France, chocolates from Brussels, and pastries from Vienna. He had connections all over the world, and while people were dying in attempts to leave our side of Berlin, Herr Franke flaunted a ridiculous level of luxury and freedom at the same time he pushed a belief in communist control. Although I was never privy to know the specific involvement Herr Franke had in the DDR, I slowly learned it was not on the sidelines watching the parade.

Part of Lena's standard duty, outside of cleaning the private rooms, was to make sure the guests were properly satisfied in the parlor. This meant their glasses were kept full and their accommodations comfortable. I'd only done this once before when Lena was called to other pressing matters. I was not as experienced as she was. Thus, when Frau Franke called for me shortly before the end of my shift, I had reason to be nervous.

"Fräulein Kühn!" My name rolled quickly off her sharp tongue.

"Yes, Frau Franke?" I hustled down the hallway the moment she called me.

"Lena is detained. I will need you to stay later tonight and see to our guests and"—she wrinkled her nose at my dirty apron—"do not confuse the *Pfannkuchen* with the *Streusselschnecken* this time!" She handed me a bright blue apron that was much nicer than my normal one and insisted I change immediately. It seemed obvious it wasn't a request and more of a demand.

I swiftly walked into the parlor with a crystal decanter in one hand and a platter of sweet pastries in the other. The men, deep in discussion, didn't even know I'd entered.

"Herr Franke, the man was an enemy of the state. His property has been confiscated and all his financial accounts seized. If his family comes to you about the body, you are to deny he was ever brought here."

"More schnapps, sir?" I held the glass vessel toward the highest-ranking officer's direction. Spotting their classification insignia was a trick Lena taught me early on. The man continued to talk, then paused as he peered up at me. His face went completely still.

"May I refill your glass, sir?" I asked again, although his stare was a bit unnerving. I was sure it had to do with the color of my skin. I braced for his reaction.

He turned to Herr Franke, still silent, yet pointed to me. I half expected him to humiliate me or demand me to leave. I stood there patiently. I was afraid if I walked out, it would be considered rude, and I could get fired.

"Herr Mielke, is there a problem?" Herr Franke noticed his guest's unusual behavior as well.

"She . . . she is your maid?" he stuttered then turned to his colleague and whispered.

"Is there an issue, sir?" Herr Franke leaned forward.

"You don't see it, Koen? Markus?"

"See what?" Herr Franke stared hard in my direction, his forehead wrinkled, confused. Each of the three men scrutinized me from top to bottom while I shifted in place.

"The uncanny resemblance this Fräulein has to Fräulein Grist." The man referred to as Mielke stood up and walked around me as he viewed my backside. I had donned a work dress that showed no skin other than my arms and legs, yet I felt exposed.

"Yes, I believe you're right!" the other guest, referred to as Markus, spoke up.

"Reri Grist? The opera singer?" Herr Franke said. It was apparent he was surprised at this sudden interruption in their business.

"Her color is lighter but look at these cheekbones" —he pointed to my face— "and the figure." His smile went wide as he continued. "They could almost be sisters." He spoke of me as if I were a mannequin in a shop window and couldn't hear or feel. My humiliation multiplied. I didn't know who this Grist woman was, but I was real and wanted to leave.

"I suppose there is a similarity," Herr Franke sounded annoyed, "but let's get back to the business at hand, shall we?"

The man was still astonished by his discovery. He couldn't pull his eyes away.

"Fräulein Kühn, take your leave, please."

I'd never been so thankful for any words out of Herr Franke's mouth before.

Once back in the kitchen, I grabbed a cool cloth and wiped my face. I remembered now why I hated serving the first time too. It wasn't like cleaning and attending to the Franke family; there was a more shameful exploit behind the assistance to their guests. It definitely felt more like bondage than service, and while I disliked both, one outweighed the other in significance.

"Are you OK, Ella?" Lena appeared.

"I guess." I put the cloth down and refilled the flask with more alcohol.

"You look upset. Did something happen?" Lena added *Buletten* to the tray and placed a small dish of white sauce next to the meatballs. She was much better at this than I was.

"How come you aren't serving today?" I tried not to sound jealous of her time away.

"I was needed in the mortuary," she said nearly mumbling.

"What do you mean, mortuary," I responded with surprise. "I didn't know we were allowed in there?"

She brushed it aside and smiled. "Would you like me to finish this for you?" She grabbed the tray gracefully with one hand and the drink with the other.

"Yes!" I jumped at the opportunity. "I think this Herr Mielke is distracted by my resemblance to some famous opera singer." I half-heartedly laughed but was still bothered by the whole thing.

Lena paused; her mouth curved into a frown. "Did you say Mielke?" She stared at me intently.

Lines between my eyebrows formed quickly. I was sure that's what Herr Franke called him. "Yes, I believe it's him."

"—An older man in his fifties with a high forehead and slit-like eyes?"

"Yes."

Lena placed the tray down before she lost her balance. I studied her curiously. Her radiant skin suddenly hovered between pale and white.

"Are you OK?" The tables had turned.

"Yes—" her response was shaky as if she was lying.

"I can do it, Lena." I reached for the tray. Her mind was elsewhere when I slipped past her with the delicacies and grabbed the glass decanter.

She never protested.

When I entered the second time, I never regarded the guests directly as I did the first time. I could still feel his stare as I moved around the room.

"Once we have the mines, gravel, and tank traps in place, not one soul will leave Berlin from this time forth," Mielke demanded, "—and if they do, we will have plenty of business for you, Koen. It's time we made a statement about what we are willing to allow."

I was able to keep a straight face while I worked but was very anxious to get out of the room once again. I knew they referred to the wall. The talk of a second wall parallel to the first had already begun. Their intent was to create a death strip, an impossible space of land where escape could never happen.

Suddenly, there was pounding on the front door. It was quite loud, alarming everyone in the house. I rushed to open it. Two *Volkspolizien* appeared and inquired about Mielke and Wolf. The officers were nearly out of breath as I led them to the parlor.

"May I get you a drink?" I asked them, more out of a curiosity to hear their seemingly urgent news than kindness.

"Yes, please! Whatever you have." I went to the bar and began to fill the two new glasses. The men appeared fatigued from their rush and struggled to catch their breath before they spoke.

"Herr Mielke! My apologies, sir, . . . we have a situation." The officer looked to Herr Franke then back to Mielke.

"It's OK, son, you can speak freely here."

"There's a standoff!"

"What do you mean a standoff?"

"The people's police refused to allow a United States diplomat access into East Germany—" the young man inhaled sharply, "—the Americans responded by bringing their M48 tanks to Checkpoint C."

Mielke and Wolf stood up, anger raging in their faces. My hands shook slightly with their sudden cursing. I wasn't sure if this was a good time to give the officers their drinks. I stood very still with my back to them. They might not have even noticed I was still present.

"How far are the tanks from the checkpoint, and are they in motion?"

"Approximately 75 metres, sir, and currently they are immobile, but their engines are on." The officer shifted uncomfortably.

Mielke's face crinkled with fury. "Those *beschissene Amis*—"

"That's not all, sir." The young man waited until Mielke faced him once again. "Khrushchev has already responded. He wants an equal number of T55s at the border immediately."

"Coat!" Mielke cried. I ran to the closet and pulled out the men's coats and hats then quickly held them forward. Snatching them, they still cursed under their breath and in a matter of seconds, everyone was gone, including Herr Franke.

Trying to wrap my head around what just happened, I rushed to the kitchen, desperate to tell someone, but found it dark and silent. Where was Lena? Had she left for the night or only for the moment?

My heart pounded, unsure if this "standoff" was the beginning of another skirmish—a war—or simply a show of power? I feared the idea of more death. Berlin had not even recovered from the last time. We were unstable and weak, and if the Allies moved against us, there could be more civilian catastrophes than military destruction. Yet, a part of me felt a sudden thrill at the prospect that maybe the Americans or their British and French Allies could somehow blast through the disgraceful wall with those tanks and set us free.

Chapter Thirteen

By the next morning, all of Berlin seemed to know what was happening at Checkpoint Charlie. Word on the street was that many people had mixed feelings, like me. Yet within a few hours of daylight, despite the potential damage a tank could do, citizens gathered in curiosity to watch the face-off.

It wasn't long, however, before we witnessed a Soviet tank at the back suddenly reverse and pull away. Then an American tank did the same on the west side. One by one, all the tanks retreated. Commanding officers subsequently released the additional border soldiers from guard duty. No obvious exchange of words was witnessed between the two parties as this equal, silent surrender occurred. Within minutes, it was all over, and the checkpoint appeared exactly as it had been for the last three months.

Once again, I couldn't quite identify my feelings as I headed to work. Was I sad the Allied tanks didn't tear down the wall? Was I relieved no destruction ensued? One thing I was sure of though, each passing day the barrier remained was another day away from Anton and Josef.

Throughout the day, military trucks with large speakers mounted on the back rolled through the city street by street. They announced the success of the DDR's ability to lead and protect its own people. This, I was sure, was an attempt to produce continued contempt against the Allies. I watched and listened with my own misgivings.

My own knowledge about the Allies or life in the West was minimal; nevertheless, in the few months of employment at the Frankes' home, I learned very quickly who the leadership in the East really plotted and conspired against. Unfortunately, it was not so much the other countries, but their own . . . the people of East Germany.

During the next three weeks, a grey *Kastenwagen* stopped at the mortuary twice daily. It just happened that the timing of the van's second delivery was always around the time I washed the windows in the back part of the house.

From this view, I could see several large, black bags being unloaded. By their size and the way the weight shifted when moved, it was easy to assume they contained bodies.

Now, I knew it wasn't unusual for deceased people to be delivered to a mortuary, I just often thought back to the conversation Herr Mielke and Herr Franke had the night of the standoff. *Have they already begun their quest to completely control the city, even if it's by deadly force?*

"Ella, you should really come out with Christoph and me tonight." I jumped at the sound of Lena's voice behind me. She giggled. "Well, aren't you skittish?" I shrugged my shoulders and went back to work as she continued, "Christoph is bringing a few of his university classmates this time."

"Lena, I'm only sixteen."

"And I'm twenty. What difference does it make? My father was twenty-eight when he married my mother, and she was only seventeen."

"I'm not getting married."

"True, but you are not dating either." Lena sighed. "Your life is dull: you work and go home . . . such a waste of your pretty face," she laughed.

"I'm perfectly fine at home. Besides, there's only one person I want to be with, and he's not here."

Lena stopped what she was doing and moved closer to me. "What's his name?"

I paused and then realized something—I'd worked with Lena for over three months, and I'd never mentioned anything about Anton and Josef to her. There was no question I trusted her, only it was rather personal.

"What's his name?" she tenderly asked again.

"It's Anton," I whispered, afraid someone else would hear.

"Where is he?"

I still hadn't moved since I said his name. Lena stared at me. "Anton," I said again, enjoying the sound of his name finally spoken out loud. If he was here, we would probably join Lena and Christoph tonight together. Possibly not, but it was a dream I would like to have.

"I know, you said Anton." Lena watched me strangely. "Where is

Anton, Ella?" Her hand went to my shoulder, and tears sprang to my eyes, threatening to spill as she whispered in my ear, "He's on the other side, isn't he?"

I nodded. Many people had the same story, but it was still hard to tell.

Lena hugged me tightly. "I'm sorry."

I shrugged. Their absence became more and more real with each passing day. My fingers immediately found Anton's tinnie pin inside my dress. I unfastened the clasp and handed it to Lena. She looked at the shield admiringly.

"Is this Anton's?"

"Yes, it's from his father. He gave it to me the night he left."

Lena smiled and handed it back. "What a special gift."

I nodded and let the grooves sink into my fingers before pinning it back inside. I pictured the pin once attached to Anton's collar and smiled at the memory.

"I need to go get more clean rags," Lena cried. "Why don't you finish up in here? I'll get you an *Orangensaft* as well. I made the juice fresh this morning."

"Is that OK?" I asked apprehensively.

"Certainly!" She smiled widely. "I'll be back soon."

I grinned sheepishly, buoyed by her high spirits. She always found a way to lift me when others couldn't. As I moved around the room, I reflected on how sweet Lena had been to me since the first day, never judgmental or cruel. She always sought opportunities to put others before herself. How lucky I was to have met her.

My hands worked quickly as I continued to wash the mirrors and await her return. This room had more mirrors and glass than any other room I'd ever seen. Of course, I'd never seen all the rooms in the house, because I only worked in the main areas on the first floor, but I was sure they were equally beautiful.

As I stepped out to get the back side of the veranda door, Stefan and a friend walked into the sitting room. I was suddenly trapped! There was very little chance he'd seen me since I'd closed the doors right before I heard voices, but now there was no way to leave except through the room, past Stefan.

I contemplated my predicament.

I could walk in and possibly subject myself to another round of deni-
gration—only with an audience—or I could wait until they left, hoping
their stay was short.

Breathing as shallowly as possible, I pressed my back against the
stone wall and eyed the two through the beveled glass. I could still see
them, but they would not see me.

"Stefan! My parents would never agree."

"They don't have to know," Stefan reasoned with his friend. I could
not see either face clearly but was sure it was a friend from the park the
first night I saw them.

"I know someone who can forge papers. We can cross the border and
be skiing in Krkonose by New Year's Day."

"What if we get caught?"

"Ralf, stop being childish. We won't get caught! Our parents already
know we'll be gone for two weeks. We have the money. I know I don't
want to sit in some boring camp when I can be on holiday."

"I don't know, Stefan. If *I* get caught, I could get in much more trouble
than you."

I rolled my eyes. Clearly, I wasn't the only one who noticed Stefan's
unique ability to get away with anything.

"I'll take care of everything."

"Ella?" Lena walked into the room with a full glass of juice, interrupt-
ing Stefan and his friend. My heart stopped. He can't know I just heard
his plan.

"Oh, I'm sorry, sir," Lena apologized and glanced around.

"Who are you looking for?" he asked suspiciously.

"I . . . I thought Ella was working in here."

"No." He peered around himself, taking a few tentative steps toward
the veranda. I pressed my back as level as I could against the stone wall
and held my breath. If he stepped out here, I would be done for.

"Nobody else is here," he added.

"Would you or your guest like something to drink?" Lena offered the
drink to Stefan. He refused.

"We must go." He motioned to the door and escorted his friend out.
Lena set the glass on a table and scanned the room. Slowly, I stepped
forward and opened the door.

She gasped. "Why were you hiding out there?"

Anxiously, I motioned for her to whisper in case Stefan was close—she didn't know our history. I pressed the door closed behind me.

"I was working and . . . afraid I would get in trouble . . . if Stefan knew I was out there." I stammered.

"Well, yes, Ella, if you're sneaking around."

"He just—" I wiped the sweat off my forehead as I struggled to explain, "—he just makes me nervous."

"Stefan?" she laughed. "He's harmless . . . rotten but harmless." I shook my head subtly . . . *not as harmless as everyone thinks.*

"Come on, have a drink." She hustled me over to the couch. "You look a mess."

I laughed nervously. My hands still shook.

"Sit down, take a sip, and then let's get going. The day is nearly over."

A few minutes later, we stepped out of the room together. She had managed to get me to forget about Stefan and almost agree to go out with her and Christoph tonight . . . almost.

As we closed the room door behind us, Stefan faced us directly. My heart stopped at the sight of him, and Lena jumped. His countenance clearly confirmed that he had his suspicions. He didn't say anything. We all realized he now knew I'd somehow been in the room the whole time. He also recognized the fact that I had confidential information against him.

We quickly turned away, arm in arm, hustling down to the staff hall—our safe zone—a place members of the family rarely went. Stefan didn't follow us. As we arrived at the back room, I finally took a breath.

"Well, that was strange," Lena chuckled awkwardly. It was a peculiar laugh, not her normal one.

"Ja." I hid my trembling hands behind my back. She didn't know the extent of my fear. I slowly untied my apron and put it away, unable to stop thinking about what just happened.

Would he corner me? Threaten me? Get me fired . . . arrested? How far would Stefan go to keep me quiet?

Never before had I felt the need to reveal *anything* said within these walls, although Stefan didn't know this about me. That thought alone was terrifying.

As I stepped outside of the house, Lena asked me again, "Are you sure you don't want to join us? It's not far, and we won't stay out late." She pulled her scarf tighter around her neck just as flecks of falling snow settled in her hair.

"No, but thank you."

I shoved my cold hands into my coat pockets and turned to walk in the other direction. Suddenly, an uncomfortable feeling crept up my spine.

I gazed around, peering back at the Frankes'. The house was a daunting silhouette against the rising moon. The shaded windows and sculpted stone revealed very little. I saw nothing to make me feel as though I was in jeopardy, yet I couldn't shake it. There's no other feeling in the world like the sensation you're being watched. I pulled my hat lower over my ears. I hesitated, then turned and waved Lena down.

"On second thought, Lena, I would love to go," I fibbed. Meeting new people truly petrified me, but in the end, it prevailed over my mysterious unease.

CHAPTER FOURTEEN

"Lena!" I called for her to sit by me at lunch. I was anxious to rekindle the vague conversation we had about Herr Mielke when he was here, weeks ago.

In passing, I recently mentioned his name to Mama G and got a similar reaction. "Master of Death," she repeated over and over, "an evil, evil man". I didn't push for a more extensive answer but wondered why it had affected Lena personally.

I diced and dressed a small potato then smothered it in a thick, brown gravy. Having a decent wage never smelled so good. I reached for a second plate, anxious to turn my ear away from the growing staff gossip.

The recent detainment and trial of Adolf Eichmann were all anyone had spoken of during the last three days. While I had no sympathy for the man who was accused of an unknown number of innocent deaths, the detailed brutalities made me physically nauseous.

"Here you go." I set the plate down for Lena as she removed her apron and placed it on a nearby hook. Her presence was refreshing.

"Good morning, Ella, thank you," she said joyfully. "I guess good afternoon, actually," she corrected herself then laughed in her usual way.

"You seem to be happy about something," I inquired with a smile.

"I am in love, Ella, dear . . . and love makes everyone happy." She giggled, and her eyes radiated. I couldn't wait until that happened to me.

"Oh, Lena,"—I remembered I was going to ask her about Mielke— "you never told me why the name Mielke bothered you so much the night he was here," I whispered, well out of the other staff's earshot.

Her face dropped a little as she pulled a stool right up next to me, apparently not in any rush to answer. "You know, Ella," —she carefully unwrapped her homemade currywurst and arranged it on the plate I provided—"Christoph's friend Rainer asked about you last night. He visited Christoph after work."

How could he possibly be interested? I wondered. It had only been two days, and I barely spoke to him the night I went out with Lena! I eyed her quizzically. Either she didn't hear me, or she deliberately ignored the subject of Mielke.

"He seems to be quite taken by you since the café."

"Lena?"

"He was intrigued by your shyness, ha-ha, your shyness, Ella!" She chuckled. "He didn't realize you aren't shy, just unsocial, but we really know what he's most attracted to."

"Lena!" I grew irritated at her avoidance.

She scrutinized me directly. Even though I could hear her voice, low and unwavering, her face seemed to remain completely still. "We do not talk about such things here, Ella," she snapped. She surveyed the other staff. "It's too risky. Don't ever do it again!"

I was stunned to silence—shocked at what just happened—and spent the rest of the lunch break stewing with frustration.

I knew she was right. It just stung coming from her. We lived in a world where you could barely trust your own family and friends. Particularly here, in the Frankes' home, you never knew what malicious plans were being industrialized and who was behind them. People like Mielke, who at the very sound of his name, sent shivers up the spine of many.

Maybe I was never part of any "side" prior to my employment here, but I wasn't entirely against the idea of a revolution either, especially as I continued to watch people like the Frankes benefit from the dirty dealings of a corrupt government. Leaders like Ulbricht, Wolf, and Mielke, all men who dominated through terror and lies, and the good people of Berlin just wondering if they would make it from one day to the next, not only economically but with their very lives.

As I worked through the afternoon without another word to anyone, my mind was on overdrive. Questions continually bombarded my brain in the quietness of each room.

Why was the Frankes' mortuary so lucrative when many other businesses failed? Why did they seem to have an adequate supply of dead bodies delivered secretly each week? Why are we restricted from the mortuary, except for Lena? Why do the state police come every Tuesday evening after we leave? Why would someone as powerful as Herr Mielke be doing business in the Frankes' home?

I, obviously, had no answers to those questions, and the later the day grew, the more ridiculous the questions got.

Why is there a pot of common hop in the kitchen? Why do they have a signed and framed photograph of the Kessler twins in the library? Why do Katharina's shoes always match the dress she wears? Do the Frankes really love their children?

I never saw any affection in the home; never with the adults and never expressed to the children. Even though I was devoid of parental affections myself most of my young life, I knew without a doubt when someone really cared for me.

"Ella!" Katharina's cry wailed from the hallway. It almost frightened me. "Ella!" she repeated until spotting me in the parlor where I dusted a lamp in the corner. "Ella! I'm glad I found you!" she gasped, nearly out of breath. "I need your help."

I immediately placed the duster down and went to her. My eyes widened at the thought of something tragic.

"Katharina, calm down and catch your breath. What happened?"

"I was—" She sighed deeply. "—I was studying my Latin in the library when all of a sudden . . ." she paused.

My eyes amplified.

". . . the most offending thing . . ." her voice constricted.

"What?"

She sniffled. "I realized I forgot to get my mother a birthday present."

My lower lip dropped a good inch from my upper one. I would have rolled my eyes in disgust if it weren't for the genuine tears that rolled hastily down her perfect cheeks. Of course, the most dreadful thing she had ever faced was the fact that she forgot her mother's birthday.

"The party is at seven o'clock, and I'm three hours away from being the cruelest daughter a person could ever have." Her dramatics were not a show. She truly believed this childish mistake would put her on the naughty list for life.

I grabbed the simple linen in my pocket and handed it to her. She grinned sheepishly. "You must think I'm a silly girl." I didn't say anything. Of all the people in this home, she had the most caring heart of all. Naturally, this was devastating to her.

"What can I do to help?" I asked hesitantly. I had no money. No gift myself. What could I do to remedy the situation?

"Well, I was thinking—" She blew her nose. "—Stefan mentioned that day in the library that you were selling a painting. Do you paint, Ella?"

"Oh . . . no . . . no . . . I—" I jumped up from the loveseat and slowly backed up. "—I dabble. It's nothing like the grand paintings you have here!"

"But that's just it, Ella. It's nothing my mom has ever had."

"Ha," I laughed. It was definitely something she didn't have because it was worth nothing.

"Please, I'm desperate."

"Yes, you are." I chuckled to myself.

"Please, will you help me?"

"Katharina, I don't have anything here. I don't have any supplies."

"Oh, it's not a problem, we have an art room."

"You have an art room . . . here?" I knew there were rooms I hadn't seen, but a whole room dedicated to art?

"Yes, I will show you." She grabbed my hand and led me to a second-floor room near the back.

She was a kid in a candy store, dancing around the room and pulling open cupboards and drawers full of brushes and paints. Every kind of tool an artist would be delighted with—and colors I didn't even know existed. I was in shock, so much so that I couldn't even move.

"It's OK to touch," Katharina assured me.

My face lit up as I scanned the room. "Who does this belong to?" I asked, my hand brushing over the nearly untouched supplies.

"It's Stefan's." My hand recoiled, and I stepped backward as she shrugged. "But he stopped painting a couple of years ago. It just sits here."

"I can't. I'm sorry." I wanted to help, but it felt wrong. Being here in this room—touching, wanting—everything about this idea seemed wrong.

"You must. Please." Her face fell.

She had been nothing but kind to me since I arrived. Indecisively, I bit my lip.

"Please?" she begged.

"Do you have chalk?" I surrendered to her pleas. She smiled widely and pulled open a small cabinet. It contained rows and rows of brand-new chalk. It was unlike anything I'd ever seen.

"What about work?" I hadn't completed my duties yet. With the party only a short time away, I knew I would be missed.

"I will take care of work! I'll be back in an hour!" And she was gone.

I sighed. *What I would give to have this room. How could it just sit unused?* I located a small stack of boards in one corner and found a plain white canvas, no bigger than a tile square. Despite my inexperience with this type of background, I knew this meant a lot to Katharina. It needed to look special.

The only thing I knew how to draw exceptionally was my butterflies. What would I do for Frau Inga Franke though?

I walked around the small room as I searched for inspiration. Within minutes, I stumbled upon a magnificent picture. A lush green hill was surrounded by an enchanting village. The thickness of the grove of trees made the houses nearly invisible, but it was the imperious medieval castle painted at the crest that demanded the most attention.

The details were staggering. From the jagged rocks to the stillness of the water under the enchanting bridge to the wisps of clouds in the sky, it nearly took my breath away. I wondered if this place really existed. The only way this artist could have been so particular was to have painted it in person. It was the most beautiful place I'd ever seen. I glanced down in the corner. The initials *SF '59* were signed with a deep red.

My face flushed. No one was around, but I was embarrassed to find something Stefan touched so appealing. How could someone like him have created something this moving? I put the picture back against the wall and chose my colors.

Frau Franke was a commanding figure. Her butterfly would be crimson and gold. It would be a reflection of how she liked the finer things in life. I would also add a small streak of mysterious orange because I believed there was a side of her I did not see or know.

I sat near the window. My thumb rubbed against the clean white fabric supported by a single flat board on the back. The texture was unusual. *Will I still be able to show precision in my lines?* I hadn't drawn anything since my front room wall. I wanted to help Katharina, but I had a lot of doubts. Then, as my thoughts turned to Anton and the orphanage, I was reminded of the only times I had ever felt free enough to express myself without judgment.

***

"Here, Ella." Anton handed me a small piece of charcoal. It was his turn to load the bucket, and in doing so, he swiped a small piece that had broken off and slipped it into his pocket. His white shirt and pants were covered in soot.

"Thank you, Anton!" I squealed with delight. I had used up the last one he got me a week ago. I hadn't been able to draw since.

"Can you draw me a dragon? Like the one in the storybook?" Anton smeared some of the soot across his face as he rubbed his nose. I peered at him and laughed. He always made me laugh.

"I can, but I'm not sure I'll be very good at those. Let's go try it out." I grabbed Anton's hand. I never cared if he was dirty or smelly or anything, and he felt the same way about me.

We waited until Nurse Gitta was no longer in the hallway and slipped out the back doors to the large concrete stairs. This was my canvas. The rain had washed away almost all I'd done in the weeks prior, so the dry ground was ready for a new set of sketches.

"I'm going to try to draw a butterfly, Anton."

"Why a butterfly?"

"Because I saw one in the book, the one that shows pictures from all around the world."

"Sounds good!" Anton settled in under the warm sun with his back against the broken railing. He watched as I got down on all fours and started to draw from memory. A thin worm-like body with two flowing wings.

"Ella, why does Nurse Gitta call you Adela?"

"Because that's my name." I didn't bother to look up as I continued to draw.

"No, your name is Ella," he insisted as he sat forward and inspected my work.

"It's both, but I like Ella. They say Adela when they're mad. I don't like it." I drew the sun shining as brightly as possible with a black piece of coal.

"What is your family name?" He asked with innocence. We had become fast friends, but there were still many questions he hadn't asked in those first two years.

"I don't have one." I drew a flower.

"Don't have one? Everyone has a family name."

"Nope." I didn't even look up. "Maybe someday if I get adopted."

"You want to get adopted?"

"Don't you?" I stopped and stared at Anton's face.

"No." His jaw grew rigid. "I don't need a family."

"We can be a family, Anton." I put my hand out for him to shake. I'd seen people do this when they made an arrangement.

Anton studied my hand then smiled. "OK, and maybe someday you can sell paintings for marks."

I giggled. "Maybe."

"Then we can have a *Haus* and food . . . and a dog. I would like a dog."

I stopped drawing and smiled at Anton. "I like your idea very much."

***

"Ella?"

"Ella?" Katharina's sweet hand was on my shoulder. I had finished the artwork nearly fifteen minutes ago but sat motionless as I savored the happy memory.

"Oh, this is the most beautiful butterfly I've ever seen!" She clapped her hands together and cried happily with joy. "Thank you, oh thank you so much!"

"Please . . ." I whispered, "Please, don't tell anyone I'm the one who drew it."

"Why not?" She picked the canvas up and inspected it closely.

"Please?" I asked again, "And the chalk can smudge if it's touched, be careful."

"Oh, not to worry." Katharina retrieved an aerosol can from a nearby cupboard. "Here, this will make it permanent. I saw Stefan use this once." She handed me the can. I pressed the button and a liquid spray spewed out. I dropped the can.

"It's OK, Ella. It won't ruin the picture; it's meant to protect it." Katharina chuckled at my ignorance. I picked up the can and pressed it again. It did appear to seal the picture through a small plume of smelly smoke.

Katharina held it up in admiration one more time. "And I won't tell anyone if you don't want me to."

"Thank you." I crossed the room and opened the cupboard to replace the aerosol can where Katharina had found it. A stack of records lay piled on the shelf next to a beautiful phonograph. My heart skipped a beat. I had never seen so many albums in one place.

I glanced at my hands; color covered up to the wrists. My eyes darted back and forth. Despite the mess I would create if I touched them, my mind reeled with curiosity. *Could it be there?*

"Ella?"

I'd forgotten I wasn't alone.

"Are you well?"

I stumbled and closed the door. "Yes . . . yes, I'm fine." I excused myself and went to the washroom.

As I rubbed my hands under the warm water and lathered soap, I contemplated how I would get back to the art room undetected. The record had to be here, *La Vie en Rose* was a popular tune for many years. Miss Piaf had become famous with the Germans when she performed for them in occupied France. Her music was cherished by all.

Katharina was waiting for me when I stepped out. Her smile never ceased as she wrapped her arm through mine and led me down the stairs. I smiled back. When I was with her, I faintly remembered what it felt like to be with someone who truly cared.

It was nearing six o'clock, and the preparations were in full swing as I slipped back into the staff room. I quickly changed to my serving apron and stepped into the kitchen to join Lena, Heidi, Eva, and Johann. We hadn't spoken since lunch, yet it was evident Lena had noticed my absence.

"I'm sorry," she whispered as we passed. That was all she said on the earlier matter.

As the evening's guests arrived, decked out in their finest dress, we kept a steady stream of gourmet foods flowing from the kitchen to the dining room and parlors: ham hock, pork sausage, sauerkraut, *Beamtenstippe,* tray after tray of *Pfannkuchen*, and an endless supply of wine, beer, and homemade *Obstler.*

"Alles Gute zum Geburtstag!" Happy birthday wishes were nonstop through the evening. All present for the festivities seemed to celebrate instead of scheming. I didn't see Herr Mielke or anyone else who had been to the house in uniform. It was a joyous occasion, and the small staff worked very hard to make it a successful one as well.

It wasn't until nearly nine o'clock when the attention was finally turned to gifts. I wasn't even nearby when Katharina presented her mother with the artwork. Yet, when I re-entered the room, I sensed something had changed, a shift in the mood.

Despite the cheers, there was one expression that could have set even the red and gold wings on fire. Stefan stewed in the background. I carefully meandered everywhere but near his corner of the room. I knew he would recognize my design. I just hoped he wouldn't destroy Katharina's good intentions.

I took my empty tray to the kitchen. As I pulled more *Eisbein* from the oven, a shadowy figure entered behind me. It didn't matter that Lena and Johann were nearby, he started toward me anyway.

"Where is your reason?" I recognized the sour voice immediately. I kept working despite the now completely silenced staff members in the room.

"Answer me, Fräulein." Stefan stepped in between me and the tray I attempted to fill. I looked directly at him. I thought of the times in the orphanage I had to stand up for myself, and this was no exception. As I peered closer, I noticed he was not his sober self. His shady blue eyes were surrounded by hints of red, and his movements were loose and uncoordinated. Any earlier trepidation I had over being alone with Stefan seemed to disappear. He was just a sad, miserable piece of a man.

"Katharina asked me to. It was for her."

"Katharina is foolish," he slurred the words. I failed to see what many women found attractive. He was a spoiled rotten child who spewed nothing but insults and, obviously, couldn't hold his liquor either.

"I need to work." I moved around him and continued. Stefan pushed the tray out of my reach. My jaw went rigid. I contemplated the consequences and knew I couldn't handle this as I had in the past. Too much was at stake here.

"What do you need . . . sir?" I fired back at him, barely able to enunciate "sir" without a jeer. He was slow to react but didn't hide his surprise. It could be that the only times someone had ever stood up to him were the times *I* pushed back.

"What makes you think my mother would want one of your . . . 'paintings' when she is privy to any of mine?"

Lena and Johann continued to watch the show. Neither one moved a muscle.

"Indeed?" I got close to Stefan's face. He exhaled. My nose wrinkled from the smell. "When was the last time you even picked up a tool, Michelangelo?" Again, he didn't move, but it was apparent I startled him with my boldness.

"None of your business, *untere Schicht*." He insulted me as he steadied himself against the counter. "I trained in Dresden, where did you train? Treptow?"

My face warmed. I knew he didn't know I lived there, but everyone knew Treptow was the poorer part of town. He was relentless, a first-class fraud.

"Always a gentleman, Herr Franke." I curtsied sarcastically. "Out of my way, I have to return to work!"

I grabbed the decanter out of Johann's hands and rushed into the parlor. Tears had started to form at the corners of my eyes, and I immediately brushed them back. There was no way I was going to continue to let Stefan tear me down. He was nobody.

Instantly, Katharina embraced me. "Oh, Ella! She loved it! She loved the colors and the whole thing! You are such a wonderful friend. Thank you, thank you!"

She still had her arms around me when her brother entered and slithered back to his chair. We carefully avoided each other the rest of the night.

Once again, I hoped it was the last interaction I ever needed to have with him. Although, back in the kitchen, Lena seemed quite determined in attaining some answers to what she had witnessed.

"Ella," she whispered, when we were alone, "what was that about?"

I spoke softly, as gently as I could, with anger still fresh on my tongue, "Remember how you said earlier some things just need to be left alone?"

Lena nodded as if she sensed where this was headed.

"This is one of those things."

CHAPTER FIFTEEN

1962

Traditionally, January 1 was a day of new beginnings, but in East Berlin, there were few affairs to celebrate. We rarely had anything to look forward to. However, when I arrived at the Franke house this particular morning, the staff room was alive with gossip.

A man by the name of Nikita Khrushchev would be arriving in East Berlin later this week. Rumor had it, Herr Franke himself had been invited to attend a private speech given by this man.

"Who is that?" I questioned Johann. His eyes scrutinized me as though I was absurd for even asking. The name *Khrushchev* came up the night of the standoff, but I didn't know why.

"Who is Herr Khrushchev?" his tone filled with contempt. "How could you not know who he is?" He rolled his eyes. "He is the premier—" I shrugged my shoulders. It didn't ring a bell. He continued, "—of the whole Soviet Union."

"Why would he come here?"

"Considering Mother Russia owns East Germany, I would assume he wants to check on his asset." Johann became snippy. From the way he acted, it was apparent he had some Soviet ties. I knew a decent amount about the German leadership but very little about the Soviets.

"Some asset!" I snapped back sarcastically. "A broken city with a prison wall and starving people."

"You watch, little miss sassy," Johann insisted, "he has done great things in Russia and will do great things here."

"Well, seeing there is no *great* here, it can't be that difficult."

"He is my premier; he will not let us down."

"He would be the first, wouldn't he . . .?" I turned away before Johann could say another word.

With apron in hand, I silently vowed no allegiance to the Soviet Union. Nor would I believe anything would ever change. Today was going to be just another day for me.

"You probably—" Heidi started to say as she walked down the hallway with me.

"I know, I know, I need to be more careful with what I say." And I cut straight into the library.

After a few minutes of dusting, curiosity overwhelmed me. I brushed along several shelves and passed many books until I found one. It was a book on the Soviet Union, published three years ago.

I took a seat as I opened the front cover. Inside was a picture of two men, titled *Nikita Khrushchev with Joseph Stalin 1936.*

As I read, I learned that the people of the Soviet Union loved this man. He had become a hero following the death of their dictator, Stalin. It seemed as though Khrushchev worked to undo many of the previous administration's ideas, as well as freed people from Stalin's *gulag* camps. The *gulag* camps were corrective camps created by Stalin. Many of the detained were legitimate criminals, but a good number of prisoners were political threats. Numerous innocent people fell victim to government paranoia and were incarcerated as well.

I paused for a moment as I read. They sounded much like the Stasi labor camps we heard about at *Hohenschönhausen,* the Labor Camp X. *If they were so bad there that Khrushchev released people, why are they utilized here if the Soviet Union controls East Germany?* I was confused but continued.

When Khrushchev gained power, he focused on repairing relations with China, Yugoslavia, and America. He promoted economic reforms such as foreign art, sports, and education for the Soviets. *With this kind of resolve . . . how could he not be seen as a hero? That would be like coming here to Berlin and suddenly removing the wall.* I paused. *Could there possibly be a specific purpose in his visit?* I forced these thoughts aside. It was never a good idea to build up any imaginary hopes concerning the wall.

I turned the page. Khrushchev worked to give the people everything they had been previously deprived of under Stalin. It appeared his vision for the country was vastly different from that of his predecessor. He seemed to be driven by change and forward-thinking. I read:

In 1956 when Herr Khrushchev addressed the 20th Party Congress in the Soviet Union, he summed up Stalin's reign in one sentence, "It is here that Stalin showed in a whole series of cases his intolerance, his brutality, and his abuse of power . . . he often chose the path of repression and physical annihilation, not only against actual enemies but also against individuals who had not committed any crimes against the party or the Soviet Government."

A strange feeling ignited within me. I couldn't stop my mind. Maybe this was the reason for his visit to Berlin. If a man can truly say those words and does not condone the brutalities of his own people, he could not possibly be a leader who tolerates the cruelty and oppression this wall generates.

Perhaps in some unusual way, Herr Khrushchev recognized how ridiculous this persecution was. Maybe his plan was to transform our lives as well. Maybe Johann *is* right! Could it really be a New Year worth celebrating?

Throughout the next few days, I continued to read privately about all the perceived successes Herr Khrushchev had accomplished since 1953. I somehow overlooked the brutalities he had carried out for Stalin prior to his own rise, wanting to truly believe he recognized the error of his judgment specifically in regard to Germany. I never let on about how I personally anticipated his arrival. This would mean I had to apologize to Johann, and I wasn't about to do that.

Therefore, even at lunch, while several staff chatted on with excitement, I secretly kept an open ear to any news regarding the premier's arrival and his unknown objective.

The 6th of January finally arrived. An eagerness grew throughout the day with the knowledge this great and powerful man was somewhere within the city limits.

Yet, no word came.

No news from the staff, the radio, or even the television upstairs in the master suite. Lena told me she turned it on while the Frankes were gone, but nothing was initially reported outside of his motorcade arrival.

Not a word was expelled. Not even later at night as I walked home from work. The wall, the soldiers, the fear, nothing had changed. Everything was exactly the way it had been for over six months, and slowly, any desperate hope I dared have started to dissipate.

The next morning, I came to work early enough to grab the newspaper before anyone would even know it was missing. I had to force myself to slow down and read one sentence at a time.

On the front page, it showed a picture of Herr Khrushchev. He was a fairly old, balding man with eyeglasses who wore a nice black suit and a white shirt. His coat was accented by three-star pins on one front pocket and a circle pin on the other. It didn't mention how old the photograph was. He seemed like an *Opa* or how I would envision my grandpa to be if I had one.

As I read farther down, I learned that he was far from kind to the people of East Berlin. He did not come to tear down the wall. In fact, he suggested it be reinforced. He only came to make sure East Germany didn't ask the Soviet Union for any more help.

When Herr Khrushchev met in front of the Communist Leadership at the SED Party Congress the day before, he was reported as having said that the wall had accomplished its purpose of stemming the exodus of citizens from the nation. He believed this action was necessary to stabilize the East German economy. However, Khrushchev insisted no additional Soviet economic assistance would be forthcoming: "Neither God nor the devil will give you bread or butter if you do not manage it with your own hands." He ended his speech with a clear warning to the East: they "must not expect alms from some rich uncle" and were to survive entirely on their own.

I dropped the paper to the ground. My eyes blurred. Stunned, I couldn't even process what I'd just read. Everything written about him must have been a lie.

How does one justify doing all he supposedly had done for the Soviet people in their own country, and here—when this part of the world was controlled by the Soviets—we were mistreated like rats in the basement: tolerated but despised.

When I entered the staff rooms once again, there was no joyous celebration. There wasn't any talk of Khrushchev at all. Even though I didn't hold any allegiance to the Soviet Union, I had briefly felt as though there was a possibility some good could come from this man. I was wrong, but I wasn't the only one.

I looked at Johann who was both silent and discouraged, and I suddenly felt sorry for him. He had a stronger connection than I did and now appeared as though he had been abandoned, the same feeling I grew accustomed to many years ago.

***

"To bed, kleine Maus!" Nurse Margret demanded. "We are waiting on you."

I scrambled under the thin blanket with my ear turned toward Nurse Margret's deep voice. Every Sunday night, like clockwork, she read to us before we went to bed. It was from a book she called, "The Word of God."

"Who is God?" I asked, the first time I could actually say the word.

"He is your Supreme Ruler, your maker, and your destiny," she emphasized dramatically.

All words I didn't know. So, to a five-year-old, all I heard was "fear him." I was frightened of this God person she spoke of. He caused scary things to happen like earthquakes, floods, and fire. I decided to stay as far away as I possibly could from this God. Especially since Nurse Margret would often say he watched us. It was from a place called heaven, and if we were disobedient or naughty, we would be caught and punished.

Now, more often than not, I was both, and I was punished. The consequences often ranged from either the closet or the switch, but I never saw this God personally. I also never spoke to Him or felt His anger. I started to believe He was all made up.

"Why do you say God punishes people?" I asked Nurse Margret. I always asked her questions.

"Because He does when they're bad."

"Am I bad?" I asked this, knowing full well what her response should be, but she surprised me.

"You are a little stinker sometimes, Adela, but you are not bad." I thought about this for a while.

"I must be bad if nobody wants me."

All the other children had fallen asleep. I stood in the dim light before her. My brown hair tangled in all directions, dirty hands, and dirty face. The answer should have been obvious, but Nurse Margret remained quiet. She lifted me up to her wide lap. I had only been there a few times before, and it was always only to get a good smack on the fanny.

"You, kleine Maus are special," she whispered so only I could hear. "God has saved you for a specific purpose. Some children have a family. Some children only have themselves, but you, my little child, are not alone. You, little one, will always be loved by God."

It was the same hope I had developed for a greater being. One who was all-powerful, the one who I hoped would be there for me. Back then it was God . . . today it was Khrushchev, and in both cases, an undeniable feeling of rejection had emerged.

As a child, I truly wanted to believe I was special like Nurse Margret told me, but over time, doubt crept in. Eventually, I stopped believing.

***

I had truly wished Johann was right. I wanted to believe this great man would come to Berlin and do heroic things. Sadly, all he really did was cut the parental strings and leave us on our own. With too many irons in the fire already, we knew from history that didn't work. The East could be facing even darker times than before.

I placed one arm around Johann. He glanced up at me surprised. No words were exchanged. It was the easiest way for me to tell him I understood his disappointment and truly cared. His moist red eyes met mine, and he nodded with reserved accord. Once again, our light had been dimmed, but even in our despair, we still had each other.

CHAPTER SIXTEEN

It was now late February 1962. I had only been in service to the family for 172 days now. Time seemed to pass quite sluggishly, especially
during this particularly harsh winter when one could not tolerate any
amount of time outdoors. For several weeks, we spent limitless hours
toiling inside in full preparation for the Frankes' annual masquerade.
They spared no expense to make their *Fasching* dinner the most festive
occasion in Pankow.

Despite the name, the event had less to do with the traditional Catho-
lic observance of Lent and more to do with an excuse to host a very lavish
costume party. Although carnival officially commenced on November 11
every year, the Frankes' event coincided with the unrestrained precursor
to the deprivation of carnal joys associated with Lent . . . it was to be a
night of errant merriment and indulgence.

In the Waisenhaus, we were taught the meaning of Lent because
Nurse Margret practiced Catholicism. She explained it to be a sacred
time when one would abstain from worldly desire . . . whatever that
meant.

We never truly participated in the Fasching celebration, except when
the nurses helped us make silly costumes out of linens to parade in the
fall or at random times throughout the long months of festivity leading
up to Ash Wednesday. This was the day Nurse Margret wore a coal mark
on her forehead all day. It was one of the few memories I tried *not* to
forget because it was one of the rare times Nurse Margret didn't show
displeasure toward us.

From the decorations to the presentation, this was something I had
never imagined in my lifetime. It made the birthday party for Frau
Franke look like a simple gathering. The dining room itself had been
transformed into an abundant garden beyond anything I had seen,
even outdoors.

The greenweed we had twisted into thick vines dangled from each doorway toward the center of the room like a Mayday pole. The bright yellow and purple blossoms aromatized the air, while the silver and gold strands that accented the braid nearly glowed as each new candelabra was lit. Lavish vases overflowed with imported crimson rhododendrons, while four life-size marble sculptures resembling Greek gods were arranged in the corners.

"Each statue represents a person in the Franke family," Lena whispered as she folded the linen napkins. "Can you guess which ones?"

"This must be Herr Franke," I laughed as I brushed my hand across the large thunderbolt that extended from the king of the gods' right hand. Koen was the patriarch of the family, but unlike Zeus, he had an impractical belief he really was in charge.

The next closest statue donned a warrior helmet, but contradictory feminine robes flowed leisurely about the sparsely covered body to which a razor-sharp spear extended. I instantly recognized the goddess Athena who represented wisdom and war. Yes, this was Frau Franke's symbolic deity. I stared at the marble eyes carved with realistic intensity.

"She looks like her, doesn't she?" Lena interrupted me.

I shrugged, "A little, I suppose." It was more than a little. I glanced to the opposite side and saw a petite figure sitting casually atop a boulder. Her figure, in perfect proportions, was covered only from the waist down.

Long, curly hair fell across her bare back. Katharina was eternalized as Aphrodite. I smiled, *she will probably be annoyed when she sees this*, humility being one of her most beautiful features.

The final figure: a perfectly chiseled, muscular build below two faces. My face twisted in confusion.

"Janus." Lena grinned with an eagerness that she knew something I did not.

"I'm not familiar with that one."

"Most people aren't. My aunt studied in Athens." She placed one hand on each face. "He is the god of choice."

"*This* was selected for Stefan?" My scorn was evident. "Maybe Hades or Dionysus," I giggled as my fingers cupped around an imaginary drinking glass.

"Janus has the ability to see into the future and the past. Thus, the two faces." She resumed her preparations.

"Well, there's no doubt he's two-faced—" I almost cackled, "—but it should be connected to the body of a snake, not a god."

Lena threw me a disappointed look. "He may be selfish, but he's not conniving."

Again, my thoughts reiterated her ignorance of our past as I finished placing the silver next to each plate.

"Who sent the statues?"

"Frau Franke's father in the Soviet Union."

"He must know something we don't." My eyes flashed one last time toward the boyish, almost desirable, countenance.

"Interestingly enough, Ella, Janus is actually a Roman god who is believed to have saved the kidnapped Sabine women from Romulus, the founder of Rome."

I remained silent. There seemed to be no logical association between Janus and Stefan. This one was a real enigma.

Lena clapped her hands together and pulled me back to reality.

"Look at this place, Ella, isn't it divine?"

"Yes." I inhaled the aroma deeply. Now *that* was something we could agree on. We quickly changed to our serving aprons and joined the other servants. Everything was ready.

Due to the nature of this particular party, the family guest list contained the highest tier of power in Berlin. Knowing this, the possibility of invitees could be anyone from Herr Mielke, Herr Grotewohl, Wolf, SED party members, or Soviet leadership. Even Ulbricht himself could be in attendance. The very thought of such power present created unspoken angst among the staff.

Thirty privately chosen guests were issued invitations. Each time the door opened, whispers circulated. Costumes ranged from simple clay masks and capes to grand illusions immersed in vibrant colored feathers, beads, or fur. They undeniably surpassed my expectations. Everything from childhood storybook characters to royalty and knights—even demons from the darkest parts of a dream. I easily controlled my mouth from reacting, but my eyes were dancing with delight as if they had entered a confectionary shop for the very first time. Even if the most powerful men from the DDR were present, we could not recognize them.

As the only "youth" invited, Katharina and Stefan were present as well. Katharina was easy to identify since she showed me her *Rotkäp-pchen* costume a week ago. Everything she wore resembled Red Riding Hood, from the red satin-hooded cape to a ruby-glittered mask and striped stockings. This matched her personality exactly as she sailed around the room and socialized effortlessly with the elite.

Somehow, I imagined Stefan to be the big bad wolf from the same childhood tale, but he was not. He wore a well-tailored, plain, black suit and bow tie, and sported a dark mask that only covered the top half of his face. He was easy to distinguish, partly due to his lack of creativity, but mostly because one can't hide a stone-cold temperament, even behind a mask.

Throughout the night, I went out of my way to avoid Stefan. Even when I served near him, there was no eye contact. I refused to repeat my run-in with him the last time I'd seen him in December at his mother's birthday party. In fact, two months had passed quite blissfully without any contact at all. He may have been on holiday, possibly even skiing across the border. Either way, it didn't matter to me.

Everyone seemed to be in a joyous mood for the event, and the cheerfulness of the evening seemed to sway the content of the conversation. There was very little talk of the wall, politics, or death.

Laughter and revelry filled the air as course upon course were presented. Plates were filled to capacity with superior meats, glazes, and delicacies. The highlights were *Weisswürste* smothered in a sweet mustard from Bavaria, sauerbraten roast marinated in red wine vinegar topped with juniper berries, and although there was an abundant pastry tray, each patron received a *Knieküchle* pie filled with marmalade, chocolate, or custard with their meal. Glasses and goblets overflowed with specialty fruit liqueurs, brandy, and Austrian wines.

The irony was tremendous. Even as we cleared the china, there were enough leftovers to feed many families. Right outside the Frankes' front door, homeless and hungry children cried, their stomachs empty for days. Yet these men tossed more food to their dogs than to the people. I tried hard not to let it bother me. I had a duty to do and only 558 more days to do it.

We took shifts in the rooms. When it was my turn to wait on the guests in the main parlor, I stood very still, my back pressed against the wall until I was summoned to fill another wine glass. I did what I was told because the money was too good to resist. The twenty marks I earned tonight, serving for the party, would be a week's worth of wages with nothing owed. Thus, in a subtle twisted way, I contributed to the senselessness, because I chose to be part of it too.

Lena joined me momentarily and handed me another two bottles of wine. They would not be the last. In front of us, one masked man pulled a woman dressed like a ballerina onto his lap and tickled her. She pretended to be offended, but her laugh told me otherwise. I fought to keep my face from reacting, but it was too difficult.

"Ella," Lena moved closer and whispered, "you need to keep your eyes still, they appear annoyed."

"The guests are acting childish."

She snickered, "I know, just try to ignore it."

"Fräulein, come." A man in the center of the room waved his hand toward us. His dark robe shrouded the bird mask he wore. It was difficult to know if it was him who spoke. The razor-sharp beak pointed in our direction, but we could not see his lips. I recognized him as the man at dinner who demanded the greatest attention. He had very little tolerance for others, which didn't impress me.

"Fräulein," he repeated. I was sure he referred to Lena, but when she stepped into another room, he said it again, only louder.

There was something unnerving about the birdman's tone. Pretending not to hear him, I curtsied to two guests as they entered the room, *please just leave me alone and let me serve.* The clock chimed loudly from the nearby mantle, and I peeked its way. Two hours to go.

"Fräulein . . ."

I was conflicted. Should I continue to ignore him and chance the Frankes' wrath for being rude to one of their guests or betray myself through obedience?

The blazing yellow eyes of his façade stared in my direction. I glanced down to my feet and then peeked up at the very moment a woman in a very revealing costume approached him, drawing his attention immediately away.

With a sigh of relief, I took advantage of the moment and moved toward a group of guests near the farthest windows. I pretended they summoned me, although they didn't. Thankfully, they didn't refuse my willingness to refill their glasses, either.

Despite putting myself in closer proximity to the younger Herr Franke, I remained near that side of the room. I glanced over to Stefan; he seemed out of sort—quiet, almost reserved—watching the guests as they played cards and socialized. I briefly allowed my thoughts to wander. This event was perfectly aligned with Stefan's shallow ways, but I didn't see him tilt a drink at any time through the night or follow his traditional path of flirting with all the women. Granted, up until now, I had avoided watching him directly, but from my view, it was impossible not to see this contrast.

Katharina had excused herself nearly an hour ago. She went out of her way to say goodnight to me before she left. While her demeanor always remained pleasant, she confided in me once that nights like this were more out of respect for her father than personal amusement.

As the night wore on, the conversation swayed between the Eichmann trial, World Cup matches, and the Grand Prix, which several men boasted quite vocally of their vested interest in. Talk of V8 engines and rear suspension grew exhausting.

"Colonel Anker?" Herr Franke called from across the room. The mask of the man who summoned me earlier turned in his direction.

However, no words were spoken.

Herr Franke hastily shortened the distance between them. Perhaps it was because the strange man's gaze didn't fall immediately upon me that I was inexplicably drawn their way, or possibly the unease I sensed. Either way, there was something peculiar about him.

Herr Franke continued, "I understand you were recently promoted within the ministry."

The man's chest seemed to swell slightly from this adulation but again no response.

"We are indeed honored to have you in our home," Herr Franke continued. The man he referred to as Colonel Anker grabbed a long cigar off the nearby table and lit it. The match remained lit in his fingers. It was an odd exchange. Herr Franke lifted his own mask and blew out the match. *Who is this man exhibiting such power over the host? Colonel Anker?* I thought to myself. I hadn't recalled hearing his name before.

As the man sank to the nearest lounge chair, he finally removed his hood and beak. I gasped and turned quickly. I didn't want him to catch me looking. A long, jagged scar crept down the entire right side of his nearly bald head. It was ghastly. I deliberately motioned toward the first guest sitting near me.

"Would you like a drink?"

It was too late to stop myself. Stefan sat before me. My hand shook the bottle. I grabbed it with the other hand so he couldn't see me trembling. I pretended my intrusion into his undisturbed stupor was intentional.

He glared but said nothing—his black mask encircled his deep blue eyes. They were clouded, but not the way they appeared before when he was drunk. They seemed pained. I remained immobile.

"Fräulein," the colonel interfered.

I didn't move.

"Fräulein, fill my glass." He had found a way to force a response. I pulled my eyes away from Stefan and turned. Even from my distance, I could see the colonel's glass was already full.

"Come, now." His scar, now completely exposed, held my attention. His fingers gripped the cigar tightly as he drew in a lengthy inhale. Herr Franke was no longer in the room. I walked toward him slowly and stopped several feet away. The colonel blew his smoke in my direction, and I struggled to conceal my cough.

"Fill the glass, girl." The colonel motioned me closer.

I stepped closer to him but did not tip the bottle. The Frankes' white carpet didn't need a permanent red reminder of the night. Herr Anker set his cigar on the table beside him. His jaw tightened.

"Your glass is full, sir." I pointed out what was apparently only obvious to me.

He held his glass in one hand while his free hand openly slid underneath the hem of my dress. It was now clear he used my proximity for another purpose. I bit my lip and froze. The colonel took a large gulp of his drink. He didn't look at me or stop what he was doing.

All present, within a fair amount of distance, could see what was happening. Nobody said or did anything. Even the woman he had accompanied reveled in her own mischief with another guest only a few feet away. I was to be Colonel Anker's sole entertainment.

I took a deep breath and tried to move. His hand caught a fistful of material. He pulled me closer, his face now eye-level with my chest. He openly salivated as he slurred with guile, "I think I am ready for dessert."

My heart beat faster. As close as he was, I feared he could hear it and would know of my fright. I turned my face to the side in a desperate attempt to locate Lena in the room, but from my peripheral vision, the colonel's face tightened. He took offense.

"I told you to fill my glass," he snapped.

Beads of sweat formed on my forehead. I could barely think. My voice cracked as I stuttered, "Y-yes, sir." I tried to force space between us as I pulled the decanter forward, but his grip was too tight.

Normally, I wouldn't hesitate to put someone in their place, but this was not an easy situation. It never crossed my mind tonight that I'd have to make a choice. What was my obligation worth to me?

"Colonel," a smooth voice sailed across the room. Anker didn't take his eyes off me. The unexpected voice continued, "Colonel, didn't you say you have an extensive art collection?"

This comment intrigued the colonel. He finally tipped his head to see who was talking.

"What is your favorite piece?" Stefan inquired; a somewhat odd question at an awkward moment—or it was just awkward for me with a man's hand maneuvering under my dress?

The colonel laughed, "You have an interest in art, young Franke?" The colonel's hand felt heavy on my thigh. I was afraid to move.

My face burned hot with each uncomfortable second.

"I do." Stefan was calm. "I have a beautiful Renoir in my room if you would like to see it."

The colonel's hand squeezed, and I released a small cry as I jumped. Everyone looked in our direction. He laughed and pushed me aside as he stood to his feet.

"Come, Stefan, show me this painting."

I hurried to the kitchen before the tears started to fall. Lena met me instantly.

"What happened?"

Angry at myself, I couldn't speak.

"Ella, I heard your cry, but by the time I got to your part of the room, you were gone. What happened?"

My fists curled as I paced. *How could I allow that awful man to even get as far as he did before . . . Stefan . . . did he really?* I didn't want to imagine the possibility that Stefan deliberately diverted the colonel's attention away from me. *Stefan doesn't care about anyone but himself. I'm sure he really did want to gloat about his painting.*

I convinced myself Stefan would never come to my rescue, a servant. A servant he hated. Yet, the colonel's intentions were clear, and had his attention not been deterred, I could have faced an awful predicament.

I quickly untied my apron and handed it to Lena.

"What's wrong?"

My hand flew to my mouth. I wanted to vomit. "I'm sorry, I don't feel well." I grabbed my coat and ran out the door before putting it on. I scrambled to cover up from the bitter winter cold but kept moving until I reached the closest bus stop, jumping on the first coach to get me anywhere away from there.

All I could think about the rest of the night was how I needed to find a way out. I needed to leave this miserable side of the city as soon as possible and get to Anton and Josef.

I had waited long enough.

CHAPTER SEVENTEEN

As 1962 wore on, I continued to work hard and serve the Frankes faithfully, despite my heart not being in it. I put the night of the Lenten dinner and the awful man's actions behind me, except for the longing it created to find a way to escape.

Every day staff gossip revealed another successful attempt across the wall, among the many unsuccessful ones as well. Most of the discussions took place in the staff room and rarely included Lena and me.

I just happened to be a good listener.

I was lucky enough in the next few months to never share words with Stefan again. We passed each other often in a room or the yard, but silence prevailed. I also never saw him and his friends gallivanting around. In fact, I never saw his friends anymore. I was sure they had all been enlisted since conscription was now the law.

Once again, however, it seemed Stefan was magically devoid of military responsibility. He seemed to spend a great deal of time in the mortuary now, not that I really cared. Although, I often wondered if his actions the night of the party with Colonel Anker were deliberate . . . I guess I would never know.

As time passed, Katharina and I became much closer. It was still beyond the watchful eye of her mother, but on occasion, we would sneak a moment in the library. She would share the details of her latest book or direct me to the next one I should read. It was something I often looked forward to.

We never talked about her family or their business. It was easier to pretend they didn't exist. Eventually, I reached a point in our friendship where I could tell her about Anton and Josef. The more I talked about them the less they disappeared from my life, and Katharina was so compassionate and understanding—a rarity I was lucky to have, both in her and Lena.

I was now almost one year down in service and one to go. The waxen "394" appeared boldly on my mirror as the end of July neared. Secretly, I had reached that crossroad again. The one I'd so gently set aside, the wish that I never stopped thinking about. I needed to see Anton and Josef again. I grew weary with loneliness.

"Lena," I whispered when we were alone in the laundry room. I had finally gathered the confidence to start the conversation. She looked up but continued to fold the linens. "Do you think Christoph knows people who can . . . um—" Her eyes grew wide in anticipation. "—get someone past the wall?"

Lena reached for the door and closed it carefully. "I told you, Ella, don't talk about such things here!" she demanded angrily; a reaction I half expected. "I thought you knew by now. All the people who come here— very powerful people of influence—you could be killed for even *thinking* such a crazy thought!"

I lowered my head but did not regret the attempt. "I miss them, Lena." My eyes were moist. "I miss them so much it hurts."

She sighed then came and wrapped one arm tenderly around my shoulders. "How do you know they are there?"

"I don't." I took a deep breath. "I have to be hopeful. I only want to be with them."

Lena reached for a handkerchief from a pile of clean cloths. She sweetly wiped my falling tears aside then whispered, "Let me see what I can find out, but promise me we will never talk of this here again."

"I promise."

I didn't realize the magnitude of it as she did. She knew too much about the inner workings of this family, but she was my closest friend, and she wanted to help. I trusted her wholeheartedly.

Within a month, Christoph had sent word through Mama G that we needed to meet. The place selected was near the edge of the city, an area I was not too familiar with, but I was eager to go. He met me after work a block away from the Frankes' and led the way.

After one bus ride and a series of back-alley turns, we entered the basement of a small free-standing home. I entered cautiously, surprised to see it was a full-service café filled completely to capacity with patrons smoking, drinking, and sharing laughs. It was precisely a gathering the East German government did not support. They believed any time people united in a common interest—despite how innocent it seemed—opposition to the cause was fueled. I knew this through the many *Zeitung* I read.

We maneuvered past the crowd toward the back and joined a small group of men mustered around a narrow table. Conversation abruptly stalled. All eyes turned to me as if Christoph wasn't there. If it hadn't been for the twitch of their lips as they blew their cigarette smoke away, I would have thought I was looking at figures in a museum.

"Ella, this is Fritz, Simon, and Klaus." Christoph wasted no time with introductions. "Gentlemen, she is the one I told you about." Christoph tipped his hat in a motion to leave.

I reached for his arm. My fingers trembled with the touch. I was suddenly alarmed. "I . . . I'm not sure about this," I stuttered.

"You're not?" Klaus, the youngest and most handsome of the three, balked. "How do we know you are who you say you are?" He smashed the lit end of his cigarette into a brass ashtray in the center of the table.

"I'm not a spy!" I defended sharply.

"Ella, please keep your voice down," Christoph insisted. "They are good men."

Christoph's confidence in his friends was reassuring, but their scowls remained. Turning, he faced them. "She wants what you want. Give her a chance."

"Wait." I didn't let go. "Why aren't you going with us, Christoph?"

He grinned widely and placed his hand over mine. "Lena is my life, and she's in East Berlin."

I smiled for my friend. She was one of the lucky ones.

Each of the men relinquished. They held out a hand simultaneously to shake Christoph's goodbye and then stretched it forth again to welcome me. I knew this was more to appease their friend, even as I took a seat.

"How are you acquainted with Christoph?" I quizzed. It didn't matter to me who answered.

Simon spoke first. A short man with a full mustache and round eyeglasses, he looked like a schoolteacher. "I'm his uncle."

My eyes widened. I hoped for a strong association, but you couldn't get stronger than family. Klaus, who still didn't seem to trust me, returned the question. "How do you know Christoph?"

I spoke immediately. "Through his girlfriend, Lena. We work together."

Klaus turned to the others. "I don't think this is a good idea." He didn't even try to be discreet, speaking in front of me. "This was supposed to be confined to just us," he added.

"I can be trusted," I stated firmly.

All three paused and stared uncomfortably in my direction.

"Look," I continued, "it seems we are all in the same situation. We want to leave and need to trust each other."

"She's right," Simon assured. "Christoph would not have brought her to us if he didn't believe in her. Let's move on."

"Why here?" My question was really irrelevant, but I was curious.

Fritz had not spoken until now. He was tall and thin with a receding hairline. "The *Volkspolizei* don't come here. This café is left alone." He lit his second cigarette since I arrived. "The owner pays for privacy with the belief he is loyal to the DDR. See the flags in the window. It has worked for years."

"But things have changed in the last few months. They're getting wise to many things." I insisted. My time spent reading with Katharina often included the newspapers they printed. I was not ignorant of their rhetoric.

"We are safe here," Fritz assured, "but once we begin, we must act fast. Are you ready to leave, Ella?"

I was surprised by his question. Of course I was ready to leave, but what he really meant was . . . *are you ready to die if it comes to that?*

"Yes!" to both.

"Meet us here again tomorrow night, same time. All the details will be in play." We stood and shook hands again.

"Oh, and Ella," Simon reached over and pulled me close, "don't speak to anyone, and bring nothing with you." I nodded and we parted ways.

As I stepped out into the warm summer air alone, I realized Christoph had brought me here—the area wasn't too familiar.

I glanced around to try and gain a perspective when I saw someone approach from the opposite corner. My face tightened and then relaxed once I recognized Christoph. I beamed as he appeared before me.

"You waited?" I smiled gratefully.

"Of course!" he said, surprised. "I knew you hadn't been here before."

As he walked me to my apartment, he told me how he and Lena met, how they planned to wed, and even how many children they wanted to have. I was happy for her—slightly jealous she was this blessed in her circumstances, but why shouldn't she be? Not everyone in East Berlin should have such a sad story like mine.

"Christoph?" I recalled the question Lena had never answered. "Why does the name Mielke upset Lena?"

He remained silent while we walked. I continued, "I asked her about him after he came to the house, but she wouldn't tell me."

"He came to the Frankes'?" Christoph was surprised. "Did she see him, or did he see her?"

"No," I answered cautiously. His question piqued my curiosity. "No, she was upset the moment she heard his name and left."

Christoph, himself, seemed visibly upset at this news. "Don't tell her I told you, Ella. She is really private about some things, and this is possibly the worst."

I nodded.

"Just promise me if he ever comes to the house again, you will keep her away from him somehow."

"OK, I promise."

"Erich Mielke murdered her grandfather."

My face pulled into an obvious frown. "Are you being truthful?"

"Yes." Christoph nodded. "Her *Opa* Anlauf was murdered in cold blood."

"How?"

"Anlauf was a good man, a police captain at a time when the communist party was gaining strength here in Germany" —Christoph held out his hand to guide me past a puddle of water. His honorable actions came without hesitation as he continued— "and her grandfather tried in vain to stop their illegal rallies."

"When was this?"

"I believe it was back in the late twenties when Lena's mom was young."

"How was the offender identified as Mielke?"

"The hearings at the trial revealed the communist leadership had assigned Mielke to be the triggerman." My eyes widened in recollection of my interaction with the man. Christoph looked around. "He was found guilty. It was never disclosed who ordered Anlauf's death, but there were suspicions. They could be the very ones running this country right now."

"Why is Mielke not in prison?" We had reached my apartment but remained outside.

"He ran off. Then the case was thrown out and somehow, over time, he became celebrated and now runs Stasi. He answers to no one—"

I shook my head, astonished, as Christoph continued, "—and his right-hand man is Markus Wolf."

"Who is that?" I recognized the name somehow, "Wait . . . the man who was with him at the house was referred to as Markus."

"Yes, that would make sense that they were together. Wolf is Frau Franke's cousin."

I gasped. It all became very clear. I suspected that Frau Franke had a Soviet ancestry. Her accent was light, and her features always seemed more Russian than German to me.

"So, Frau Franke is the actual reason why their family is close to the government?"

"Well, she's a big part of it. She was raised in Moscow. I even think theirs might have been an arranged marriage."

"I didn't think people did those anymore. It would explain why they don't seem to be in love." I summoned my earlier thoughts of never seeing any affection in the home.

"Oh, arrangements definitely exist, especially when it's politically advantageous."

"All this time, I thought it was Herr Franke's doing—"

"Some. They both have dirty hands, stories that would chill you to the bone."

Just the imagery of Christoph's words made me shudder. "Why does Lena continue to work there?" I knew my debt was the only reason I remained, but she had a choice.

"Nobody knew the family connection to Wolf until later. Additionally, I'd never heard of Mielke being at the house before." Christoph sighed. "Lena's father was the Frankes' lead gardener at the time of his death. She was only fourteen when he passed away. Herr Franke felt compelled to offer her a job. I guess Lena feels obligated in a strange way. Her income helps support her mom and sisters."

I hadn't realized we had this in common. I was torn, especially after I had pushed her so persistently for answers. She never even let on that she had such sad secrets.

"When will you meet my friends again?" Christoph changed the subject as he realized how late it had gotten.

"Tomorrow evening."

"Will you be able to find it on your own?" he asked.

"Yes," I said confidently. "I can get there."

"Goodnight, Ella—" Christoph shook my hand, "—and be careful!"

"Goodnight, Christoph. Thank you very much." I placed my hand to my heart. "Thank you for helping me!"

As I entered my apartment, I was wrenched with emotion. I was thrilled with the idea I could actually be in West Berlin by this time tomorrow night, searching for Anton and Josef, only my mind was also clouded with fear.

I knew the depths to which this country would go to prevent people from being successful in their efforts to escape. I, likewise, understood I faced the very real possibility of death or tremendous misery if I was caught.

Either way, I knew tomorrow night my life would be very different.

Leah Moyes

CHAPTER EIGHTEEN

The next day couldn't move fast enough. I sped through my duties and was nearly completed by early afternoon. I even did it with a smile on my face. It seemed silly to work this hard with the knowledge that this was my last day. However, my new acquaintances made it very clear. I needed to act as though nothing was changing.

"Don't bring any attention to yourself, and keep your normal routine," Fritz insisted.

Thankfully, no one noticed my unusually high spirits or cared to pay any attention to my permanent grin—except for Lena of course. I wanted to tell her the details but respected her warning. She gave me a tight hug before we parted and told me how much she loved me.

I wanted to say goodbye to Katharina, but again, I knew it was a risk I could not take. I stepped out of the house and took one last look back . . . back at where my life had been spent the last eleven months. I would miss very little from here. I shed no tears as I walked briskly toward my destination.

I was on time, but only Simon sat at the table. This made me a little nervous. It's possible I read too much into it, but that wasn't uncommon for me. Most people tend to overreact when engaged in unlawful activities.

I didn't remove my mother's sweater, the only item I brought with me, as I sat down. Simon seemed as nervous as I was, and the trust game began again. We sat there in silence for a few minutes. I couldn't handle it much longer.

"Why do you want to leave East Berlin?" I spoke up.

Simon scoffed, "Same reason as you. My family is there."

"How do you know my family is there?" I responded quickly.

"Christoph told me."

"Oh."

I could hear the barmaid's conversation. This was her evening job.

She worked as a hairdresser during the day. My fingers tapped anxiously on the table.

"My wife and children were visiting her parents at the time the wall went up." Simon's voice was low and regretful. "They became permanent citizens of West Berlin that night."

My heart softened for him. I could only imagine how much harder the separation if Anton and I were married.

"Have you tried any of the legal ways?" I questioned. "I heard married people have a better chance at getting a travel visa." I personally had already tried three times and was denied all three.

"Yes, . . . a dozen times." He stared out the window. "It is impossible."

Right then, Fritz and Klaus arrived. It wasn't until they sat down that I recognized a similarity.

"You are brothers," I said with some surprise.

They glanced at each other, but Simon ignored it. "Why are you late?"

"Doesn't matter, we're here now." Klaus was definitely the feistier of the two.

"Did you place the vehicle where I told you?" Simon continued. I was in the dark about their plan. It almost scared me that I was so desperate to leave without even knowing what I was willing to do.

"It is there. We spent the afternoon reinforcing it. It's ready."

My eyes grew wide. Slowly I pieced it together. *We're going to run the checkpoint.*

My heart rate increased. I said nothing. I'd heard of a few successful tries, but there were many more unsuccessful attempts. The newly fortified checkpoints had deep ditches and concrete barriers. The weapons unleashed on the vehicles alone most certainly cut through everything, including bodies.

My eyes closed tight. I imagined Anton and Josef's faces, and it only confirmed my inability to turn back now.

"The metal bars are mounted on the front, the mattresses and sandbags are sec—"

"Shhhhh," Klaus hissed as quietly as possible. My eyes opened at the urgency in his voice. He nodded toward the newest patrons of the café. Two men in uniform had entered and walked straight to the bar.

"This is very unusual," Fritz spoke quietly. The officers turned and looked right in our direction.

My face went numb. I felt the blood drain from my cheeks as I stared.

What have I done? My mind started reeling. *How could I be so careless?*

Klaus saw my expression and steamed, "Relax! You must compose yourself! If they suspect anything at all, we could be arrested."

"They're coming over!"

"Get it together!" Klaus whispered.

I turned my head to try and catch my breath. By the time I turned back, the officers were right next to us. The official gray uniform of the NVA was close enough for me to touch.

Nationale Volksarmee was a large military group used to strengthen the presence of the government all over the city. It wasn't often they worked in pairs like the border guard. Whatever was going on was highly unusual.

My legs started to shake uncontrollably underneath the table. Klaus grabbed my knees with his hand, subtly enough that the soldiers wouldn't notice, but firm enough to get them to stop. They looked each of us in the face before they stopped at one.

"Are you Simon Alger?" the officers questioned.

"Yes, sir," he answered clearly, but I was sure his stomach was in his mouth.

"We need to speak with you outside."

"What is this about?" Fritz spoke up. He was instantly shut up with a dagger of a look.

"None of your business, unless you are Simon Alger!" The officer reached for his baton. He lifted it halfway up in a threatening manner.

I hadn't been this scared since the August night my life turned upside down. I knew I could not hold it together for long. My teeth started to chatter. I bit my lower lip as hard as I could. I tasted blood but did not stop.

"Get up!" The second officer had lost his patience.

Simon rose to his feet, but he was still slower than the soldier wanted him to be. The man grabbed his neck and shoved him aggressively away from the table.

As the men moved toward the door, Fritz whispered low enough for only us to hear, "This is going to end badly. We must leave as soon as they are outside." My eyes widened, but he didn't look at me as he continued, "There's a back exit through the kitchen to an opposite alley."

All faces were fixated on the windows out front. Because we were lower than street level, all we could see were their legs from the hips down.

In a matter of seconds, a strong swipe of the baton cracked against the back of Simon's knees. He was on all fours against the ground. His shrieks could be heard throughout the room, which had gone completely silent moments before. Another swipe of the baton connected across the back of his head. His body writhed in pain and curled up fetal style on the sidewalk. Patrons started to run for the exits out of fear.

"Now!" Fritz cried, "Now, now, *now!*"

He pushed me out of my chair. The three of us sailed in the opposite direction and through the back. This led us up to a vacant road. We ran until we could no longer hear Simon's screams.

I had no idea where we were headed, we just kept moving. I didn't want to be alone; I kept up with the steady pace of Klaus and Fritz. They guided me to their apartment building off Falkoniergaße in Mitte. This location was closer to my old home than my new one.

We paused on the empty, narrow street before we rushed up the side stairs to the fourth floor. Once inside their apartment, we only had a brief moment to rest.

"They will come looking for us here if Simon gives us up. It is only a matter of time," Fritz spoke candidly.

"If this was about the escape plan—" I coughed hard in between labored breaths, "—why didn't they have us all go outside back there?"

"I'm not sure."

"Surely they would have known we would run if they knew." I tried to make sense of it all, and the harder I tried, the harder my head hurt.

"She's right." Fritz paced back and forth. "There is no way they would have only taken him out if they knew . . . if they knew about the plan, they would have detained all of us."

"What if he cuts a deal?" I asked in a panic.

"What do you mean?" Klaus asked.

"You know . . . a deal . . . a trade . . . us for less pain, or his life."

"Would he do that?" Klaus looked at me with a new fear.

"Would *you* do it?" I shot back . . . then asked myself silently, *Would I do it?*

Now the brothers lost color.

I stood up. "He knew everything, right? The whole plan, right? Why did they only come after him?" I pushed. "Think! We have to figure this out."

"I don't know," Fritz groaned. "It was a pretty firm plan."

"No," Klaus mumbled, "it wasn't."

"What?" My eyes narrowed.

"Klaus? Are you aware of something?" Fritz sat next to him on the couch.

His brother shook his head. Small beads of sweat formed on his cheeks. "I . . . I'm not sure." He buried his head in his hands. "He may have stolen the van."

Fritz and I shot horrified looks in his direction at the same time.

"Stolen the van?" Fritz raised his voice. "What happened to the van belonging to his friend?"

"It was his friend's van, but he wasn't as cooperative as we hoped."

"How long have you known this?" Klaus shrugged.

"Are you kidding me?" I cried angrily. "I can't believe I was stupid enough to trust you."

"What are you screaming about, you crazy girl?" Klaus fired back, "You almost got us all killed back at the café!"

"Shhhh," Fritz cried, "we have neighbors! Keep your voices down!"

"I only wanted to leave East Berlin," I whispered hotly between gritted teeth. "I was under the impression you had a good plan."

"We all want to leave Berlin!" Klaus broke. His eyes filled with tears. "Our whole family is over there living a life of freedom and happiness, and I . . . *we,* are stuck here in this awful, miserable place."

"That's enough." Fritz lifted his hands calmly. "We need to think clearly. It won't take them long to figure out we ran."

I rubbed my temples. Losing my temper wouldn't help our situation right now. "Is there a possibility Simon could lead them here?" I joined them on the couch.

"I don't think he would."

"Does he have this address?"

"Yes," Fritz answered, "this was where we met the first time."

"Well, the police can be very persuasive." I stood up and turned off the light. At the window, my view was limited, but the street seemed bare.

"How do you know about the police?"

"Let's just say I happen to see and hear more about the government than I want to sometimes."

"How?" Klaus snapped. He was back to his old self.

"Does it matter?" I retorted.

"Shhhh." Fritz put his hands up.

I ignored him. "Since Simon knows this address, there is a chance he could . . ." The hair on the back of my neck rose. "We must leave. We must leave now!"

Fritz and Klaus stood still.

"Now!" I cried more forcefully.

Fritz quickly grabbed a bag and filled it with a few necessities. Once again, we raced out the door, and despite our best efforts to avert attention from our flight, our footsteps thumped much too loudly down the stairs.

A door creaked open on the first floor. I pressed tightly against the perimeter walls, but the others didn't stop. My mother's sweater snagged as Klaus grabbed my wrist and dragged me out the back entrance.

By the time we reached the end of the street, a canopy of chestnut trees provided a small cover as a white and green Wartburg Coupe passed us unseen. The car, known by many as the choice of vehicle for the Stasi, drove well below the recommended speed, slowing the closer it got. It stopped directly in front of the apartment building we recently exited. We held our breath, unsure whether we should remain hidden and watch or chance being seen and flee.

The car idled quietly in the muggy summer air. "Nothing's happening. No one's getting out, and no one's getting in," Klaus reported hoarsely. His sweat ran down his face, and it had nothing to do with the humidity.

"I don't think we have a choice," Fritz whispered. "Even if this car isn't here for us, it's only a matter of time before someone will be."

I steadied my trembling hands against the smooth bark of the tree, afraid I would pass out. I peeked to the right. The car didn't move. Turning back, I braced myself for support and suggested, "If we cut back through the park over there, we can head west to my old home on Bernauer."

"Bernauer?" Klaus barked. "Right to the border guard?"

"My apartment was evacuated. Nobody is there. If we're careful and can get in, it will be a good place to hide."

"Aren't they checking?"

"They've already been there and seen that it's empty. They boarded up the front door, but we can go through the back window." I fought hard to keep my thoughts from returning to that terrible night.

"We need to go somewhere, Klaus," Fritz insisted, "a place Simon doesn't know about."

"Fine," Klaus snapped, "but we need to go now, the car seems to have no intention of leaving."

"Can you see inside?" I inched forward.

"Not well, I think there are two people."

We shared looks of agreement and one by one slipped carefully across the street. We hoped the darkness provided enough camouflage from the driver's rear-view mirror.

None of us even looked in the direction of the vehicle as we crossed. Its engine continued to idle smoothly as we ran swiftly and discreetly through the park. It was a terrorizing sound, lingering in my mind even after we were streets away.

Despite the familiarity of the streets the closer we got to Bernauer, I was running on fumes. What should have been no more than a ten-minute jog turned into much longer as we cautiously inched our way past vacant apartment buildings blocked by barricades and pockets of soldiers.

We scrambled to a stop behind a large dumpster a street away from my old flat. My neck ached from constantly looking around. Again, we surveyed the area for our safety before we moved.

Although my kitchen window was dark, a strange sense of warmth surfaced as we stood before it. It was my home.

Klaus reached into a container and tossed rubbish around until he found a soiled rag. As quietly as possible, Klaus wrapped the rag around his fist and pressed the glass pane until a corner broke. It was the same window Josef and Anton had crawled out of, only this time, we crawled in.

The shattered dishes from the night the soldiers broke in crunched beneath our shoes. I fumbled for the flashlight under the sink. The small beam illuminated a path to the living room where shards of broken wood scattered about reminded me of the night of the intrusion and the careless destruction of my mother's clock.

"What happened here?" Klaus mumbled irreverently. I ignored him and parted the front window curtains. I'd forgotten about the solid wall of red brick. With the lights out and only using the small flashlight, the brothers turned the couch right side up.

"You don't think they'll track us here, do you?" Fritz asked as he brushed some dust off a pillow.

"Simon never got my last name," I recalled, making my way down the hallway. "There are hundreds of girls by the name of Ella." I was being dramatic.

"Yeah, but how many look . . . different?" Klaus pointed out as he helped me upright my bed.

"It doesn't matter," I sneered. "This house was in my father's name; besides, Simon knew very little about me." Klaus followed my beam of light to the living room where Fritz had fixed several chairs back on their legs.

"Well, we definitely can't go home again." Klaus slumped to the couch discouraged. He had irritated me since the moment we met, but it was true—Simon knew a lot more about them than me. I suddenly felt sorry for them. Their lives would never be the same.

"You can stay here as long as necessary," my tone was softer. "We just need to be aware of the soldiers' post checks in the alley. They used to be fairly predictable, about twenty-five minutes apart. If we monitor the times, we'll be OK. Until then, we need to rest."

"*To Anton . . . and Josef, may you . . .*" Fritz ran his hand across the front wall where I'd drawn months ago. He attempted to read the expression that was quickly fading. I paused in the doorway but remained silent. "I can't seem to make the rest of this out." He turned to Klaus who took no interest in it. "This is quite a fascinating picture . . . Ella?" He turned and saw me staring.

"It says . . . '*be as free as a butterfly,*'" I whispered.

"Did you?" He pointed to the picture. "Did you draw this?" It was apparent he was impressed.

I nodded but brushed it off.

"Who's Anton and Josef?"

"My family in the West. Here's a blanket. I'm sorry there's only one."

"I'm fine." Klaus scowled and pulled the collar of his jacket up as he stretched out on the couch, leaving the floor to his brother.

"Thank you, Ella." Fritz reached for it. "Goodnight."

"Goodnight."

I went to the room I shared with Josef. The clothes I had taken refuge behind in the closet were strewn across the floor as if the Volkspolizie had revisited the flat, but I was too tired to care tonight. I was exhausted and scared, yet as I lay there in my old bed, an odd sense of comfort developed as well.

Despite the unknown I faced, I gained strength from this place. As I stared at the dark, empty walls, a calming peace came over me. It was though I could feel the souls of my family will their might into me . . . it was simply enough strength for me to press on.

I was a Kühn. Not by birth but by choice. It confirmed to me, that with their help, I could face whatever lay ahead.

CHAPTER NINETEEN

When I opened my eyes the next morning, I temporarily forgot where I was until I glanced around the room. An untouched picture was pinned to the wall. While practically everything in this house had been tossed or destroyed, it was a tender mercy that this specific item remained intact. It was one of my earliest memories of the Kühns.

***

"Do you like butterflies?" I asked the quiet boy who sat very still in the corner. It had been two days since my arrival, and my new brother hadn't spoken one word to me yet.

It was nearly bedtime, and as we waited for Frau Kühn to tuck us in for the night, I sat at the edge of my bed and brushed my doll's hair. It had been brushed nearly nonstop since I arrived, and not a strand was out of place, but I did it anyway. Josef remained distant, his head hung low with his legs curled tightly up to his chest, only his finger moved, twisting a strand of his hair over and over.

"I like butterflies. Especially the blue ones," I continued even though the conversation was only with myself. "I think if I could fly, I would fly to the top of a mountain." I stopped brushing as I imagined seeing the world from that perch. I smiled broadly then whispered, "Imagine being closer to the sky, to feel the sun or touch the stars."

I peered at Josef, his face no longer hidden by his hands, and although he didn't speak, he seemed to somehow suddenly see what I described. He appeared captivated. "Imagine jumping from cloud to cloud," I giggled, "or flying over a big ocean." Josef scooted a step closer as I continued. "I can draw you a picture if you like. I'm still learning, but I will draw whatever you want me to." I pointed to his toy horse a few feet away. "Even that horse if you want."

"All right children, it's time for bed now." Frau Kühn walked in. "What story would you like to hear tonight?" She pointed to the shelf where a handful of storybooks rested in a pile. I shrugged. I hadn't ever been asked such a question.

How about *Rübezahl?*" She picked up a book that showed a large man with a long beard walking on top of a mountain. Again, I shrugged my shoulders. I'd never heard of it. She turned to Josef. "Would you like me to read this?" He nodded subtly before he scrambled into his bed.

I sighed and climbed into bed as well. My doll, whom I'd named Mary, at my side.

As Frau Kühn told the tale of the mountain spirit who kidnapped a princess and then turned her turnips into friends so she would not be lonely, my breath swayed with the pace of the story. It sped with suspense then slowed with relief. I'd never felt this way when Nurse Margret read the Bible. Suddenly, all sorts of images came to mind—my whole world shifted, and that was the very night I fell in love with books.

At the end of the story, Frau Kühn pulled the covers to our chins and kissed us each on the forehead. I had never felt so important.

Darkness filled the room when she closed the door behind her, then out of the silence a small voice rose softly, "Will you draw me a horse?"

***

As I stared at the picture I'd drawn nearly six years ago, I laughed at the skinny legs in comparison to the fat body. It was my first and last attempt at a horse, but Josef loved it so much that he never took it down.

I stepped out of bed and quietly folded the paper and placed it in my pocket. Although it was still dark, I knew morning was emerging and it was time for me to leave. The door creaked slightly as I stepped into the next room. I tried to be as discreet as possible, but when I reached for my sweater that hung over a chair, my foot accidentally tapped the leg.

"Are you leaving?" A startled Fritz sat up from the floor.

"I have to get to work."

"Today?"

"Yes. I must not change my routine. I've never missed a day of work. It will cause suspicion."

"It will cause death if you get caught." Klaus joined us from the kitchen.

It appeared he had been up for a while. "Simon knew you worked with Christoph's girl."

"I must go," I insisted, although I knew he was right. There was a possibility I was walking into a death trap. If there was the slightest chance Simon turned over Christoph and Lena's names, I needed to warn her.

"I will return this evening with food. You shouldn't leave."

Despite their silence, I could sense their conflict, but it didn't stop me. I rushed to the Frankes.

With only a small annoying quiver in my fingers, I went about my regular duties. It wasn't until there was a loud knock at the door in the early afternoon that my worst fears were realized.

Lena led a handful of soldiers to the drawing room, and I panicked, hiding in a doorway near the main hall to watch. As she shuffled toward the kitchen, I called to her quietly.

"Pssst, Lena."

"Ella, what . . .why are you hiding?" She joined me, confused.

"Who were those men?"

"Soldiers I've never seen before . . . very official. They seemed to be here on business."

"The Frankes have many soldiers come here on business," I reasoned. My anxiety was apparent.

"Yes . . . and no." Lena paused and eyed me carefully. "All the soldiers who visit rarely come unannounced." I stiffened. She noticed.

"What happened last night?"

"You knew?" I whispered. Lena pushed me further back into the empty room.

"Christoph told me he introduced you to some men . . . men who could help you. What happened?"

"Something went wrong. Christoph's uncle, Simon, was dragged off and beaten, and the other two are possibly being hunted. You might not be safe either," I cried.

"Do they know it was you? Is that why they're here?"

"I don't know. They never got my last name, but" —my legs went weak as I continued— "Simon knew I was friends with you."

"But Simon doesn't know enough to send the soldiers here," Lena assured. She had only met Simon once.

My mind wandered on the chain of events. Was there any possibility the soldiers' visit was random or for a purpose other than me? My hands flew to my face. I couldn't look Lena in the eyes. It was a mistake to come back here.

"Stay here," she whispered with strength. "I need to notify Herr Franke they're here, but I'll find a way to stay close and listen."

The ten minutes before Lena returned were torturous. When random shouting exploded somewhere beyond the door, I entertained the idea of running, that possibly things had gone badly. It frightened me to think what could be transpiring all because of me.

"Ella, are you still here?" Lena slid into the dark room undetected.

"Yes, I'm here." Despite the shadows, I hid behind a bookcase.

"What happened? I heard shouting."

"Oh, Ella." She reached for my hands. "It's not good."

"What?" If a light had been on, she would have seen horror cover my face. "Tell me!"

"Herr Franke was immediately handed a notice the moment he appeared in the parlor. No introductions or anything. The officers promptly demanded that he comply . . . I was filling glasses at the bar and literally cowered at their words. You can imagine Herr Franke's response . . . I don't think he has ever been spoken to that way and in his own home!"

"What did he do?" My voice trembled.

"After he read the contents, he crinkled the paper in his fist and threw it to the ground. Within seconds he was face to face with one young soldier, pressing his finger against his chest screaming how this was an unacceptable intrusion into his personal affairs. He cursed and then brought up the many political associations he has, including both Herr Mielke and Herr Wolf." She seized a short breath, then continued. "I've never seen his face turn that color of red before, Ella. He was enraged. Even the walls seemed to shake when he spoke. The young soldier was practically quaking in his boots. His apologies could barely be heard above his whimpering as he and his comrades ran from the house. Herr Franke followed him out—even to his automobile."

"That is good, right?" I watched her face, but even with the limited lighting, I could see her countenance fall. "I read the paper after they left the room, Ella. It was a declaration of an arrest." She sniffled hard, and a tear slipped down her cheek. "It described you."

"Oh." The word was barely recognizable.

Lena grabbed my hands as they began to shake. "I'm scared for you." Her words came out in a whisper but echoed in my ears.

My skin swelled with heat. The room suddenly felt very small and constricting, I needed air. I cracked the door and inhaled sharply as I contemplated the news.

I knew it wasn't that I was worth the risk Herr Franke would take to defend me. It had to be about his appearance. A man of his caliber could not afford to have menial soldiers question him or his household. I knew it was a humiliation he would not ignore.

Although Herr Franke promptly drove the soldiers from his home, I sensed the matter was far from over. Even if I somehow endured his anger toward me or the consequences that would come, the ministry rarely dropped a case. It most likely would be pursued without his knowledge or involvement.

Lena moved behind me and wrapped her arms tightly around my shoulders. I sighed heavily. There was little relief. My mind reeled with questions.

I turned back to Lena. "I'm sorry I've put you in this position. I should leave."

"No!" Her response surprised me. "No, you are safer here. Besides, maybe the matter really is closed. Maybe the soldiers think Simon lied."

"But it couldn't have come from Simon." My mind spun. "It had to come from someone who knew I worked here at the Frankes' . . . with you . . ."

The room remained silent for several minutes.

"Ella, it's over now." Lena tried to sound hopeful.

I nodded then stopped. A terrible thought came to mind. My face turned ashen. I mumbled incoherently.

Lena stared at me. Her eyebrows twisted. "What?"

I grabbed Lena's hands and spoke louder than before. "Christoph . . ."

"What about him?" The alarm in Lena's voice elevated. I turned my head. It was all coming together now. Lena's muscles went rigid.

"Ella, answer me. What about Christoph?"

"Simon . . ."

"Simon?" Lena's eyes narrowed. "NO!" Her scream amplified in the small space as she finally realized what I was trying to say but couldn't. "He . . . no, Ella . . ."

Lena started to tremble. Her knees buckled under her, and she collapsed to the floor. I dropped with her, my arms cradling her. The sobs caused her body to shake with grief.

"Lena, please, don't. We don't know anything yet. Maybe Christoph is OK." Even as the words left my lips, there was no truth behind them. I was sure Simon gave up his name . . . his own family.

Everyone knew the tactics the Volkspolizei and Stasi used to get names. It was always about more names, and very few people survived to tell about it.

"Lena, please don't cry, please?" It was hard not to feel the full weight of guilt. I knew this was my fault.

"Do you . . ." her words became incoherent.

"Lena, I'll send for Christoph. He will come, you'll see." I laid her gently down and ran to the back door. I motioned to one of the young yard boys in the cemetery nearby.

"Please," I cried, "please come. I need your help." He followed me back to where I left Lena.

"Will you help me get her to the guest bedroom upstairs?" I pleaded. "Then I need another favor. I'll pay you." He agreed.

After he laid Lena on the bed, we were able to get her to tell the boy where Christoph lived.

"Please, boy," I reiterated, "do not tell anyone where you're going. Just see if Christoph is there. If he is" —I looked over to Lena's fragile form— "tell him to come to Lena immediately."

"And if he's not—"

I cut him off. "Just bring us word. Hurry, please."

I found Johann in the staff room. He, like everyone else, seemed to recognize the heightened anxiety in the home. Thankfully, Frau Franke had left for the day prior to the soldiers' arrival. If she had been home, she would have turned me over, this much I knew was true.

I ignored Johann's questions and begged him to cover both my and Lena's whereabouts for the day. He only accepted when I offered him money.

I returned to Lena, locked the door, and crawled next to her. She hadn't stopped crying—it was difficult to watch.

The clock on the desk ticked slowly, second by second, confirming that time was dragging agonizingly slower than normal. The wait was excruciating. Lena stopped crying, but her thoughts were elsewhere. She seemed frozen still.

Tears started and stopped at a steady pace with me. I knew this was my fault. If anything happened to Christoph, she would never forgive me. I wouldn't forgive myself either.

Thirty minutes went by. Johann appeared. "Ella, Herr Franke is looking for you." I took a couple of deep breaths and then pointed to Lena, who sat on the edge of the bed, rocking slowly with her back toward us.

"I can't leave her alone right now, Johann." He stayed in the doorway. He could see she was not herself. "Please, Johann, can you help me? Tell him I had a predicament."

"He seemed angry." Johann's eyes narrowed. "It could be something about the visit from the soldiers. Ella, . . . what have you gotten yourself involved in?" Despite Johann's ability to suppress emotion, his face grew rigid and dark.

"Please, Johann, please."

He glanced back at me, frustrated. He owed me nothing, but he was fond of Lena.

"OK!" he relented. "OK, I will address it." And he was gone.

The boy had now been away over an hour. Another thirty minutes passed before I heard a knock on the door. It was him. The fear that spread across his face was all too familiar, I knew his news would not be good. I stepped out into the hall with him.

"He . . . the man you, y—" the boy stuttered, unable to speak clearly.

"It's OK, slow down." I placed my hand on his arm. He inhaled a long breath.

"He's gone."

I tried not to let my face respond with distress. "Gone?" I whispered.

The boy looked around him, his hands were trembling by his side. "The door was open, and his flat was muddled." He shifted nervously to his other foot. "I found this near the door." He held out a silver button, perfectly chiseled, dark green threads trailed underneath. It appeared as though it had been ripped from a uniform. I reached for it, gripping it tightly as I stared at the ceiling.

Please no, please, I begged silently. My head whirled with emotion.

"May I please be relieved?" The boy pleaded.

I nodded but didn't say a word as I moved back into the bedroom. My fingers gripped the door in an effort to close it quietly. Tears slid down my cheeks; I could no longer stopped them from coming.

I climbed gently onto the bed where Lena lay. The moment was surreal; her sobs had finally slowed to a purr, only I knew what was about to come and it terrified me. I pulled a pillow up near her face and whispered into her ear. Her fingers gripped the sides as she screamed violently into the pillow.

It muffled the brunt of the noise, but the bed shook. Her body convulsed as I attempted to hold her tightly. Lena's heartache seared through me. The guilt crushed my will to live, a stark contrast to the exhilaration I felt less than twenty-four hours ago.

Although words were never uttered, the dark reality of the world we lived in weighed heavily in the room. We both knew enough about this government to know anytime a person disappeared, chances were we would never see them again.

I held her for the rest of the day and through the night. I thought about Lena nonstop and how my choice had affected her so directly. *How will she ever move on? Christoph was her life.*

At first light, I awoke to an empty bed. Panic set in when I didn't see Lena. A moan led me to the floor where she shivered restlessly, curled in a ball. A dark stain covered her sleeve. My throat constricted and smothered my cries in grim speculation.

I rushed to her side. A letter opener slipped to the ground from her other hand. From the broken skin at her wrist, it appeared the dull blade hadn't accomplished the job she had hoped for, but the damage was done.

"Lena, . . ." I choked through rapid tears. I grabbed the doily on the nightstand and wrapped it around her wrist. The blood soaked through as she grew pale and unresponsive. *What is wrong with me? I knew Lena was vulnerable, why didn't I see this coming?* I scolded myself for not watching her more closely. It should have been obvious she wouldn't want to survive without Christoph.

I needed to get Johann; he would know what to do. Rushing down the hall, I turned the corner to the stairs and nearly knocked Stefan down in the process. My heart sank; he was the last person I wanted to see.

"Excuse me!" I cried both exasperated and frightened. As I struggled to maneuver around him, he grabbed my wrist. I coiled my hand to hide my blood-stained fingers. His touch was neither soft nor hard but enough to stop me from continuing.

"What's wrong?" His voice demanded an answer. I glanced at him, then down the stairs. If I didn't reach Johann in time, Stefan might be my only hope of saving Lena.

"Please, follow me." I led him back to the guest room. Stefan's eyes went wide the moment he saw her. It was as bad as I believed. Without hesitation, he swiftly scooped her up and was gone within seconds.

Numb, I stood there well after their departure. It was pointless to follow, she was in the best hands possible. The irony of the situation was overpowering—I, her best friend, was the one who caused harm, and Stefan, the "enemy", would save her life.

In despair, I finally sank to the bed, unable to take my eyes off the bloody tool.

It was I who should die.

I was solely responsible for not only Christoph's disappearance but possibly Lena's life as well. My mind weighed the options. I didn't deserve to live, but Josef didn't deserve to lose anyone else. The blade stared back at me for an hour before I left the room.

In my desire to care for Lena, I'd forgotten about the two men hiding in my old house. I had assured them I would be back the previous night with food. When I didn't return, they must've believed the worst. I needed to get there as soon as possible, but when I reached the bottom of the stairs, I froze.

"Fräulein Kühn." I knew this particular voice would soon find me. Afraid to look Herr Franke directly in the face, I turned but did not peer up. The silence coated the room for several minutes. I could feel his eyes boring into the top of my bowed head. The blood-stained apron clenched tightly in my fists for concealment, I fought to remain still. Memories of a failed task in the orphanage competed with images of what my fate might be. *Just get it over with!*

Finally, he spoke. "Do you know why the soldiers came for you?"

Despite rehearsing a multitude of answers in anticipation of this confrontation, my mind went blank now that we were face to face. A rivulet of sweat slid down the back of my neck.

"Fräulein, answer me." His tone increased in volume. My eyes found the button at his collar, and I nodded. He was growing impatient. "Now!" His voice continued to rise.

Finally meeting his eyes, I stuttered, "I w-was at a café with . . . some friends." My pulse quickened. "Soldiers came and took one of them away."

Herr Franke watched my every move.

"I ran because I got scared. I didn't do anything wrong." It was the truth even if the details of what I'd planned to do later that night were omitted.

He turned sharply as if the conversation was over, but the heaviness in the air attested otherwise. Even though his pacing was silent, every step he took seemed to imprint on my soul, it felt like an eternity before he stopped and faced me once more.

"Don't put me in this position again, or I will personally see to your arrest myself."

I nodded, but he was already gone.

Sighing heavily, I knew the conversation could have gone many different ways. It was suddenly apparent to me which parent was the more lenient of the two.

I did not see Stefan return. Although I wanted to know about Lena's condition, fear of additional scrutiny prevented me from searching for him. In my heart, I had to believe she was recovering nicely in a hospital bed, thanks to Stefan's quick jump to action. Had I not seen it myself, I would not have believed it.

Precisely at five I departed, boarding the first bus that got me closer to my old address. A block away, I watched until the soldiers doing their rounds had passed, then entered the alley once more. I looked through the window before climbing through, but even as I whispered their names, it was evident the brothers were gone.

I maneuvered through the room with caution, even holding my hurried breath more strictly for fear of the unknown. The dark emptiness confirmed, yes, they were gone.

In discouragement, I fell to the couch. Had I sentenced them to their death as well? Were they caught as they waited for me? I was the one who told them not to leave.

So here I was . . . a walking death sentence. In the course of twenty-four hours, I possibly had the blood of four people on my hands; a burden that crushed my core.

Suffused with guilt, I buried my head in the couch cushion that was more like a shredded ball of stuffing and brought less comfort than I hoped. When I tossed it aside, it came to a stop a few feet from the front door or what was left of it. After the soldiers' break-in, someone had nailed a barrier across the busted frame with a sign that declared *Kein Eintrag*. The demand of "No entry" carried little weight with the holes. Anything could get through . . . even a folded piece of paper that I hadn't seen before. I stood and retrieved it.

The paper was closed tightly and covered in dirt with no indication of how long it had been there. At first, I hoped it was from the brothers, bearing the news they were safe and had chosen to leave, but the paper's fragile condition told me it had been there much longer than one night.

I carefully opened it. Scribbled in faded ink was a message. A quick glance to the bottom showed it was signed by Brauner. It was difficult to read due to its condition. I grabbed the flashlight as darkness started to fill the room with a setting sun and read slowly to decipher the correspondence:

To Fräulein Ella K   3   1961

On recent visit to West Berlin, I was approached young man by the name of Anton Schultz.

My heart pounded. Overcome with emotion at the mere mention of Anton's name, I tried not to read too fast and just take in one word at a time.

He is employed as a bricklayer at company in which business in Charlottenburg. shared with me gripping escape from the East the nig of Aug , along brother Josef and pleaded I bringword of their safe arrival. They could give this address, however, he the fact mailed letters were returned this note now finds well and of good health. I had misfortune of losing many friends in the business I have with providence to travel freely, If you wish to relay a message to Anton Josef, I reside in the neighborhood # 2 Bernstrasse

Your humble r
Brauner

I could not believe my eyes. I had waited so long to hear of their arrival and survival. Anton was working, and I'm sure Josef was safe in his care. I had to find this Herr Brauner, though it would be difficult from the faded letter. Even part of his address was missing, but I had to try.

It seemed my fate has suddenly shifted . . . a fate I was sure was doomed mere minutes before. I read the letter three more times before carefully folding it up and placing it deep in the pocket of my dress. There was no reason for me to remain here.

I watched carefully once more until the soldiers passed and turned the corner then slipped out the back again and ran home, eager to share the news with Mama G.

CHAPTER TWENTY

13 Aug 1962

One year to the day Anton and Josef disappeared around that alley corner, a loud commotion originated from the West at high noon. It didn't matter where you were in the city or on which side, everyone heard the clear exaggerated honking from automobile horns pressed hard in a synchronized protest of the wall.

I still hadn't found Herr Brauner. His correspondence said something about the fact of his location being in —*Bernstrasse*. It narrowed his location down to the partial name of a street, but it was still a broad search. Since his apartment number had also been smudged, I decided to blanket what I could with the little information I did have.

So far nobody I'd talked to even knew a family by the name of Brauner. I wasn't ready to give up. I left my address with multiple shop and café owners in several neighborhoods. They agreed, that if they had contact with anyone named Brauner, they would give him my information. It was a frail attempt, but since I had no other connection to Anton and Josef, I had to try.

I continued to venture over to the old house once a week to see if any other letters turned up. Although searches under the boards, through the garbage, and even in the hallway produced nothing, I had to remain positive. It was all I had.

Six weeks had passed since that awful day when Lena fell ill. A week after the incident, Stefan found me cleaning the dining room and initiated conversation. I was as surprised at this as I was by his news.

"Your friend is going to recover," he said as he watched my reaction carefully.

"She is?" I cried, overcome with emotion.

"Yes," he replied impassively, "we got her medical attention just in time."

I felt like screaming hallelujah! She was my best friend, my closest confidant. I clasped my hands together to thank a God, whose possible intervention was the only logical explanation, despite my feelings that "God" seemed to disregard our little corner of the world.

I owed Stefan my gratitude for his quick response, but when I turned to say thank you, he was gone. I really was grateful for his assistance. Even though I knew it was solely his intervention that saved her life, it was still hard for me to accept where the help came from.

As time went by, the names Simon, Fritz, and Klaus became a distant, sorrowful memory, never to be seen or heard from again.

Although our alliance came from difficult circumstances, my wish that Fritz and Klaus had found a successful path to freedom never changed while I continued to crave finding my own way across the border. I just had to be much smarter about it and much more discreet. I knew very well Herr Franke's threat was real, as well as the government's intentions to find those who plotted an escape.

Tonight, the first anniversary of the wall going up, demonstrations were being staged on both sides of the border in protest. Despite my fears, I always kept an eye and ear peeled for further secret opportunities.

By a small chance of fate, Mama G's daughter, Khloe, set up a meeting for me with a friend who thought he had found a weak link at the wall. He wanted to talk at a pub in the Prenzlauer Berg neighborhood. Pubs were my least favorite place in the city but always made a great cover to be able to talk without drawing additional attention.

That night I rode the bus to an area of town that initially seemed similar to the rest of the city, yet on approach appeared somehow less run down and forgotten.

It was my first time in Prenzlauer, and I surprisingly felt at home. There were amazing displays of artwork on the sides of buildings, musicians and mimes performed on the streets, and people were out and about, including a large group of youth assembled to march near the wall.

I say *near* because everyone knew by now it didn't matter if your proximity to the wall was an accident or not, the tower guards had itchy trigger fingers. They even received awards for their valor in protecting the perimeter.

My mind went back to the night when I ventured too close just weeks after the initial closure. I would have become a wall fatality had the senior officer not halted it. I'm sure that same officer now gives the order to shoot without hesitation regardless of who is watching.

Over the course of this last year, much had changed. The increase in nightly action near the wall often confused the skyline with lightning, minus the rain. It had become so normal to hear the single pop of a rifle or the continuous rounds of a machine gun that we no longer held our breath like before.

Many times, when the Western media outlets crossed lines, we could hear the reports in uncensored facts. The number of death and injuries caused by the Berliners' desperate struggle for liberty was shared as well as the blood lust of the border guard.

However, in the daily reports of the *Neues Deutschland* newspaper, the official paper of the Socialist Unity Party in East Berlin, the language was vastly opposite. It defended the ongoing boundary shootings as justified breaches on the border, emphasizing that the lives of members of the border security were often put in "extreme danger".

Once I arrived on Eberswalder Straße, it took only a few minutes to find Mosse's on Kastanienalle. The pub was small and dark, packed with patrons. My eyes subtly scanned the crowd as I recalled the conversation Khloe and I had barely a day ago.

"How old did you say he is?"

"Eighteen, I believe." Khloe put her steaming mug to her lips. "He said he will be wearing a brown cap."

"Will he be alone?"

"Peter will be with him, maybe others."

"Do you think it's safe?" I reached for an apple as we whispered in the kitchen.

"Mosse's? Oh yes. It may be a pub, but it's . . . different—" Khloe grinned widely. "—well you'll know what I mean when you get there."

I was puzzled by her comment until now. Three small children played *Topfschlagen* in a corner, giggling as they filled a cooking pot with rocks. Josef and I had played it on occasion, but somehow Mama Kühn always found a treat to hide.

I was sad for these children until I realized they didn't seem to mind their treasure wasn't edible. A baby's cry pulled my eyes toward a table where an infant bounced on his papa's knee while he balanced his stein of beer in his hand. There were nearly as many children as adults present. I'd never been anywhere like this.

I continued to search the room when a teenager who matched Helmut's description glanced in my direction. The expression on his face told me I'd found the right group. It was the same look of desperation I saw on the faces of Simon, Fritz, and Klaus when I first met them.

"Helmut?" I approached cautiously.

"Ja, you must be Ella." A young man with a slender build and bright eyes rose to shake my hand. He was followed by three others, two boys and a girl.

"This is Peter, Jakob, and Frieda."

I nodded and shook all their hands before taking a seat.

"I ordered you an *Obstler*."

"Oh, I appreciate the gesture, but I don't drink." The disbelief in their eyes was not masked. For what did East Berliners have to look forward to but their spirits?

"No problem," Helmut cried. In one swift motion, he grabbed the glass, swallowed the contents in one gulp, then wiped his mouth with his sleeve.

"You have family in the West?" Frieda asked quietly, although nobody could hear our conversation above the noisy crowd. It was precisely why they chose this particular establishment in the first place.

"Yes. Yes, I do. Do you?"

"My mother and sister."

"And you, Peter?" I asked one of the other boys. "Do you have family in the West?"

"No, my family is here. I just want a better life. I know there's a brighter future in the West."

I nodded, but his words seemed strange to me. Yes, it was confining and smothering here, but if my family—Anton and Josef—were here, I could possibly be content.

"Peter and I work for the same company," Helmut interrupted.

"We are rebuilding the former Kaiser-Wilhelm-Palais, a palace on the Unter den Linden. Are you familiar with the area?"

I was since it was in Mitte, but the other two were not.

"We happened to come across a shabby building on Schutzenstrauss, and inside were the run-down remains of a workshop."

Helmut leaned in and whispered, "The back windows lead straight to Zimmerstrasse and very close to the wall."

Peter added, "—and no signs of regular guard patrol either." He looked around. "We walked in and out twice, completely undetected."

"The windows weren't bricked up?" I asked with surprise.

"No, not at all," Helmut confirmed.

"Dogs? Lights? Do you know if the fence has motion sensors?"

They looked at each other uncomfortably. I knew they hadn't even considered this.

"So, what does this mean?" I questioned cautiously. My previous experience was fresh on my mind.

"Mean?" Helmut looked surprised. "It's an opportunity."

"To run the border?" My face lifted skeptically, but all eyes looked at me with surprise. They were convinced their idea was unrivaled.

"Have you ever read the papers on border runs—" I looked at each member of the group then brashly continued, "—seen the photographs of the bodies?" The irritation in my voice was evident. "Have you watched someone be tortured by the Volkspolizei or had to run for your life because you were being pursued?"

Despite the fact the three boys were all approximately two years older than me, I was the one who showed the more mature reasoning, . . . yet they blew off my skepticism as if I was an ignorant girl.

"I thought you wanted to leave?" Helmut's eyes narrowed.

"I do . . ." I assured them, ". . . more than anything in this world, but there has to be a reason the shop is not secured, a trap or something you aren't seeing."

"Maybe they just haven't gotten to it." Jakob had been silent until now.

I shook my head. "This doesn't sound right." I knew this was the approach I should have taken with my first escape attempt.

"I don't think it will work," I insisted.

"It could," Peter protested. "Maybe, if we had more—"

"—more people?" I questioned.

"Yes, if we had at least ten or more of us running simultaneously. It would cause chaos, confusion, and with such a short distance, chances are we could surprise the border guard and all make it."

"And chances are one or more would be shot." I was discouraged. I came here looking for a credible proposal but knew this was too high-risk.

"You're not interested?" Helmut asked.

"I don't know, Helmut." I looked around the room. It was a motion I did more often lately. "I just think if you study it a little more, maybe watch the border a little closer, . . . it just seems precarious."

Frieda and Jakob seemed to have their own reservations as well. My exhilaration deflated. I didn't come here to change people's minds, but after what I'd seen and read and experienced, this was not the direction I wanted to go.

I stood to leave. "Helmut, maybe give it some more thought or possibly time."

"Time?" Peter scoffed. "It's just a matter of time before the East has no one left to kill."

I bit my lip and forced myself not to respond. I've seen this desperation hundreds of times. It wasn't his fault. I turned to the others.

"Thank you for the evening, Peter, Frieda, and Jakob. Nice to meet you all. I wish you the very best in your efforts."

"You too, Ella." Frieda touched my hand sweetly.

I nodded and turned to Peter. "Please be careful and think it through." We shook hands and parted as friends.

As I moved to push the exit door open, the words, *Voilà le portrait sans retouche* reached my ears. I stopped. My eyes darted around in an attempt to locate the source.

Helmut noticed my concern and approached. "Ella, are you well?"

I nodded but still focused on the woman's voice. Translated, it evoked an image of a man taking his woman into his arms. It was the only French I knew.

"Can I get you something?" Helmut's hand went to my shoulder, his eyebrows pulled together tightly in concern.

I whispered, "No," as I jockeyed around him again drawn to the instrumentals in the background.

I exhaled softly. Papa took Mama's hand. Her brown curls bounced as she giggled and moved toward him. This was the only time I forgot Papa had a bad leg. If it hurt at that moment, we never knew. He twirled Mama around the room. Her smile was infectious. Then came my favorite part, Papa cradled her gently as he dipped her smoothly to his side. They always ended in a kiss...*la vie en rose.*

The vision had driven me back to the bar. I stood awkwardly silent in front of the *Barmann*. He stared at me with a similarly confused expression.

"Is . . . is that a record playing?"

The stocky, hairy man wrinkled his lip but made no response. Leaning to the side, he pointed to the box radio behind him. The song was over. Edith Piaf's voice ceased. Disappointment swelled inside me. Helmut appeared at my side, a brotherly countenance I recognized on Anton's face many times.

"Ella, are you alright?" he asked, possibly for the third time.

"Yes, Helmut, I'm fine. Thank you."

"Did you . . .?" he stopped himself short. I focused on his eyes. "Did you change your mind?" There was a lift in his voice.

My thoughts went back to my family. I couldn't believe I was saying this, but my heart was not lying, "Yes, I believe so."

Helmut's face brightened, instantly delighted.

I continued firmly, "The plan needs work. Let's meet again. I'll send word through Khloe."

I walked home from the bus stop feeling numb, unable to pinpoint the sentiment that lingered. *La Vie en Rose* definitely triggered the emotional side of me, but surprisingly, the rational side didn't argue this time. I knew I was ready to try again. I missed my family. It was time.

Less than a week later just after two o'clock in the afternoon, the nasal-sounding Western reporter repeatedly announced over the air, "Junge erschossen! Junge erschossen!" Johann turned up the volume as I happened to be passing by the room. The small staff crowded curiously around the radio in the back room.

"Boy shot at Charlottenstraße. He remains on the ground bleeding to death."

I held my breath as I moved my head a little closer. How many people were witnessing this horrific event live?

"He is still alive!" The newsperson nearly shouted through the speaker. "He is calling for help!"

The entire staff was glued to the broadcast, completely immobilized for another twenty minutes in a play-by-play dialog detailing how people from the Allied sector of the wall were trying to help a badly injured teenager who had been shot the moment he rushed the wall. Bandages were thrown over the wall from the west. Hands and voices tried to encourage from afar, and the Western media photographed the gruesome scene for all to see. This boy, who suffered immensely from multiple gunshot wounds, was left to die in no-man's-land mere steps from freedom.

"What is going on here?" Frau Franke demanded angrily at the door of the room. We all instantly shot up to attention.

She turned her ear toward the radio and heard, "Western patrol cannot intercede!"

"What are you listening to?" Unaware that we listened to an Allied station, her face wrinkled with each passing word. She stomped over to the radio and ripped the knob off the face of the receiver, hoping that would solve the problem—only it didn't actually stop the sound from coming through.

"East German border troops are descending into the Sperrzone under a wall of fog that is now covering the body . . ."

Frau Franke was particularly enraged by the report but not for the same reasons we were. Grabbing the box, she pulled it from the wall, ripping the cord. "You will get back to work immediately or look for alternate employment." She stomped out; the radio clasped in her hands like an enemy by the throat.

We knew we shouldn't have spent so much wasted time, but it was hard to pull away. Despite the DDR's best efforts at shrouding the truth of the event, a monument had spontaneously begun to develop on the west side of the wall. Random flowers appeared both pierced by the wire on top and scattered along the ground near the boy's final resting place. Residents of both sides of Berlin mourned.

It wasn't until the next day that it was fully reported on the front page of the newspaper. A young man by the name of Peter Fechter had run the border with a friend. He was shot in the process and declared dead at the Berlin People's Police Hospital shortly after.

Karl-Eduard von Schnitzler, a representative of the border patrol, was quoted in the press as saying that the border guard's brutality in the boy's case was good for and in the interest of the state. "When this kind of element is wounded directly on the border and not retrieved immediately, then a huge fuss is made. The life of each of our brave young men in uniform is more important to us than the life of a lawbreaker. By staying away from our state border, blood, tears, and screams can be avoided."

My stomach curled. This boy only wanted freedom and now has been used as propaganda to prove an evil point. As I glanced over the rest of the article, I couldn't read the words fast enough,

". . . due to the treasonous act, the body of Peter Fechter will not be released to his family and remains in custody of the DDR. A warrant has been issued for the apprehension of his accomplice Helmut Kulbeik who illegally crossed the border minutes before. Both Peter and Helmut were eighteen years of age and—"

Wait, Peter and Helmut?

Panic came in the form of perspiration. I searched frantically for a photo that did not show the bloody scene. Something, anything that showed his face, but I could not find it.

Yes, they were both eighteen and colleagues in the same construction company. I needed to sit down. My mind spun. I knew in my heart it was the boys I had just met. The ones I'd seen less than a week ago . . . alive, breathing, and talking.

Why didn't they wait? Why didn't they plan better?

My face heated up and bobbled between anger and sadness. Why do so many have to die in such desperate desires for independence, for family, for choice . . . and way too young?

I thought of my brother, Josef, now twelve years old. He was growing up without a mother, father, or now his sister. Would he forget me? Will he remember the games we played or the walks we took? What about the times he would fall asleep curled up in my lap on the couch while I read Storm's *Immensee* at night?

I was not much younger than Peter, and Peter had just begun to live. He had his whole life in front of him, and now it was gone. *Will I die young too?* Die, before I see my brother and Anton again?

I had to believe there was a better way.

CHAPTER TWENTY-ONE

The next two months seemed like a blur. I abandoned my thoughts of escaping momentarily in light of the events that surrounded Peter and Helmut. Khloe confirmed within days after the tragedy my assumption was indeed accurate. Our friends had run the border on a whim.

Thankfully, Helmut survived and made it to the West, but Peter, everything he spoke about the night in the pub had vanished. Everything he desired or hoped for was taken from him in a rash matter of minutes.

My longing to be reunited with Anton and Josef never failed. I simply lost any strength in pursuing a plan that could jeopardize my life. As long as I was breathing, there was still a possibility of being reunited with my boys.

Instead, I decided to focus my energy on trying to locate Herr Brauner and left my contact info in nearly every store in this half of the city. From the first correspondence, which I often carried with me, I took solace in at least knowing they were safe and free, but I longed for more.

By October I'd all but given up. It seemed Mr. Brauner was no more than a figure of my imagination, come to haunt my dreams. I continued to count down my days of service for the Frankes. It was all I had to look forward to.

The day, 27 October 1962, started out like any other. Heidi and I were assigned to serve a morning brunch and had prepared accordingly as we had for dozens of other meetings. But what should have been routine evolved into anything but mundane.

Herr Wolf was the first to arrive. Frau Franke's elbow nudged me briskly out of the way the moment I opened the door. Her hand extended for a handshake, but her other hand reached gently for his forearm . . . almost tenderly. I turned my back, careful to hide my irritation.

By the time I reached the kitchen doors, I heard the voices of several other men materialize near the entrance. I glanced back just in time to see Herr Ulbricht appear with a handful of soldiers accompanying him—his personal guard. Nobody of importance went anywhere in the East without protection.

The workers' uprising and growing tension over a constant lack of resources had made them vulnerable. Although the people, for the most part, were too scared to do anything, history had proven over time that desperate people have the ability to change both the course of their future and governments alike, and this, I was sure, the Germans knew better than anyone.

"Heidi!" I whispered sternly to get her attention once we were reunited. She had just finished placing the *Quarkkeulchen* on a separate platter; I could smell the sweet scent of cheese. She peeked in my direction but didn't stop working. "You should see who the guests are for this meeting." I smiled but couldn't hold it in very long. "Wolf and Ulbricht!" I stretched my neck as I spoke through gritted teeth. She stopped. Her eyes grew wide.

"Are you certain?" Heidi ran to the door and peered through a small crack in the door. The guests had already been shown into the parlor, and all she saw was an empty hallway.

"Ulbricht?" she questioned.

"Yes, I promise it was him. I've seen his picture in the *Morgenpost*."

Heidi giggled; she was still naïve enough to confuse admiration for these men with what should have been trepidation. I, on the other hand, was more interested in overhearing their designs.

Throughout the morning, Heidi and I worked feverishly to make sure all the needs were met in the drawing room, despite our presence never actually being acknowledged. Much of the conversation was unhindered, yet beyond our understanding . . . that is until the door suddenly burst open, and an exasperated Johann entered, to our surprise.

"Herr Ulbricht!" he cried, nearly out of breath. This startled everyone present. One soldier reached for his weapon as Herr Ulbricht stood. He put his hand up to relieve the young man and approached Johann. Johann handed him a telegram. I could see from my proximity it was stamped "сро́чный". A word I was unfamiliar with.

Herr Ulbricht adjusted his glasses and brushed his fingers across the hair on his chin. His eyes poured slowly over the words on the paper before he read it aloud to his anxious company.

UNARMED AMERICAN PLANE SHOT DOWN OVER CUBA STOP DO-BRYNIN MET WITH R KENNEDY STOP KENNEDY SAYS AMERICA PRES-SURED TO RESPOND WITH FIRE STOP KHRUSHCHEV WARNED CUBA IS A SECURITY RISK

AND WILL BE BOMBED STOP WAR IMMINENT STOP KHRUSHCHEV WILL NOT CONCEDE STOP

The tray I was holding began to shake. I quickly set it down as my mind attempted to grasp the full reality of what I had overheard. The men, too, appeared stunned, dazed to the point I could have probably done anything at that moment and still not drawn their attention away from the telegram.

"Quickly, Koen," Wolf demanded, "Turn on the radio." Herr Franke reached for the large upright radio in the corner. They had a television in their bedroom, but I doubted he would invite them there.

"This was a confidential telegram, Markus," Ulbricht spoke realisti-cally. "The media does not know it has escalated to this."

Herr Franke continued to scan the stations to see if anything hap-pened to be broadcast.

"What do you think Khrushchev will do?"

"He is Russian!" Wolf cried. "He will not fold to the Americans!"

Herr Ulbricht walked over to the bar. "I wonder if this was the first time our ambassador met with the president's brother?" He spoke with an eerie calmness in his voice.

"Castro cannot be trusted." Herr Franke joined him at the bar. He barely acknowledged my presence as he held up his glass for more vod-ka. I filled both glasses and wiped the sweating decanter with linen. I knew I shouldn't be there, but I was driven with curiosity and Herr Fran-ke had not excused me yet.

"Cuba is ideal for missiles; they can reach parts of America swiftly, including Washington." Ulbricht returned to his seat. Although his face did not appear as uneasy as the others from the news, his continual tug-ging at his collar and tie indicated his discomfort.

"But Cuba used to have an alliance with the United States. Their loy-alty is weak." Wolf reasoned.

As I pretended to stay busy and useful, I contemplated the position this put East Berlin in. Just across the wall, American troops were ready and armed, fortified by military units from both France and Britain. At a moment's notice, war could break out not only overseas but here as well.

The very thought of hostilities erupting, forced my heart to palpitate a second faster. I reached for the edge of the bar and gripped hard for balance. Voices continued to buzz around me but were muffled against the ringing in my ears. My only interest now turned to Berlin and the destruction and scars that lingered from the last war.

The door opened, and Heidi walked in with a tray of S*enfeier*. I watched as Herr Wolf's eyes immediately bounced from Heidi to me then turn to the other men in the room. He stood up quickly and waved his hand toward us both. Herr Franke seemed to understand the silent warning.

"Fräulein Kühn, thank you for your assistance." Herr Franke joined Wolf and pointed to the table with urgency. "Fräulein Frederickson, please place the dish on the table. You may both leave."

I bowed my head in acknowledgment and moved to walk out quickly when Herr Ulbricht reached for my arm to stop me. This surprised all who were present.

"Your family is Kühn?" he inquired openly, although his face eyed me skeptically. I knew he questioned the validity of my German heritage.

"Yes, sir. My adopted family is Kühn." Although I did not need to include that fact, I knew that's what he really wanted to know.

He smiled. The long lines that surrounded his mouth deepened, and he seemed to momentarily forget the pending disaster. "My Lotte is a Kühn. Perhaps you are a relative." His eyes lit up. He must be very fond of this "Lotte" woman.

"I'm sorry. I have no living family." I nodded my head in respect and left the room.

I waited in the kitchen for Heidi to appear.

"Ella," —Heidi rushed to my side— "I didn't know you are alone." Her eyes were full of compassion.

"It's all right; it's been a long time." I quickly changed the subject.

"Heidi," I looked to the door as my eyes started to well with tears, "I know I'm not supposed to talk about this here." I grabbed her hand and moved her toward the back wall, "The Soviets are going to war with America!"

"What?" she cried a little too loud. The door opened, and Johann walked in. "What are you two gossiping about?" he demanded.

I waved him over. His eyes rolled as if I'd asked too much of him. He shuffled over casually, but when I repeated what I had heard, he froze.

"I knew it was an urgent telegram from Moscow, but I dared not read the contents." Johann took a seat, appearing quite pale.

"Do you really think?" Heidi whispered.

"I don't know," I whispered in return.

"Khrushchev will not yield." Johann stood up firmly. Despite some reservations, Johann was Russian through and through. "It's about time we contested the Americans. They have never been our friends."

My eyes widened. "But Johann, we could be crushed here. The Americans could break Berlin like a twig . . . we could all die."

"Pshhh. Fräulein Kühn, you underestimate the Soviets." And Johann walked out. I looked to Heidi. Her family was all here in the East, but she still felt the same as I. The unknown was alarming.

Throughout the day, men came and went. Telegrams arrived, and tension increased as the hours passed. Heidi and I spent the time preparing more food and serving; however, Herr Franke was much more aware of our presence than before. Therefore, our time in the room was limited and monitored. We heard very little of the progress.

"I need you to remain here at the house tonight," Frau Franke announced upon finding Heidi and me in the kitchen. "We will have guests throughout the evening."

We had already assumed we would be needed since the number of guests had swelled to over a dozen. I was initially surprised the meeting was not held at the SED headquarters, but of course, the food, drink, and comforts were not as pleasant.

Each time we entered the room, the tension seemed more and more heightened. The radio was on, and the men paced. The large television had been moved from the bedroom to the parlor, as well as the telephone from the mortuary. A long cord had been brought in just for that purpose. The alcohol consumed was three times the normal amount.

"Yes, Frau Franke," I acknowledged. "Is there anything specific you would like prepared?"

She glowered. "Everything."

I nodded. "Of course." She walked out with an air of offense like she should not have to answer such trivial questions. If Lena were here, she would not have to deal with such ignorance. I rolled my eyes as the door swung behind her. Heidi muffled a laugh as the door opened again. I bit my lip, afraid she had returned and seen my facial rebellion. I stared as a man's hand reached around and then caught my breath as he came into full view.

It was Stefan.

Heidi and I hesitated; surprise covered our faces. He rarely came into the kitchen.

"*Kaffe,* please." His voice was uncommonly relaxed. I didn't move.

Heidi jumped forward and grabbed the kettle. "Yes, sir." She proceeded to pull a teacup from a cupboard.

I remained still. Given our previous interactions, including one in this very room, my hesitation was warranted. Stefan glanced at me while he waited. I turned away and moved toward the oven. I probably should've been kinder, given the way he assisted with Lena, but it was safer, I presumed, to stay distant.

"Anything else, Herr Franke?" Heidi's voice was sickly-sweet. I wrinkled my nose.

"No, but thank you, Heidi," he responded genuinely. Neither one of us hid the shock that he knew her name. Only I kept my back toward them both until I heard the door close once again. I silently recalled the conversation in the library with Katharina, quite some time ago, when he claimed to not know who Lena was after her many years of service here.

"He's quite handsome," Heidi gushed.

"Barely tolerable," I mumbled.

"Are you jesting? Do you not have eyes?" she giggled. ". . . and so kind . . ."

I groaned.

"No, really. I didn't even think he knew my name." I could practically see her daydream.

"He is not who you think he is," I insisted.

"You're wrong, Ella."

"Am I?"

"I heard he helped Lena, back when she—"

"—Uh-huh." I cut her off. I didn't even want to think of that day. Heidi continued, "I also saw him help Herr Schneider."

"The lead gardener?" I questioned, skeptically.

"Yes, his wife was quite ill."

"I didn't know."

"Stefan gave him time away from work and money for the doctor."

"I doubt it."

"I saw it myself," she insisted.

I brushed it off. "Let's get back to work. It will be a long night."

We pulled out the ham hock, bratwursts, schnitzel and capers with cream sauce. But as the night wore on, I had trouble getting Heidi's comments out of my head. *Stefan actually helped someone unselfishly? There had to be some gain for himself.* Then I grew annoyed at myself for even wasting time thinking about him.

A little after two o'clock in the morning, Frau Franke entered the kitchen and slammed the door upon entry. I had been resting on my arm and had fallen asleep. I jumped to attention immediately. I wobbled a little as I tried to focus.

"You may leave," she demanded. "Everyone has departed. You can tidy the parlor in the morning."

Heidi, who had fallen asleep in a chair, jumped to her feet. I rubbed my eyes and nodded in compliance.

"May we come in a bit later tomorrow?" I hesitated to ask. I almost knew how she would respond.

"No." She walked out.

"Ella, I live quite close." Heidi yawned, "Come stay with me."

I squeezed her hand. "I suppose since the men have retired for the night, World War III must have been averted."

Heidi smiled faintly. "We should be safe for tonight at least."

We walked out arm in arm with no further talk of our impending doom.

Several days later, the *Berliner Zeitung* reported an agreement had been reached between the American President John Kennedy and Nikita Khrushchev at a late hour on the 27th—there would be no war at the present time. The Soviet Union consented to remove all missiles from Cuba, and the Americans would remove the navy blockade. Both countries agreed to take their weaponry out of Turkey as well.

The news was not received well. This action angered many Soviets in East Berlin as it appeared weak to them. Some people chanted in the streets, raised signs near the western part of Kreuzberg at the American portion of the wall, and threw rotten vegetables across, nearly hitting border guards and residents. Others even went as far as to say this could be the end of Nikita Khrushchev's political career.

This reaction was not just found on the streets of Berlin or Moscow; it came dangerously close to home as both Herr and Frau Franke were also in sour moods for weeks.

Personally, I was quite relieved. Despite Cuba being far from here, the one thing I did know from all my reading about past military conflicts, the target was always the weak link.

Berlin was a weak link.

CHAPTER TWENTY-TWO

When Katharina turned sixteen, 17 January, she prepared to attend *Gymnasium* in Nonnenworth, a private school far away from home. I knew about this possibility for months, but as it neared, I felt as though my world would come crashing down again.

Despite the fact I finally broke through to 190 days remaining in service at the Frankes', I was unsure how I would survive the next six months without seeing Katharina's sweet face every day.

Since Lena's absence, Katharina had become the main reason I was able put one foot in front of the other. I'd gotten quite close to her, comfortable enough to even share my darkest secret—my failed escape attempt to see Anton and Josef. I knew it was always a risk saying anything within these walls. It was an even greater danger sharing those same thoughts with someone whose parents thrived on keeping people like me trapped here, but there was something different about Katharina.

"Ella," her voice cracked as she reached for my hands. Only a small lamp shed limited light in our direction. Katharina's parents had retired to their bedroom, and we were alone in the library. "My heart aches for you—for your loneliness and sorrow."

I met her eyes but had less tears. Time has helped me bury the more painful recollections. "I'm all right, Katharina. I know someday I'll see them again. I have to believe that. It's what gets me out of bed every day."

"Let me help you find them, Ella." Her countenance instantly brightened. "I have many friends in the West. They can look for Anton and Josef. I'll write to them immediately."

"Oh, no Katharina." I held onto her hands as she began to stand. "Please, please don't get involved."

"I want to . . . I want to help."

I didn't know how to say that her parents would forbid it, and they would probably go as far as having me detained for even allowing their daughter to feel sorry for me.

"No, Katharina." My voice grew firm. "No, I cannot let you get involved. I have a plan, please don't worry about me." It may have been the tone or the stare, but Katharina reluctantly sat down.

"Then—" she smiled, "—let's read something jovial for our last night together." I smiled. Now that was the Katharina I adored.

As February approached, I learned from Johann that Herr and Frau Franke planned, once again, to host another pre-Lenten Fasching dinner.

Sadly, the city was even worse off this year than last. It was apparent to me they continued to have little regard for the majority of working poor in the city or anyone who was below their class. Like snobby peacocks, they flaunted their worldly gains at every possible opportunity.

"Ella, you are one of the most efficient staff here," Johann pleaded. He was tasked with heading the preparations for the annual event.

"I'm not available that night." No matter how many times he asked me to serve, I repeatedly refused. No amount of marks would ever be worth the risk of possibly seeing the cruel colonel again.

"Lena will be back," he dangled. I swung around and met him in shock.

"Lena?"

"Yes, she starts next week."

"She's recovered?" I wanted so badly to visit her at her home but feared she hated me. I could not bear to face her rejection. Even if by some small miracle she forgave me, she would always be a reminder of what I'd done to her.

"She's doing better and will resume her duties . . . including the Fasching dinner."

"I'm glad she is well." My heart was torn; lifted she was coming back yet worried the sight of me would undo any recovery she achieved away from here.

"No, Johann, don't ask me again. I won't help."

"Fräulein Kühn!" Frau Franke cornered me in the hallway. Johann quickly excused himself.

"I need to speak to you at once!" Her tone sent a small chill through my body.

What could she possibly be upset about? I'd never been late to work and never missed a day, even coming in sick. There hadn't been any complaints about my responsibilities, and I worked harder than most of the staff. This was even pointed out by Johann. Every possible scenario rushed through my mind as I followed her into the study. She pointed so indignantly to the end table that her finger shook uncontrollably.

"My watch is missing!"

"Your watch, Frau Franke?" I thought hard. I had just cleaned in here and didn't see anything.

"My diamond watch was on this table, and now it's gone!" She looked at me hard. I knew nothing about it but still began to sweat. I inhaled and then exhaled as quietly as possible. She eyed my every move.

"I never saw your watch, Frau Franke." I spoke with as much calm in my voice as I could muster, her very presence caused my heart to race. "I was just in here, and it wasn't there." I realized I was putting myself at the scene of the crime, but she already knew this; that's why she accused me.

"It didn't simply disappear." One of her eyebrows rose suspiciously as she stared obviously toward the pockets of my dress.

"I didn't take it," I spoke softly.

"You were the last one here!" Her voice rose well above ladylike and most likely alerted others to her status.

"I am not a thief!" I said carefully but deliberately.

"It is missing!" She clenched her teeth. I could see blood begin to rush to her cheeks.

"She didn't do it." A bold voice declared from the doorway. I was stunned to see it belonged to my adversary.

"What do you mean, Stefan?" his mother demanded, angrily. "What do you know?"

"Nothing, except she is honest in her dealings."

"That means nothing."

"That means everything, Mother. She has worked here for almost a year and a half, doing exactly what you've asked, day after day, with access to many more valuables than a lady's watch. Why would she jeopardize her time here and possible imprisonment over a small piece of jewelry?" Stefan stood in an unfamiliar way. Not that I watched him often, but he now actually appeared as a man.

"A very expensive watch!" Frau Franke reiterated.

"Check the area again, she does not steal." He never made eye contact with me, but I was shocked into silence as I watched him come to my defense. Who would have ever guessed my greatest witness would be the man who loathed my very presence and right now had an opportunity to destroy me . . . but didn't.

Frau Franke glanced from me to her son. She was angry but did not move.

"For heaven's sake, Mother!" Stefan moved toward the table. "As a child I used to lose my toys in here daily, remember? The table tilts slightly to the right from a cracked leg." He got down on his knees and patted the carpets underneath the sofa. He stopped and then rose slowly from his knees. He held the silver band in his palm. My heart leaped with relief and gratitude.

Frau Franke's lips tightened then forced a whisper. "Thank you." She seemed to say this more out of obligation than sincerity then snatched the watch and stomped out of the room. She was ready to send me to the gallows but could not utter a small apology in my direction.

Stefan himself possibly waited for a thank you, but I had difficulty forming any words. He instantly recognized the awkwardness of the moment, excused himself, and disappeared.

I stood there for another few minutes alone, unable to get my brain to tell my muscles to move as if I was paralyzed standing up. I struggled to process what had just happened when Heidi walked by.

"What are you doing, Ella?" she cried, legitimately worried. "Get back to work before the mistress sees you and you get fired." I grinned at the irony and followed her out.

I fell into work quickly but could not stay focused. I had to know why. *Why would Stefan not just let the pieces fall where they may and be done with me?* I found myself walking toward the mortuary.

Through simple staff gossip, I'd heard this was where he spent most of his days. I surveyed the area, never having been this close to the heavy wooden doors that separated the business from the house. I pulled the handles and stepped inside. It was dark and musty. The hall was decorated in an old medieval style, almost like the castle pictures I'd seen with the red velvet fabrics and mahogany woods. It was a stark contrast to the residence.

I was forbidden from being here yet continued forward. The smell of burnt flesh was prevalent. I hadn't been around it much, but it was a smell you never forget. There was only one room where the light seeped under the door. Pulling my sleeve to my nose, I knocked.

"Come in."

I knew Stefan expected someone else, but I entered.

He worked intently at his desk and when he looked up, he appeared surprised at my presence. "Fräulein Kühn?"

I was shocked to hear he knew my name, similar to the time with Heidi, but I didn't hesitate and jumped straight to the point. "I have to know why."

"Why what?" Stefan paused.

"Why you came to my defense back there . . . with your mother."

He pulled his eyes away from his paperwork and stared at me silently for a few seconds. I shifted uncomfortably as I peered around at the office, at anything but him.

"Because—," He waited until I faced him directly again, his eyes burrowing through me "—it was the right thing to do."

The silence was thick. Neither one of us budged on our stare-down. It was as if we both tried to read beyond the surface. He was unrelenting, I could read nothing.

"I'm confused," I whispered. I wrung my hands nervously at my side. I should've left it well alone and departed, but I had always been one who wanted answers.

"Confused about what?" With his reading glasses on and studious appearance, he seemed older—different.

"When did you start to care about the right thing?" It was a fair question but probably came across as more sarcastic than it should have. I shifted once more; his smile emerged. It seemed genuine.

"I deserved that." He chuckled a little then removed his glasses and wiped his face. He looked back at me, still smiling. It was completely unnerving. I didn't even know he knew how to smile without mocking. He continued, "I overheard you tell Johann you are not working the Fasching dinner this year." His blue eyes softened but never strayed. It seemed they were saying more than his lips.

"I have a prior engagement."

"Good," was all he said.

What an odd way to respond. My forehead wrinkled. I started to move toward the door but turned. Once again, staying silent was too difficult for me.

"Did you . . ." I wanted to know. I *needed* to know if he had really planned to show Colonel Anker the painting last year. "At the previous dinner, did you intend . . ." but I couldn't finish the sentence.

Stefan continued to stare at me. He waited for the question to come out, but I cowered. "Did I intend what?" he urged.

"Never mind," I whispered, "You have work to do. I'll leave you alone." Stefan watched me. I reached for the door and turned.

"Thank you," I said humbly. "Thank you for helping me."

The gratitude was for more than solely his mother or Lena; it was for the colonel as well, even if it wasn't warranted. I couldn't even believe I was saying this, given our history, but it was true; he deserved it.

He nodded subtly. "You're welcome."

I finished the week without seeing Stefan or Frau Franke at all. While one seemed less daunting than the other, I feared my emotions with both.

I was still having trouble understanding Stefan's motive. I'd heard from the other help, over time, Stefan had been maturing. He was taking his place in the family business and spent less time with his mischievous friends and more time becoming an adult. This was no small change. He seemed almost like a different person.

I brushed any thoughts of this aside as I stepped in line to receive my weekly pay. My plan tonight was to get to *Fruchs Bäckerei* before it closed.

Often, it took waiting in line a couple of hours to find out they had completely run out of product before your number was called. I had to try—I was going to make Mama G a dumpling stew my father had taught me and needed a loaf of bread for it. She had been ill recently, and I wanted to repay her kindness for letting me rent a room from her.

I grabbed my coat in a rushed attempt to put it on before the brisk wind hit the moment the door was opened. A hand appeared behind me. It held the sleeve of my left side as I readjusted my right. I turned to thank my assistant but stopped short.

It was Stefan.

He rarely appeared in the staff rooms. This caught me completely by surprise. I was instantly nervous and avoided his attentive eyes as best I could. I pulled my scarf tightly around my neck as I slipped my money into my coat pocket. "Thank you," I said, feeling slightly indebted.

"Are you in haste?" he questioned with a kind tone I hardly recognized from his lips.

My mind had to be playing tricks on me. I subtly pinched my arm behind my back for confirmation. *Ouch!* The sting seemed real, but I said nothing.

"May I interest you in a drink?"

"Uh—" Disbelief covered my face. I recovered. "—I don't drink . . . alcohol."

Stefan smiled. "Then coffee or tea?"

Stuttering again, it was as if I had forgotten how to speak, "I . . . I need to get to Fruchs."

"Why Fruchs?" His voice was smooth and natural.

I pulled my mittens on but still avoided his stare. "I need bread." I didn't have to explain, but somehow the words sprang forth. "I'm making dinner . . . for someone."

He paused and seemed to think hard on this answer. "A gentleman?"

My mouth flew open. I was offended by his boldness. "Excuse me, Herr Franke—" I suddenly found my footing.

"Stefan."

"OK, Stefan . . . with all due respect, it's none of your concern." My temper started to flare. His personal inquiries instantly put me on the defense.

"Ella?"

I flinched, astonished my first name slipped off his tongue so easily.

"Yes?" I snapped.

"Ella, please? I mean no offense." He said it again slowly. I was irritated. I glanced around and saw half the employees watching from a distance. Now I would be the topic of discussion all next week.

"I need to go."

"I owe you an apology," he whispered.

"For what?" I finally made eye contact. *I knew why of course, but I wanted to hear him say it out loud.*

"Not here," he pleaded.

"Why not here?" I was unrelenting.

"I need to explain something. At least come and sit with me in the parlor where we can speak privately."

"No, . . . I really have to get going."

I grabbed the handle and whipped the door open. I braced for the blast of winter air, which could bite through any layer of clothing. I stepped to the ground and pulled my scarf over my mouth. I turned around. Stefan was gone.

That didn't take much.

Although I was surprised at the conversation to begin with, I was startled at the twinge of disappointment I suddenly felt with him gone.

I chastised myself severely as I walked quickly toward Fruchs Bäckerei on Treskowstraße. Suddenly, Stefan appeared again right next to me. Nearly out of breath, he must've run to catch up. I rolled my eyes, but inside I was slightly gratified.

"I told you I need to get to the bakery. Why are you here?" A sharpness in my voice surfaced.

He held out a fresh loaf of bread. A swirl of steam floated above it, surely losing its warmth as he exposed it from the towel.

"Here," he said proudly. "I took it from home, now you don't need to go."

"That doesn't belong to me." I pushed it aside, recalling his own mother's threat regarding their food, and turned the corner.

Despite the frigid temperature, the line in front of the bakery snaked nearly half the block. It was payday for most of the neighborhood. My chances of getting pneumonia tonight seemed to outweigh the possibility of getting bread.

Frozen in place, I physically fought the temptation to turn back to Stefan who I was certain still stood where I left him.

The angel on one shoulder tried to convince me if I accepted his offer, I wasn't necessarily accepting his past behavior. It was merely a token of apology, that's all. However, the devil on the other shoulder reminded me of the pain and humiliation he had caused. This was my opportunity to return the feeling. I remained motionless.

Despite the number of people nearby, winter had a way of silencing speech. A strange quiet enveloped me as I continued to contemplate my choice. A small tree branch, heavy with snow, cracked and fell close by causing me to jump. Staring hard, I recognized a connection to that branch. There were many times I questioned my own ability to endure beyond a breaking point.

I nearly forgot about Stefan, but with my heightened senses, the crunch of snow underfoot told me he was approaching cautiously.

"Here, Ella." He held out the bread in front of me. "No obligation, I promise, I only wanted to apologize."

I didn't move. He set the bread on the park bench next to me and started to walk away. I sighed heavily with frustration. I knew if my parents could see how I behaved right now, they would be disappointed, despite Stefan deserving it.

"You know this is quite unfair." My hands reached for the small package.

He hadn't gotten too far away. "Possibly, . . ." he said calmly.

"Fine!" I cracked. "Meet me tomorrow after work, and we can talk."

His mouth curled in a half-grin as he tipped his hat. A few strands of hair fell loosely across his eyes. I did not return the smile and walked in the opposite direction. I attempted to focus on how happy Mama G would be when I got home, but the thought quickly took a backseat to what had occurred moments before.

Did I really agree to see Stefan after work tomorrow? I must be completely out of my mind. There is no way I can go through with this. No matter how much he had changed, there were too many reasons why I shouldn't forget. It started with the Friedrichstraße station almost two years ago. How could I possibly overlook the way he treated me then and the night of Frau Franke's party? Granted he was fairly drunk, but from what I'd seen, it was still the real him.

No, there's no way I can see him, even as I held the fresh loaf in my hands. *Maybe I can pay him for it.* That would be fair, and it would be over. I could simply make it clear his apology was accepted, and we would be cordial to each other from now on. *Yes, that's the plan.*

CHAPTER TWENTY-THREE

It was another night of restlessness. Despite convincing myself it would all work out, I was troubled . . . even angered. Another way the spoiled child—well, now man nearing nineteen, I believed—had his way. All he ever had to do was snap his fingers and it was done. Whatever Stefan wanted, Stefan got. Well, I was not going to fall for his charms that easily . . . *did I really think he was charming?*

Ughhh, it had been a horrible night and now an even more horrible day. I peeked around every corner to make sure we never met. I knew I was acting weird. By their small comments about the scene he had made the night before, everyone else noticed it too. I denied whatever they conjured up. I wanted nothing to do with Stefan.

Finally, at four-thirty p.m., I decided I wasn't ready to face him and rushed out of the house. It was very risky. If Frau Franke somehow found out I left early, she could follow through with her threats, but I justified it.

I couldn't see Stefan.

At home, it was all I could think about. I knew I couldn't avoid him forever. It was better to be honest with him. The Kühns taught me a great deal about integrity, and it was being tested. Now, I had a chance to prove I backed up what I believed.

I decided if Stefan found me at work, I would arrange to see him after, but only long enough to tell him his apology was accepted, and that was it.

"You disappeared last night." Stefan emerged much sooner than expected. I'd only been working for forty-five minutes the following morning when he entered the dining room.

I spun around to face him, but words did not come easily as he stood tall in the doorway. He wore a vivid blue, button-up shirt that made his blue eyes appear brighter than I had ever seen. I quickly turned away.

"Sorry," I mumbled. "I needed to be somewhere." Instantly, I realized

I had undone the very speech I'd sworn to give, the one which spouted honesty. Reluctantly, I faced him again. "No, I'm lying."

Stefan's eyebrows rose with curiosity. He slid into a chair at the table as if this was going to be a long discussion.

"I don't want to see you at all, Stefan. I actually don't even know why you all of a sudden keep showing up, but I simply can't forget the past. The Friedrichstraße station, the names, the painting, your mother's birthday . . ." He nodded subtly with each item on my list.

"I only wanted to apologize, Ella," he spoke evenly, with no emotion. "I can't take back what I said or did. I want you to know I really am sorry."

I watched him carefully. He *was* different. His forehead wrinkled slightly as he waited for me to respond.

"It's done," I whispered. "I accept your apology."

Stefan grinned slightly as he stood to leave. An awkward silence filled the room as he realized we had reached the end of our conversation. He hesitated and then added, "I saw Lena enter the back door fifteen minutes ago. You should go see her." He excused himself.

I quickly put my duster down and followed him out the door only to find Lena right there in the corridor. She gave an odd stare when she saw us both exit the dining room at the same time.

"Lena," Stefan spoke up first, "you look well."

"Thank you . . ." Her gratitude was reserved. "I understand I have you to thank for that." She blushed a little. My brows rose curiously.

"I didn't do much. It was actually Ella here who sought help for you. I only assisted."

"Well, whatever you did, thank you."

"You're welcome." He laid a hand on her shoulder, and again her cheeks brightened a shade darker. "I must get back to work. Good day, ladies."

Lena's forehead crinkled in confusion.

I waited until she met my eyes but kept my distance. I wasn't sure what she thought of me. Lena ignored the hesitation and reached for me, embracing me tightly. I couldn't hide the tears.

"Lena," I stuttered, "I am so . . . so sorry."

"Ella, it wasn't your fault."

"It was! If I hadn't asked"—she put her finger to my mouth to silence me. I'd forgotten once again how careless I could be—"Why would you ever forgive me?" I relived that day often in my mind. My breathing accelerated.

"Stop." Lena insisted. "It wasn't your fault. It was I who . . ." She caught herself. ". . . It's over Ella." It was still the same sweet, beautiful Lena, but her smile did not carry the same weight. Even her eyes did not sparkle like they used to. I found myself glancing down at her arm.

I saw the scar before she pulled her arm behind her. "It's the past."

No matter how much she tried to get me to not feel guilty, I knew it would be there, in front of me, all the time.

Lena's expression instantly changed. "Was that man really Stefan?" She circled around to the direction he had left and pointed down the hall.

"Yeah." My thoughts started to wander. "Yeah, it really was."

Her mouth soundlessly formed the word "truly?"

"My sentiments exactly," I snickered.

"But—" she contemplated "—but didn't the two of you just come out of the dining room together?"

"No, . . . no, I mean yes, . . . we came out the same time, but it's nothing, Lena. He apologized, that's all."

"How is this nothing, Ella?" The old Lena appeared, briefly. "The biggest *Arsch* who ever lived said he was sorry, and you say it's nothing?" Lena snickered. "That's front-page news."

I nodded my head. Yes, I guess she was right. My desire to hold onto my anger somehow challenged any reason. It was the only thing about my life I could control.

Johann appeared and picked Lena up and swung her around. "We have missed you!" he said truthfully. The temporary help came nowhere close to her abilities, and it was obvious the house suffered in her absence.

"This calls for a celebration!" Johann cried, "Tonight!"

"Oh no," Lena declined, "too soon."

He nodded understandingly but insisted on another night. I laughed. It actually seemed like our little work family was whole again.

"And maybe you can convince miss 'I'm too good for the job' over there to work the Fasching dinner . . ." Johann would not let it go!

However, Lena remembered how upset I was the previous year.

"No, I actually don't want her there," she chuckled. "She messes everything up."

I smiled. It was good to have her back!

CHAPTER TWENTY-FOUR

A week later, Lena met me in the staff room as soon as I walked in. "Ella, I saw an old acquaintance last night." She had a wide, sneaky smile. "Remember Rainer?"

I didn't flinch. Of course, I remembered him, but I kept quiet.

"He asked about you too," she slipped in slyly.

I grinned, but it was a fake one. The only reason I even knew this man was because Lena and Christoph convinced me to go to the café one
night. Bringing up anything that had to do with Christoph made me uncomfortable. She read through me.

"It's OK, Ella," Lena whispered.

"Did Christoph . . ." I couldn't even finish the sentence. I had not heard his fate.

"We haven't heard anything."

"Nothing? You don't even know where he is?"

"No." Lena's voice was strained. I'm sure she had done everything to find him.

I turned away, my eyes filling with tears. "It's my fault, Lena."

"No, Ella. Don't. It—," she stopped herself and placed a hand on my shoulder. "—Please don't."

I should've been the one who consoled her, not the other way around.

"I'm sorry. I shouldn't even mention his name."

"No, Ella . . ." Lena insisted, "I like talking about Christoph. His memory brings me peace."

I smiled . . .genuinely this time.

"But . . ." she grinned. ". . . Rainer?" I groaned. "Rainer asked if you would meet him at a café this weekend."

"Oh no, I don't think so." I shook my head nervously from side to side.

"Come on. Have you even gone out since that night?"

I already knew the answer but pretended to think it through. Lena laughed. She knew me too well.

"Ha, don't fib. I already know your response." She grabbed my hand and patted it tenderly. "You are going, even if I have to drag you there myself."

"Well, in that case, Lena, I would love to go with *you*," I chuckled.

When Friday night rolled around, I was sure I'd made a mistake. Going out with Lena is one thing but having a man there too? Especially one who seemed interested in me even though that interest was not reciprocated. It would be a waste of time I thought, but I agreed . . . *for Lena.*

As we entered the warmth of a place called Dafne's, not too far from work, I removed my coat and left it on a hook by the front door. Lena and Rainer did the same. I circled around. A pair of baby blue eyes instantly met my gaze as I unraveled the scarf over my hair. My shoulders dropped.

Stefan . . . here with a friend, a female friend. I tried not to stare, but he seemed quite happy to have seen us, immediately waving us over to his table. I wanted to pretend I didn't know him, but Lena responded happily.

"Come join us." Stefan pointed to the extra chairs that surrounded his unusually large table for an intimate dinner.

"Oh no, we don't want to bother you," I spoke quickly.

"No, it's no bother." He motioned for us to sit down.

Rainer seemed to love the idea. Lena appeared intrigued. I wanted to crawl under the table and hide.

"This is Marion, an old classmate of mine," Stefan introduced his date. "These are my friends, Ella and Lena and . . ."

"This is Rainer," I mumbled. They all shook hands as I scouted the exits.

As the night wore on, Rainer and Stefan hit it off. I barely spoke to anyone, and Lena was her usual enchanting self.

I stood to leave precisely at nine o'clock.

"I'm going to say goodnight." I had literally counted the minutes until my exit would seem appropriate. Stefan stood as I did and extended his hand.

"Let me see you home," he suggested.

I shook my head. "No!"

It was suddenly awkward. Rainer eyed us both, then stood as well. "*I* should walk you home, Ella."

I scrutinized him and answered the same way. "No," I snapped and then backpedaled, "I mean no, thank you." I realized I was a horrible date.

Lena sat back and watched. Her grin was evidence of how ridiculous this must have appeared.

I smiled uncomfortably and turned to Rainer, "Thank you for tonight." He nodded.

I wanted to hug Lena goodnight, but instead, I searched for a way to get out of there quickly and rushed for my coat. Bursting out the front door, the agonizing cold hit me fiercely and caught my breath, but it didn't stop me.

Once again, Stefan appeared behind me as I struggled to secure my coat in the chill, something that had become a bad habit as of late. He grabbed the loose sleeve.

I shook my head and confronted him, "What are you doing, Stefan?"

"I'm trying to be a gentleman."

"A gentleman doesn't leave his date to help another woman."

"Marion is not my date. We're friends out for coffee, and didn't you just leave your date?" He smiled.

I groaned. I was tired. "Just friends, Stefan, no date. Goodnight."

He grabbed my arm and brought me to a solid stop. "Ella, I only want to be your friend."

Agitated, I pulled my arm away. It was rude, I knew this even as I rushed farther down the sidewalk. It was irritating that this man had such an effect on me. Somehow—being around him—carefully concealed emotions seemed to rise to the surface. Anger, sorrow, grief, revenge, all present and accounted for.

Instantly, my thoughts surprisingly turned to Lena. She too had suffered a great loss that came at the hands of someone else's choices. *My* choice changed her life, and she had every reason to hate me, but didn't.

I stopped walking and turned around. Stefan hadn't moved. This man, who for so long had reduced me to nothing, stood there facing me with a perplexing countenance. He appeared discouraged. *I* was being the jerk this time. It wasn't who I was, and it bothered me enough to force a surrender.

"OK, . . ." I relented, "friends." I closed the distance and reached out to shake his hand, the same way a businessman would seal a contract. He smiled. I said good night and walked briskly to the bus stop.

When I got home, a strange feeling materialized. It had been such an emotionally exhausting night. I was completely spent from the conflict I'd fought with myself. Stefan simply happened to be there, but it was myself I battled.

The apartment was dark. Mama G had already retired even though it was only half-past nine. Her bad health seemed to take a toll on her. This caused great concern since I'd seen this happen too many times in my short life. By instinct, I went to her room and checked on her. She wasn't anything like Mama and Papa. She had a loud snore. Once I opened her door, it reassured me to hear the snorts come at a steady pace and brought a smile to my face. She appeared well. As I approached my room, a paper tucked into the crease of my door attracted my attention. I retrieved it as I turned the handle then quickly flipped my lamp on and carried it to the bed. It was in Mama G's handwriting.

A man by the name of Lenin Brauner stopped by this evening.
He said you have been looking for him.

My heart raced. *Why wasn't I here?* The only night I go out in months, and I missed Herr Brauner, the very man who saw and spoke to my Anton last!

His home address is Strabenstrauβe 12. Lichtenberg.
Mama

I nearly shouted my joy. Finally, after all those months of tracking neighborhood after neighborhood, shop after shop, leaving so many notes and messages, he finally found me!

I sat on the side of my bed and cried my first tears of happiness since the boys left. It felt oddly similar to the very day I left the orphanage—unsure of whether I would see Anton again and then all of a sudden, there he was.

***

The woman who would be my new *Mutter* took my hand gently. It was the softest hand I'd ever felt. She smiled as if she meant it, and it didn't seem like she was hiding anything. The man, Herr Kühn, walked with a funny limp and used a black cane for assistance. When he opened the automobile door, he smiled as he waited for me to enter.

I'd never been in a car before, but at eleven years of age, I realized I'd never done a lot of things. There on the back seat—sitting straight up—was a doll, a real glass doll with brown hair and a dress and both arms and both legs. I was afraid to touch it, afraid they would tease me and say I really couldn't play with it, but as the man opened the door for his wife, he motioned to the doll from up in front.

"It's yours, Adela." He smiled widely. "She belongs to you." He pointed to her and encouraged me to pick her up.

Next to the doll was a small boy. He appeared to be no older than six or seven. His wide brown eyes stared at me.

"Adela," —Frau Kühn shifted around in her seat— ,"this is your new brother, Josef."

Neither one of us moved.

"Ella," I whispered. "My name is Ella."

"OK, sweetheart." She smiled. "Are you ready to go home?"

I wanted to cry. I was afraid this was all going to suddenly disappear. In one day, I received a mother, a father, a brother, and a doll.

I sat back against the seat. The smell of plastic permeated the car. Everything in it was blue and felt warm to the touch. As the Kühns settled in the front seat, the vehicle made a loud noise. My legs shook as a weird vibration rumbled beneath me. I gripped the edge of the seat, afraid to let go. Frau Kühn turned back to me and laughed. "It's OK. It's safe, it's an automobile." I had often seen them from the upstairs window, but never this close and never inside.

"Look," Frau Kühn continued, "there on the door is a round knob. If you turn it, the window will roll down."

She pointed to a small button with a handle. I reached out and moved it then gasped out loud as the glass dropped simultaneously to my turn. I let go, anxious, but I could feel a taste of the warm wind slip through the crack I'd created and wanted more. Two more turns until it was halfway down, and I touched the edge of the glass. It wasn't sharp. I stuck my hand out and felt the air slip through my fingers as we started to pull away from the curb.

Then I saw him.

He wore a shirt I'd never seen and a pair of trousers too big for him, but Anton was there. He ran on the sidewalk and kept a steady pace with the car.

My eyes lit up. I waved but was careful not to say his name. Without knowing what kind of people, the Kühns were, I feared they would lose him on purpose.

One . . . two . . . three . . . the streets passed, and I continued to count *. . . seven . . . eight . . .* but I didn't know any more numbers. Despite the new sights and sounds as we traveled, my eyes were glued to Anton who never lost pace.

We came to a stop in front of a tall building where there were two windows on each side of the main doors. *One, two, three, four, five stories high.* My eyes were like saucers, my mouth gaped wide. It was the best building I had ever seen.

When Herr Kühn opened my door once again and said, "Welcome home, Ella," he held out his hand for me, but I did *not* reach for it. I had never been around adult men. He and his cane scared me. Frau Kühn then met me on the sidewalk.

"You forgot your doll," she whispered as she reached back into the car and pulled the figure out and cradled it gently in her arms. I didn't move.

"This is where we live." Herr Kühn pointed to the window in front of me on the left side. Relief filled my soul. Despite my delight from the building's magnitude, remaining close to the ground provided a much-needed security.

As we moved toward the large doors that were the front entrance, I hesitated and then spun around. Across the street, part of Anton's body peeked around a streetlamp. I smiled, thrilled with the idea he knew where I lived. Anton would not be gone forever as I'd previously thought. Maybe, in just a short time, we could be on our own together.

As I neared the door, I suddenly felt guilty about turning away from Anton. I glanced forward then behind. I couldn't move.

"Let's go in, Ella . . ." Frau Kühn smiled down at me, ". . . as a family."

Conflict seized my heart. I had to walk into my new home with my new family and leave Anton alone outside. I never wanted to feel that way again.

CHAPTER TWENTY-FIVE

I didn't wait long. Immediately after work the next night, I went straight to the bus stop. I rode the coach to Herr Brauner's neighborhood in Lichtenberg. It was an area closer to Treptow than Pankow but, once again, an unfamiliar one.

I knocked on his door a little too anxiously. He was slow to respond.

With growing fears of who would show up at your door next and whether they were there to take you away, I understood his reluctance. I saw his peephole grow dark and knew he was home. He finally cracked the door.

"Herr Brauner? I'm Ella!" It all came out at once.

The crack disappeared and the jangle of the chain was reassuring. As the door opened wide, he eagerly motioned me inside, a warm smile spread across his face. His wife was in the kitchen making dinner. It smelled like sauerkraut.

"Well, little lady," Herr Brauner was a tall, thin man with a small curly mustache and thick-rimmed eyeglasses, "you are a difficult person to find!"

I smiled and sat down; the anticipation of this moment peaked as I scooted to the edge of the couch.

"Please, tell me everything!" I gushed.

Herr Brauner invited me to join him and Frau Brauner for dinner. I didn't see any children in the home but felt it would be rude to ask. He spent the next two hours describing his visit to the West and how he met Anton.

I hung onto every word.

Often, my tears sprang through spontaneously. My heart swelled with the knowledge of their good fortune and security.

The construction company Anton worked for was assigned to lay brick in a building where Herr Brauner oversaw improvements. It wasn't until the job was nearly done that Herr Brauner was approached by Anton, so they didn't have a great deal of time to talk.

Herr Brauner assured Anton he would do all he could to assist him in his search for me when he returned. The short conversation they had made it sound like Anton was doing well. He also told Herr Brauner Josef was going to school. I couldn't believe my ears. Josef was being educated in a public school! He was smart and was getting good marks as well.

"Do you have an address?" I asked. The eagerness in my voice was dampened quickly.

"No, Fräulein Kühn." He wiped his nose with a handkerchief from his front pocket. "Our visit was too short, I apologize. I do know they lived in a migrant camp for the first two months after their arrival."

"A migrant camp?" I pondered. "I hope it was decent."

"Oh, they're decent. In fact, what they consider to be squalid living conditions in the West would be quite comfortable here."

I smiled. It brought me a great deal of reassurance knowing they were safe.

"Will you be going to the West anytime soon?"

"Yes, I leave next Monday."

I lit up at this news. "Herr Brauner, may I please give you a letter for Anton and Josef, if you happen to cross paths?"

"Yes." He wiped his nose again and then handed me a pencil and paper.

"You know, Ella, it's been well over a year since I met Anton. It's possible he isn't employed with the same company." He pulled his glasses off his face and rubbed his eyes. They appeared tired and worn, and he seemed a bit unwell. I knew it was time for me to leave.

"Yes sir, I understand." I didn't want to dwell on any doubtful possibilities. We had come too far.

"But I will try my best to locate him."

"Anything you can do to help is appreciated. They are my only family."

"I'm sorry you are not all together, dear." Frau Brauner's sentiments were very kind.

"Do you get to travel to the West with your husband, Frau Brauner?" They kept their mutual glance subtle, but I saw the expression in her eyes. She was probably forced to remain in the East as a "hostage" of sorts, forcing Herr Brauner to return. I wondered if his work was sanctioned by the DDR. This could be the only logical reason he was allowed to travel quite freely, but alone.

"Ella," Herr Brauner spoke as he stood up to help Frau Brauner clean the table. "Please be careful what you say in your letter. The work I engage in is quite . . ." he stared at his wife again, ". . .delicate. I can be searched at any time."

I stopped myself from guessing. I didn't want to know the details; I only wanted to find Anton and Josef.

I skimmed over the simple words I'd written. How do you sum up all that happened in eighteen months in a few short sentences? How do you describe the pain, anguish, and fear? All the emotion experienced from one decision made in one night?

I'd often thought about my choice to stay with my papa, and despite what I know now, I still could not have chosen differently.

Anton and Josef,
8, Feb 1963

I hope you get this letter. I've missed you more than you can imagine!
I had to leave our home and now live with a woman by the name
of mama G. My address is Rotherstraße 34 Treptow, 1012 Berlin,
Germany. Please write to me!
I love you both with all my heart, Ella.

I folded it and handed it to Herr Brauner, hugging him, very grateful for all his help. He and his wife seemed more than understanding.

As I stepped out, away from their apartment, a small amount of anguish lifted off my shoulders. Finally, a possibility, a small sliver of hope with a long-awaited chance I could be reconnected with my family—even if it was only by post—was something.

CHAPTER TWENTY-SIX

I needed to find a way to keep my mind off the letter, Herr Braun-er, Anton, and Josef. I knew that even if Herr Brauner saw them and they wrote back to me, the correspondence could take weeks, possibly months. East Berlin was not only effective at keeping people in but very good at keeping the world out.

The night of the Fasching dinner came in early March this year. I tried hard to get out of the house before the guests arrived, but time and time again, my friends needed help. I still refused to serve but felt an obliga-tion to make sure the preparation for the event was a success. However, late in the evening, I became trapped—unable to slip outside without being seen, as nearly all exits on the lower level were blocked by people.

I decided that trying to reach the staff exit from the back rooms would be my best attempt. Stepping out of the kitchen, my body froze stiff and my knees began to shake. The voice that reverberated through the hallway fired a sharp chill through me. The vision of his ugly, scarred face jeered on the backside of my eyelids as I squeezed them shut. The voice moved.

Is it traveling toward me or away?

My legs failed to budge. Colonel Anker's laugh paralyzed me even now.

With a mixture of fear and willpower, I mustered the strength and quickly shot up the nearby stairs, maneuvering down the dark hall on the second floor until I could no longer hear his voice. With my back pressed against the wall, eager to clear my head and catch my breath, I rested and remembered the art room nearby. It would be a suitable place to hide as it was rarely used and far from the celebration.

I turned on the light. Although I hadn't been in here since the night I drew the butterfly gift, I thought of this room often since then. Not only because of my burning desire to draw, but also my hope to return in search of the record.

It had been impossible up to this point for me to come here without question; my movements were monitored regularly since Frau Franke's unfounded accusation—if not by her personally, it appeared she employed others in the cause. I was rarely alone.

Gazing around, not much had changed . . . except . . . an easel, centered in the room with a large canvas against it. I approached it from the back and was surprised to find a painting resting on the front. The image was serene.

My finger curiously brushed the front. I pulled away surprised—it was still fairly wet. *Had Stefan started painting again?* There was no indication it was him except it was exceptional. I doubted anyone else in the family turned to such a hobby.

I moved to the window. The lights on the street were dim, though I was sure the lights in the Frankes' "castle" lit up this half of the city alone. From this view, the crest of the Brandenburg Tor lit up from a distance.

The large, arched structure stood boldly with its imposing sculpture—The Goddess of Victory steering four horses by chariot on top. It was a commanding statement, slightly damaged from the war, but not destroyed. It remained a bold reminder of our division because just past those pillars stood a free land. A place where you could be educated, work where you want, eat what you want, and whisper or shout as well—if you want—all without a price to pay for your choice.

I longed for that place. I couldn't see the tanks, the guns, or the guards from my position, but I knew they were there, and I ached to be on the other side. Suddenly, I saw movement in the reflection of the window. A man's silhouette in the doorway startled me.

Although my breath was controlled, my chest stirred. Relief washed over me once I realized it wasn't the colonel who had followed me up. Despite the mask covering his face, I recognized the black suit and bowtie Stefan wore from last year. It was striking. I stared with unforeseen admiration.

"I'm so sorry." His apology sounded sincere. "I didn't know anyone was up here." He paused. "I thought you had other plans tonight." Stefan removed his mask.

"Unfortunately, I got held up here." I turned away, embarrassed. "I'm sorry I trespassed." I stepped around him and toward the door. I didn't know where else to go.

"You don't have to leave," he said quietly.

I stopped and faced him.

"Don't you have a party you need to get back to?" I reasoned.

"Now, we both know what kind of guests are down there." He smirked. "Do you really think I'm missing out?"

My thoughts went immediately to the reason I fled upstairs in the first place. I nodded my head and smiled.

"See, there it is," Stefan joked. "There is a smile in there, somewhere."

I walked to the painting in the center of the room, eager to take the focus off me. "Is this yours?"

Stefan joined me. "It is."

"When did you start painting again?"

"When I realized my life was full of tedious, monotonous work, and I needed vision and color again."

I suddenly realized that was my problem too. I was always happiest when I drew. The times I could indulge in my pastime were too few and far between.

I pointed to the picture. "A river?"

"Well, it was until somebody smudged it." Stefan reached for my hand. He pointed out the blue paint on my pointy finger.

I smiled again and pulled it away.

"It was an accident."

"You just couldn't keep your hands off it, could you?" he teased.

I watched Stefan closely. His eyes were fully blue, with no hint of red this time. His walk was smooth, not inebriated, and his voice was kind, not full of malice. I liked this Stefan much better.

"It's a village in Saxony along the Elbe River. Have you ever been there?"

"I've actually never been outside of Berlin," I whispered.

He didn't conceal his surprise. "There's a big world out there, Ella, so much to see."

"Yes," I agreed, "but when you're held captive in a place with a restricting wall, it makes it hard to see anything, right?"

He nodded solemnly in agreement, although I knew he could not relate. Even with the wall, the Frankes had the connections to go any-where they wanted.

"Can you hold on a moment?" He didn't wait for my answer. "I'll re-turn shortly." Stefan excused himself.

Minutes later, he arrived with a small tray of delicacies, and two gob-lets of sparkling water balanced in his left hand. He set everything down on the nearby counter and reached for an unused paint cloth in the cor-ner. Without saying anything, he spread the cloth on the hardwood floor and laid the treats in the center.

I stared at his display. My face started to twist with worry.

"Ella, don't." He seemed to know I was trying to think my way out of this. "It's just food, come join me." He removed his outer black coat, loosened his bow tie, and sat down on one half of the linen.

I shifted nervously. He patted the other half with his hand.

"Do me a favor and don't make me go back to that awful dinner." He laughed.

I struggled to come up with an excuse.

"Besides," he sighed, "you aren't there for me to rescue this year."

My mouth flew open. *I knew it!* He did do it on purpose! "Janus." The name slipped out before I could stop it.

"Janus?" he repeated.

I nodded, still trying to let his confession sink in. "Your mythological sculpture—he saved the Sabine women—"

"Oh, that's right . . ." he chuckled to himself. "Yes, Janus. God of choice."

My mind was spinning as I continued, "—with the ability to see the past and future." Who would have ever guessed the reality of that image a year ago? The two faces, like two different people.

"Yes, my grandfather always did see something more in me than I ever did myself," he said with unrestrained admiration.

"But why?" I questioned.

"Why what?" Stefan patted the blanket once more.

"Why me?"

"Why did I coerce the octopus from you?" Stefan did not hide his shock at my query. "Why would I let a woman be handled for sport against her will?" he asked back.

"That man is . . ." I stumbled on my words.

"He's a deplorable human being. You aren't the only one he's tried to . . ."

My face shot up as I hoped he would elaborate. Stefan seemed to sense it.

"He's offensive to many. He's one associate of my father's I'll be relieved to terminate my affiliation with when I take over the family business.

"Why *me* though, Stefan, you hated me. Why did you help me?"

"I didn't hate you . . ." He glanced down. He lied. I stood in front of him with hands on my hips and waited for him to look up.

"OK, I disliked you, but that was a different time. Sit down, let me explain." He had definitely piqued my curiosity about where this conversation was going. I finally joined him on the other side of the blanket.

"I owe you my thanks first." I held my hand out to him. It seemed insignificant compared to what he had done for me the night of the dinner.

"You're welcome." He shook it.

I reached for a small plate and started to place some random desserts on it as I spoke. "I noticed you were different that night, Stefan. Something had changed in the two months from your mother's party and last year's Fasching dinner."

"Yes, the party . . . Ha." He laughed uncomfortably. "I think I owe you an apology for that night—"

"One of many," I cut in.

"Yes, I know." His head hung low. "I was drunk."

"You weren't drunk in the library when you accused me of being with the resistance in front of Katharina."

"No, . . . I can't say I was then—"

"What about Friedrichstraße, were you drinking then?"

"Yes, but not drunk . . . OK, Ella, I surrender. I really am sorry for all those situations. I was young and stupid—"

"Stefan!" I snapped at him unintentionally. I was irritated he blamed his behavior on weak reasons. His face met mine. "These all just happened in the last two years! You were not that young—seventeen, eighteen—old enough to know better." I caught myself and calmed down. "What really happened in the two months after the party? Something happened, I know it."

His eyes closed, and instantly I regretted attacking him like that. The room suddenly grew very quiet.

I waited as he gathered his thoughts. "I'm sorry, Stefan. It's personal, and I shouldn't have pushed." He didn't answer. "I should leave."

I began to stand up, but Stefan's hand reached for my arm. A few strands of his long bangs had fallen freely across his face, but his deep blue eyes, now wide open, pierced through them with a profound stare. Something in that moment compelled me to sit down again. His touch remained gentle but intensified as if he spoke without words. At that very moment, I realized he *needed* me. What a crazy world I lived in . . . *Stefan Franke needs me.*

"Do you remember the day in the library when my friend Ralf and I were talking?

I nodded. We both knew I overheard his plans.

"What you may not know is we got caught at the Czech border with our forged documents two days after Christmas" —he definitely had my attention now— "and were put in jail."

I tried to picture him there. I knew nothing about jail other than what I read in books, but it didn't seem pleasant.

"I thought your family . . . because of your . . ." I didn't want to sound like I knew his family secrets. ". . . I thought because of your family connections you could cross any border without a problem. Why did you have to forge documents?"

He exhaled slowly. "Ralf and I were assigned to attend a communist youth leadership camp in Poland. Our documents didn't allow us to go anywhere else at the time. We used forged copies."

"I see." I chewed on my bottom lip and waited for him to continue.

"My father used his high connections to get me home, but it came at a steep price." This part didn't surprise me. You could not ask a favor here without owing in return.

"My father owns only half of the mortuary now; the DDR owns the other half. I, myself, was given two options upon my return to Berlin. Enlist or learn my father's trade and become a full partner within five years."

I groaned. "That's not a choice! Weren't you going to take over your father's business already? It has been handed down to the sons four times."

"No, Ella. Actually, I wasn't. I had no plans of working around dead people at all and . . ."

"And what?"

"I saw how my father had become someone else through the years. He became a puppet, dancing to the demands of every powerful man in Germany. I didn't want anyone to own me." Stefan showed a side of himself that surprised me. "Ironically now, they not only own me but half of the business, as well."

"But Herr Franke is not that old. Why replace him so soon?"

"He's not necessarily replaced . . . the DDR recognizes the wisdom in a long-term investment such as the son of their lead mortician." Stefan whispered the next sentence, "Many more years to hide bodies."

I cringed. "Why didn't you enlist then?"

"My father saved me from jail, Ella. He risked everything for me. I couldn't turn my back on him then."

"Your father saved you from a couple of nights in jail, and you felt like you owed him your entire life . . . your freedom?" It was hard for me to wrap my head around this. I wasn't trying to sound unsympathetic, but it's possible it came out that way.

"Ella, it wasn't a couple of nights . . ." Stefan sounded frustrated, "it was eighteen nights in a Czechoslovakian jail, but they had already sentenced me to five years. My father gave everything for my release. Yes, I owe him that much."

"I'm sorry, Stefan, I didn't mean to—" I touched his hand. "I shouldn't have been so quick to judge, I'm sorry!"

He turned my hand over and traced his finger along each of mine. I watched him do it. It was gentle and comforting, and I had no desire to pull away.

"What happened to Ralf?"

Stefan shook his head. I could've sworn I saw his eyes get moist, but he glanced away.

I knew the answer. Ralf wasn't freed.

I could hear the laughter from the party below. The sound continued to amplify in the quietness of the art room. This was an indication the liquor had finally kicked in. I was glad I wasn't there. I watched Stefan, who still held my hand. I could see the lines of remorse weigh heavily on his face.

"The day I painted the butterfly for your mother, I came across a charming painting." I stood and retrieved it from the far wall. When I sat back down, I faced it in his direction. "This is the most beautiful place I've ever seen, is it real?"

Stefan had been reclining and raised to take a full look. He smiled. "Yes, I haven't seen this for years, ha." I was quite relieved when he laughed. The dark mood had shifted.

"It's a place called Cochem, located in the Moselle River Valley. Years ago, my family would travel to the wine country on holiday. It was a peaceful little village surrounded by vineyards and that castle." His face lit up with the memory. "Some of the stone remains are 900 years old."

I smiled with my own recollection. "There was a world book in the Waisenhaus that showed pictures of jungles and mountains and places I never dreamed were actually real. It's where I saw the picture of a butterfly for the first time."

Stefan stared. His eyes reflected pain.

"What?" I became uncomfortable.

"You were in the Waisenhaus?"

Then I realized what I had let slip. "It was a long time ago." I rose to put the painting back but faced it toward him again, "You are a very talented artist, Stefan."

"You, as well," he added, "I was jealous when Katharina had chosen you to paint mother's picture. The butterfly was exquisite."

"Nothing like this . . ." I took one more glance before I set it down. "I love this painting, Stefan. It makes me feel like there is beauty outside of all this darkness." I sighed. "Just looking at it gives me hope."

"Then it's yours, Ella."

"No," I protested, afraid I may have come across as coveting it. "I can't take this; you could sell it. It's really good."

"I don't sell my paintings. I really want you to have it. It just sits up here hidden and doing no good. Yet it brings you happiness, and that's a good thing."

"Why is that a good thing?" I laughed as I sat back down.

"Because I get the feeling you haven't had many good things happen in your life."

Stefan held my stare for a moment longer, then stood and moved to the back of the room. I brushed some stray crumbs off the linen, attempting to hide my smile. The night was turning out much different-ly than I ever expected. Although there was more to come, nothing fully registered in my mind until the snap of a record clicked onto a turntable. I sat completely still.

The notes were faint at first. When Stefan returned, I found myself straining to hear the woman's voice whir softly from the speaker.

Dans un amour. . .

I flew from the floor just as Stefan sat down. My hands shook when I pulled the small record off the phonograph. The words that illuminated across the bright red center spelled out *Un Refrain Courait Dans La Rue*. Edith Piaf, Side B.

Tears were already forming as I flipped it over. Stefan was instantly at my side. My fingers traced the small grooves in the black vinyl until they reached the title "La Vie en Rose", in bold, white lettering.

Overcome, I could not believe I was holding this record. I had dreamt of this moment for so long. Little did I know it really was right here all along.

Stefan placed his hands over mine and smoothly retrieved the record. I didn't move. He deliberately placed it down on Side A and then replaced the needle. The instrumental beginning of "La Vie en Rose" caused chills to form all over my body. The trumpet thumped simultaneously with my heartbeat.

Stefan didn't even ask. One hand slid across my lower back while the other reached for my fingers. He pulled my body next to his as we swayed gently to the song. It felt as though I watched our movements from above. He made dancing seem more effortless than it ever had been.

I closed my eyes to the elongated curling notes that only Piaf could perfect. Tears still slipped through, but I didn't bother letting go to wipe them away. It was as if we were dancing in a different time.

Each time Papa played this song, I grieved the anticipation of the end, and today, like then, I wished for it to play forever.

Stefan repeated the song three times without my even asking. Some-how, he knew that at this very moment I needed it. Finding this *one* song here tonight—with this person—made it seem more like fate than chance. And that very conclusion terrified me.

It was nearly midnight. I hadn't said more than two words since the song ended and our dancing stopped. It was a feeling I didn't want to lose, and Stefan seemed to know this. He never pushed. I helped him carry the dishes to the kitchen and then motioned to leave.

"Ella, may I please offer you a ride home?"

I hesitated, ". . . It's late. You don't have to do that."

"It wouldn't be proper for me to let you leave the house alone at this hour."

"I've taken care of myself so far, Stefan," I said playfully. I pulled my scarf up over my mouth. "Plus . . . I live in Treptow." I eyed his response. I wasn't even sure he'd ever been to that part of the city.

"I know you can take care of yourself, Ella. I've seen you withstand many pressures . . ." he leaned in and whispered with a laugh, ". . . including my mother." Then he continued, "I guess I'm just not ready for the night to end." The way he looked at me caused me to forget why I ever questioned him in the first place. It was as if I was the only person in his world.

I turned my head to conceal my smiling eyes and led the way. Stefan alerted Max, the driver, as we walked to the free-standing garage in the back. I hadn't been in an automobile since Papa sold ours and never one as nice as this. The drive was quiet. The city was dark and mostly asleep. When we reached my street, Max cautiously pulled over to the curb. He peered around nervously as though he hadn't spent much time in this neighborhood. Stefan held the picture as we walked quickly in an effort to reach my apartment building faster than the cold could slip under our coats.

We stepped into the hallway with a sigh of relief as the warmth of the radiator nearby took some of the bite out of the frost. Stefan wanted to walk me up the three flights of stairs, but I refused. It was here where we would say goodnight.

"Ella, can I ask you a question?"

I nodded, curious.

"Why didn't you tell anyone about the ski plans you overheard in the parlor?"

"Why would I?" I was surprised he even asked.

"I don't know. I guess when I realized you had been in the room the whole time we were talking, I expected our plan to somehow come crashing down. Nobody keeps secrets."

"I do—" I shrugged my shoulders. "—But it really wasn't my secret to tell. Only now, after hearing what you went through, maybe I should have."

"Actually . . ." Stefan paused, "I've thought about this a lot." His face grew very solemn. "I can't change the fact that I ruined Ralf's life. It's something I'll have to live with forever, but in a way, it saved my own."

"What do you mean?" I probed.

"It's hard to explain." His eyes were on me, but his thoughts were elsewhere. "I guess I found myself. Somewhere between imprisonment and my duty of death, I found the person I needed to become, not that I'm there yet—" his eyes finally connected with mine, "—but I'm getting there, and if I hadn't gone on the trip, I possibly would have never changed."

I stared at him with unusual respect.

The moment seemed perfect. Our walls finally lifted, our perspective altered, but I knew in my heart I wasn't ready for what naturally wanted to come next.

I extended my hand. It was awkward. Stefan chuckled and met my hand to shake.

"This evening was . . ." I paused, choosing my words carefully. It was difficult to pinpoint exactly what I felt. ". . . It was really special. Thank you."

"For me too." Stefan's fixated eyes took on a completely different look. It could have been the low lighting in the hall, or maybe I just saw something I didn't see before.

"And thank you for the painting," I laughed as he passed it to me. "Goodnight, Stefan."

"Goodnight, Ella."

As I entered the door to my apartment, Mama G was in her recliner reading.

"What are you still doing up, Mama?" I questioned, concerned it was my fault.

She put her book down. "I couldn't sleep."

I went to her side and pulled the blanket up closer to her chest. "Are you well?"

"Just a small ailment, I suppose. I'll be fine." She smiled slyly at me.

"What?" I grinned at her reaction.

"You look different."

"Different?" I was suddenly self-conscious. How could she know? We didn't even kiss!

"Yes, your face looks completely relaxed. I'm not sure I've ever seen you without that wrinkle above your nose." She was still grinning. Now I was *very* self-conscious.

"Wait a minute," she laughed. "It's back." She was still chuckling when she picked up her book again. "Whatever it was that made it disappear must've been pretty great."

I grinned and headed toward my room.

"Oh. Wait, Ella!" I turned in her direction. "This came in the post for you."

She held up a tan envelope, and I rushed to grab it. I'd never received a letter before. Could it really be from . . . *Yes!* In the left corner were the names Anton and Josef and their address! *An actual address!* I kissed Mama G on the forehead and ran to my room. The seal was broken, but I half expected that. Not from Mama but from whoever delivered it. I glanced at the date it had been written, nearly four weeks ago.

14 Feb, 1963
Dear Ella,

We were so happy to hear you are alive! When all of my letters were returned, we thought the worst. The stories coming out of East Berlin are horrible reminders of the life we left, and I will never forgive myself for leaving you there. Once here we were sent to Marienfelde, a factory that was set up to be a shelter to help people who escaped from the East. We were amongst thousands of people who fled but many found the camp upsetting. I, on the other hand, had never had much to begin with, so it was a good change.

They also helped us find a job. The Allies offer many opportunities here. It's very different. Josef is healthy and in school. He is smart and getting good marks. He has taken over my learning where you left off. As you can see from this letter, he is doing well with me.

I have work as a bricklayer again. I met Herr Brauner the first time when he came to inspect one of his buildings. This time he searched for me. He is a very nice man and I'm thankful for his help.

I'm saving my money, Ella. I will get it to you to find the right people who can get you here. There are many agencies over here that work to free the people of East Berlin and I've heard many stories. We can do it. I know we can. I feel good about this.

Josef misses you . . . I miss you. We have never been apart this long. It's not the same without you here. I've included some of the news clippings of stories where people succeeded in escaping. Maybe it can help. Everything is open over here. Nobody censors anything. Please respond soon and send it to the address on the envelope. We wait to hear from you soon!

Love Anton and Josef.

There were no clippings inside like Anton had said. They must've been removed. It's possible from his words, my name would now become an interest of some sly informant somewhere, but I didn't care.

I laid the letter down on the bed next to me. I could not describe the mixture of emotions that engulfed me right then. I was relieved and happy Josef was safe in Anton's care and that they thought of me often. I hadn't been forgotten . . . and I was especially pleased they were experiencing the very life I dreamt for them.

Then my thoughts turned to Stefan . . . confused with the stirring that occurred within my soul. As I replayed the night's events in my head, my skin tingled spontaneously. A year ago, I would never have believed that was even possible.

I put my nightgown on and studied myself in the mirror. My smile faded. Enormous guilt suddenly washed over me. How could I even allow myself to smile or laugh with anyone other than Anton? Anton had been true to me since we met. He had never hurt me, never said anything to degrade or criticize. He had protected me from day one and, even now, protected my brother because I couldn't be with him.

I knew I needed to put any and all thoughts of Stefan away. He contradicted all I believed about my future. I owed it to Anton to keep my thoughts faithful to him.

CHAPTER TWENTY-SEVEN

Only 170 days left . . .

21, March 1963

Dear Anton and Josef,
I cannot tell you how wonderful it was to receive your letter. I do have to warn you though, even now our correspondence could be read. Please be careful in whatever you say, for my safety and yours.

I was removed from the house on Bernauer but live with a wonderful woman called mama G. She is good to me. I also work as a maid for a rich family that runs a mortuary. It's very strange to be around people who have much when most of Berlin has so little, but they have been successful despite the challenges. I've made some good friends finally. It shouldn't surprise you it took me a while. I even went to a café for fun.

I'm happy to hear about your employment and your good circumstances. Keep working hard, but don't send money. It will never reach me. Just know I'm looking into many things.

Josef, keep working hard at your studies. It's hard to believe you are almost 13. I'm proud of you and love you dearly.

Anton, thank you for looking after him as family. I wish I was with you, but until then delight in the memories . . . I do!
All my love,

Ella

It was hard to actually let go of the letter. I envisioned Anton's hand as he received it. How long would it be before I would see them face to face? I ached to be in their presence again and feel the closeness we shared.

About a month before they left, before Papa got really sick and before the threat of the wall was realized, life seemed good. Even now, looking back, I realized I never comprehended the extent of how much I meant to Anton until that July day in 1961.

Anton went with me to deliver a package to Herr Krzinsky. It was fairly common for Papa to send me with correspondence, and it wasn't unusual for Anton to accompany me. This particular time, something had changed.

***

"Anton . . ." I tugged at his shirt. ". . . why are you walking so slowly?" I teased. Normally he bounced all over the place, but for some reason, today he was distracted. "Are you well?" My hand naturally rubbed his cheek; his skin glowed from all the time he spent outside.

He shrugged his shoulders but kept very quiet.

"You don't have to come with me," I suggested. "You probably want to get back to Geoffrey's, huh?"

Geoffrey was a bricklayer who had taken Anton in. He offered to teach him the trade. Only his long days often started before sunrise to avoid the hot summer heat later in the afternoon. It was during this time we walked.

"I'm fine. He had to go to Kopenick for supplies today."

"Are you tired?" I asked as I watched his broad shoulders slightly bend forward as we walked.

"Yes."

"You still don't have to come." I tried to make it easier on him.

"I want to." His smile lifted partway. I knew Anton nearly as well as myself and there was definitely something wrong.

We dropped off the package. Herr Krzinsky insisted we take some Pfannkuchen for our trouble. It was Anton's favorite pastry. I suggested we eat them as we walked near the Spree on our way home. Anton didn't disagree.

I found an empty bench and soaked up the warm sunshine. I removed my shoes and let my bare feet sink into the grass. Anton sat next to me but kept his shoes on. Generally, I could get him to smile under any circumstance, but today he remained distracted.

"Anton!" I grabbed his hand and squeezed it. "Tell me what's going on!" He looked at me briefly then scanned our surroundings. "Anton," I insisted, "this isn't like you, please talk to me."

His face flushed. A bead of sweat rolled down his cheek. "Ella . . ." he whispered, but he was looking at the river.

"Yes?"

"What do you think of me?"

"What do you mean?" I was confused. Anton had to know my world couldn't function without him.

"When you see me, what do you think?"

I thought for a moment. I glanced at his anxious face and spoke up. "I see one of the greatest people I know. I see my best friend." I smiled.

"Friend?" Anton looked at me. His darkened eyes squinted from the afternoon sun.

"Not just a friend, Anton." I nudged him playfully with my elbow. "You're my *best* friend."

He leaned back on the bench and rubbed his short hair with one hand. He had kept it the same way since he left the orphanage.

"Do you love me?"

I scrutinized him like he was crazy. "Of course, Anton, you know this already."

"No, I mean . . . really love me?" His voice was very serious.

A couple of girls walked by and giggled in his direction. In the last six months as Anton worked with Geoffrey, he had grown. Not only in height but the width of his shoulders as well. Everywhere Anton went, girls smiled at him, but I looked at him the same way I always had, my Anton.

"Are you sick?" I cried, surprised at how strange he was acting, ". . . or drunk? Geoffrey gave you some vodka, didn't he?"

I moved closer to smell his breath. I leaned in and teasingly pressed up against his chest when he pulled me even closer. Both his hands went to my shoulders and squeezed. He met my lips with his. They were warm but conveyed an intensity I was unfamiliar with. For some strange reason, I didn't pull away until I needed to catch my breath. Even then, I didn't want to.

Having never been kissed before, it surprised me how natural it seemed . . . especially with Anton. I remained still, only inches away. I gazed at his face. He was so impassioned. His eyes clearly focused only on me. His arms wrapped around me like they always did, but this time, everything was different—the flutter I suddenly felt in my chest, the pounding I was sure he could hear, and the irregular breath that escaped my lips, which now felt unexpectedly numb.

I nuzzled my head against his neck and rested my cheek comfortably on his chest. My arms folded around him as well. We just fit. No words were spoken. They could have ruined the moment as we sat on the bench and watched the sunset's reflection against the water. It may have been the most perfect night I'd ever had in my life.

***

It was less than a week later that Papa fell ill. Little did I know everything would change soon after.

I often thought of that day. Anton and I actually never talked about what happened or repeated it. I wasn't even sure as I reflected on it, what it was. I knew I loved Anton, but with us separated, our future looked unclear.

And for the first time ever, another man's face came to mind and added perplexity to an already uncertain situation.

Chapter Twenty-eight

I hadn't seen Stefan since the Fasching dinner a week ago. Despite my resolve to forget him, I still made sure I fixed my hair, cleaned my face, and stayed in my routine—in case he ever came searching for me, but he didn't.

A small twinge of disappointment arose before I reminded myself this was the way it was meant to be. Yes, the picnic in the art room was pleasant, better than I was willing to admit, including the escort home, but it was unrealistic for me to believe it would go any further. We were far from equals.

The following Friday, near the end of the day, I was oiling the wood shelves in the library. Normally, the books distracted me, but as I slowly moved about, other things were on my mind. When I turned, my heart jumped. Stefan had entered the room unseen and was sitting on a sofa lounge watching me.

"You scared me!" I cried as I set the jar and cloth down and wiped my hands on my dirty apron. Stefan laughed but appeared apologetic.

"I'm sorry," he said, although he couldn't stop chuckling at my reaction. "Really, I am. You were working hard, and I didn't want to disturb you."

"Next time," —I shook my finger at him— "disturb me!"

"OK, I promise. Come sit with me." He casually patted the seat next to him.

I knew the oil on my apron would stain the fabric, thus I sat opposite him on the vinyl chair.

"How has your week been?" he asked sincerely.

"Good, nothing too eventful." Overall, the job itself was quite boring; it was the staff and guests who seemed to spice it up from time to time. "And yours?" I asked politely.

"Busy." His answer was short.

I watched him carefully, forcing myself not to think of why his week was busy. I hoped it wasn't due to more "law breakers" according to the government's definition of the word.

"I've wanted to see you all week, but with Mother and Father out of town on business, I've had much to do. Will you join me at Dafne's tomorrow night?"

I wasn't sure if he was asking me on a date or wanted to meet as friends, like the last time he was there with his "friend". I tried not to stare. He wore a casual brown coat over matching pants and appeared quite handsome for a workday. I gazed down at my hands as they rested on my soiled apron. *Why in the world would he want to spend time with me?*

When I didn't answer right away, Stefan chuckled. "You're trying to think of an excuse not to go, aren't you?" He sat forward and leaned closer. "I don't bite." He smiled wide. His teeth were perfectly straight.

I matched his laugh because despite the short amount of time it had been, he'd had me figured out from the beginning. I thought about my struggle. The more Stefan's face inched closer, the more Anton's face slowly faded. I took a deep breath. I was sure I was making a mistake.

"OK." I surprised us both when I said it. "What time?"

"Is seven o'clock a good time for you?" He moved close enough for me to feel the energy radiate from his skin. My chest rose half a second faster than before.

I nodded, yes. He winked and then he was gone.

If I thought I was distracted before, it hardly compared to the next twenty-four hours of my life. The best way to describe it would be a thrilling agony.

As I faced my bedroom mirror the next evening, the woman standing in front of me was barely recognizable. Since I started at the Frankes', my hair had always been worn in a braid or bun every day. Tonight, as I prepared to meet Stefan at Dafne's, my dark curls fell softly past my shoulders and down my back. Being fortunate enough to not have to crimp my hair with a fire iron to make it roll, it waved naturally on its own despite the limited freedom I allowed it.

My pale-blue, sleeveless dress narrowed to barely above my knees. I had only worn it once before when I went out for coffee with Lena. It was like the dress at the Waisenhaus, the one used only on special occasions. I added a small amount of black liner to my eyelids and pink gloss on my lips.

Mama G whistled when I walked out of my room. "Heaven help that boy!" she cried as she washed her dishes.

"Wh—what boy?" I stuttered.

"The boy who will be staring at you all night," she snickered. "Have mercy on his soul!"

I smiled, kissed her on the cheek, and grabbed my mother's sweater before walking out.

I arrived at Dafne's in time but paced slowly back and forth on the walkway. *What am I doing?* I started to play the ping-pong game in my head. *We are opposites in every way . . . Opposites attract. How can I possibly believe Stefan is interested in me . . . we're just friends though, right?* I struggled hard to keep Anton's image in my mind.

"Fräulein, you dropped your sweater." A man held it up. Horrified I'd let Mama's sweater fall to the ground, I reached for it. I brought it specifically hoping it would will some strength into me.

"Thank you," I said as he held the door open.

"Are you coming in?"

I glanced at the door and then at the nice man and nodded my head. "Yes, thank you." Maybe, in some strange way, this was the sign I was waiting for from her.

I stepped inside and thanked the man as he joined his party. Stefan sat in the corner behind a small table. His head lifted, dropped, and then shot up in my direction once again. My face grew warm with embarrassment. I shouldn't have tried this hard.

As I approached Stefan, he was slow in rising from his chair. His face told me he did not expect to see me this way.

"Your hair . . ." he stuttered, "it's . . . really pretty down."

I blushed. I don't think I've ever blushed. Thankfully, my skin hid color well. He held out my chair like a perfect gentleman as if we were on a date. I assumed this was how dates would go, although, I'd never really been on one alone with a man. Was I supposed to pretend this is what we were doing? I sat at his request, but the wrinkles on my forehead gave away more than I planned.

"You seem concerned?"

"Um . . ." I didn't want to tell him I'd never done this before. He waited without pressure. "I'm not really good at this."

He chuckled. "Do you happen to have a mirror at home?"

I was instantly self-conscious. *Do I have something on my face? Did I do something wrong?* "Yes, . . ." I paused.

"Because if you saw, what I see now, I can assure you . . . you're good at it."

My eyes dropped to my hands.

"Relax, you're doing fine," he urged with a smile in his voice.

I took a breath and peeked back up as he carried on.

"If I remember correctly," —Stefan handed me a menu— "you didn't eat the last time we were here."

I giggled, remembering that night. It was the time I came with Lena and Rainer. I drank a glass of water as I waited impatiently for the time to pass quickly. It was awful.

Stefan seemed to understand my humor and added, "It was a strange night."

I agreed.

"The food here is fantastic. You have to try the *Erdbeerkuchen*." He lit up like a schoolboy as his eyes danced around the menu. "It isn't like any strawberry tart you have ever tasted."

I'd never tasted any type of tart. Money made all the difference as to whether your food had pretty words like "tart" or not. I'd grown accustomed to soups, noodles, or beans as opposed to desserts and pastries.

When the waitress appeared, Stefan faced me and asked what I would like to order. Having recently been paid, I knew I could afford something small. Stefan sensed my apprehension.

"Two *Erdbeerkuchen* please, and a large plate of *Currywurst und pommes*." He smiled and handed her the menu. "Traditionally, the man pays for the date." He smiled again.

So, this is a date . . . It was a relief to have that clarified. Though that word now awakened my nerves. All this time, I wanted to be angry with him, but he was doing everything right. He apologized. He was charming, handsome, and funny. I suddenly realized it was a dangerous combination for trouble.

I gazed around the room reassured by the fact that nobody watched us. Nobody cared what happened in our tiny corner of the café. Stefan's full attention was all on me. I took a deep breath and relaxed.

"Stefan, you mentioned the night of the dinner you never wanted to go into your family business. How do you feel about the mortuary now?" I asked as I placed my napkin on my lap. "You know, now that you don't have a choice of whether you're taking over the business or not?"

"I struggled at first," Stefan reasoned. "My heart was never into it."

"Then what happened?"

"A few months ago, a body was brought to me; a body presumed to be dead." Stefan hesitated. His jawline went rigid, the muscles constricting and his eyes becoming glass-like as he appeared to recall something only he could see.

He faced me, but his lips didn't move. Finally, he whispered, ". . . but the woman wasn't dead."

My eyes grew wide.

Stefan took a long sip of his drink before he continued. "Her heart rate was quite faint to the point she was declared deceased in haste, yet due to the nature of her injuries, she died in my arms. It was—" My mouth fell open. I quickly closed it. "—It was really difficult . . . but a blessing . . ." He paused. ". . .It changed my thoughts on life and death."

Stefan poured a bit of sugar on the top of his dessert as if it wasn't sweet enough. I smiled as I watched him do this. He continued, "After that experience, I craved knowledge. Anything to teach me about human life, the organs, the tissues, the respiratory and circulatory systems. I found a great deal of fascination with life and death, but it was the spiritual dimension that caused me to really pay attention."

"Spiritual as in a *God*?" I questioned.

"Well, yes, that's part of it."

I was shocked. Someone else was as confused as I was about this higher power.

He continued, "Look, Ella, show me your hand." Without hesitation, I held it out. As he reached for it, his touch made my skin tingle. He turned it over and pointed out the fine lines in my palm and the shape of my fingers and nails. "See the detail? The perfection? And this is only a hand. Imagine your lungs, eyelashes, even lips."

My face heated up again as he studied my lips.

"Our bodies are flawless" —I listened with fascination— "sure, there are deformities and ailments, but from the design of a toenail to the intricate valves of the heart or the nerves of the brain, only a God in his perfectness could design such a complex, absolute being." Stefan stopped long enough to take a sip of his coffee. His energy about this subject was unexpected. I was riveted by every word.

"As I received the bodies and prepared them for burial, I realized I wasn't only receiving a corpse or a *nobody* with a number, although sometimes, the tag was all that was attached. But they were a real person who had loved, lost, experienced fear, pain, happiness, or hope at some time in their life. I knew such a perfect being could not have been subjected to all time had to offer if our physical existence in this desolate dark time was all we had."

Suddenly this man before me seemed perfect, absolutely perfect.

"I now felt my duty, the job of preparing their burial, had become a noble task. It was placed solely upon my shoulders. I had the opportunity to be the 'transporter' in a sense. Like the Egyptian God *Anubis*, the one who would help souls arrive at their next destination. This idea suddenly made my role more invaluable to me." Stefan's white skin radiated as he stopped to take a breath. "I now view each individual as they arrive with enormous respect, and as I go through the steps to prepare the body for burial or cremation, it is quite a sacred motion."

I was nearly moved to tears. I thought of my father and his final moments. The way Stefan spoke of the change he had experienced and the personal care he engaged in for each body, I had to stop myself from reaching across the table and embracing him. I was overcome! This man only a year ago was the most selfish creature who ever lived and now has been given a second chance. It suddenly scared me how appealing he had become.

I watched Stefan carefully. I didn't want to stare, but I couldn't help it. He met my gaze. "What an honor you give the deceased family, Stefan. Whether they know it or not, you give them an unparalleled gift."

Stefan's azure eyes were misty. "I actually have never told anyone what I just told you." he chuckled nervously, "not even my father."

My hand moved to his across the table. "Thanks for sharing it with me. It means a lot."

"Thank you for listening." Stefan smiled again. Although I wasn't used to seeing him this happy, it was comforting.

"You're different," I whispered.

Stefan's eyes dropped to our hands, still clasped in the center of the table.

"Is that a good thing?"

"Yes, . . . it is," I said honestly and then anxiously removed my hands from his.

We had spent such a long time talking, that we didn't realize the café was waiting for us to leave. It was eleven o'clock and closing time, vastly different from the last time I was here. Tonight, I actually regretted the fact there wasn't more time.

We had arrived at the café separately, but Stefan insisted on escorting me home, once more. I didn't protest.

Back near the entrance to my apartment building, I motioned to say goodbye, once again holding out my hand for him to shake. He laughed, then gently pulled my hand toward his lips and kissed it. My heart raced as if all my nerves were ignited. I was not used to these strong feelings stirring inside me.

"Thank you for an amazing night, Ella." Stefan's eyes fixated on mine. They had a way of making me feel defenseless. Not that I needed to shield my emotion as I've had to in the past, but those eyes, those beautiful blue eyes held me captive more than I wanted to admit. My face flushed as I rushed up the steps. On the small landing, I hesitated and turned.

"Thank you, Stefan." I wanted to say more, but all that followed was a simple, "Goodnight."

CHAPTER TWENTY-NINE

"Good morning, Ella!" Lena met me on the street before we entered the Frankes'. She stared at me strangely. "Something's different." My eyes gawked in her direction. Could she really read my face that easily?

"Oh, it's your hair! It's in a ponytail and not a braid." She giggled. "I've never seen you wear it this way."

"Yes, trying something new." I brushed it off. I was glad she didn't suspect anything else.

We walked in together and were immediately met by Johann.

"Change in plans today, Fräuleins. We have some dignitaries coming for a working lunch. Please make sure the parlor is your first priority. I'm assigning you both directly to serve."

I nodded. Johann was always slightly dramatic over these events despite their frequency. The best part of the plan was I would get to work with Lena all day. It had been nine months since Christoph disappeared, and she was barely starting to seem like her old self again. It was bittersweet.

As we prepped the room, I wondered if I should tell her about my date on Saturday, but then argued against it. I knew she would keep my secret, but if it did get out somehow, there was one person I feared more than anyone else. I knew Frau Franke would not hesitate to have me fired but suspected she could find a way to have me arrested as well, anything to keep my distance from her precious son. No, this was a secret I would have to keep entirely to myself.

"Lena, Ella! They're here. Please show the guests into the parlor."

It was strange to me why Johann always got excited. They were only people. Lena was placing the last of the appetizers on a tray; it would be I who opened the door. Four guests awaited my welcome. I didn't recognize anyone from previous visits, but I also hadn't seen everyone who came to the house. I did recognize the official uniform of the People's Police though. That was impossible to miss.

Two of the four guests were likely in their late teens or early twenties and were definitely part of the border guard. The senior officer wore the shoulder insignia with four diamonds indicating he was a captain, and the other gentleman was in a regular black business suit with matching fedora.

I graciously showed them the way to the parlor. After they each took a seat, I offered to get them a beverage of choice. They all asked for vodka, except for the man in the suit who asked for orange juice. Lena passed me with a tray of *Buletten* wrapped in *Eierkuchen*. She went around the room offering delicacies one by one while they waited for Herr Franke to join them.

As I returned with their drinks, I politely delivered their requests and was met with engaging smiles. Nothing at all seemed out of the ordinary until Stefan himself entered the room. It caught me off guard, and I nearly dropped the tray on the lap of one of the border guards. Thankfully, it was shortly after I had handed him his drink, and it was empty.

"Oh, I'm sorry, sir." I cried as I gained control of the metal plate in front of one of the young men. Despite a near collision, his face lit up. The dimples on both sides of his wide smile led me to believe he couldn't be more than a few years older than me. As I peered closer at his youthful face, I wondered if he really understood the tasks he was required to do.

"No harm done, Fräulein." He laughed and held his drink high for a toast. The others followed suit.

It was quite obvious this was their first time at the Frankes'. They were eager and showed very little sophisticated experience. I turned to Stefan and mouthed, "I'm sorry," out of the view of the guests. Here, being the first time Stefan saw me work a private lunch, I was clumsy.

He winked and smiled before he turned and graciously introduced himself as Stefan Franke, the new supervisor for the mortuary. I ran quickly to the kitchen to compose myself.

Lena didn't miss a thing.

"Did Stefan just wink at you?" she cried from the door. I reached for the food I'd already placed on the lunch tray and pretended to rearrange it.

"Ella!" Lena went right to my side and whispered, "I know I saw Stefan wink at you and you smile at him."

I knew this wouldn't work. I peeked around to confirm our privacy.

"Promise you won't say anything?"

Lena's face lit up. "Are you teasing me?" She was too loud.

"Can we talk about it later and not here?" I pleaded.

"OK, please tell me one thing . . . has he kissed you?"

"No, . . . I'm really scared." My eyes darted to the door, and I whispered, "I kind of make it so I shake his hand when we say goodnight." Lena half laughed and half cried.

"It's pathetic, I know!" My head fell into my hands. "It's not that I wouldn't want to, I mean, look at him . . . of course you know, you see him too, but . . ."

"But what?"

"But... I've only had one kiss. It was good—actually it was great!"

"Anton?"

"Yes, but I'm sure Stefan is more experienced than me. I could really mess it up."

"You could . . ." Lena giggled, "but wouldn't it be fun trying?"

I joined her laugh then sighed. "I never thought I would be having this conversation with you . . . ever." I grinned.

"Yes, me too!" Lena hugged me. "Ella, you really deserve to be happy."

"I'll tell you more later, I promise."

As the afternoon carried on, Lena watched me carefully. I was professional as I worked. I attempted to only look at Stefan when he spoke directly to me, and even then, he presented himself in an unemotional manner. It fascinated me to see him at work, as well. He had somehow become an adult recently, mature and responsible.

"Herr Franke,"

"Please, call me Stefan, Captain Scharf."

"Thank you for your hospitality, Stefan. We have a few details to discuss about a delivery arriving later today and an issue that has come up before Congress, a rather delicate issue." The captain stared at me, and I knew this was my cue to leave.

"Whatever the SED requires, we are more than happy to accommodate," Stefan announced right when I left the room.

I closed the kitchen door behind me and frowned.

"How do they do it, Lena?" I was unsettled.

"What?"

"How do they simply go along with whatever people tell them to do?"

"Who?"

"The Frankes. Is it for the money?"

Lena shrugged her shoulders as I continued, "Obviously, they're well compensated for their alliance, but . . ."

Lena glared.

"I know . . . I need to be quiet like always . . . I simply think it would be nice to live in a world where people didn't control one another, where you truly are free." I poured a fresh kettle of coffee into the teapot and set out five teacups while I waited to be summoned again.

"Coffee, sir?" I asked each of the men. They were still engaged in conversation and barely acknowledged my entry.

"We look forward to a long and productive relationship, Stefan Franke." The man in the black suit raised his cup to Stefan.

"Well, thank you for your confidence." He then pointed to the young soldiers. "I assume these are two of your finest People's Police, sir?"

"Absolutely," the captain gushed with pride, "These men are being honored today with a medal for exemplary service at the border. We thought it appropriate to recognize their bravery with a delicious meal before we are required before Congress."

"Oh?" Stefan appeared hesitant to ask why, but Captain Scharf did not delay in sharing the details of their actions.

I tried not to listen, but the way the men joked about a man's failed escape attempt across the wall, horrified me. My face shot irritation toward the group. I couldn't help it.

Stefan peered in my direction and caught sight of my nose wrinkling with disgust. Of all the people I didn't want to offend, it would be him. I hastily turned my back before I drew the guest's attention. Yet, the image was difficult to expel; I knew exactly what exemplary service at the border meant. They killed this man and then continued to talk about the incident as if it was some great accomplishment.

"The man thought he was quite smart," one of the guards inserted. "He inched his way through the canal, but Dietrich spotted him first and pelted the water with bullets."

"At least thirty," hooted the other one, who I assumed to be Dietrich.

Tears started to build. I thought of Peter and wondered if the border guard who shot him was honored as well. My cheeks burned. I knew if I faced the men, they would see my torment. I needed to step out.

"Fräulein?" The commanding officer called for me. I could not turn. I feared my rage would surface.

"May I refill your drinks, gentlemen?" Stefan distracted him. He stood up and retrieved their glasses.

He moved swiftly to where I leaned over the bar. He set the glasses down and reached for my hand and squeezed it gently, completely out of sight.

"Are you OK?" he whispered as the men continued to gloat over the details of what happened at Teltow and the botched recovery of the man's body. It was difficult to focus on Stefan's touch. My heart crumbled more and more with each word. He quickly refilled their glasses and whispered for me to go. I nodded and stepped outside the room then outside the house.

"What's going on, Ella?" Lena opened the back door and found me sitting on the steps with my head in my hands.

"I need some fresh air." I didn't even glance up.

"You're lying. What's going on?"

I kept my voice low, but even as I spoke, I knew the content was dangerous to say.

"I'm tired, Lena. I'm tired of how these men mock our pain, bragging about shooting innocent people and receiving awards for killing common citizens . . . can you believe it? Killing someone earns you a medal of valor!" My voice began to rise with each word.

"Ella, take a walk."

"I'm fine!"

"No, go!" Lena anxiously pointed me in a direction away from the house. I knew she was trying to help, but I was angry. "Now!" she cried and closed the door behind me.

I walked but had no idea where to go. Everything in front of me reminded me of the prison I lived in. I stumbled desperately toward Papa's grave. Images of broken and bloodied escapees somehow clouded my way. Their desperate cries and fear filled my ears. Reprieve seemed unattainable until I finally reached the grassy mound. Even though there wasn't a marker to bear his name, I knew the exact spot of Papa's body. I desperately needed to feel his strength at this very moment.

Papa had to do tough things in his young life, one of which was to help round up Jewish people from the Barn Quarter and board them on a train to Auschwitz. He knew the slaughterhouse he sent them to. It killed him to do it, but he was bound by duty.

It was ridiculous I was so weak, much weaker than I should be having him as a father. He often told me he wished he had refused. That maybe at some point, if he had said no, one person would have been saved. He knows he could have been killed, but he said, "dying doing the right thing would not be a bad way to die."

Removing my apron, the linen fell carelessly to the grass. Watching it drop, I realized I was one crack short of shattering.

I was done.

I didn't want to live this way anymore, to feel small and helpless, insignificant and unimportant, pretending to be happy when, in fact, life here was confining and crippling.

No place to go, like a fish in a fishbowl, waiting for the hook or net to destroy me. Papa was right, I needed to take a stand. Maybe I couldn't stand up to these men physically, but I also didn't need to serve them as they tittered on about their revolting conquests.

By the time I made my way home several hours later, the sun had set and the distinct call of the crickets expanded the closer I got.

As I approached, there, sitting on the steps of my building, was Stefan. He appeared handsome but tired. My eyes found his but didn't light up at the sight of him as they had barely two days ago.

"Ella!" He stood immediately.

"What are you doing here?" I whispered.

"I came to see if you were all right."

"How long have you been here?"

"Not long," he lied. The crease in his pants was evidence that he had been sitting a long time.

"I needed to walk."

"For seven hours?"

I moved around him to go inside. His hand reached for my arm. "Talk to me, Ella." He didn't let go.

I scanned around by habit, even though I didn't care who listened.

"How can you do it, Stefan?"

"Do what?"

"Listen to those men speak so callously about a person's life? How can you knowingly participate?"

"I have a duty, Ella," Stefan defended calmly. "I'm in charge of the mortuary now, and I have a responsibility to maintain a relationship with this administration . . . even if—" he gazed around himself this time, "—even if I don't agree."

"But it's not who you are, Stefan." Tears started to roll down my cheeks. "I saw a man, an inspiring man, speak on Saturday of how precious life is. Then, today, that same man submitted to the will of evil men who take every opportunity to silence innocent life."

Stefan wiped my tears with his fingers.

"Do you burn innocent people, Stefan?"

"Ella, . . ." Stefan's hand lingered on my face, "please don't do this."

"Do you?" my voice strained.

"Ella, . . ." His eyelashes lowered.

My eyes shifted to a single vine of ivy climbing the concrete steps, I needed to see anything but his face. "You can't be both, Stefan. You are either one or the other," I contended and then brushed his hand aside, walking inside the apartment building without a backward glance.

I could not sleep. Stefan's expression appeared every time I closed my eyes. The pain of my words injured him. I saw it over and over again in my mind, the tenderness of his heart and the struggle he must be having trying to please everyone but himself. Who was this man who had me unexpectedly ensnared? What power did he have to make me feel like I was on top of the world one moment then below it the next?

I thought about my decision to go or not go back to the Frankes'. I contemplated the consequences of my choice and knew Papa would be proud of me either way, but he had also taught me that giving your word was invaluable. If you agreed to something and didn't see it through, you risked losing your integrity. What kind of person did I want to be?

I walked to the bathroom sink and splashed cold water on my face. As I dried it with a towel, I scrutinized the woman facing me in the mirror. She had every reason to be angry, every reason to hold a grudge or even seek revenge. Her history was as porous as the war-torn buildings around her, but did she really want to be defined by her hardships? Her weaknesses? Or rather she overcame those trials, time and time again?

As I contemplated this, I recognized my greatest error. All this time, I chastised Stefan for his inability to stand up against wrong, yet I was willing to jeopardize my own character by not standing by my word and fulfilling my own contract with the Frankes who, at my time of fear and hopelessness, came to my desperate need and provided a casket and plot for my papa.

It suddenly seemed I was in no position to judge . . . anyone.

CHAPTER THIRTY

I arrived at work on time the next morning but was met with fierceness in the air. Frau Franke stormed into the staff rooms and called for me, immediately. I knew there was a possibility of this happening. I had left the house shortly after one o'clock yesterday, and despite their good intentions, Lena and Johann couldn't possibly account for my whereabouts the whole time I was gone.

"I warned you, Fräulein Kühn." Her jaw set as her nostrils flared. This familiar expression made it hard for me to envision her as Stefan and Katharina's real mother.

"I'm sorry, Frau Franke. I wasn't feeling well. It won't happen again."

"You're correct. It will *not* happen again!" She walked over to my shelf and ripped my nametag off. "You're dismissed! And . . ."

"Mother," Stefan entered behind her and gave her a light kiss on the cheek. This stunned me. I'd never seen him do that before.

"Calm down, dear Mother," Stefan grabbed the tag and replaced it.

"I gave Fräulein Kühn the day off myself."

Frau Franke's eyes grew wide and rivaled those of the rest of the staff present as well.

"She was feeling ill, and I thought it best she did not infect our guests."

She glimpsed between us both. Her face revealed nothing.

"Are you feeling better, Fräulein Kühn?" He stared directly at me.

"Yes, much better, thank you." I tried to hold his gaze, but the others were still present. Stefan then put an arm around his mother and gently guided her out and down the hall.

I was somewhat relieved, but Stefan's rescue may have conflicted things between us even more, if that was possible.

Not too much got past Frau Franke. She had to suspect something was amiss. My thoughts returned to Stefan and the wrangle that filled my head the night before. I knew Stefan was burdened with a fairly difficult situation. It wasn't hard to see now that he had scarcely any room for choice and freedom. We had much more in common these days than we ever had before, and I felt guilty and ashamed for the way I treated him. I needed to find a way to see him, to not only thank him for preserving my job but also to apologize.

I knew I had to be extra careful today. Frau Franke would jump at any opportunity to find me at fault. To avoid the risk, my plan was to try and locate Stefan during lunch, since realistically, the break was my personal time.

I slipped back through the large doors to the mortuary a little after noon but hesitated. Stefan hadn't been forewarned of my visit. He may not even want to see me. I stood still in the hallway as I debated the options in my head. It didn't take long for me to convince myself that Stefan was worth the risk.

I checked the office, but it was empty. After searching the back receiving area and the waiting room, my quest still came up empty-handed, but I didn't give up. As I came to the only other room I hadn't checked, besides the crematorium, I stepped inside. The light was on, and the air was unusually cold. A strong, strange odor permeated my senses forcing me to cover my nose with my hand as I moved about. I was not even sure why I stayed, but it might have been the organized rows of doors that piqued my curiosity.

As I approached, I noticed each individual compartment had a handwritten note attached. The closer I got, the more I realized they were people's names. I ran my finger across them slowly, *Hoffmann Y, Madler P, Frankert J, Schwarz S* . . . When I reached the end, I intrusively grasped the handle.

"Ella?"

I jumped at the sound of his voice and my hand jerked, popping the lever. The door cracked open.

"I'm sorry," I stuttered, gawking between him and the flesh that suddenly became visible through the gap.

Stefan calmly moved toward me and casually sealed the compartment once again. "I didn't mean to scare you, Ella. What are you doing in here?"

"I-I'm sorry." I regretted snooping . . . again. I knew I wasn't supposed to be in the mortuary, but my intentions were good. "I'm looking for you."

"Why in here?" Removing his work gloves, he washed his hands as he waited for my answer.

"I checked all over. I knew you had to be somewhere nearby."

He smiled. "Why were you searching for me?" He grabbed my hand and led me out of the room. Happily, I took a deep breath of clean air.

"Are those names of people? Are those all dead—" I couldn't even get an audible sentence out.

"Don't think about it, Ella. Please come sit down." I let him grasp my hand and direct me to a nearby sofa. My thoughts battled between both the people in the room and the closeness with which Stefan sat next to me. His cologne masked the awful smell that had imprinted in my nose. His hand still intertwined with mine, rested on my knee, but his eyes never left my face as he waited for me to speak.

"I—" *Focus, Ella!* I reprimanded myself for being juvenile. "I wanted to say thank you for what happened back there, with your mother." Stefan smiled humbly, then I mumbled, "And . . . I'm sorry."

"For what?"

"For everything!" I blurted.

Stefan's eyebrows lifted inquisitively.

"I'm sorry I judged you, Stefan. I know the decisions you must make can't be easy. I was wrong to assume you are willingly . . . you know . . ." I was afraid to finish the sentence.

Stefan's touch was soothing, his fingers moved from my hand to my cheek. Despite where we were, it was a very tender moment.

"Ella, you're right. It seems wrong to feel one way and act another, but I'm merely trying to do what is necessary to carry on. I'm slowly realizing everything has a price." Stefan now placed both his hands over mine. "Every time I think things are getting better in Berlin, something happens to make it worse, but please don't lose faith in *me*. I'm still the same man from the café."

I shook my head, the familiar sting in my nose that always came prior to the tears beginning. "It's not you . . . it's the system we're a part of. It's the deceit and control and lack of conscience I'm struggling with. I'm petrified that one day we will blink and not even realize we have become the very thing we feared."

"Not everyone has to concede. We can find a way to rise above it." Stefan's finger moved to retrieve the tear sliding down my cheek. He smiled. "Just think, we're actually the lucky ones. Imagine being separated from your loved ones by the wall."

My mind was filled with confusion . . . *did he always believe this, or was this empathy part of the new Stefan?*

When I didn't speak, Stefan pressed, "Are you OK?"

I took another deep breath. "Do you really care about those people?"

"Why are you asking?" Stefan seemed startled by my question; his face twisted as if my inquiry offended him. "Why wouldn't I?"

"Because . . ." I stuttered, ". . . because your father . . . he's involved with making the wall, you know . . . a success . . . and now you are a part of it too." I watched Stefan carefully, nervous I had possibly crossed the line, again.

"My father does what he has to in order to survive—"

I crinkled my nose a bit. Our definitions of the word "survive" were extremely different.

"—Ella, you have to believe I will do all I can to do the right thing," he continued. "Why do you ask?"

Was I ready to tell him? I remained quiet.

"I'm not my father."

"I know . . ." I really did know there was a difference. It was hard for me to believe the son of a communist devotee wasn't molded by his father . . . like Anton. Even at his young age, I was sure Anton was taught to hate the Jews by his father. It seemed natural for a child to follow the same path as a parent.

"Stefan," I stared him in the eyes, "I'm one of those people you´re talking about."

"What do you mean?" His eyes narrowed.

"My brother, Josef, and my best friend, Anton, left me for the West the night the wall went up."

Stefan was silent as he processed this, then he whispered, "Why didn't you go with them?"

"My father was ill" —my eyes became moist again thinking about it— "and then . . . well, you know the rest . . . you were there when my papa was buried. I saw you on the patio, do you remember?"

"Oh, right," Stefan realized. "I forgot, it was only you and the priest. You seemed really angry . . ." My face went blank as he retracted. "Of course, you had every right to be upset . . . you'd just buried your father."

"He was my adoptive father. Actually, my only real father."

Stefan's arm went around my shoulder, his hand rubbing gently against my sleeve. This unintentionally triggered the memory of another man's touch in the exact same place hundreds of times. The recollection of Anton caught me off guard.

"How old were you when you were adopted?"

"I was eleven when the Kühns came. I'd been an orphan since birth and . . ." I paused. ". . .They could have picked any blond, blue-eyed little girl, and they chose me, a mixed-race tumbleweed." I always recognized the significance of their decision but rarely spoke of it out loud. I braced for a reaction, but it wasn't the one I expected.

Stefan leaned in, his whisper tickled my ear as he spoke, "You have more people who care about you than you think." Both his arms wrapped around me and pulled me toward his chest. The embrace was both welcome and intoxicating.

"Ouch." Stefan pulled back and rubbed his chest.

"Are you all right?" I tilted my head, my eyes dropping to where his fingers patted his shirt, but I didn't see anything.

"Yes, I just felt a pinch." His hand reached for the top of my dress, and there, sticking out, was the sharp end of Anton's pin. Somehow, it had unclasped.

"Oh." I quickly retrieved it and turned it over to inspect the back. Stefan reached for it. My hand froze. *What would I say about its origin if he asked?*

"This is beautiful." His eyes followed the detail. "Why don't you wear it on the outside?"

"It is special to me," I whispered. "I don't want anyone to see it and take it."

"I understand." Stefan smiled and placed it in my palm. Every time he touched me, my skin quivered. "Be careful, Ella, it looks like the clasp is loose."

"Thanks." I slipped it into my dress pocket.

Stefan brought the conversation back to the orphanage. "Do you know who your parents were?"

"Not the ones who gave birth to me. I don't really consider them my parents though; the Kühns were my mama and papa."

"Was it difficult in the orphanage?"

I remained silent. My feelings were unclear. There were many things about the orphanage I wanted to forget, but every good memory involved Anton.

"I'm sorry, am I upsetting you?"

"No." I shrugged. "I'm all right." Truthfully, I didn't want to talk about my life anymore, but I knew Stefan was only being curious.

"I can't imagine how hard it must have been," Stefan mumbled sincerely, his hand reached for mine once again.

I knew there was much more to say, but this was neither the time nor place. I glanced at the clock on the wall above us and panicked.

"I'm sorry, I have to get back before my lunch time is over." I stood in a rush to leave. "I can't get fired twice in one day." I chuckled, even though it really wasn't funny.

"Thanks for coming." Stefan was not ready to let go. "Will you meet me tomorrow night at Dafne's?" he asked with a wide smile as he led me down the hall. I squeezed his hand and reached for the large door handle.

"Sure. Is seven o'clock OK?" I matched his smile.

"Yes, . . . oh, and Ella," Stefan turned toward me once again before I stepped out. "I almost forgot . . . I wanted to tell you this last night, but the timing wasn't right." Curiously, I waited for him to continue.

"I would love for you to use the art room."

"The art room?"

"Yes." His eyes lit up simultaneously to his smile.

"Are you sure? It's your personal space, Stefan."

"Of course, I'm sure. I know drawing is important to you, and I want you to feel comfortable in there anytime you want."

"Thank you, Stefan. That means a lot!"

I was still smiling when I reached the staff room. It was impossible to shake.

"Uh-oh." Lena noticed. "You saw him, didn't you?" she whispered.

My grin broadened, but I was mute. Words could not express my feelings at that moment. I wanted to hold on to the sensation as long as I possibly could.

As I placed my apron in my box at the end of the day, Lena was at my side. I knew she would appear at some point, only I didn't know when.

"I happen to be free tonight, Ella." She smiled slyly. "I would like to treat you to coffee . . . only, if *you* are available."

I laughed. "Yes, let's go."

We walked out together and down the street to a coffee shop called *Karlina's Kaffe*. I'd only been in there once before, and it was with Lena, of course.

I spent the next two hours filling her in on the recent events involving Stefan, including the Fasching dinner night and the café. She, herself, had noticed a change in him but wasn't aware of the jail time in Czechoslovakia. I was careful not to give her too many details regarding Stefan's personal confessions to me since they deserved some privacy.

It felt like a couple of school friends chatting about the cute boy at school, something I had wondered about but never experienced—mostly because I was homeschooled with the Kühns and partly because I never had a close female friend before Lena.

"Have you told him about Anton?"

"Kind of."

"What do you mean kind of?" Lena took a sip from her second steaming mug but never took her eyes off me.

"I told him Anton was my best friend and with my brother in the West."

"So, you didn't really tell him about Anton."

"What's there to tell?" I cried defensively. "I don't even know what we were when he left. It wasn't like I was his girlfriend. We kissed— once— it was amazing. Papa got sick, life got hard, and now he's gone. How do I explain that?"

"Well, how do you feel about Anton now? Do you love him?"

"Of course, I do!" I announced with confidence. "We went through a lot together, Lena. He's everything to me." Then my certainty wavered a bit. "Besides, I'm not Stefan's girlfriend either . . . we've only seen each other a few times." It almost seemed like I was trying to convince myself I really was neutral. "It's not too complicated . . . right?"

"OK . . ." Lena waved the waitress down to pay. "Whatever you say, Ella, . . . I don't want to see this get confusing and you find yourself caught between two men."

"Two men?" I mocked. I never would have imagined a scenario like this in my lifetime.

Lena kissed me goodbye on the cheek. "Two men who have fallen for my sweet Ella."

As I walked home, I thought about what Lena said.

I love Anton. I've spent most of my life with him, and I think he feels the same way about me, but he's not here, and right now I can't get to him. I can't even talk to him. I don't even know if I'll ever see him again. The thought brought tears to my eyes . . . but if I could . . . if I could actually find a way to the West, would I leave right now? *Of course, I would go,* I insisted . . . almost berating myself. Then doubted. *Would it be for Josef or Anton? Could I leave Stefan? We're only friends anyway, right? Friends who hold hands . . . is it possible things could get more serious? If so . . . would I leave Stefan then?*

I didn't want to think about it. It didn't seem fair that any one person should have to face such decisions. Decisions I never could have anticipated . . . ever.

CHAPTER THIRTY-ONE

The next day, I reached into my work dress to retrieve the tinnie pin, but it was gone. I frantically pulled both pockets inside out and then desperately checked every dress I owned. Devastated, I retraced my steps. I knew the last place I had actually touched it was the mortuary, but I had walked through town and the apartment quite freely since. I got down on my hands and knees checking every square inch of the flat.

"For heaven's sake, child, what are you doing?" Mama G inquired as she saw me patting the boards under the table.

"Anton's tinnie pin, Mama. I lost it!" Tears streamed readily down my face.

Mama G quickly scanned the room then knelt next to me. Her arms wrapped around me instead of reaching to the floor to assist.

"You need to leave for work, Ella." Her hands cupped my face gently and wiped my tears.

"I can't . . ." I sniffled loudly and wiped my nose on my sleeve.

"I'll look for it, dear. I'm sure it will show up somewhere. It is part of you. I'm convinced it will find its way back."

She helped me up and led me to the door where she kissed me on the forehead.

I tortured myself the entire way to the Frankes'. I lost more and more of Anton every day and losing his one token of friendship felt as though I'd lost him completely.

"Ella," Lena found me in the library. "I haven't seen you all day, not even during lunch, are you well?"

I nodded. I had watched for every opportunity to get to the mortuary without anyone seeing me, but it was impossible. Herr and Frau Franke had gone in and out multiple times. Frequent business today had forced my distance. Frustration consumed me.

"I am well." I forced a lift in my voice to keep Lena from knowing the truth. She placed her arm around me.

"When do you see Stefan again?" she whispered quietly into my ear. My smile could not resist his name. My eyes sparkled with only a mere mention of him. "Ah, I see," Lena chuckled. "It must be tonight." "Yes." I blushed.

"What are you going to wear?"

I thought about it for a moment. I hadn't even considered anything but finding the pin. My face curled in confusion. "I actually don't know." I didn't have a lot of choices, but I knew I wanted it to be impressive. The last occasion would be hard to outdo, but I couldn't wait to try.

"Here, Ella." Lena reached into her pocket and handed me some coins. I tried to give them back. "No, Lena, I can't take this."

"Yes, you can, please. I want you to get a new dress. It's not much, but you are my friend, and I want to help." She clasped my hand with the coins, "Go to Alexanderplatz after work. You are sure to find something at *Zentralmarkthalle.*" Then she kissed me on the cheek.

When I got home after shopping, Mama G was already asleep in her room. I needed to ask about the pin but didn't want to disturb her. Her health caused her to fall asleep at all hours of the day. It would have to wait until tomorrow.

This time, when I stepped through the door to meet Stefan at Dafne's, I wore a short, red dress with a black belt and a pair of black knee-high boots Khloe gave me. It was obvious I was a force to be reckoned with the moment I entered the café.

"How do you do it?" Stefan questioned as he met me near the front.

"How do I do what?"

"Appear more beautiful each day I see you!"

I smiled, embarrassed again. I had hoped he thought that but struggled to hear it said out loud.

As handsome as Stefan appeared in his gray turtleneck sweater and black dress pants, I could have asked him the same thing, but I just admired him silently. He took my hand and led me to a corner table. Holding out my chair, he squeezed my shoulders gently from behind as I sat down.

"Thanks for coming."

"Thank you for the invitation." I scooted closer to him and whispered,

"Our time in the mortuary was too short."

One of his eyebrows rose adjacent to a sly grin. "I couldn't agree more."

The waitress approached the table to take our order.

"Are you ready to order, Ella?"

I hadn't even looked at the choices yet. Stefan stared at me as I tried to focus on the words.

"What?" I smiled and peered over the top of the menu.

"Red is definitely your color," he said boldly.

I laughed. "You're distracting me."

"Really?" He smiled devilishly. "I can do better than that," he responded playfully. Now both his eyebrows rose as if accepting a challenge. I knew he would win so I changed the subject.

"Did you finish your painting of the Elbe River?" I asked him. I really wanted to see it again.

"Almost, you can come and see it tomorrow if you like."

"I would love to." My eyes lit up. "Will you be there also?"

"Possibly . . ."

The waitress returned. I ordered *Konigsberger Klopse* at Stefan's urging, "well known to be the best meatballs and capers in town." Stefan stared at me for a few seconds before he spoke.

"One thing I'm curious about, Ella, is with your family gone . . . why haven't you tried to get to the West since?"

I studied him carefully. Then naturally glanced around the room. This was personal.

He waited then asked, "*Have* you tried?"

I nodded.

"Really? How?" His interest seemed piqued. I scanned the café again. You never knew who would be listening. "It didn't turn out . . . of course, you know that since I'm still here."

"It was multiple times?" Stefan's face didn't hide the shock.

"Yes, I pursued it twice."

"What happened?"

"Terrible things."

"Like what?" He appeared quite interested. It was uncomfortable talking about such a delicate topic, especially with someone whose family was directly involved in keeping people from crossing.

"People died," I whispered. Stefan shook his head then leaned in closer. I could smell the mint from his tea on his breath. It tempted me.

"Are you still trying?"

I thought about this for a minute. "Depends—"

"On what?"

"—Depends on whether staying turns out to be better than leaving."

Stefan stared at me, he seemed unsure whether he should believe he knew what that meant. A little surprised at my audacity, I changed the subject. Despite the euphoric feelings that kept arising in his presence, my heart dangled with vulnerability.

"What did you want to do before the mortuary became your life?" This was my attempt to turn the conversation. He responded easily or else just let me believe I was in control. Either way, he was a gentleman.

"I had many different ideas." He chuckled. "I wanted to travel abroad and paint. I also wanted to be a musician and" —curious, Stefan had my full attention now— "lastly, I wanted to open a discotheque here in Berlin."

I snorted out loud. "Dancing?" It actually didn't surprise me.

"Are you laughing at me?" he asked spiritedly.

"No—" I backtracked, "—the um . . . tea tickled my throat, and . . ."

"Uh-huh!" He didn't buy it and grabbed my hand. "You are making fun of me." His touch was playful and exhilarating.

"No, I actually have never been out dancing."

"Really?" Stefan appeared surprised. "Sorry, I thought every teenager in Berlin had been to a nightspot."

"Nope, but I don't think I'm a normal teenager either."

"You're right—" Stefan's half-grin emerged "—and that's a good thing."

Stefan reached over for my other hand and now held them both in the center of the table. It seemed so natural.

"How did I find you?" he whispered.

I heard the words, but I was caught up in the moment. His face not far from mine, I watched Stefan's eyes as they lit up at the same time his lips curled into a smile, the kind that bowed just enough to appear devious. His blond bangs fell slightly over his forehead and swept to the side when he moved. I could not take my eyes off him. He could possibly be the most handsome man I had ever seen. Not that I'd seen many with my sheltered life, but it wasn't only his appearance anymore that sent goose bumps up and down my arms. Stefan had become a man. A man who I discovered was as incredible inside as he was outside.

"What?" He matched my stare.

"Nothing." I pulled my eyes away and tried to glance around the café, but it wasn't anywhere near as appealing as his face.

"Don't tease," Stefan laughed.

"I'm not," I joked but still didn't gaze back at him.

He spent the next couple of minutes jockeying to get me to face him again. In spite of my stubbornness, this was one game I was fine with losing. The mood shifted to light and enjoyable, and we spent most of the night laughing, which was such an unusual experience for me. I'd never done that before.

Later, as Stefan walked me home, he kept his arm around me the entire way. It was comfortable and sweet to think that everyone we passed knew we were together.

Before we arrived at my apartment, Stefan stopped at the corner and wrapped both his arms around me. We were in the shadows of the nearest streetlamp, therefore, a fair amount of darkness concealed his embrace. Stefan's tall, lean frame towered over me. I tilted my head back to face him.

"Are you going to put your hand out for me to shake tonight?" Stefan leaned in close enough for me to feel the heat emitting from his skin. My heart thumped so loudly, I was sure he could hear it. When I shook my head "no" it was subtle enough to miss if he wasn't so close.

The sweetness of his breath mingled with the salt from his lips as they merged with mine. His touch, both strong and gentle, magnified my senses in a way my body had never experienced before. As the kiss deepened, I closed my eyes and felt my spirit enter a place I had only read about...complete and utter ecstasy.

As our silhouettes emerged from one to two, our eyes remained locked. The limited light from the streetlamp cast shadows on half of Stefan's face, but even in the darkness, his eyes seemed to glow. Streaks of mesmerizing blue appeared brighter than a gem. I suddenly perceived precise details in an altered state. It was like the kiss created a whole new dimension of communication. This startling awareness stunned me.

I smiled bashfully, "Did I do that OK?"

He kissed my forehead with a smile. "It was perfect." Holding my hand, he led me home. I stood on my tiptoes and kissed his cheek before stepping into the apartment and could not stop smiling from that point on.

As I got ready for bed, I kept touching my lips. They remembered every move Stefan made, and it was one I couldn't wait to repeat.

Everything about tonight was exactly how I hoped it would be.

Chapter Thirty-two

The next day after work, I slipped upstairs to the art room. I hadn't seen Stefan all day and hoped to see him here, finishing his painting as he had suggested at the cafe. Disappointed, I found the room dark and empty. All day, my thoughts focused on our kiss the night before, goose bumps appearing every time I relived it in my mind.

Two years ago, when Anton kissed me, it was the first for us both— exciting, new, and a tiny bit awkward as we figured it out together. With Stefan, it was different. Despite my lack of experience, the kiss seemed nearly flawless. He'd left me wanting more of whatever it was, and that rarely happened to me.

As I admired his nearly completed painting, it tempted me to indulge in my own drawings. It had been too long since my fingers had touched chalk, and I missed it immensely. Glancing down the empty hallway, I carefully closed the door, lucky the art room was the farthest away from the master bedroom. Herr and Frau Franke usually retired by seven o'clock each night unless they had an evening meeting. It should be safe for the next couple of hours.

Placing "La Vie en Rose" on the phonograph, once again, was like satisfying a hollow void, a thirst quenched by little else. Nearly more excited about this than the art itself, I closed my eyes and allowed the music to penetrate my senses before I began.

Like before, the limitless supplies at my access overwhelmed me, but with the music playing and a new canvas on the easel, a curiosity developed to experiment. I had never actually painted with a liquid before— always using chalk or wax for my designs—but tonight, something new and intense raced through my veins. As I randomly selected bottles of colored paint, a different person emerged. When I set out the supplies, it occurred to me how much fun it would be to combine both chalk and paint, so I quickly grabbed Stefan's painting shirt, which hung on the closet hook nearby. His scent still lingered, so I pulled the collar up to my nose. The memory of being so close to him put a smile on my face.

I dipped my yellow chalk into the small blob of purple paint on the pallet. I spread the double wing wide on one side of the canvas and then mirrored the image on the opposite half. With the fingers of my left hand, I fanned the wet paint out, extending it to the tip of the wings. The image developed beautifully.

I now dipped the blue chalk into the green paint continuing the process on both sides. A vibrant butterfly emerged against the white background. It was taking flight as I went to dip the chalk once more when suddenly, a gentle touch transpired on both sides of my arms from behind. This was a good surprise; I didn't even hear Stefan enter the room.

His hands mischievously slid down my shoulders the length of my arms to my wrists. His touch was light but electrifying, and my skin tingled with anticipation. When his body moved close behind mine, the hair on my neck quivered with each exhale.

"I've missed you." His whisper ignited chills. I remained still as he moved my ponytail to one side, and his lips maneuvered from the back of my neck around to the curve under my jaw.

My pulse raced. I could not concentrate on anything but his touch.

When his fingers teasingly traced my hand before he pulled the chalk free from my grip, a faint gasp escaped my lips. He placed the chalk on the easel shelf and turned me slowly around to face him. An unusual hunger dilated his eyes. He interlocked his fingers with mine regardless of the wet paint that I now shared with him. His lips wandered very close to mine and brushed them faintly enough to make me yearn for more. I closed my eyes, recalling the kiss the night before. Stefan's mouth moved across my cheek and grazed my ear as he whispered my name. I licked my dry lips as my breathing amplified.

"Ella," he playfully repeated then drew back.

My head lifted to face him, and I saw the corner of his mouth raise in his traditional half-smile. *A cruel tease.* I didn't wait for him to continue his game and immediately reached for his shirt, pulling him to me. His lips were ready, unexpectedly urgent in the kiss. When his arms fully engulfed me and brought me tightly against his chest, immeasurable strength and passion surfaced. An unquenchable thirst had been tapped as the kiss lasted several minutes.

It was the most compelling feeling I had ever experienced. I wanted more but backed away, stunned by the overwhelming sensation.

Facing each other, nearly out of breath, I lowered my eyes unable to speak. My lips quivered as I replayed the last few minutes in my mind, and when I peered back up at him, blue and green fingerprints appeared all over his neck and face. I couldn't help but laugh.

"Oh, no." I chuckled as I pointed out the colored paint that not only covered Stefan's skin but his nice clothes from where my painting shirt had pressed against him as well.

Instead of getting mad, he seemed determined to get even, swiping his finger against the pallet and rubbing a purple streak down my nose. When I went for the wet paint on the pallet, this most romantic spell suddenly turned into a paint war with drops of different colors flying in all directions. We were laughing so hard, that when a knock came at the door, we weren't really sure it was a knock until it repeated, only louder.

I panicked. I could not get caught up here and ran to hide behind the corner cabinet. As Stefan cracked the door, I peeked just enough to see confusion cover Johann's face. He deliberately stretched his neck for a better view of the room, so I recoiled further out of sight.

"Your mother is requesting your presence, sir."

"Let her know I'll be there shortly," Stefan laughed as he spoke, "After I clean up, of course."

"S-sir," I heard Johann stutter, "would you like me to have the room cleaned?" Without the ability to see them, I was sure Johann referred to the paint that had been flipped in all directions, barely touching the canvas. I giggled quietly to myself.

Stefan addressed it quickly, "Oh—no. Thank you, Johann, I'm experimenting with a new technique. I'll take care of it".

"Of course, sir," his tone sounded doubtful. "I will let your mother know you are on your way."

The door clicked shut. Stefan was immediately at my side as I burst out laughing, "I'm going to get fired . . . again!"

He grabbed me tightly. I couldn't move, but I didn't want to, either.

"Please, stay here." Stefan beamed, but there was a twinge of seriousness in his tone. "Stay here and live in the art room where I can find you every day."

"Oh, Stefan," I groaned, "if only life were that simple." I wiggled free.

Not that I didn't want his arms around me, I just feared who the next intruder could be. I grabbed a wet rag and started wiping my face.

"It can be . . ." he suggested.

Suddenly, Frau Franke was calling Stefan's name down the hall. I froze as he rushed to the door. "One moment, Mother, I will be there shortly."

Stefan turned and despite his reassuring smile on his way to the back closet, I subtly shuffled toward the safety of my original hiding place and watched with admiration as Stefan removed his shirt, his bare chest rising and falling before he covered it with a clean one. It was hard to believe a man as beautiful as Stefan would even glance in my direction.

He caught me watching him. His smile broadened, then he winked and left the room. I stood there silently; the happiness clearly departed with him. I finished washing my face but could not get his words out of my mind and added my own. "Life will never be that simple."

I knew as long as Stefan was a Franke, we would never be able to get away from the talons of his mother and the aspirations of his father. I wanted to believe there was a future for us. In fact, it surprised me how badly I suddenly wanted it. Yet, I was a realist—maybe even a pessimist. How long could we go on pretending this . . . whatever *this* was . . . could be headed somewhere? I quickly cleaned up and slipped out unseen.

Chapter Thirty-three

June had historically been a beautiful time in Berlin. Despite the broken buildings and general lack of color, it had its possibilities, but you would have to pretend there was no wall, no soldiers, no guns, and no death.

Wild hop sprouted through cracks in the sidewalks. Common hop, an ingredient for homemade beer, flourished in between concrete building slabs. Wild berry grew against fences, and the open market would finally have tulips and daisies for sale. Flowers were a luxury few could afford; men would buy them for their wives to celebrate a *Jahrestag,* symbolic of their years together, lovers would exchange them, and lucky for me, Frau Franke demanded fresh flowers throughout her home all summer long.

It might have been that nothing had actually changed around me, except now I viewed the world through the rose-colored glasses called "love", but it did seem, overall, things weren't as depressing as the previous winter had been. Even border shootings seemed to slow down for some reason, or we just didn't hear about them; either way, life appeared enjoyable again.

Despite my current interruption from pursuing freedom, I still often thought of my future. I had less than three months of service due to the Frankes. I didn't know if I wanted to stay on after my obligation was fulfilled or try something else, assuming another employer would hire me.

Since Stefan and I met so often in secret, it almost didn't seem like a real relationship. Except for the times when we were truly alone. Those were the times I felt confident in his love and gained strength from his certainty.

"Keep your eyes closed, Ella. Don't peek." Stefan held my hand and guided me forward with every word. "It's close. There are seven small but wide steps coming up, be careful."

I inched closer and felt the first one tap my shoe to a stop. "Don't let me fall." I put my free hand out, ready to catch myself if I did.

"I would never let you fall." He reached for both my hands now and gently led me past the bumps and to the top. My sense of smell came alive. A strong floral aroma erupted all around me, but it wasn't merely one type of scent. It was a mysterious mixture of many.

"OK, you can remove the blindfold."

I reached up and pulled the handkerchief off my face. It took a minute for my eyes to readjust to the bright lights of a noonday sun. Instantly, color consumed me in every direction. The foliage and blooms were breathtaking as far out as I could see. I never knew such beauty existed within the borders of my limited world.

Stefan turned me slightly to the left where a white-columned structure emerged. I held my breath as my eyes gazed over its grand design. A dozen arched niches sheltered perfectly chiseled basins as sculptures of children and animals appeared like lattices along a cascade of flowing water.

I remained motionless, except for my eyes. "Oh, Stefan, where are we?"

He smiled, seemingly pleased his surprise was successful. "Volkspark. The Fairy Tale Fountain."

A warm breeze picked up and kissed my face as I engraved the word into my memory. "Fairytales, . . ." I whispered. "It's so beautiful!"

From behind, Stefan wrapped both his arms around me as his lips brushed against my cheek. I could not imagine another moment that would possibly make me happier. Everything seemed perfect.

"It's Hansel and Gretel!" I pointed to the statues that greeted us first.

"Yes," Stefan added, "and Snow White, Little Red Riding Hood, and Rübezahl. He's just through that opening in the brush to the right."

After stepping up a short walkway, a full-size statue appeared. I brushed my hand over the spirited face and flowing beard of one of my favorite childhood characters, Rübezahl, a story that flooded my mind with memories of Mama and Josef, the three of us huddled in delight over the mountain man's adventures. I stopped suddenly.

"We are still in Berlin?" I caught sight of a brick building nearby.

"Yes, between Friedrichshain and Prenzlauer."

"This is—" I inhaled deeply unable to finish my sentence. How could I have not known such a treasured gift was so close? The sweet smell of pollen encircled me in every direction. I squeezed Stefan's hand.

"Thank you." I reached down and plucked a cluster of forget-me-nots bundled in a flower patch. Tears filled my eyes as I recalled the last time I held them in my hands.

"The best part is yet to come, Ella." Stefan winked.

It was hard to even imagine anything better. He held my hand again and led me under the intimidating stone arches where antlered deer reigned from above and past another circular fountain centered in stone.

"This mountain here" —Stefan pointed to a large hill dotted with chestnut trees and wild brush— "is called *Mont Klamott"* He smiled. "It's not really a mountain, it's *Schutteberge."*

"War rubble?"

"Yes, as well as the smaller one over there."

Stunned, I remained speechless. How could something so remarkable have come from such destruction? Stefan placed his free hand on my lower back and guided me past a heaping pile of rocks. The vegetation became much thicker the farther we walked.

"There were flak towers and bunkers built back here. Most of the bunkers were broken down after the war. You can barely recognize any parts of buildings anymore, but look at this—"

We entered the hidden center of a garden completely filled with bishop's weed. The wildflower was in full bloom. It could be found all over Berlin in the summer, but I'd never seen so many all in one place. Thousands of little white puffs of corn surfaced, intertwined with random splashes of red, blue, even green and purple.

"Oh, Stefan! This is breathtaking."

He laughed. "Look closer."

I stepped forward and was brushing my hand over the top of the flowers when suddenly they moved; the petals started to fly away. It startled me so much that I jumped back until I detected the flutter of the butterfly wings.

There were more than I could count.

I stood still. Some flapped above my head, others moved back to the flowers, while some were attracted to the bright-yellow shade of my dress. I lifted my arm gradually. I marveled as a sole butterfly stood completely still on my wrist. It moved its wings slowly as though more for balance than flight.

I had never been this close to one. The black antennas swayed with the breeze. The blue color spread across the wings matched Stefan's eyes and extended all the way to the edge where only a small black streak outlined the magnificent spread. I wanted to cry. It was the most beautiful thing I had ever seen.

I reached for Stefan's hand. I knew my touch alone could convey the thrill that resonated, but I gently squeezed so there would be no question. No other gift he could offer would ever compare. This was priceless.

We spent the rest of the day wandering through the extraordinary gardens Stefan's *Kindermädchen* introduced him and Katharina to when they were children. It was one of his favorite places in Berlin, and now it had become one of mine.

Along with flowers and simple pleasures, June also brought word from Anton and Josef—something I eagerly anticipated since my last letter went out in March. When Mama G gave it to me, I raced toward my room, ripping the long-awaited letter from the envelope, letting the excess fall to the floor as I dove with little propriety onto the bed. I had to stop myself from reading too fast, every word fueled a hunger for the next.

8 April 1963
Dearest Ella,

Despite your circumstances and our separation, you sound well. We were happy to hear you are employed and have friends. We have also had the good fortune to become well acquainted with some wonderful people here but none compare to my best friend, Ella!

I miss our walks and talks. I miss the way you wrinkle your nose and how your eyelashes flutter faster the angrier you get. I miss your fiery temper and the way you made me feel better when I was down. I know you said to be careful in our correspondence, but I need to know that you are trying to find a way here . . . home. I need to have hope you will be with us shortly. I'll do all I can to assist you. Please let me know what I can do.

Josef misses and loves you. He has a girlfriend. He didn't want me to tell you because he said you would be upset but I know you are only being protective. Don't worry, Ella. He is a good boy, and it is only a crush. I'm taking good care of him. He is happy and does not lack anything. Imagine that, Ella, we have a home, food, and comforts. The only thing we are missing is you.

I've heard of places we can see over the wall-- would you meet us? Can we plan a day and a time that we will all be there? I know it takes a while to get a post so I'm going to say watch for me across from Potsdamer Platz on July 3rd, six o'clock in the evening. I need to see your face, Ella.

With Love,
Anton

I folded the letter and put it in my pocket. It warmed my heart to know they were doing quite well . . . then conflict arose. Anton's pin never resurfaced. The thought of how careless I had been with his one gift crushed me. Anton would be hurt if he knew.

Anton . . . even his name had started to sound foreign. Too much time had passed since I saw his face. So many questions . . . would I be as happy if I were in the West now? Things had changed. Stefan and I had now courted for two full months. They were the most joyful months I'd had in years.

I could never forget my life with Anton, but the memories were all I had. Yet, knowing his feelings were still strong and that he thought of me too and wanted to see me, worried me. *Are Anton and I only meant to be friends, or am I supposed to seek my fate in the West?* These thoughts clouded my mind; I tried hard to keep them hidden. *I'm happy with Stefan.*

I finally felt I had something worth living for.

During our time together, Stefan continually searched for new ways to surprise me. Even though we had busy work schedules, there wasn't a day I wasn't reminded of him. Occasionally, I would reach onto my shelf at work to retrieve my apron and find a lily blossom or a stem of forget-me-nots. Stefan noticed the day he showed me Volkspark that with all the blooms I could take home with me, it was the stunning blue forget-me-not flower I clung to the longest.

While Stefan and I kept our affections hidden in the house so as not to alert his parents, I couldn't keep my positive countenance from Lena and Johann. I had become a different person. I still exhibited moments of sass, but rarely a day went by when I didn't smile. Stefan made me happy. So happy, any possible thoughts of trying to escape again were set aside.

A week after reading Anton's letter, I became unexpectedly detained late in the parlor. As I attended to the neglected stain from a recent business lunch, I contemplated my thoughts. Guilt consumed me. *Josef is my brother. The one remaining family member I have left. I should be the one providing for him and caring for him and seeing him have feelings for a girl.* The more remorse I bore, the harder I scrubbed, but the stubborn spread of the dated red wine against the white plush carpet had made it nearly impossible.

I tossed the linen into a bowl of cleaning suds, splashing the contents in all directions. *I hate thoughts of regret. Am I being foolish these last eight weeks? Playing a role that has no possibilities?* This was hardly the way I wanted to feel when I met Stefan tonight at Dafne's. I glanced at the stain once more. *Of course, if I can't get this out, I might be here all night.*

"Stefan! Where are you going?" Frau Franke's sharp tone caught me off guard. I held my breath and moved closer to the door, unseen. She must be in the nearby corridor.

"I have plans." It was obvious he did not know of my delay.

"What plans?" I envisioned the way her lips curled as the words were spoken.

"Nothing is being delivered tonight, and the Huhn body is under process. I can't do anything until morning."

"This is the third time this week you've been out late . . . why?"

I inhaled sharply at what I'd overheard. My face felt moist . . . *does she know?*

"I'm only meeting friends. I still have a life outside of the mortuary, Mother."

"But Markus is on his way here."

"He's not coming for business. He's having dinner with you and Father."

"It's always business, Stefan. He's asked to speak with you."

"About what?"

"He only mentioned a program he's working on."

"I won't be gone long."

"I want you here."

"I'll see you in the morning."

I heard the front door close shut and knew Stefan was headed to Dafne's. I also knew Frau Franke enough to know this would not settle well. Fearful she could somehow sense that her conversation was overheard, I moved slowly back to the floor. My mind whirled with possibilities, all with the same conclusion. She must know Stefan is seeing someone, but did she have her suspicions on whom?

"Johann!"

I froze on my knees. Frau Franke was not finished.

"I need to see the new grounds boy, Thomas. Send him to me immediately, please."

I moved once again to the door at great risk. If she knew I was there, it could be my demise. The hair on my arms went rigid, just the idea that the destroying angel was so close was frightening, but I needed to know what she was up to. I bit my lip and waited. Within a few minutes, footsteps approached.

"Frau Franke, you asked for me?"

"Yes," She hesitated. I could not see them but assumed she was assessing him. "I have a task for you, but first, you must promise to keep this between us."

I could sense the boy's fear even without seeing his face. Frau Franke was intimidating and powerful.

"Y-yes, Frau Franke. What would you like me to do?"

"I would like you to follow my son." My face heated up. *Am I imagining this?*

She continued, "I want to know where he goes and who he sees."

I cupped my hand over my mouth to stop myself from gasping aloud, but truthfully, I wanted to scream.

"Stefan?" the boy questioned, even though she only had one son.

"Yes, go now. He may only be a few minutes ahead. He likes to go to the cafes down on Pappelallee. Check there first." I fought the urge to cry.

She must've handed him something, money possibly. I could hear him thanking her with a lift in his voice. It must've been ample enough to give him much encouragement.

I immediately took a seat in the parlor and tried to process what just happened. She was having Stefan followed now, maybe only for tonight, maybe always. I wasn't sure, but I did know that this changed everything.

Reaching for the handkerchief in my pocket to wipe my face, I glanced at the stain. It was no longer my priority as I pushed a chair slightly to the left for obscurity. Pacing the room, I waited a good twenty minutes before I grabbed the cleaning supplies and walked out. The hall was empty. The sigh I released was both for relief and composure as I entered the staff room, but something didn't feel right.

"Fräulein Kühn?"

It was her. She came from behind.

I pretended I did not hear her and fumbled around in my box as I reached for nothing.

"Fräulein Kühn?" The tone was louder and firmer.

I turned but did not look her in the eyes. "Yes, Frau Franke?"

"Have you seen Fräulein Kerner tonight?"

"Lena?" I barely choked out the name.

"Yes! I need to speak with her immediately." I wondered how Lena played into her plan.

"I—I think she left when her shift ended. I didn't see her though. I had a job I needed to complete."

"Very well." She scanned me as if she could see through me. I shifted in my stance.

"If you see her in the morning, make sure she knows I need to speak to her."

"Yes, Frau Franke, I will." It came out quietly, almost a whisper, but she didn't flinch.

She continued to stare. My breath caught in my throat until she spoke again.

"Goodnight."

Something was definitely up. She'd never said goodnight to me before . . . ever. *Does she know? Will she interrogate Lena for answers?* Questions consumed my thoughts. I was sure she could read my mind.

Discouraged, I stepped outside. It was impossible to see Stefan without being exposed. If this boy had already located Stefan at Dafne's, I could not risk showing up only to tell him he was being watched. Making my way to the street opposite the café, I stayed far from the streetlamp and watched with jealously as patrons moved in and out.

I did not see Stefan but imagined him inside wondering where I was. I did not see the spy either, but I only had a faded memory of him when we were introduced a month ago. Taking a seat on a nearby bench, I wanted to cry. I knew my relationship with Stefan was fragile, I just didn't want to admit how much.

I rubbed my sweaty hands on my dress and stood up from the bench. My head hurt from all the thinking. Frau Franke had to suspect something, *but does she know it's me?* That's probably why she wanted to talk to Lena.

Inga Franke was very smart and very manipulative. If she had been born a man, I imagined *her* in charge of Stasi instead of Mielke. She had a gift for terror and coercion. My head dropped heavily into my hands.

After another miserable thirty minutes, I noticed a man and woman approaching my direction. They held hands as they strolled along the sidewalk. This was it. Maybe I could ask them to pretend they were Stefan's friends, at least for tonight. It was imperative I get a message to him somehow. If he didn't see me here, he might feel the need to go to my apartment, and then such info could get back to Frau Franke as well. I didn't think she knew where I lived, but again, her little spy could be tasked to find out who does.

Completely out of my element, I stood in their path. "Excuse me?" I murmured just enough to draw the couple's attention as they approached.

"Ja?" The man held the woman back apprehensively. His body subtly wedged between us. My petite form was hardly threatening, but size didn't necessarily mean anything here, deceit had no standard in the East. They stopped directly in front of me.

"I'm so sorry to interrupt." My apology was genuine. It could have been the pleading in my eyes or the quiver in my voice that induced sympathy, but as I explained my predicament, they were more than happy to help.

After giving them Stefan's description and the message to be relayed, they disappeared inside Dafne's. I wanted to wait and hear the result of the exchange but was frightened it would all lead back to me somehow. I quickly left the area and boarded the bus home.

Completely disheartened, I entered my front door alone. This routine had become part of the excitement as we dated. Stefan always made sure I arrived home safely, and even though we didn't like saying good-night, the moment was anticipated all day.

This morning when I awoke, a completely different scenario was pictured for tonight. I hated the outcome. Once inside, without a word to Mama G, my dampened spirit fell hopelessly in bed. *How will I ever see or talk to Stefan again without getting caught?* Everything I trusted about my relationship with him seemed to suddenly swallow up and disappear.

The next day, I woke up physically sick and spent most of the morning at the base of the toilet until there was nothing left to heave. I knew being late or absent was not an option—on top of everything else that was happening—yet I could barely lift my head.

"Please, Ella, go back to bed." Mama G held my hair back as I puked air once again.

"Mama," I groaned and laid my head against the basin. "I can't. I'll lose my job." Mama moistened a piece of cloth and wiped my brow.

The chill was a nice contrast to my rising temperature.

Mama G insisted I stay, even as I pulled my coat on in 80-degree weather. She did not know my dilemma or Frau Franke.

"I'll go tell Frau Franke myself." She stomped her foot with both hands on her hips. Even as weak as I was, this made me smile. Mama G was barely five feet tall, but her spirit was the height of a giant.

Knowing this would only make things worse, I declined but accepted her licorice tea and mother's kiss on my way out.

I arrived to work nearly an hour late, but once Johann saw my appearance, he knew it was unintentional. My face was as pale as someone with my skin color could get and my eyes dull and clouded. When I walked, my gait appeared slow and unsteady, but I was here.

I hoped with all my might that I could get through the day without having to face any Franke, including Stefan. I didn't want him to see me under such unappealing circumstances, . . . and I especially did not want his mother to see us together at all.

I worked slowly and steadily. By midafternoon, I realized I had fallen a good two hours behind. I hadn't seen Lena since early morning when I had passed on to her Frau Franke's request, and I was curious as to why she was absent. It hurt my head to think, so I didn't dwell on it long.

Entering the library, I started in on my tasks but was unaware someone watched me from the shadows. As I reached to turn on a lamp, hands appeared, and I was swiftly transported to the veranda. Startled, I couldn't even scream.

It was Stefan. I broke down crying, my body nearly collapsing from the stress.

He quickly closed the door and held me close. I did not want him to see me this way, but I also yearned for his touch. Without saying anything, he simply let me cry.

When I finally raised my eyes, I didn't see the face of a man who was disappointed or repulsed but one whose own eyes were full of worry and concern.

"Ella, we will be OK."

I couldn't get a single word out before starting to cry again. It was as though every thought, every feeling, every discouraging moment of my seventeen years came out in that one instant. Stefan pulled me in tightly. He rubbed the back of my head gently with his hand, his touch soothing and kind.

"You need to go, Stefan," I whispered. "We could be watched right now."

"I don't care. My only concern is you."

"I'm not ready to lose you, please go."

Stefan cradled my face in his hands and forced my view upward. "Ella, you will never lose me." I started to cry again. His lips kissed my eyes. "Please don't cry. It will all work out somehow. Meet me Saturday night at Harald's in Prenzlauer Berg."

I lowered my face. "We can't."

"I will lose the spy, Ella. I'll make sure no one knows where I'm going. We'll figure things out then." Stefan lifted my chin, his lips brushed across my cheek where they ended next to my ear. "Promise me you will be there, Ella." His whisper tickled but did not bring the same fluttering of my heart as previously. The heaviness in my chest refused to let me enjoy it.

"I promise." It was a weak attempt, yet I wanted it as much as he did.

Stefan's lips lingered on my cheek. "Stay here, love. Wait a few minutes after I leave before you return." He squeezed my hand then he was gone.

It was more than a few minutes. My limbs were futile and weak, caused nearly as much by the illness as the woe. By the time I walked to the bus stop that evening, it was well after dark—but my chores were complete.

When Saturday night arrived, I had fully recovered physically, but my emotional state was still in turmoil. I stepped into Harald's shortly after seven p.m. My hat hung low and tight over my ears. The pub wasn't crowded, and feeling safe enough to remove it, I wandered to a quiet corner near the back. I knew Stefan would find me.

It was nearly seven-thirty when a grungy-looking man in a ripped coat twice his size slid into the seat across from me. When he went to remove his poor excuse of a hat, I could see the man's hands and face were caked in dirt.

"I-I'm sorry, this seat is . . ." A familiar pair of blue eyes stared back at me from underneath the blond tousled hair. My surprise turned to a half-smile, half-laugh. It was the first time I'd felt this way since this whole nightmare began. Stefan grabbed my hands across the table and squeezed.

"I told you I would lose the spy." He winked.

"I think he's still waiting for me to come out of the bathroom back at the S Bahn. I took two buses and a sidecar to get here . . . and a romp in the dirt." Stefan grinned wider. "I promise, Ella, we are alone." I sighed, with guarded relief.

He removed the filthy layers and stuffed them under the table. "I paid some Obdachlose for this," referring to the coat.

I couldn't imagine it even being worth a pfennig to the homeless man either. It smelled awful.

"Stefan?" I went directly to the point. "Do you think she suspects it's me?"

Stefan said no, but his head moved in the wrong direction. My face twisted confused. He continued, "I don't think so, but . . ."

"But what?"

He said it before he realized how it would affect me, "My mother is quite sharp."

The panic on my face returned. I already knew this.

"What if she set us up?" I peered around frightened. "What if she only made us think she had one spy but really has several?" I fought the tears from coming. All the happiness from being together seemed to dissolve in a matter of minutes.

Stefan scooted his chair around next to me, "We are safe." His arms found their way around my shoulders and pulled my body securely next to him. My heart wanted to stay, but my head told me to leave.

"I'm sorry, Stefan . . . this is too hard!" I stood up. Stefan reached for my hands, but I pulled them away. "I can't live this way." I rushed to the door before he even realized what happened.

"Ella!" His cries faded as I ran harder. I wasn't even sure what direction to go, just anywhere away from him.

Once again in the security of the only place and people I knew were real, I locked myself in my bedroom. Only Mama G wasn't about to let me have an additional moment of pity. She knocked on my door until I opened it then proceeded to sit on my bed and vowed to stay there until I told her what happened. She had always been a great listener.

"Two buses, a sidecar, and a disguise! What kind of life is that?" I cried, frustrated by the end of the story. She patted her hand on my knee.

"Two buses, a sidecar, and a disguise? That tells me someone tried very hard to be with you tonight." She sighed and then walked out. I buried my head into my pillow. Uncertainty and longing waged a war in my mind. *I want to be with him too.*

The next morning, I found a note in my box. The seal on the envelope confirmed that it hadn't been tampered with. I set it in my pocket and waited until I was in the water closet before I read it.

Ella,

I can't tell you how much it breaks my heart to not only see you discouraged but not see you at all. These last couple of months have meant so much to me. Not one day goes by where you are not in my every thought.

I know this relationship is difficult. I asked you once to not lose faith in me regarding my duty, but I ask again about us as well.

I'm doing what I can to make changes. I can't disclose the details

*yet. I know I have no right to ask you to be patient or wait this out,
but I'm hoping you will. Know that I love you and am faithfully yours.*

The letter was not signed. I understood why. I wanted to believe Stefan's words. There was so little good in my life, that it was difficult to suddenly imagine that would change.

"Ella." Lena caught me the moment I walked out of the water closet. I folded the envelope tightly in my fingers.

"Ella, I need to talk to you." She gently pushed me back in and closed the door behind us. Her face confirmed what I already knew.

"Frau Franke has suspicions," she whispered tensely. "You know when you told me she wanted to see me?" I nodded. "Well, she was asking all sorts of questions about you . . . personal questions."

My throat was dry. I couldn't speak as she continued, "I told her I didn't know anything, and I'll never say, but you two—you need to be careful . . . she is . . ."

"I know, Lena." I wiped my forehead. "I know." I opened the door to walk out, but Lena grabbed my wrist.

"She has something of yours."

"What do you mean?" My eyebrows curved with confusion. How could she have anything of mine?

"She has your . . ." Lena pointed to my dress. "She has Anton's pin."

I rapidly closed the door again and moved closer. "How do you know? How did she get it?" I peppered questions angrily, not realizing how it appeared to Lena.

"Ella, stop." She grabbed my arms softly. "I don't know, she just held it up when she was talking to me and said she found it in the mortuary and was sure it belongs to the woman who is seeing Stefan. I told her I didn't know anything."

I leaned against the wall. I was suddenly very sick. "She knows."

Lena sighed. "Maybe she's guessing, maybe it's why she hasn't come to you yet. She's not sure."

"She knows," I repeated then walked out in a daze.

I knew what had to be done but could barely face the thought. *Stefan and I can no longer be together.*

CHAPTER THIRTY-FOUR

"Hey, beautiful." Stefan grabbed my hand and pulled me through the heavy doors into the mortuary. I didn't even get a word out before his lips covered mine.

"Stefan!" I protested once I could breathe. "Stop, please." My conversation with Lena was still fresh on my mind despite the few days that had passed. "Your parents—"

Stefan ignored my pleas and kissed me again. It had been over a week since the night in Prenzlauer, and while I tried to be reasonable, my heart wanted this as badly as he did.

"Stop . . . your mother!"

"They're gone," he said and kissed me again.

I could feel the desperation in his touch as he pressed against me. I missed him more than I could bear. After several minutes, Stefan pulled back. "Spend some time with me today, Ella. I've missed you."

Tempted, I bit my lip.

He squeezed my hands. "Please?"

I wanted to be near him more than anything, but I was desperate to tell him what I knew. "We need to talk." I struggled to focus again on what lie ahead.

"We can talk—" Stefan smiled slyly, "—and kiss." It was a sexy look. He was incredibly attractive when he appeared that way.

"I have to work." I was trying very hard to resist, conflicted. With his parents gone, I wanted to be with him, but I also knew this could be our last time. It was painful.

"I'll take care of it. Wait here." Stefan disappeared momentarily.

"What are you up to?" I questioned upon his return.

"Nothing!" He grinned again. This was the first time our conversation felt somewhat normal again.

"They can do without you for today. I want your help in here."

"What help?"

"I need to be next to you." He pulled me in again, his lips melting against mine. My whole body shuddered. It had been too long since he touched me last. I placed my hand against his chest with barely enough pressure to halt him momentarily.

"What did you say out there?"

"I told Johann I needed your help, and you would be unavailable this afternoon and . . . he would need to have your duties covered." Stefan kissed my neck then spoke up, "A very strange expression was on his face, does he know?"

I bit my lip, "Yes, he and Lena are the only ones unless you make it obvious to the rest of the staff by always getting me out of my duties!" I pushed him back and forced him to face me. "Stefan, your mother is suspicious of me."

"I'm sure she doesn't know." His hands rubbed my shoulders.

"She has my pin!" I cried. His fingers stopped moving.

"Your shield pin?" He pointed to where I wore it on my dress. "Yes." Tears started to form.

"How? How did she get it?"

"She found it in here and told Lena she knows it belongs to the woman who is seeing you."

Stefan stepped back. He put his hand to his forehead as if to think it through. He reached for me again and held me.

"I will get your pin back, Ella. I promise. She won't know it was you." Stefan kissed my nose.

I sighed as Stefan caressed my neck with his lips. My body hovered between weakness and exhilaration. Just the touch of his skin against mine created sensations I never knew existed, but his hands yearned for something more. I wasn't ready. Maybe intimacy scared me, or maybe I was old-fashioned, but as I recalled the Kühns and how much they truly loved each other, it just seemed simple. Why not give the most personal part of you only to the one you're committed to forever?

The likelihood of marrying Stefan was slim. I knew this even as I found myself falling for him. Although I dreamt of being Frau Stefan Franke, we both knew his parents would never let that happen.

He grabbed my hand and led me down the hall. I spent very little time in the mortuary. It wasn't my favorite place to be, but if it meant being close to Stefan, nothing else mattered today.

"What are you working on today?" I asked.

"Let's not talk about work, mine or yours." He winked as he closed the door to his office and led me to the couch.

I smiled as Stefan took a seat next to me. We were truly alone. It was hard for me to really believe it was possible. All I wanted to do was stare at him, study every detail, memorize every line, but Stefan had other plans.

His hands went immediately to my face and drew me in as his kiss stretched over several minutes. His lips sparked a heat that ran the length of my body and tingled my toes. Desire pulsed through his fingers as they roamed over my shoulders, down my arms, and clutched my waist. As his grip intensified, my chest tightened, and my breath shortened.

I wanted him more now than ever before, but I couldn't. I placed my hands gently over his to stop them from sliding upward. He smiled through the kiss.

This had become routine.

"Ella, . . ." Stefan whispered, "you drive me crazy."

"You drive *me* crazy!" I groaned. The temptation to concede drifted close to the edge.

"Then why do we stop?" he questioned honestly. His thumb brushed against my lips, paralyzing me, as usual. "Do you love me, Ella?"

My forehead wrinkled. "Of course, Stefan." I was surprised by his question. "You know this!"

"Then why don't we—" His hands squeezed mine.

"Because . . ." I cut him off. I knew exactly what he was asking. My face grew serious. I bit my bottom lip hard. My eyes blurred, and the room seemed to get very small. I wasn't sure I could finish.

"Because . . ." Stefan encouraged.

I took a deep breath. "—because that's a really personal thing for me and—" Stefan watched me carefully as I continued, "—I only want to share it with the man I will be married to."

He showed obvious surprise by my statement. His forehead wrinkled with confusion as he drew back. "What do you mean?"

I could sense his frustration and I turned away. I didn't want it to come out this way.

"Forget it, Stefan," I reasoned, still unable to face him. "I don't want to ruin this day. It means a lot to me." In my heart, I spurned reality, but in my mind, this could very well be our last time together, and I wanted it to be perfect.

"No." He pushed with apparent exhaustion over the subject. "I want to know what you mean by that."

I finally faced him again, but hesitated. I knew the price of honesty already, but I couldn't stop myself. "We both know there's no way you can marry me."

"We do?"

"Yes!" Now it was my turn to be frustrated. "How can you know all that's happened with your mother recently and not believe she'd use every ounce of her strength to stop us from being together if she knew it was me."

Stefan appeared wounded. "I don't care what she thinks."

"In secret," I fired back.

I inhaled swiftly, it had been a long time since I'd used a sharp tone with Stefan and the stunned expression on his face confirmed our joint uncertainty. The subsequent stillness was thick, but far from calm.

Stefan stood up and walked back toward the window. He left the curtain untouched and pushed his fingers through his long bangs, a sign he was upset.

I tried to be rational, but even as I said it, the words sounded harsh. "We will always be sneaking around because whether you like it or not, your parents will never allow you to be with me. It's why we hide in the first place, right? Why you had to wear a disguise a week ago and why you're afraid to tell them how you really feel." It all rolled out at once. The room got very quiet again.

"Stefan?" I stood up to join him, but on my approach, the atmosphere changed. Even the air that swirled with warmth and love just moments ago, bristled like icicles the closer I came. Leaving some distance between us, I stopped, his silence bothered me. "Am I not telling the truth?"

He didn't answer. I reached out and touched his arm, but he didn't react. My chest physically ached. I longed for him to stop thinking, stop being angry, and just hold me and protect what little time and moments we had left. Stefan's gaze remained detached as he whispered, "This really isn't about my parents, is it Ella?"

"What are you talking about?" I cried defensively.

He continued, "You have no plans of staying in East Berlin, do you?"

"Where is this coming from, Stefan?" I was surprised and worried. I was afraid he had somehow read my mind concerning Anton's last letter.

"You said it yourself. You attempted to escape twice before." His eyes glazed over. *How did this get turned around to me?* I was stunned.

"Yes, my family is in the West. Yes, I miss them. Josef is my brother."

"What about Anton?"

"What about him?"

"You carry his letter everywhere. Don't you think I notice you reading it so often it's nearly in shreds? Do you want to be with him?"

My eyes stung with tears. The very thought of them brought my tender feelings to the surface. Stefan saw through me.

"You love him, don't you?"

"Stefan, I've known Anton since I was six. We only had each other in the orphanage. He watched out for me, and I, him."

"But it's more than that, isn't it?"

"I don't know. I haven't even spoken to him in person for almost two years!"

"Is the pin from him?"

I lowered my head.

"The shield you hold close to your heart?" Tears slid down my cheeks.

"Have you kissed him?"

My hesitation answered his questions. Stefan tucked his shirt back into his slacks and walked over to his desk.

"I'm sorry, Ella," his voice suddenly formal, "I forgot I need to get some paperwork finished."

I stood still. I was shocked at how this afternoon turned so quickly.

"Why are you doing this?" I wiped the tears off my face and walked to the edge of his desk as he sat down.

He ignored me.

I slammed my fist on his desk. He glanced up at me, the deep blue in his eyes turned to ice. They were unsympathetic and cruel—the part of Stefan I wished no longer existed. He appeared hurt and betrayed. I was confused. How could he be injured from the past—by a memory, *my* memory?

"OK, I'll leave you alone—" Anger consumed me. Tears continued to flow down my face, my eyelashes blinking rapidly, "—but Stefan, you have no idea what it's like to be alone. You've had a family your whole life. I've always been abandoned . . . my real parents didn't want me. My adoptive parents died, and when Anton and Josef left, I literally wished to die. Before you go punishing me for my feelings and join the list of deserters, you should know I've fallen for you. I love everything about you but can never see a future for us because of *your* parents. They would have me dragged away before they would ever see us together . . . and you know I'm right!"

I slammed the door behind me.

When Johann saw me polishing the silver in the dining room less than an hour later, he attempted to inquire why until he saw my tear-stained cheeks. He quickly retrieved Lena, and when she came to me, I cried hard in her arms. She knew enough to not even ask.

Relationships are complicated. Ours was doomed from the beginning; I just didn't want to believe it.

CHAPTER THIRTY-FIVE

For some reason, the next several weeks got very busy for all of us. The Frankes' lower-level rooms had never been quite this clean in all the time I had worked there. From the crown molding on the ceiling to the smallest piece of china, I worked until my fingers bled. Then I started again the next day.

During this time, Frau Franke had also found countless reasons to be nearby. Her meaningless tasks in the rooms I cleaned were more out of annoyance than necessity. We rarely spoke, her silent scrutiny loitered in every corner. I knew she watched me, but now it didn't matter. I had nothing to hide.

The chimneys for the crematorium smoked nonstop due to a larger-than-normal delivery the day after Stefan and I got into our argument. It was a horrible smell. As the summer heat increased, it felt as though my hair and clothes carried the permeating odor the moment I stepped on the property.

Suddenly consumed by images of sorrow and death, the beauty I'd seen a short time ago seemed to shrivel up next to my crushed heart.

Now everything appeared empty, black, and gray once again.

The social visitations also increased to the point where there was a dignitary once or twice a week. Congress was on hiatus for the month, therefore, a greater variety of guests made appearances in the Franke home. Some notables arrived from neighboring communist countries, yet the greatest number of representatives derived from local leadership. Regardless of their origin, the home had become the center of all extravagant entertaining.

The first time I saw Stefan after the quarrel was in one of those very lunches. I tried to prepare myself for such an occurrence, but truthfully nothing ever could. Despite my intentional avoidance of contact, his eyes fell upon me. He watched my every move. It took all my strength to resist. I knew if I returned his look, everything would break. My body and soul, barely held together by my skin, would dissolve in front of everyone. It was unbearably difficult. Outside of the parlor, I scarcely functioned. The pretense was a game I no longer wanted to play.

Day or night, I could think of nothing but Stefan. *How could he profess such deep feelings for me then stop cold?* Was he still angry, hurt, or just being careful? Did he know I was under the watchful eye of his mother, or had he found a way to move on?

Inside the home, the few times we crossed, he appeared completely unaffected. His emotions were either well-hidden or easily cast aside. He never found a way to reach out to me or see me. Not at home, on the street, or even by letter. It was as if our entire existence together had been suddenly erased.

My fingers brushed across the number 74 shortly after I marked it on my mirror Wednesday morning, the 25th day of June 1963, . . . *74 days and I'll be done.* There was a time I considered staying on at the Frankes' only to see Stefan. Now I realized it could never happen. He would find a woman who would turn his world upside down. He'd court her and marry her under the approval of his parents, and I could not be there to watch that happen.

As I prepared to leave the apartment that morning, I found Mama G huddled up to her radio, and the voice of a reporter announced loud and clear:

"A twenty-one-gun salute welcomes President Kennedy as he steps onto German soil; a chance for the American president to meet the German people on his four-day trip that coincides with unique international developments with Western Europe on the brink of political change as the East Bloc falters in ideological disunity."

"Disunity is correct . . ." I kissed her on the cheek before I walked out.

Once I reached the Frankes', the whole staff was in a heightened mood over the news of the American president's arrival. I found it strange to be excited over something that had very little to do with us. Especially since he would not be coming to the eastern side of Berlin, all his speeches would be presented on the free side. Thus, no reason to celebrate.

I immediately went to work. The day before, I was advised we would have several honorable guests during lunch this afternoon. After I thoroughly cleaned the parlor, I met Lena in the kitchen, and we set about the arrangements for another display of refinements. Today, it would be roast pork knuckle with creamy brown gravy, small potatoes, and cauliflower.

As I removed the *Eisbein* from the oven, Lena's face lost color. I followed the direction of her eyes and there stood Stefan, just inside the kitchen door. *I can't do this at work.* I'd fought the urge to cry time and time again as I walked through this house every day since we argued.

Lena immediately excused herself. I shook my head and begged her not to leave. Stefan inched closer but kept a fair distance.

"Shouldn't you be with your guests?" I forced emotion out of my voice.

"This is my father's meeting. I need to talk to you."

"Why now?"

"I . . ." Stefan was more flustered than I'd ever seen. "I need to explain myself."

"I'm working." My response was cold.

"I know, but . . ." He leaned sideways, trying to make eye contact with me. I kept arranging the plates. This was too hard.

"Please look at me." He moved forward.

I turned my back.

"Why are you being stubborn?" he questioned, tersely.

I stood in front of the ice box for a moment. I could feel myself losing strength, yet I said nothing.

"I know I can be a jerk sometimes, but you are being cruel."

I swung around quickly and faced him. Angered by his words, I motioned to contradict. "You are taunting me."

"Not intentionally." Stefan moved closer but seemed to sense I wasn't ready. "When you said you didn't believe we had a future, Ella, it hurt. Then I feared you would try to leave again and . . ."

"And what?"

"I was jealous of Anton."

His words struck me hard. "Why?"

"Because . . ." Stefan's eyes fell, "because I know you share something special with him."

In silence, my irritation melted away.

"Please, Ella." His voice matched his pleading eyes, now burrowing into me.

My breath skipped, moved by his confession, but halted by reality. "It's too complicated, Stefan."

"It's worth the fight," he appealed. "You're worth the fight, Ella!"

I studied his face carefully. His sincerity tore my heart in opposite directions. "I don't know what to say," I cried, conflicted.

"They're ready for us, Ella." Lena peeked in tentatively. I stared anxiously at Stefan.

"We shouldn't be talking about this here anyway . . . please go," I whispered.

Stefan reached for my hand. I hungered for his touch. My eyes filled quickly.

"Promise we will talk later. We need to talk."

I nodded yes when I really meant no. I could never resist him.

"And El," he whispered, "I'm going to tell my parents today."

My eyes met his. I wanted to believe this would make everything better—to trust that what we shared was stronger than our opposition, but I knew the truth. I forced a smile, and even though he matched mine, I knew in my heart once he told them about us, he would never be mine.

Before Stefan left, he reached into his pocket and pulled something out. He held my palm open and placed Anton's tinnie pin in the center. I cried at the sight of it, and Stefan leaned in to kiss my cheek and walked out.

It took me a few minutes to compose myself after he left. I was a mess, torn between the return of both the shield and Stefan's presence at the same moment. Lena held me as she often had in the last few weeks. Sobs racked my body. I knew I needed to pull it together, but I could barely stop shaking. I couldn't think straight or focus. This was a terrible way to begin a work lunch.

"El, I will do the lunch, please sit down."

"No," I insisted stubbornly. "I can get through this. It's too big for one person."

I had very little energy but pretended I was fine. I clasped the tinnie pin on the inside of my dress and gripped it tightly on the outside. If ever I needed its strength, it would be this very moment.

I grabbed the tray of drinks and entered the dining room, my thoughts distracted. *Why did Stefan come right then when he knew I needed to serve? Maybe he doesn't realize how much his proximity affects me . . .just being next to him, smelling his cologne, and feeling his touch.*

He made me defenseless.

Suddenly I felt relieved knowing that Herr Franke himself was conducting this meeting. It was comforting to assume I wouldn't see Stefan's face again so soon.

Balancing the crowded drink tray, I pushed the door open with my back, my thoughts still far from reason. As I turned and took one brief glance at the nearest guest, terror choked me and before I could compose myself, the platter slipped through my hands and crashed alarmingly to the floor.

The deafening sound of shattering glass and gushing liquid erupted in all directions amidst the bellow of the one who took the brunt of it all.

I quickly fell to my knees to retrieve the shards of broken glass that littered the ground. "Please forgive me, sir," I begged. "I'm sorry."

"You should be, Fräulein!" The man who stood before me, growled as he examined his stained uniform.

"My sincerest apologies, sir." I continued to reach for broken pieces of crystal as the weight of every eye in the room descended upon me.

"You intentionally harmed an officer of the law!" Rage had surfaced in the man's tone.

"It wasn't intentional," I cried, barely able to look in his direction. "It was an accident. I'm sorry, I tripped."

I knew I hadn't tripped. It was the dreadful scar I'd hoped to never see again in my life staring back at me. I stood to wipe the man's coat with my apron when Colonel Anker roughly grabbed my wrist. My trembling hand dropped a fragment of glass.

The dining room had suddenly swelled with more occupants as the angry sounds amplified through the house. Stefan and Johann arrived the moment Colonel Anker shoved me backward to the floor.

Stefan stepped forward, his jaw protruding as his eyes flashed between me and the colonel. I subtly shook my head *no*. He stopped.

Johann came to me and helped me back up to my feet. I wasn't hurt, only concerned that all the attention had now been shifted to me.

"Don't go to her!" Colonel Anker barked. "I'm the one she offended."

"It was an accident," Stefan spoke up. His father shot him a strong look.

"It was on purpose, young Franke. You were not even present."

Johann quickly knelt and picked up the remaining pieces of glass cluttered around the colonel's boots then noticed one small piece had lodged into the colonel's hand.

"You are bleeding, sir." Johann pulled a linen napkin off the table and handed it to him. He snatched it heatedly.

"I want her arrested!"

Stefan immediately moved in front of me, his feelings instantly became apparent to all. My body shook, both from shock and fear. "No!" he yelled. "She did nothing wrong."

Herr Franke slowly stood up from his chair and began to process the situation. Lena entered the room followed by Stefan's mother. Inga's cheeks changed from white to crimson. She too seemed to realize what was transpiring.

"Stefan!" she demanded. "Come over here!"

He didn't even acknowledge her as he retained his protective stance in front of me. Her lips tightened as she stomped furiously from the room.

The colonel's eyes squinted. He wiped the blood from his hand even though it continued to trickle. He smiled. It was the lethal smile of a snake. I was sure his forked tongue would protrude as he spoke.

"I see . . ." He walked toward us. Though Stefan's eyes followed his every movement, I lowered my head. I could not watch him.

The colonel stood next to us. He touched my sleeve and left a bloody fingerprint on the edge. Stefan's body nudged me back farther behind him.

I peered up when the colonel laughed wickedly. "So" —he examined me with eager eyes then shifted them back to Stefan— "she has become *your* dessert."

He referenced the horrible dinner over a year ago . . . he *did* remember me.

Stefan's face turned red. A low growl rumbled in his throat as he appeared to lose restraint. His fists curled at his side as he placed himself fully between me and the colonel.

Colonel Anker laughed again then turned to the two Volkspolizei present and calmly said, "Arrest her."

They immediately moved toward me. Stefan pushed one of the soldiers away as Herr Franke grabbed Stefan and shoved him against a wall.

"Verdammtes Arschloch!" Stefan screamed expletives at the colonel. Never had I seen him that enraged before.

"I will have you arrested as well, boy! Learn your place!"

Colonel Anker spat on the floor.

Herr Franke continued to hold Stefan back, but pleaded, "No, please, colonel, let me manage him." He then motioned for Johann to help him the moment Anker waved them off.

Together they physically dragged Stefan out of the room.

Lena stood there completely helpless; her face turned ashen. Tears filled her eyes as one officer pulled out a pair of cuffs and placed them on my wrists. I started crying. Escorted through the house, we passed Frau Franke who remained still near the front entrance.

Contempt spread across her face as though she now realized her suspicions were true. She made no attempt to intervene. I was sure this was exactly where she believed I belonged. As the Polizei guided me down the front steps, people on the street stopped to watch.

Everyone could hear the angry sound of furniture and glass being broken from inside the house. The noise faded the moment I was placed in the back seat of their vehicle.

I glanced back to where Lena and Johann's faces were pressed against the front windows in horror. Tears streamed down my cheeks as I wondered if this was the last time I would see them . . . *any of them.*

Chapter Thirty-six

I was driven to a plain, gray one-story building in the middle of a labyrinth of similar structures in the center of Friedrichshain. I only knew of this area as I passed through to Treptow by bus. Many Berliners, however, knew this neighborhood to be the center of communist control, specifically Stasi headquarters.

Nothing was said on the ride here, and only the two Volkspolizei accompanied me. The shock hadn't worn off yet; I was mute. The colonel and the two other men from the lunch rode in a separate vehicle. They did not follow us inside.

Forcefully pushed into a group cell, I cowered. Three other women were in the room, two of them I was sure were sex workers from their apparel. The other one resembled a mother. She appeared as frightened as I was. There were no chairs, therefore I sat on the floor, pulled my legs in tight, and rested my chin on my knees. The floor was covered in dirt, urine, and feces and smelled worse than the crematorium if that was possible.

There was nothing behind the bars but us, yet it was filthy. I thought about Stefan in a place like this for eighteen straight days, and I became nauseous. No wonder he was willing to do whatever he was asked. I couldn't imagine another day of this, much less the five years he was sentenced to.

Did he think of me?

He was quick to jump to my defense. I'm sure he wouldn't have done that if he didn't care for me, especially in front of his parents. I had to hope Stefan was searching for me. I had to believe he would find me.

My stomach ached, and my head throbbed as my swollen eyes fought to stay open. I was afraid to close them not knowing what would happen next. As nighttime came upon us, more women were brought in. The small cell was now crowded with eleven, none of whom had any intention of making friends. I avoided their glares.

The woman who reminded me of a mother took her place next to me. I didn't feel like talking, but her presence was comforting as time passed. I fell asleep leaning against the wall.

***

"Adela. You must learn your place." Nurse Gitta grabbed my arm. She dragged me because I refused to use my legs. I knew exactly where we were headed. Nurse Gitta was not as large as Nurse Margret, but she was strong for an old woman. At least she appeared old with many wrinkles and silver-colored hair. She continued to scold me for my most recent fight. Jasper had taken my cracker from lunch and ate it. I was going to get it back in blood if necessary. I was hungry.

When we reached the closet, I put my heels down. I did not want to go in there. It scared me and smelled bad, but it would be years before my little seven-year-old body would be strong enough to resist, and with one final push, I was in. I heard the door slam and the knob clink locked.

My screams bounced back at me the harder I pounded. This got me nowhere, but I persisted because my mind convinced me I was not alone in there. Images of spiders, snakes, long-legged bugs, or even ghostly spirits swirling around, frightening me.

I curled up and cried myself to sleep. Only this particular time, I awoke to the sound of a key being turned. Unsure of whether I should be afraid of a beating or anticipate a release, I remained still. I doubted enough time had passed for it to be morning yet.

Why would my captors be back this soon? I questioned in the dark. The door opened. Anton's scrawny little hand reached out for me. I peeked up at this boy whom I'd only known for six months but regularly risked his own neck for me. What was it about me that kept him coming back?

***

My eyes shot open. Darkness engulfed me, and Anton's hand was not there to save me this time. I was alone. Not physically, because there were other bodies stretched out in the cell, but I was alone.

A path of earlier tears had dried on my cheeks, but they became moist once again. I thought about Anton and then Stefan. Anton had rescued me time and time again at the orphanage and even when my mouth got me in trouble at the Kühn's. But he could not save me now. Stefan, I had to believe, would be here if he could, but he may not even know my whereabouts.

Now that his parents knew his feelings about me, would they let him try to find me or tell him to know his place too?

Feelings of fear and anxiety kept me up for the rest of the night. It wasn't until the light finally hit the hallway windows that an officer appeared near the bars. He scanned the room.

"You!" he cried, pointing right at me. "Come."

I stood up slowly. The eyes of envy appear on all the others' faces, and I shuffled to the entrance as the man unlocked the cell door.

"Step out!" he yelled. I was not far from him, but his voice raised with every word. I brushed off my once-white working dress, which now emerged mostly brown from the dirt.

"You're leaving."

"To where?" A small twinge of hope kindled. Maybe Stefan had come, and I would get to go home, but the man was harsh and cruel. He ignored me and pushed me forcefully down the hall, the same direction I had come last night.

We arrived at a back room where two officers waited for us. My heart sank. My nightmare was not over. One of the men placed cuffs on my wrists once again while the other handed papers to the man who had brought me over. They were all whispering.

The small television on the corner desk was on with the volume unusually loud. The black and white image showed a man in a dark suit with a strange accent speaking to an enormous gathering. The words, **President John F. Kennedy / Rathaus Schoenberg** appeared in the bottom left corner of the screen. One of the officers glanced over at the television and drew the attention of the others as well.

The president spoke out confidently to the cheering crowd as an interpreter translated his words into German. "While the wall is the most obvious and vivid demonstration of the failures of the communist system, for all the world to see, we take no satisfaction in it, for it is, as your mayor has said, an offense not only against history but an offense against humanity, separating families, dividing husbands and wives and brothers and sisters and dividing a people who wish to be joined together . . ."

"Blode Amerikaner!" One officer raised his fist to the screen.

The other screamed, "Tod dem Prasidenten!"

Both men showed extreme hatred for a man they never met. Their vicious words wished death upon him. It frightened me to be in a room with so much anger.

Within seconds, all eyes immediately came back to me and the duty at hand. The one who was harsh to me earlier, yelled for us to leave. He pushed me from behind toward the door. I nearly tripped, unable to catch myself with my hands detained behind me. Thankfully, I hit the doorframe first.

As we stepped out, the words from the voice on the television rang painfully and ironically in my ears, ". . . this generation of Germans has earned the right to be free, including their right to unite their families . . ."

Once again, I and the backseat of an official vehicle were reunited. I struggled to make sense of the process. I'd never been to jail before and assumed this was how it worked, although my name and information were never taken at any point. It scared me to think my very presence here could be easily erased.

"Where are you taking me?" The two men exchanged looks but ignored me. "I have a right to know where you're taking me," I yelled louder. "I didn't do anything wrong."

"Halt den Mund!" The one who drove told me to shut up. They whispered low enough I couldn't hear what they said.

Gazing out the window, I noticed that we passed five streetlights by the time the sun peeked well up and over the tallest buildings. This entire drive was unfamiliar to me, and another three city blocks passed before they pulled up to another plain, gray building.

Please, no, not another cell, I pleaded in my mind as I examined my dress and the stained and torn hem. The rancid smell from the last one still lingered.

The officers escorted me up a single flight of stairs, I remained silent this time. They knocked on the only visible door. It was solid brown with no numbers, only a small symbol; a shield with the Soviet flag flying from a gun. The words *Ministerium für Staatssicherheit* appeared at the bottom in black lettering.

My cheeks heated up with a sudden shortness of air. I gasped but re-mained still. My eyes adjusted hard to what I'd just read . . . the seal of state security was known by every German; I had been brought to the secret police.

CHAPTER THIRTY-SEVEN

There was no answer at first. The officers knocked repeatedly until the door opened.

"Komm herein." We were invited inside as if expected.

My heart pounded heavily as I was led through a series of rooms, all decorated in a very basic way: a couch, a table, a desk. Confused, I peered around, taking in as much of my surroundings as possible. It did not appear to be a prison, but some sort of occupational area. I held my breath wondering if that might be good or bad.

The last room we entered had no furniture.

"Unlock her cuffs."

"Yes, sir." The officers obeyed. Relief flooded through me as the tight restraints were removed, and I rubbed the raw, red flesh of my wrists.

"You're dismissed." The man waved the officers off as he retrieved a chair for himself.

He didn't look at me right away, so I studied him. His composure rivaled that of a stone statue—no emotion or expression. The only movement he made came from the wiggle of the pencil in his right hand, a blue folder resting casually on his lap. As the silence stretched, my nerves were tested. My whole face felt wet from tears, sweat, or both. I wiped my nose with the back of my hand while I waited for the man to speak.

Time continued to pass. When he finally glanced up and met my stare, he remained silent, watching me. I shifted my weight to my other leg, a minor relief from the aches that had developed in my muscles from standing so long. *How long will it be before my knees buckle beneath me?*

"Sir? May I sit?"

Silence.

My eyes narrowed in on a face that started to appear familiar the more I stared. An older man with a heavy build, his round face bore thick eyebrows that almost seemed to connect in the middle, contrasting with a small mustache resting on his upper lip. His commanding officer's uniform had a patch that identified him as a captain.

It was hard to know exactly how much time had passed, but I knew it would not be long before my body would succumb to fatigue.

The silence continued. The only sound above the whirling buzz in my ears was the scribbling of a pencil against paper . . . until suddenly it stopped.

Finally, he spoke. His voice emerged serious and monotone. "What is your name?"

The throbbing in my head distracted me.

"What is your name?" he repeated.

"Ella," I whispered.

"Ella what?"

"Kühn." Then I realized I'd made a mistake.

"Sorry, my given name is Adela Kühn, but I'm called Ella."

He kept his face down to the papers. Another few minutes went by.

"Where do you live?"

I hesitated, frustrated over my treatment. I felt the rebellious gene inside me stir. "Why do you ask?"

He ignored me. "Answer the question."

"Why am I here?"

I could sense his growing agitation, "Answer the question, Fräulein Kühn . . . Where do you live?"

"Treptow," I obeyed. I realized he could be the only one who stood between me and freedom.

"Your full address."

"Rotherstraße 34 Treptow, 1012 Berlin."

He silently scribbled. "Do you live alone?"

"I . . . I do not." My lips started to tremble.

"Who do you live with?"

"I live with an elderly woman, Frau Genau, and her daughter Khloe."

"With whom do you associate?"

"My friends?"

He arched a brow.

"I don't have many."

"Name them."

I was instantly unsettled. This was the one subject I knew too well. I had overheard conversations at the Frankes' where the officers spoke freely of their interrogation tactics including coercion for more names. It was never a good thing when you gave the secret police more names. My mind instantly went to Christoph.

"I really don't have any, sir, I mostly keep to myself."

The captain seemed like a patient man, but for how long I did not know. My mouth closed tightly. His eyebrows rose.

"Their names, Fräulein Kühn."

A strand of hair had come loose from my braid, and I nervously pulled it behind my ear and wiped my forehead. *What should I do?* My mind spun . . . *was he talking about Stefan, Lena, and Johann, or Fritz, Simon, and Klaus? Did he know about the escape attempt?*

I swallowed. My throat suffered from dryness. I hadn't had any water since yesterday.

My interrogator stared at me carefully. "Names, Fräulein," he asked again, only there was something different in his tone, almost cautionary.

My breathing elevated. I knew I had little time to answer but could not bring myself to form the words. Several more minutes passed in silence.

"Gentlemen . . ."

The captain called for the officers to enter the room once again and with a flick of his wrist, the motion was made for the restraints to be returned.

"Fräulein Kühn will be going to the remand room. Please see to her removal." His voice remained calm, but the word "remand" should have warned me.

As the cold steel once again pressed into my flesh, my throat tightened. Fear smothered me but not enough to give up the names of people I cared about. Better that I was the only one to suffer. I had less to lose.

The officers led me to a windowless room with peeling white walls splattered with dark red paint in different directions. It was an odd combination. As I moved closer to the sides, I realized it was not paint after all.

My chest swelled anxiously, my lungs stretching as I attempted to take a deep breath but choked. I covered my mouth to muffle my gasp as my eyes frantically spun around the room. A large metal basin stood in one corner while variously sized ropes and chains hung from the ceiling.

I bit the inside of my cheek to stop myself from crying. If they saw me weep, they would know they had gotten to me. *I need to stay strong.*

The Polizei set me down on the only chair in the room, positioning my clasped hands directly under my bottom and securing a thick belt attached to the chair around my chest to prevent mobility. It was uncomfortable, but not painful. Confused, I tried not to rejoice too early. With all they could use in this room to force me to talk, this seemed like the least invasive. I glanced around, the two ropes above me had been tied into knots as if to clench hands or possibly a head. I shivered.

"Sir," I whispered, as the officers entered again with two small bowls. "Please," I pleaded to the captain.

His chin raised sternly. "Had you been more compliant, Fräulein Kühn..."

I watched anxiously as bowls were placed on the ground directly beneath my arms. My body continued to tremble. *What is their purpose? Do they intend to bleed me out?*

"I'm not who you think I am." A tear escaped and slid down my cheek.

"I will give you some time in here to think about your future cooperation."

"Please, please," my final petition was ignored as the door sealed shut behind him.

Blackness swallowed me up. Nothing—not even a crack under the door—offered relief. Only the sound of my heavy breathing could be heard until an unearthly moan awakened inside the walls. A groan as if something abnormal stirred.

My breathing accelerated as a swoosh of air was released through nearby vents. It wasn't until the thick, hot air reached me that I realized the noise must be a very large furnace. The scorching air continued to burn and sear against my face and body as if it cast out fire. Moisture coated my skin and pooled on my lap. I could no longer hold back the tears, yet I somehow knew this was not going to be the worst of it.

I didn't know how much time had passed when the whispers started. Even as my eyes adjusted to the blackness, I saw shadows and movement and voices. I remained seated in the position they left me, but jerked rapidly, opposite to the sounds that shot out from behind, above, and what seemed right in front of my face.

My terror grew with each passing moment.

The perpetual blast of heat winded me, allowing perspiration as the only source of wetness on my parched lips. My drenched hair weightily stuck to my face, and the salt stung my eyes. When the whispers paused, I heard a steady drip of fluid. It hurt to think. *Where is the water coming from?* I assumed it was a faucet on the tub then realized the sound was much closer . . . the bowls. With my hands still positioned underneath my body, liquid easily rolled off my skin . . . they were collecting my sweat.

I read once that the Stasi found an escapee because they turned their dogs onto the scent they had collected from interrogation. Now it all made sense . . . *but why me?* I had no intention of running away . . . at least not lately. I could not possibly be a threat.

The noises started and stopped randomly. Hours must have passed—possibly even a day. I no longer had any feeling in my hands; they were numb. The whispering continued, ghostlike voices repeated over and over that I was guilty, and I would be punished.

By the time the door finally opened again, I was barely coherent. Unable to lift my eyes against the bright light that filtered in, I kept them closed with no concept of how much time had passed. Someone stood before me, and the weight of their eyes penetrated but I could not look up to see who it was. The captain's voice resonated.

"Are you ready to comply, Fräulein Kühn?"

I nodded. I wanted this to be over. Every part of my body screamed with weakness and pain. My eyes remained closed. Even when I heard the officers enter once again and remove the bowls from beneath me. A significant amount of liquid sloshed as they carried them out.

Upon their return, more lights were turned on. The strain was more than I could bear; I kept my head lowered and my eyes shut as they released the body restraint.

Still bound at the wrists, men on each side of me gripped my arms tightly and forced me up into a standing position. My legs wobbled. I couldn't find the strength, and my body fell weakly to the floor. I was dragged upright again, but my arms and legs were practically useless. The metal restraints cut deep into my skin with each attempt. Finally, they left me on the floor. My chair was taken, and the deep sound of the captain's voice continued.

"Your friends' names, Fräulein."

I sobbed as blood began to move through my arms again—the sting nearly unbearable.

"Their names." His tone bore no sympathy.

"I—" my voice cracked, "—I work with a butler by the name of Johann. He is Russian." I coughed, but it felt like I had fabric in my mouth, the dryness amplified.

"Continue . . ."

"There are three other maids: Lena, Heidi, and Eva. I believe they are all German."

"Where do you work?"

Depleted of strength, my muscles protested as I used my shoulder to brush aside some of the hair that had stuck to my face. "Captain?" I whispered. His heavy breathing halted. He seemed surprised I knew his rank. "I'm a simple maid. I have no political ties to anyone. I only clean and serve. I don't understand why I'm here. I've done nothing wrong."

Silence.

My eyes blinked rapidly. I was finally able to crack them open. "Sir, I've done nothing wrong."

"Whose home do you serve?"

"Herr Koen Franke," I whispered. "He and his son, Stefan, run the mortuary in Pankow. He has many friends in the government, do you know him?"

The captain's face flinched just enough to confirm that he did. He was an intimidating man, but there was something about him that didn't seem too threatening to me. Maybe it was the way he reminded me of Herr Krzinsky, or maybe he was the age of someone's father, but he seemed sure I had information he needed.

Could it be possible that Herr Franke was the target, and they wanted information on him? I could only describe his visitors; I didn't know many names. I tried not to even listen to the conversations and most of the time I was excused from the room.

Then it occurred to me where I had seen this man before. "Wait, I remember you." I squeezed my eyes tighter to clear my sight. Even though the hot air had ceased, I continued to sweat profusely. "I remember you." I was sure of it now.

I adjusted my position and licked my cracked lips with an equally dry tongue. "You brought the two People's Police officers to the Frankes' for a meal . . . the day they were honored."

He remained silent but I could tell my words affected him. He kept his head down and continued to write.

"I served you. The officers spoke of an incident that involved a man at the Teltow Canal. Stefan Franke was your host." I was wasting my breath. My words were completely ignored. The little hope generated from this connection slowly disappeared.

Tired and worn, I scanned the room defeated. I knew there was a great deal more that could be done here to get answers, answers they believed I possessed, but I knew nothing of worth. *I could die for nothing.* It was hard to know how much time passed between his questions, but this pause seemed insurmountable.

"Do you have family in the West?" His next question frightened me most of all.

I knew spies regularly hunted people who had escaped to bring them back and face charges of treason.

"No," I whispered but turned away.

"Where are your parents?"

"They are dead."

Scratch, scratch, scratch, the tip of his pencil moved swiftly across his paper.

"Do you lie, Fräulein Kühn?"

My face heated up; I could not look at him.

"Anker said you are a liar. Do you lie, Fräulein?"

"Anker? Colonel Anker?" My heart stopped. "What does he have to do with this?" I sat up off the floor. My arms were still cuffed and limp at one side.

"You are familiar with Colonel Anker?" He probed.

"No . . ." I paused. "Well, yes . . ." My sudden energy piqued his interest. "He has been to the Franke home." I stared at the captain. He met my eyes. "Colonel Anker was at the Franke home yesterday. I think it was yesterday . . . for lunch. I spilled a drink on him—it was an accident." I took a breath then continued. "He became very angry with me then had me arrested."

The captain remained silent as he processed this. I shifted my legs into a different position. He didn't talk for what seemed to be another uncomfortable spell.

"It was an accident, sir," I pleaded. I hoped to somehow get him to believe me. "I tripped when entering the parlor, and the glass went everywhere. I'm sorry. Please captain, please go to Stefan, he will speak for my innocence."

Suddenly, the door flung open. Before it registered who entered the room, Colonel Anker's hand flung angrily against my cheek. Tears immediately shot forth from the sting, and I fell to the cold cement floor once more, my cheek numb.

The captain appeared as surprised as I was.

"Colonel." The captain stood. "I have this under control."

"She is lying, Scharf. She's a spy, I know she is."

My eyes widened with this news. That's what this was all about, *his pride*? He was trying to frame me to get back at me or possibly Stefan for what happened.

"I'm not a spy!" I sniveled back through gritted teeth.

He lifted his hand again, and I braced myself, but the hit never came. I glanced up to see the captain's hand restraining the senior officer's forearm. My eyes shifted back and forth between the men. Colonel Anker's face was blanketed in shock. The captain quickly released his grip.

"S—sir," Captain Scharf stuttered a bit, "we need to follow protocol on this one."

The colonel's jaw locked, his eyes filled with rage, but he stepped back. "We need to break her," Anker said.

Captain Scharf responded, "We will *if* she's a spy." The way he said it, gave me hope. Maybe he doesn't believe I am.

The colonel paced the room. His hands alternated between wringing and tightening in a fist. The mumbling was incoherent, and his apparent agitation became distracting, like he wasn't himself, although I didn't know him well enough to know if he was always this dreadful or not.

"Where do you meet with your friends, Fräulein Kühn?" The captain ignored Anker's aggravated movements and continued with his questioning.

"Um . . ." The colonel's presence made me nervous. ". . . we go to this place called Dafne's café." There was a strange shift in the mood. Despite Anker's restless presence, I now realized my best chance for a release was to cooperate with Captain Scharf.

"What do you talk about?"

"Normal stuff . . ." I glanced fearfully toward Anker. The veins in his neck protruded. ". . . stuff like work and music." I cleared my throat. "I'm only sixteen, sir." I was actually seventeen now if we went by the birthday the Kühns gave me, but I hadn't celebrated since Papa died. There was nothing to celebrate . . . and maybe sixteen sounded more innocent at the moment.

Colonel Anker slammed his hand against the wall, impatiently. It made me jump. He was different from last night . . . or whatever night it was. He seemed worse.

"Colonel, may I speak with you outside, please?" Captain Scharf pointed to the door, then once outside they started talking, although Anker did not know how to whisper.

I tuned in as best I could.

"You know she works for Koen Franke, correct?"

"Yes," Anker snapped as Captain Scharf continued.

"I think we need to proceed carefully. We have a specific relationship with him."

"She is the maid. She means nothing to them."

His words imprinted deeper than I thought they would. Maybe that's what they all think of me.

"Still, there is also Inga Franke's family connection with Wolf. Let's not create a reason to disrupt any association."

I held my breath. Who could have imagined it would be Frau Franke's bloodline that could ultimately set me free?

"I want her convicted, Scharf. I want it done tonight!"

"I'm not certain she's a spy, sir. There are some . . ." he tried to whisper lower, ". . . doubts." Papers shuffled loudly. "This is not a high-priority target. Who did you say reported this?"

"It doesn't matter," the colonel snapped. "She is, I know it. We need to press her harder."

There was silence for a few minutes. Then Captain Scharf spoke up. "Well, let's give it some more time, sir."

"Do not be mistaken about who the ranking officer is here, Scharf." Anker's irritation was evident. "You may have influence in high places, but I am still in command."

"Yes sir," the captain conceded. "I understand. I'm only suggesting more time. She's not going anywhere, and I'm due to meet Honecker this afternoon. I can return and proceed shortly after."

"Fine!" The colonel's disgust was clearly evident as he conceded.

"Are you feeling all right, sir?" I could see the captain hand the colonel something, "You look tired and a bit out of sort this morning."

"It's nothing."

"All right, sir." Scharf gazed back into the room, but I had already turned away. "She'll be fine in here. We have two officers who will remain close. They can keep an eye on her while we both go about our business. Let's reconvene at four this afternoon."

When Captain Scharf re-entered the room, he held a glass of water and offered it to me. This action surprised me, and I hesitated, wondering if it was somehow poisoned.

He motioned for me to turn around, and as I did, the metal bands released. Shifting forward again, I rubbed my wrists and reached for the glass. I gulped hastily. Poisoned or not, my mouth ached for it. When I finished, he held the cuffs out again but kindly restrained my arms in the front and not nearly as tight.

I thought about the conversation he had with the colonel and wondered if I had imagined the uncertainty he might have in my guilt. A sliver of hope blossomed in my heart and gave me the courage to plead my case once more. I thanked him for the water and proceeded in a whisper, "I didn't do anything wrong, sir. I'm not who you think I am. Please . . . please ask Stefan Franke."

The captain didn't respond to my statement. "Make sure you are ready to tell me everything I need to know when I return." His stance was less domineering than before. Or so it seemed. "I will return shortly. Do not consider running away, I have soldiers posted at the doors." He turned before he left. "This will all be over soon."

Then he closed the door.

I wasn't sure if I should feel reassured by his last comment or not. It was a double-edged sword.

The tingling in my arms subsided as I scooted awkwardly toward the back wall and leaned up against it. Now that my hands were restrained in the front, I could rub my stinging cheek gently with my palm. I welcomed the silence.

The psychological terror the Stasi deployed was notorious. I had heard the stories. The tales of people who were in the wrong place at the wrong time, accused of crimes they never committed, interrogated relentlessly, and sentenced to horrible outcomes.

Hohenschönhausen Prison in East Berlin was one of those places. Many received life sentences there, but those who didn't and were
released after a few years were never the same. I wondered how long
it would take for me to prove my innocence—if innocence was still
an option.

I thought of Stefan. Was his family keeping him from me, or had he
realized what they always knew—we were never meant to be together. As time continued to pass, any trace of hope or courage diminished
with it.

Chapter Thirty-eight

As the hours passed, my eyes started to droop. With very little sleep recently, fatigued by both the duress and lack of strength, my head fell lifeless upon my bent knees. I slipped easily into a deep sleep.

I immediately saw Stefan. He appeared quite real. In my mind, I attempted to tell myself to wake up, that he had come for me, but my eyes refused to open. Somehow, I saw a bridge not far off where Stefan lingered on the other side. His face appeared calm and peaceful. He smiled and called my name, extending his hand toward me. I tried to get to him, but my feet wouldn't move. I glanced down. Nothing was holding them back, but it felt like I was paralyzed. Panicked, I called to him, but he couldn't hear me. His face crinkled in confusion. *Why didn't he come to me?* He turned away, his back facing me now.

"Stefan!" I yelled.

No reply.

"Stefan!" I cried again. Finally, my legs moved, but the bridge was gone—only a cliff remained. By then I couldn't stop myself from walking forward.

At the helpless feeling of falling, I shook awake. Reality set in as recognition of my circumstances resurfaced. The room seemed darker than before. I felt wetness against my skin and assumed it was from crying in my sleep.

"You know he won't come for you."

Instant panic gripped my chest. Colonel Anker's voice generated a tremble in my hands so great I buried them in my lap.

"Stefan's not coming," he chuckled darkly. I was as frightened now as ever before. I narrowed my tired eyes to make out his form but could only see his silhouette as he lingered in the shadows directly across from me. He must've been watching me sleep.

I didn't respond. I wasn't even sure I was capable of speech as my throat constricted in fear.

"No words?" the man mocked sarcastically. "You had plenty to say to my colleague."

Completely awake now, I could see my adversary lean guardedly against the farthest wall. The outline of a glass appeared as he lifted it to his lips. I glanced toward the door. It was cracked slightly open, but I couldn't see or hear anyone else. The colonel watched and grinned shrewdly.

"Oh, you think Captain Scharf will come?" He laughed his ugly laugh. "He left . . ." I blinked rapidly as he continued, ". . . and the officers, I dismissed them." His voice rumbled low and unsettling. "No one to play innocent for, no one to deceive." My breathing accelerated, but I concealed it as best I could as he continued, ". . . It's just us . . . Adela."

My name rolled off his tongue in a slippery manner. He must've looked at my file to call me by my given name. His movement seemed awkward, but his intent was clear. He was now my greatest fear.

Inhaling deeply, I continued to watch him cautiously. He had to be insane.

It was impossible to prevent my eyes from growing wider as he moved from the shadows through the streak of light the parted door provided to stand directly in front of me. His heavy breathing rivaled my own as he placed the glass on the floor in front of me. The whites of his eyes practically glowed as he glared and pointed to the drink. The contents were only half-full, but from my proximity and serving experience, I recognized the distinct smell of vodka.

"Drink!" he demanded.

I didn't move.

"Drink!" his voice echoed loudly through the empty rooms.

"I . . . I don't drink," I stuttered.

His face tightened at my perceived defiance. "Drink!"

I swallowed hard. I made the mistake of turning my head, just as the back of his hand swung, smacking me squarely across the nose.

Blood left a splattered trail across my face and the floor. It now matched the walls. The sting was indescribable, and my hands went to my nose. My fingers inched up the bridge and felt a decent-sized cut oozing blood. It suddenly occurred to me that this man could kill me. Right here, right now, and nobody would even know. Stefan would not even know.

Tears steadily fell. I sniffled hard to control my breathing. Blood now drizzled down the lines of my mouth and covered my fingers. Anker stood unsympathetically in front of me. My elbows rested on my knees as my arms instinctively covered my face.

"Drink this now!" He bent down, his face inches from mine—the jagged scar visible in the open space between my arms. I closed my eyes tight. Only the stench of sour liquor seeped through. "Now!" he bellowed angrily. His fist grabbed my hair and forced my head toward the glass.

I picked it up awkwardly, my wrists still chained together. The tumbler rattled against my teeth as I placed it to my lips, my hands shaking uncontrollably. I tipped the glass slightly and pretended to drink, but it barely grazed my top lip—I could not allow the alcohol to penetrate my virgin system. It was vital I kept my wits about me.

Satisfied, the colonel turned his back and stepped out of the room. I struggled to move the glass behind one side of me and poured the liquor onto the floor. The fluid seeped into the backside fabric of my dress.

I peered at the nearly empty glass. Thoughts started reeling in my head . . . I held a weapon in my hand. If he tried to hurt me again, I could break the glass on his head or face, but if I failed, it would only make him angrier.

I was still staring at the glass when he returned with not only another glass but a partially full decanter. He filled my tumbler once more and then gulped his down in three swallows. Once finished, he set it down next to mine.

The repulsion in *Scarface's* eyes amplified as he commanded me a second time to drink. Once again, I pretended to obey. This time he watched.

This time he realized my pretense. Anker's face turned a deep, unearthly red. The lines around his mouth expanded as his teeth clenched with fury, and even though there was no smoke, it was as close to a volcanic eruption as I might ever witness.

One hand slapped the glass out of my fingers, shattering it against the wall. Simultaneously, his other hand reached for my braid and yanked me roughly forward, flat to the floor. The movement happened swiftly enough that I couldn't catch myself, and my face slid painfully across the cement floor. A shard of glass tore through my abdominal flesh as the weight of my body smashed the second tumbler.

When I finally realized what had happened, my screams begged for freedom. There had to be someone nearby who would hear my cries and come to my rescue, but nobody came.

Anker shouted unrecognizable words while his hands lunged for me; I could barely see through the tears. His grip was tight and painful when he lifted my body off the floor. He threw my back against the nearest wall. Something cracked, and I gasped unsuccessfully for air.

In a matter of seconds, he grabbed my legs and dragged me back to the center of the room. Instantly, Anker's body pressed on top of me, his weight pushing me heavily into the floor.

Coughing and choking through desperation, air still refused to enter my lungs. I was suffocating. The serrated piece of glass lodged deeper into my skin. A sticky wetness seeped freely between us, but nothing seemed to distract him.

He grabbed the chain that held my hands together to stop my thrashing arms and easily held them tightly with one hand. His other hand ripped the top of my dress down the middle. The buttons clinked as they hit the hard floor, my chest exposed.

The colonel froze long enough for me to wiggle a knee free from underneath. I shoved it up with just enough force to connect between his legs. Groaning, he rolled stiffly to my side as I gasped for much-needed oxygen, but his paralysis was short. I had very little time to act. My screams could have awakened the dead, had there been anyone to hear them. The colonel quickly straddled me once again.

In an effort to silence me, he pressed his hand tightly over my mouth. I bit his finger firmly until I tasted his blood on my lips. The colonel's cries shrieked nearly as loud as my own, but he wasn't finished. Instead, he doubled up his fist and swung widely to the right, connecting squarely with my cheekbone. My face went numb.

I kicked hard again, my legs flailing wildly about, but this only seemed to increase his adrenaline. His knees pressed heavily, forcing a gap, then drove my legs apart. His fingers dug sharply into my wrists to restrain me harder.

With his free hand, I could see him trying to undo his pants. I mustered all the strength I had left for a piercing scream. He pulled his loose belt out to the side and whipped me twice in the face with the buckle. I recoiled in unbearable pain, gasping desperately as blood and sweat rolled down my face to my neck and chest. Something hard and forceful then connected with my stomach. I cringed in agony as Anker grabbed another fistful of material and shredded what was left of my dress, completely exposing me.

I was utterly defeated. This man was a soldier and an experienced fighter with a fiery rage. I was losing, and he would kill me. My body fell limp, and my arms and legs slumped lifelessly. I could no longer see or think. There was no fight left in me.

At the moment of my submission, a door suddenly slammed. Anker's weight was unexpectedly lifted. Indistinguishable words filled with hate preceded horrendous groans and cries.

Frightened, I pulled my body tightly into a ball. A loud crash vibrated too close to me. Painful sounds mimicked kicks or a series of blows.

"Please, please don't hurt me," I mumbled. Afraid I was next, I remained still. My eyes squeezed shut as I braced for more pain. Unearthly moans echoed. I wasn't sure if it came from me or someone else. A familiar hand touched my face.

"You are safe now," whispered Stefan, his face next to mine.

I sobbed as I pulled my arms tightly into my torso, the throbbing was excruciating. Stefan removed his shirt and laid it over my naked body, gently caressing my hair.

"I'm so sorry, Ella," Stefan's voice cracked with torment. He held me close as more loud noises filled the room. I reached out for Stefan's arms as they were yanked from my grip. The cuffs once more tore my already raw flesh.

Stefan was instantly seized.

"No!" I cried out, stretching for him but finding only empty handfuls of air. Forcing one eye open, the other swollen shut, I watched as soldiers filled the small room.

Chaos was everywhere—men shouted and hollered instructions, and then I saw him . . . the colonel. He lay crumpled in a heap on the floor nearby, broken glass scattered in a puddle of blood beneath him.

He didn't move.

Stefan was held at gunpoint. I struggled to keep myself covered in my attempt to sit upright.

"Ella, stay put," Stefan pleaded under strain. "Someone get a doctor!"

"Please, please release him." New tears flowed as I sought to reach the closest Polizei officer present.

"Be quiet and don't move!" He pushed my arm aside. Despite my appearance, the officer gave me no immediate sympathy. That is until Captain Scharf arrived. He looked around to me, Colonel Anker, and then Stefan and back to me.

"Stefan!" he yelled angrily, "what were you thinking?" Scharf immediately went to my side. "You should have waited for me!"

"She would be dead if I had waited. Look at her. Let me go to her. She needs help!" The sounds that followed indicated he continued to fight his restraints. I tried hard to make sense of their conversation . . . *Stefan came with Scharf?*

Captain Scharf ordered a towel to be moistened and a blanket to be delivered to him immediately. "Keys!" he demanded of the closest soldier and then pointed to Stefan, "Get him out of here!"

"No!" I lunged, desperate to not be shut down again.

Scharf, who only moments ago seemed to make my apparent connection with Stefan, held me back surprisingly gently. He unlocked the handcuffs and then whispered, "Procedure." He then motioned once again for them to leave.

His touch was mild as he placed the blanket around me and handed me the moistened towel. My sight was limited, but I held Stefan's gaze until the moment he disappeared. My body ached immensely, but the agony of my heart outweighed any physical pain I endured.

The captain then called for another soldier, "Retrieve Dr. Tischer at once."

I was sure it was to see Scarface, but the captain moved aside and led the doctor directly to me.

Colonel Anker must be dead.

The doctor examined my wounds, none of which were life-threatening, possible broken ribs and a dislocated shoulder. The pain was agonizing as he maneuvered it back into place. He carefully cleaned the cuts and bruises on my face, wrists, and body with alcohol. Fortunately, they were mostly superficial. Only my nose and the front part of my hip needed stitches.

He handed me a small towel and then took out his sewing kit. It would have hurt if the rest of my body didn't already throb in agony, but it was quick.

Once finished, he went over to the colonel. The doctor's face confirmed what we all assumed. Captain Scharf motioned for the soldiers to cover Anker with a blanket then led me to the door.

"These men will take you home, Fräulein."

"Please," I pleaded, "Please let me explain." My fingers squeezed his hand desperately as the soldiers nudged me forward and toward the door. Captain Scharf simply nodded for them to proceed.

"Later. We will speak later," he said as they led me slowly down the steps.

I could barely walk. The path to their car, one of several military vehicles parked in front of the building, was slow and tedious. There were no words, not even a sound as they drove me to the address I provided. It was my home.

I collapsed before reaching the door. One of the men carried me the rest of the way. The moment we entered the apartment, Mama G ran to me. She'd been beside herself when I hadn't come home for, what I learned was several nights, and had kept a constant watch.

I was a horrible sight, covered in dry blood, and the swelling and discoloration had already begun on my face and body.

"What happened?" she asked the men, but the only response they gave was that I had already been attended to by a doctor. She turned to me and repeated her question.

I mumbled incoherently as Mama directed them to my bed, thanked them for their assistance, and excused them to leave. At some point, I lost consciousness . . . Mama's gentle touch brought me back.

As soon as I recalled the earlier events, the tears were unstoppable. I was nearly raped and killed, but all I could think about was Stefan . . . his touch ripped from me, and his face. The expression he bore before he disappeared around the corner was as if *he* was the one who caused me harm. I could barely stomach the thought. *Stefan saved my life!*

Mama's soothing hands placed clean linen over me before she began to administer. "Hush, Ella, calm yourself." The warm washcloth pressed carefully across my wounds. The way Mama cringed as she wiped the dried blood seemed as though it hurt her nearly as much as me.

"To heal broken bones might take months, but the other scars—" Mama hesitated then brushed my hair back softly, "—they may take longer," and kissed my forehead.

She stayed with me until I fell asleep then returned each time I awoke screaming. The image of the colonel's evil face laughing at me, the crude scar, his determination to crush me, all of this kept rising from the darkness and pierced any chance I had at peace.

He had nearly taken everything from me, including Stefan. Even though he could no longer harm me physically, he taunted me from the grave . . . I could not get the tormenting images out of my head.

Chapter Thirty-nine

As I watched the sunlight enter my bedroom window, I saw Mama's petite form curled up in the chair beside my bed. She must've given up on staying in her own room through the night.

My hands went instinctively to my face. I could feel the bumps and the cuts. The spiky, raised stitches that stuck out at the top of my nose sorely reminded me of yesterday's nightmare. I tried to move, but my body ached severely, and I couldn't even get out of bed. My attempts woke Mama.

"Ella," she cried and reached for me. She lay my head gently back against the pillow. "Don't move, love, stay in bed."

"Please!" I pleaded. Tears spilled limitless down my cheeks. "I need to know if Stefan is OK."

It took me a while to tell Mama the abbreviated version of events. At least what I could recall. A severe headache clouded my memory on top of all the other aches and pains. Mama struggled to hide her shock, but I saw her lip trembling as she listened.

"Please, Mama," I cried, "Please . . . I need you to talk to the Frankes." I knew something must have gone wrong because Stefan would be with me if he could.

Mama didn't want to leave me, but I wouldn't let it go—I needed to know. Therefore, she made me tea from licorice root and watched me drink it as she dabbed my skin with mineral oil before she left.

She returned two hours later with not much to share. "Herr Franke is gone."

"Gone?" I whispered.

"Possibly to find answers of his own," she conceded, ". . . but it was Frau Franke who quite forcefully objected to my inquiries. When she found out who I was, she demanded I leave at once."

"I'm sorry," I said. Mama knew very little of how she treated me. Guilt overcame me. I should've been more forthcoming, then she might not have been surprised.

"However, as I walked from the residence, I was overcome by a gentle soul." Mama smiled and placed her hands on mine. "A woman by the name of Lena followed me out. She was quite distressed and concerned for your welfare."

"She's my closest friend, Mama"

"Well, that is good news then, because I invited her over tonight." I matched her smile faintly, then my mouth curved into a frown. ". . . but we still don't know where Stefan is. I must know. Help me decide what to do, please?"

"Rest yourself, love, we will figure something out."

Discouraged, I knew that reaching Captain Scharf might be the only answer. He was the only one who could possibly prove Stefan's innocence.

Again, I tried to get out of bed but fell to the floor. Even if I wanted to, I could not physically move yet. I would have to wait, and I had never been good at waiting.

Later, when Lena entered my room, she gasped at the sight of me. Unable to hold back her tears, she sat at the edge of my bed, afraid to touch me—worried that I would continue to break. I convinced her I needed her hug more than I needed distance.

Her closeness calmed me as I relayed the events to her. She couldn't restrain the horror that covered her face as a result. "Oh, Ella." She squeezed my hand. "All of this happened because you spilled a drink on him?"

I shook my head and told her about our first encounter at the Fasching dinner the year before. She remembered my abrupt departure, but I had never told her why.

"He's in hell." Tears slid down her cheeks. "He will burn for his sins."

I wanted to believe it, but my only concern now was Stefan. "Do you know anything?"

She nodded her head up and down slowly. "Herr Franke was gone all day. I deliberately waited beyond my shift for his return" —I held my breath as she continued— "I placed myself within earshot of his conversation with Frau Franke." She hesitated, "It's not good, Ella."

"Please, Lena, please tell me the truth."

"Stefan was arrested."

"For what?" I cried.

"For murder."

Instantly dizzy, I grabbed my head. My fingers curled in my hair as I pulled on the strands. It was my shrieks that caused Lena to run to Mama for help. They found me curled in a ball when they returned.

"No, please no." I cried hysterically.

"What happened?" Mama questioned as she dropped to my side and pulled me to her lap. She hardly had the strength to lift me, but somehow embraced my entire body.

Lena sat at the end of the bed. "I—" she whimpered, "—I told her about Stefan."

"Hush, love." Mama held tight. "We will find him."

Despite my broken body, I suffered beyond physical at this point.

Lena sobbed quietly. She knew this feeling all too well. Stefan was not missing like her Christoph, but his fate was unknown. With the accusation of killing an officer—a high-ranking one—the outcome was most likely headed in a deadly direction.

"Find Captain Scharf," I pleaded with them both. "Find him, he will fix this."

"We'll do our best, Ella. You need to rest, or you won't recover."

I stopped fighting. Mama was right. I needed my strength to save Stefan as he did me.

"I'll visit you tomorrow. Take care of yourself." Lena kissed me on the cheek and left.

Three days passed before I could bring myself to look in a mirror again. The deep purple and blue had started to fade into an ugly yellow. I could finally see my own skin color reappear along my neck, shoulders, and parts of my cheeks. The swelling had finally reduced with around-the-clock ice pads and mineral oil, and the herbal teas Mama prepared, helped the pain in my sides diminish.

I tried to sleep, but it remained sporadic. It seemed every time I closed my eyes and fought to see Stefan's face, somehow Anker would appear. The squint of his eyes, the grit of his teeth, and the dreadful-looking scar tormented me nonstop.

Lena visited every night but had nothing new to report—except that I was "released of my duties". I figured this would happen, and if for some miracle it didn't, I would have never returned anyway. There's no possible way I could have walked through those halls and rooms and functioned knowing Stefan was gone because of me.

If I hadn't dropped the tray . . . or if I hadn't worked the Fasching dinner the year before . . . or if I hadn't fought Scarface off, maybe once he was done with me he might've passed out and I could have escaped.

Maybe Anker would have left me to die somewhere, thrown me in prison or a work camp, and Stefan would not be arrested for murder. Or . . . I continued to develop a hundred what-ifs, but it all came down to one thing. *It was my fault.*

One week passed. The third of July came and went. My heart ached as I thought about Anton and Josef watching for me from the newly constructed platforms that had popped up on the western side of the wall, all to get a glimpse of the "detained".

I knew it was a desperate endeavor, one that meant the world to many people, but I couldn't bring myself to even try to leave the flat.

I knew if Anton saw my condition, it would enrage him. The distance would not have allowed me to properly explain, and he would naturally feel helpless and troubled. I could not do that to him or my sweet brother, Josef. Thus, when the six o'clock hour passed, I suffered silently.

Within days, I was finally able to move from my room to the kitchen and living room. I was recovering, but at quite a slow pace. My thoughts focused entirely on Stefan and where he was or what was to become of him.

Lena continued to visit me nightly and brought different treats to lift my spirits, but it didn't help. She knew the only thing to make me feel better right now was seeing Stefan. However, tonight she brought a friend.

It didn't register right away when she opened my door, that it was Katharina who stood in front of me. My heart fluttered with delight, something that had eluded me for too long. I cried out loud, "Katharina!"

She smiled and moved to my side. "Oh, Ella. I'm so sorry!" She hugged me gently. "Lena told me the truth."

I considered her curious choice of words.

"There is quite a different version of the event circulating at my house!" She frowned. I shook my head. Of course, there would be. Katharina squeezed my hand. "Stefan loves you, Ella." Tears filled my eyes quickly at the mention of his name.

"He wrote to me at school." She laughed. "I bet you didn't know that, did you?"

I shook my head. I didn't think he'd told anyone about us.

"He was conflicted," she continued, "he had an obligation to the mortuary, and after his mistake in Czechoslovakia, it was a legal obligation, but he was trying to figure out a way you both could disappear together."

"Really?" I wanted to smile. I had no idea he felt that strongly.

Instantly, remorse consumed me for doubting him. "Where would we go?" I cried. "I'm an anchor to him."

"He said he wanted to somehow get you to Cochem, even if it took everything he had. I don't know why he chose there," Katharina sighed. "I remember how beautiful it was as a child, but he didn't tell me why this particular village was important to you two."

I smiled and pointed to Stefan's painting, which hung on my bedroom wall. "That's why." My heart swelled. The thought of Stefan planning a future for us was astounding. The possibility of a future that took us far away from Berlin . . . even when I had trouble seeing it myself.

Katharina and Lena stayed for a few more minutes. Katharina promised to keep me fully informed on Stefan, though no one in the family had been allowed to see him yet, including their father. He was using every possible connection he had to negotiate Stefan's release and refused to stop until it happened.

That was the best news I'd heard all week. There had to be some good to come from all the sly negotiations and corrupt associations at the Franke house. It was all I could hope for.

Chapter Forty

Captain Scharf,
6, July 1963

I'm sending this note to you to plead for your help. I know you know what happened that night. I believe you understand Stefan was defending me from Colonel Anker. Doesn't the attack against me carry any possible weight? You saw what he did to me when you were present and the condition you found me in. He would have killed me if Stefan hadn't gotten there when he did.

Please, I am very grateful to you and your kindness when you found me, but please, please, don't let Stefan be put to death because of me.

Ella Kühn

"Mama, I know this is hard for you, but you are my only chance. Please, please get this to Captain Scharf."

"Ella, I will do whatever you ask," Mama sighed heavily, "but you need to prepare yourself for any outcome."

I knew she was right, but I couldn't think about it. Even though I was a victim, the word of a woman was rarely trusted. In this case, it was my word against a dead colonel.

Mama had always been honest with me, and this was no time to ignore the probabilities. She told me people had been sentenced to death for lesser crimes against an officer, and if it was true that Stefan did kill Colonel Anker . . . I turned my head when she said this and pleaded with her not to say it out loud. It may be true, but I just couldn't bring myself to hear it.

After she left, I walked to the window. Summer was in full swing, but you wouldn't know it from my view. I glanced at the damaged building directly across the street.

Mama said it had been bombed in April 1944. She was home when the air raid sirens went off but could not get to the basement before the strike hit. The impacts shook both the walls and floor nonstop for hours. At the time, she didn't know what the target was or where the missiles hit. As a young, frightened mother, she hid in a closet with her two small daughters for three days.

The crumbling walls that had continued to degrade over time had never been removed or rebuilt, along with three additional structures nearby.

It was a constant reminder to a war-torn people, but there was something about the building that held me hostage. Maybe it was our parallels. I, myself, had taken a beating like that building and resembled an inability to rebuild or start over.

I brushed my hair back and ran my finger across the bruises on my face and wondered if reconstruction was even possible.

There was too much about that night that was still confusing. I didn't know how Stefan found me. Somehow, Scharf brought him. I know he was the one who pulled the colonel off of me, possibly the one who threw him against the wall and carried out the blow that killed him.

The reality of the dreadful event continued to press on my mind, and I suffered significantly each time I relived the moment Stefan was ripped from my grasp. It was a painful recollection.

Mama returned by afternoon the same day I wrote the letter saying she could not get to Captain Scharf himself. The man she left the letter with assured her he would deliver it.

I had never felt this helpless in my entire life. Now all we could do was wait.

Three days later, a letter arrived addressed to me, delivered by a Volkspolizei officer. Mama immediately brought it to me in the living room, where walking more freely about had led me to my latest perch, the rocking chair.

The only remnants of my facial injuries were the slight discoloration and the scar where my stitches had been. Mama removed them herself.

It was my broken ribs that took more time to heal. I rushed to open the letter, the envelope dropping to my feet.

Fräulein Adela Kühn,
9 July 1963

I received your post and appreciate your desire to clarify the situation, however, I was recently removed from the case for multiple reasons I cannot disclose. I assure you I included specific details in my final report including the nature of your injuries and the condition in which I witnessed Colonel Anker prior to my departure. It was during that particular absence I made a call on the house of Koen Franke who you mentioned as your employer. It was then I confirmed the information you gave regarding the incident two days before.

Herr Franke was unavailable at the time, but Stefan, whom I had been acquainted with, insisted not only on your innocence, but since you were an employee of his, he should accompany me back to where I left you. Through my respect for our professional relationship, I conceded. I had no indication, other than his concern, that he would not handle things appropriately, at least until we arrived. He managed to reach the room before me or the officers who traveled with us. It is because I cannot explain Herr Franke's actions before I arrived and found the colonel deceased that has presented the greatest doubt. Yes, I believe you sustained terrible injuries—I hope you are recovering well—but the death of Colonel Anker must be accounted for, and that is what Stefan will face trial for. I am sorry I cannot offer better news.

Sincerely, Captain Scharf

I crumpled up the letter and threw it angrily to the ground. "I should be the one to die!" My first reaction was filled with wrath, then heartbreak convulsed through my body. I slid to the floor as sobs saturated the room.

Mama G picked it up and read it before kneeling by my side. The same hand that had spent countless hours mending me, soothed in a familiar fashion, but I could not be consoled.

"Stefan is paying for me!" I curled up, my legs pressed against my stomach, shaking relentlessly in repeated cries, "It's all my fault! It's all my fault!"

"Please, Ella. Don't do this." The quiver in Mama's voice confirmed the situation was as bad as I imagined. *I'm going to lose Stefan.*

Stefan, who saved me, will pay the ultimate price because of *me*.

CHAPTER FORTY-ONE

14 July 1963

The number 74 remained on my bedroom mirror even though it had now been three weeks since that awful day. Unable to bear looking at the number any longer, I reached over and smudged it off.

The reflection before me suggested I wore another person's clothing as my dress slipped off my shoulder. I pulled the loose sleeve back in place as I stared at the glass smear. The memory of that day was imprinted in my head every waking moment, and from the dark circles that accented my weary eyes, I was sure it plagued my dreams as well.

Despite the few visible wounds and only a small scar where my nose and hip had been cut, I appeared hollow and empty, unable to even force myself to smile.

By early afternoon, I made my way to the rocking chair even though Mama had placed a warm bowl of *Linsensuppe* on the table. She had studied the healing powers of lentils and garlic, but even the lovely aroma of that and the *Kalter Hund* sweet cake, baking in the oven, couldn't entice me to eat.

Time had not been kind to me. I was thin and weak. Daily, Mama tried hard to get me to consume something, but I refused. My appetite after the attack hadn't returned, and with Stefan's subsequent arrest, eating seemed like a luxury I didn't deserve. I punished myself harshly. If Stefan couldn't indulge in anything, neither could I, including food.

Katharina sent word with Lena last night—she had news. I could not allow myself to be hopeful until she arrived in the next few hours. If I imagined the possibility of Stefan's freedom and it was a lie, it would destroy what was left of me. I had nothing more to give.

I reached for a new book Mama had brought home in hopes of lifting my spirits, *The Flight of Icarus*. In past conversation, she had learned of my interest in Greek mythology and with what little money she had, she attempted to brighten my world.

Since leaving the Frankes' vast library, I read *Immensee* another two times, only to find myself in an emotional quarrel knowing full well it reminded me of Anton. Another indulgence to refuse.

In this book, Icarus had been given a pair of meticulously crafted wings by his father, Daedalus, to escape a labyrinth, which he had created at the demand of King Minos to imprison his enemies with horrible creatures like the minotaur. Daedalus warned his son not to fly too high or the sun would melt the wax that secured them nor too low that the dampness of the sea would weigh them down. Icarus, caught up with the thrill of flying, ignored the warnings and fell into the sea when the sun melted the wax . . . the Icarian Sea became his final resting place.

I too had been given a great gift. The gift of love, companionship, and devotion and, in a similar manner, did not recognize the value or heed the warnings, and because of my carelessness, everything came crashing down. Nothing will ever be named after me and my foolish actions—no, instead, someone else will pay the debt.

Even in my reading, I could not find relief.

Each day grew darker. I couldn't imagine what the future held, much less the next hour. I couldn't even bring myself to write Anton or Joseph. Somehow, if my thoughts turned to Anton, I assumed I had turned my back on Stefan, and I couldn't do that.

"Ella?" Mama shuffled in holding something tight in her fist.

My eyes shifted in her direction, but I didn't speak.

"I found this under the chair this morning." She held out a folded piece of paper as she shook her head. "I'm just not as thorough as I used to be."

Confusion covered my face. I knew she struggled to keep the floor as immaculate as she desired, but why would I want a piece of rubbish?

"Ella, here." Insistent, she pushed it into my palm.

Immediately, the familiar shape of a pin poked against my fingers. I choked back a sob. It had been a few days after the incident that I sadly realized Anton's tinnie pin was attached to my clothing . . . the clothing left on the floor of the remand room. I quickly unraveled the paper and read a simple message.

"This jewel was found on your dress, I hope its return will bring you some peace." C. Scharf

I had been separated from Anton's shield pin several times, and every time it somehow found its way back to me. *What does this mean?* My lip trembled as my thumb glided over the details. My spirit yearned for Anton in my life, but it was my heart that belonged to Stefan.

A mere moment later, Mama happily announced from the door, "Katharina is here." Her voice always carried a lighter tone when she spoke to me, a vast contradiction to the emotional pleadings I heard her cry at night in her prayers. Even though we were not related, she cared for me like a daughter.

I stood up from the rocker and let my book fall to the ground, the pin still gripped in my hand. My dress annoyingly slipped off my shoulder once more as Katharina approached. Her hand flew to her mouth, and a wisp of air escaped despite her attempt to stop it.

"Ella." She reached for me. Her arms had never completely enclosed me before. Her hands lingered on my arms as she released her embrace. "Ella, you're . . ." She glanced at Mama, then the table where my food remained untouched. "Are you eating?" The concern on her face increased as her eyes visually scanned the length of my body.

"I'm not hungry," I whispered, steadying myself against the arm of the chair. Even standing for a few minutes, drained what insufficient energy I had.

"Oh, love, . . ." She kissed my hand sweetly. "Please, sit down." She waved her hand. "I have something to tell you."

From the lift in her voice, my own heart sensed a dormant charge. Maybe she really does have good news.

"Stefan . . . is not being sentenced . . . to death." She wept in between her words. I watched her intently, *not being sentenced to death does not mean free.* "He has still been sentenced though." My face fell as she continued, "He faces ten years of active-duty service in the Nationale Volksarmee."

My mouth fell open. "Ten years?" I wasn't sure how to react. A decade was an exceptionally long time. Normal conscription was only eighteen months. His sentence seemed unfair. I shook my head. The news really was better than expected—he would not be in prison or a Stasi labor camp . . . or . . . executed.

I cried. Both of us did as we clung to one another. It was overwhelming. Picturing Stefan as a soldier was difficult, but a much better image than the one I had been preparing for.

"He leaves in two days—the six-a.m. train to Strausberg." She smiled through her tears. "We get to see him off at the train station."

"We?" My eyes lifted with hope.

Katharina's hand pressed against her chest. "Oh, Ella, I'm sorry . . ." She bit her lip and turned away as if it was she who betrayed me. "Mother and Father will be there."

I nodded.

"It would not be a good idea right now if you came," she whispered. I sensed she was trying to be kind in her rejection, but it still felt as sharp as a blade.

My eyes dropped again. *Of course, nothing has changed their opinion of me. I know they despise me . . . and they are his family. They need to say goodbye.*

I was instantly jealous.

It wasn't Katharina's fault. I couldn't change what happened. If I could . . . what would I change? The only thing I could imagine is not serving that day. Every other decision I've made since Papa passed led me to Stefan in a strange but destined way. He was part of me now.

"I have to go" —Katharina kissed me on the cheek— "but I'll let you know how we can get letters to him. I know he would want to hear from you . . . and, Ella, if there is something you want me to tell him, I could whisper it in his ear."

I choked back a cry. "Tell him I'm sorry—" My eyes once again filled with tears. "— and I love him."

I said goodbye to Katharina and waited for her to leave before I tumbled to the floor once again. The sensation of touching, pressing against something, seemed to be the only comfort I could find. I held my sides tightly. *Please!* I begged aloud. If there really was a God, I needed Him to hear me right now more than ever. *Please! Please! One chance! I'm only asking for one chance to see him again!*

Mama's footsteps, although dainty, slapped my direction in a hurry. She scooped me up in her arms and cradled me in her chair with minimal exertion. Either her strength had improved, or I really had really lost a great deal of weight . . . or both. My head fell gently into the curve of her neck as she hummed.

"Ten years," I mumbled. My chest heaved as the tears flowed. "Ten years." Just saying it was immensely painful.

Stefan was given a chance to live—he would be breathing, talking, and maybe even laughing again— but it was difficult to find optimism in the length of our separation.

Ten years was not forever—but ten years could change everything.

CHAPTER FORTY-TWO

I couldn't sleep at all the night before Stefan was scheduled to be transported to a military training camp far away from Berlin. I tossed and turned endlessly as my mind reeled with thoughts. The NVA was a large army. Much of it was made up of former Wehrmacht like my Papa—that is until the draft was enforced.

I struggled to find comfort in the consequence, despite knowing that this part of the military primarily served the interests of East Germany. They rarely saw conflict overseas, so the possibility Stefan would remain close to the city was real. Not close enough to see unless he marched in a parade or . . . the very thought frightened me . . . unless he was assigned to border guard at the wall, but again his fate could have been much worse. For this I really was grateful.

The moon cast uninvited light through the bedroom window and steered shadows eerily across my plastered walls. Staring at the ceiling, my eyes traced the cracks from one end of the room to the other, then followed a diverging fissure down the opposite wall. As my sight focused on its jagged path, I cringed. Its similarities to that of the colonel's scar, made me shiver.

I rolled to my side as the ticks of a nearby clock, second by second, echoed through the room presumptuously, forcing restlessness, but it was the thought of not seeing Stefan for ten years or longer that truly haunted me.

Today he would be leaving Berlin and leaving me, I could not just lie here and do nothing. How do you say goodbye to the man whose love altered your life forever? A man who had envisioned the better part of me when I couldn't see it myself.

I had to go, even if it was only for one final glimpse.

It was still dark when I arose and located my blue dress from the closet, the one I wore on our first date to Dafne's. The black belt positioned around my waist was tightened to its last hole so the dress would not look as big as it felt, and then I slipped my feet easily into the tall boots. Only my bony knees were exposed.

I let my hair fall to my shoulders, grateful its length camouflaged my thin torso quite well, and wrapped a matching blue ribbon around my head, sliding the bow underneath. I wanted to look my best for Stefan, even if he may never see me.

Except for the way my defined cheekbones protruded more than before, my face almost appeared as though nothing had changed.

I rolled the black liner above my top eyelashes to pull the view away from the dark circles that formed underneath and brushed on just enough red to hide my cracked lips. I was almost eighteen years old but appeared thirty.

I stared in the mirror. I was different. Despite the image facing me, it was what blazed beneath the skin that had really changed. I knew I appeared frail, but I was not broken.

Before leaving, I peeked in on Mama. Her steady snore told me she had settled into a deep slumber, perhaps the most peaceful sleep she had received since the attack. If I awoke her and told her of my intentions, she would either try to stop me or feel obligated to accompany me, and I couldn't allow either result.

I tiptoed quietly out of the flat. Despite the predawn darkness looming, a calm peace confirmed I was doing the right thing, and even though I had no assurance I could get anywhere near Stefan, I trusted my heart. I wanted to see his face, and I needed to know if he blamed me.

The twenty-minute walk to Friedrichstraße station took thirty with all the stops I made. It had been almost a month since I'd exerted that much energy and my body just couldn't keep up with my desire. Yet nothing could stop me from going.

How ironic Stefan's departure would be at Friedrichstraße, considering that's where we first crossed paths two years ago. I reflected on that experience and how far we'd come. The transformation was undeniable.

As I entered the station, numerous military police stretched out along the deck underneath the bowed shed. Some paced with dogs, others with guns, and a handful were checking every crack under the train. It was routine. People in the East used any opportunity to escape, no matter how risky or dangerous.

I glanced around and there, on the far side of the platform, a small emotional farewell took place. I slipped behind a ticket station and watched. Stefan stood in the center, barely a bus length away, and my heart leaped as I peered around the corner for a better view.

Although Stefan's shoulders bent in a way that indicated fatigue, he was still as handsome as ever.

Dressed in military green, he no longer appeared as though he came from wealth. No more dress slacks, sweaters, or suits. And although he was one of many soldiers, I could easily distinguish the outline of his jaw and the curl of his eyelash from anywhere. He would always be *my* Stefan.

Emotion built in my throat as I watched him gently embrace his weeping mother. This was the most sentiment I had ever seen from her. I didn't even know she was capable of tears. One of his arms then reached for Katharina and pulled her close. Her body shook as well with obvious sobs. Herr Franke closed the gap, placing both arms around his family, and their farewell circle became quite intimate.

I pulled away as tears glided down my face. I should not have come. This moment was meant for family only. I didn't belong here.

The train whistle blew.

I peeked around to see one final embrace between them all. Stefan glanced past them. His eyes scanned the area behind his family. It was as if he expected something else. A skip in my heart made me want to believe he wished I was there, but maybe he too held me responsible for his dire circumstances.

They parted. Katharina handed Stefan the pack they had prepared for him and leaned forward to whisper in his ear. Stefan's face twisted with distress. He kissed her on the cheek and the family departed in the opposite direction.

Stefan reached the door of a passenger car and hesitated. I watched him. My lips parted as if to cry for him, but no words came. He turned his back and boarded.

Stepping away from the sanctuary of the structure, I shuffled slowly toward the rails. Vulnerability raced through my veins as I approached the now nearly vacant platform. Most everyone had either departed or boarded. Even the Frankes had vanished.

I observed Stefan maneuver through a train car and position his baggage above his head. I couldn't pull my eyes away. I wanted so badly to be next to him—to feel his face, see his smile, and receive his touch. I yearned to memorize every detail I could.

I inched my boots closer to the edge of the deck as I stretched forward to see every move he made. He seemed content. He even smiled at a fellow soldier as the conductor made the final preparations for the train to leave. I lowered my head in defeat. *This is it! In a matter of moments, he will be gone.*

The train whistle bellowed piercingly as the last of the military police boarded. A thick, gray cloud of smoke puffed in increments simultaneously to a constrained squeak of the engine. Every second seemed to last an eternity.

I peered up. Stefan's hand was pressed against the window, his eyes firmly on me while he called my name. I tried to smile with assurance, but my mock happiness only disguised deep sorrow.

I lifted my hand to wave when Stefan's face suddenly disappeared. A commotion stirred at the door as Stefan jumped off the train and onto the platform. Regardless of its noisy intentions, the train had not yet started to move, and Stefan was instantly at my side.

The police jumped off the train to detain Stefan. However, they never reached us. They may have stopped once they realized he was not trying to escape, but my concern no longer fell upon them, my eyes fixated only on Stefan.

Everything happened so fast, that I hardly had time to react, but my shock melted to relief as he wrapped his arms around my waist and pulled me close. The urgency in his kiss and the charge in his touch awakened the numbness in my senses. I barely heard the whistles blowing all around us.

Stefan pulled back and gazed at my face. His fingers brushed my cheeks, my forehead, and the fresh scar on the bridge of my nose. He touched everything as if he needed reassurance that I was real and in one piece.

He drew me against his chest and whispered in my ear, "I love you, Ella."

My heart raced. I couldn't speak.

"I'm sorry I didn't protect you," he added with pain in his voice.

Although I yearned to keep my resting head against him, I withdrew just enough to absorb his presence face to face. My palm cupped his cheek. My eyes held every inch of him, yet even at this distance Stefan appeared restless and clenched my body tightly against him once more as if our closeness was his only relief.

His lips vibrated against my ear as he spoke. "It's not your fault." My chest swelled. It was his response to Katharina's message to him from me. This was the precise memory I wanted to seal in my heart.

The train whistle blew one last time as the wheels thrust into motion. One guard grabbed his arm and yelled, "It's time!"

Our bodies remained intertwined.

"I love you, Stefan," I finally spoke. My words were soft but full of conviction. There was no doubt in my mind how I felt about this man.

Stefan exhaled. The guard grabbed his arm and pulled him away, "That's enough," he demanded.

Stefan shook loose and reached for my face with both of his hands. The intensity of his lips left a warm imprint. His reassurance brought me to tears.

I grabbed the ribbon from my hair and placed it in Stefan's hand. He gripped it tightly as the impatient guards became more physical, nearly dragging, then pushing Stefan toward a train that increased in speed.

"I love you, Ella," he yelled as all three men jumped to the opening between cars. While the police moved to the inside cabin, Stefan held the railing on the outside and never took his eyes off me.

Within seconds, I no longer saw his face or the end of the ribbon flapping in his grasp. The train had disappeared into a maze of brick buildings and took with it my hopes and dreams. I buried my head in my hands.

"Ten years!!" I cried. Grief seared through me. *Ten years was forever.* I sobbed nearly uncontrollably. I clutched my chest, my hands turning white from my grasp. The pain was excruciating—as if my heart was physically ripping in half.

Pulling in deep breaths, I opened my eyes. The station was now empty, all evidence of a train, soldiers, or Stefan had disappeared.

I reflected on what brought us here. Because of one moment, the happiness I had once shared with Stefan was stolen from me. My mind spun with fear.

Anything could happen in ten years. Anything could happen in one! What fate awaits us? Will our love survive? Will we survive?

I stumbled awkwardly forward, weakly forcing myself to take a step— the first painful step in a new direction. One that would no longer have the foundation of a man who loved me, even cherished me, despite my many imperfections.

I glanced one last time at the empty track. A long curl had stuck to the wetness on my face, and as I pulled it behind my ear, thoughts of the smudge on my mirror earlier in the week resurfaced, and I pondered my fate.

I would never be the same.

For nearly two years I had tallied the remaining days of service on that glass, but now . . . now a new number would be etched each morn- ing . . . the countdown to Stefan Franke's return home.

ReadMore
Press

GERMAN GLOSSARY

Straße and strausse – Street
Nationale/Nationalen Volksarmee – German Military
Tasche – Knapsack
Kasperle – Famous childhood puppet in Germany
Kleine Maus – Little mouse
Pfennige, Mark/Deutsche Mark – German currency
Schweine – Pig
Geschaft – Store
Geschlossen – Closed
Polizei – Police
Wehrmacht – Early German armed forces
U-bahn – Train/subway system
Ruhe in Frieden – Rest in Peace
Brandenburg Tor – Brandenburg gate
Stasi (Staatssicherheit) – State Security
Heir – Here
Waisenhaus – Orphanage
Morgenpost – Newspaper
Fräulein – Miss
Herr – Mr.
Frau – Mrs.
Stehen Bleiben – Stand/stay
Gehen sie – Get going
Mach ich – I will
Halt – Stop
Erschieben sie mich – Push me
Nachgeben – Give in
Bitte Beachten – Please note
DDR – Deutsche Democratic Republic

Beweg dich – Move
Wilkommen – Welcome
Danke – Thank you
Sind das die waisen – Are these orphans
Ja – Yes
Rübezahl – Childhood folk tale
Schuchtern – Shy
Regierende – Ruling
Nein – NO
Verschwindet – Disappear
Obdachlose – Homeless person
Guten Morgen – Good Morning
Schmetterling – Butterfly
Ein Mensch – A human
Ich liebe dich, bis bald – I love you, see you soon
Straßenkind – Street kid
Kommt! Ich habe jemanden gefunden! – Come, I found someone
Beschissene Amis – Shitty Americans
Kastenwagen – Van
Haus – house
Alles Gute zum Geburtstag – Happy Birthday!
Untere Schicht – Lower class
Opa – Grandpa
Fasching – Carnival
Rotkappchen – Little Red Riding Hood
Topfschlagen – Child's game
Barmann – Bar man
Junge erschossen – Boy shot
Сро́чный – "Urgent" in Russian
Bäckerei – Bakery
Arsch – Ass
Mutter – Mother
Zentralmarkthalle – Store
Verdammt du Arschloch! – Damn you asshole
Blode Amerikaner – Stupid American
Tod dem Prasidenten – Death to the President

German Foods
Zweibelkuchen – Onion pie
Apfeltasche – Apple tart
Pfannkuchen – Crepe/pancake
Struesselschnecken – Sweet pastry/scone
Buletten – Meatballs
Orangensaft – Orange juice
Beamtenstippe – Sauce generally served with potatoes
Obstler – Brandy
Eisbein – Pork knuckle
Liqueurs – Liquor
Sauerbraten roast – Beef roast
Quarkkeulchen – Egg/potato dumpling
Weisswürste – White sausages
Senfeier – Mustard eggs
Kaffe – Coffee
Erdbeerkuchen – Strawberry cake with custard
Knieküchl – Fried pastry
Eierkuchen – German pancake
Konigsberger Klopse – Meatballs with Capers
Linsensuppe – Lentil soup
Kalter Hund – Fudge brownie

ACKNOWLEDGMENTS

I would like to thank my family for their love, support, and patience with me. To my husband, Greg, my biggest fan, my daughter Taylor, daughter-in-law, Harlie, and sons Ryan, Alex, and Chad, I love you—as well as my part-time kids, Jace Thatcher, Bubba Taunima, and the boys' soccer team at Combs High School. Thank you for being a part of my life.

To my writer friends who through their time and dedication have helped mold me as an author and continue to help me strive to become better each time we meet. You're the best, Jennie Durkee and Stacy Johnson!

To those who were willing to read, edit, reread, and fact check, I owe you everything, Jennie Durkee, Melanie Laczko, Taylor Moyes, and Greg Moyes. Special thanks to Jennifer Griffith for your wonderful advice.

To my editor, Irene Hunt, for the many hours you locked yourself away and for your love and dedication to the written word, thank you for stretching me and helping me bring this story to light. Your talent and insights were invaluable.

Thank you to Helena Kürten from Pressestelle der Stiftung Berliner Mauer in Berlin for your department's dedication to keeping the facts and memory of the Berlin Wall alive and for allowing me to share your knowledge with my small corner of the world. More information can be found on their website: http://www.berliner-mauer-gedenkstaette.de/en/grenzsoldaten-456.html

And finally, thank you to the people of Germany (and my ancestors). I am grateful for the opportunity I have had to study and research your beautiful country and heritage. My characters' strength and resilience to the challenges faced through the decades are only a sliver of your true spirit and veracity. I will always be moved by the memory of those lost by such a senseless act as the Berlin Wall.

ABOUT THE AUTHOR

L eah Moyes is a wife and a mother, a former teacher, and a coach with a background in Anthropology and History. Her best-selling historical fiction novels have won multiple awards and come from unique stories she has stumbled upon around the world. She loves popcorn and seafood (though not together) and is slowly checking off her very long bucket list.

Her *Berlin Girl* series is inspired by a dream and through great love and respect for the people of Germany including her great grandparent's history, it has become a reality.

AUTHOR'S NOTE

It has been quite a journey researching the events both prior to the Berlin wall going up and throughout its existence and subsequent fortifications. Many nights my heart ached for those who experienced these dark moments first-hand.

Although Ella is a fictional character I created, I have always believed she represented many strong women of East Berlin who suffered loneliness and grief through separation the morning of August 13, 1961. Unnamed women, whose very survival remained anonymous in the history books, yet somehow through perseverance and determination found happiness and many times, even love.

Historical characters depicted in the book with Government or Stasi ties such as Marcus Wolf and Erich Mielke are factual, however, relationships derived and conversations between them and the fictional characters are assumed based on both their duties and involvements and invented for the purpose of storytelling.

Victim/shooting scenarios mentioned in the book were taken directly from the Berlin Wall Memorial records (used with permission). Although once again the associations preceding the tragedies were created in attempt to bring their names and stories to light. A complete list of the victims and their biographies can be found at www.berliner-mauer-gedenkstaette.de

As you follow the journey of Ella, Stefan, Anton and Josef, you will find their lives intertwined with factual places in East Berlin such as the border neighborhood of Bernauer, Acker, and Anklamer, Brandenburg Gate, Schönhausen palace grounds, Volkspark/Friedrichshain and the fairy-tale fountain, the river Spree, Alexanderplatz, Friedrichstraße train station and more to come.

On the following page, you will find a sneak peek
of the second part of three in this series,
The Berlin Girl's Promise, which continues Ella's story.

Thank you for reading!

Printed in Great Britain
by Amazon